The Secret Agenda

The Secret Agenda

James Best

To order additional copies of this book, contact:
Xlibris Corporation
0-800-644-6988
www.xlibrispublishing.co.uk
Orders@xlibrispublishing.co.uk
303973

CHAPTER ONE

"The leaders of Afghanistan, Pakistan and Turkmenistan have agreed to construct a $2 billion pipeline to bring gas from Central Asia to the sub-continent . . . ."—Article 'Afghan pipeline given go-ahead' (BBC—30th May 2002)

"Condemnation without investigation is the height of ignorance"—Albert Einstein.

" . . . if liberty means anything at all, it means the right to tell people what they do not want to hear." George Orwell.

16th September 2001—Vice President stated: "We also have to work sort of on the dark side, if you will. We've got to spend time in the shadows, in the intelligence world . . . . (it) will have to be done quietly, without any discussion, using sources and methods that are available to our intelligence agencies . . ."

James Miller—ex MI5 Agent: "It is like layers of an onion and the more you peel them away, the more you feel like crying. There are two laws running this country: one for the security services and one for the rest of us."

Within the "Operations Northwood" report released under the U.S. Freedom of Information legislation . . . . is a proposed 1959 project to use remote-control technology, then in its infancy, to crash a plane into a U.S. building and destroy a US ship before blaming it on Castro, as an excuse to invade Cuba:

" . . . . participation by U.S. personnel is limited only to the most highly trusted covert personnel . . . . if the decision should be made to set up a contrived situation . . ."

Subsequent Newsweek Report:

"On 10th September 2001, high-ranking Defence Department and Pentagon officials were advised to cancel travel plans for the morning of September 11th for security reasons." On the same day, a military report states: "Mossad are extremely cunning . . . . with a capability to undertake an attack on the US and make it look like a Palestinian or Arab attack."

No significant evidence of Osama bin Laden's involvement with the 9/11 events has ever been offered. They have produced a "confession" video, but the man does not resemble bin Laden, does not have the greying beard of bin Laden; he writes a note with his right hand, (bin Laden is left-handed), and he wears a gold ring, (forbidden by bin Laden's religious beliefs). Professor Bruce Lawrence of Duke University has officially gone on record as saying the 9/11 confession is a fake. Furthermore, there is a complete absence of any corroborative evidence of the US Government line on the 9.11 events, whereas there is overwhelming scientific, engineering and corroborative evidence to support the contention that the Twin Towers and Building Seven were part of a controlled demolition.

The official theory is disproved as completely as any theory could possibly be and the likelihood of it being true is zero, whereas all the evidence can be explained by the alternative theory of explosion. The official theory is an outrageous theory and the alternative theory is the only possible theory.

The official theory defies the whole basis of Newtonian physics—Professor of Physics. "The whole building collapses upon itself symmetrically, (through the path of greatest resistance), at almost free-fall speed, as if there is no resistance in the massive protected steel columns and five inch packed concrete on every floor, (pulverizing 90,000 tons of concrete and steel decking in mid-air), even though the buildings were designed to withstand the collision of a packed Boeing 747 flying at 600 miles per hour. Thousands of pieces of bone, steel and concrete are projected outwards as far as 600 yards from the WTC, with six hundred bone fragments only half an inch long found on the top of adjoining skyscrapers."

Multi-ton steel sections explosively eject laterally, many 20-40 stories below the demolition front.

S tation." The duty desk answered in its customary manner.
"Station Chief, please." Osama bin Laden asked politely.
"Protocol Code?"
"Sheikh 1." He replied gruffly, hating the clandestine nature of the Agency's procedures.
"I can't see the code?" The operator replied.
He sighed heavily. "Check your level 4 classified directory."
"One minute please." A few moments of silence followed, then a different voice spoke.
"Station Chief."
"It's the Sheikh. I'm at the American Hospital here in Dubai."
"I know."
"Do you have something for me?"
"I can deliver the package tonight."
"The Egyptian is with me and he'll be waiting in reception for you at nineteen hundred hours." He said, before adding reverently. "Inshallah."
"Is there a direct telephone line in your room, if I need you?" The Station Chief asked.
"Ask for room number thirteen on the first floor, but the Egyptian will take the call."
"Fine."
The Sheikh replaced the receiver. He dismissed the Egyptian, his mentor of many years, with a wave of his hand, glancing briefly at the chrome clock on the far wall of his room. It spelt out the time in digital figures, with the date underneath it, 10th July 2001. He had three hours

until his meeting with the Station Chief and he settled himself for sleep. At nineteen hundred hours precisely, he awoke from a fractured sleep to a knock on the door. The Egyptian entered with the Station Chief, a bespectacled man with light casual trousers and a short-sleeve white shirt, its front pocket full. He carried a package, heavily taped and sealed and walked up to the bed, placing it to the side of the man he would refer to as the Sheikh.

The Sheikh lifted himself up, stroking sleep gently from his eyes and placing a prayer cap on his head. "Do you know what's in the package?" He asked.

He shook his head. "I'm told the package doesn't even exist." The Station Chief was surprised at the softness of the Sheikh's brown eyes, strangely compassionate, he thought. "It's not come from the usual source."

"Have they told you anything?" He asked, preferring his links with the Agency remained secret.

The Station Chief knew he could never acknowledge the existence of a black operation unit, running parallel to the operations of the Agency, but under the direction of the corporate front organization and the FBI's Division Five in the tradition of the infamous Permindex Corporation. "I know nothing." He replied, the tone rising.

The Sheikh looked at him with penetrating eyes, feeling uneasy dealing directly with a Langley operative. "If you know what's good for you, you'll forget this meeting ever took place."

The Station Chief's face relaxed, expressionless, showing no outward sign of stress. He looked directly at the Sheikh. "I'm just the messenger and know nothing at all."

"So there'll be no difficulties leaving Dubai by private jet on the 14th July?"

The Station Chief shrugged. "Of course not."

*   *   *

The uncomfortable trek from Peshawar across the bleak mountains of the Hindu Kush, passing the polo fields in the Chitral Valley through into Afghanistan, had made Mohammed tired and stiff. The slow journey along rutted paths and tracks, unfit for vehicular traffic in winter, had taken its toll on his body, now more used to the decadent lifestyle and diet of the West. In the clear sky above the ridge, he noticed white vapour trails, reminding him of that different life.

"Wah Salaam Alaikum, Sheikh," Mohammed offered the traditional greeting of peace, placing his hands together, as if in prayer, then touching his head and heart with the right hand, slightly bowing in the process. As with all double agents, he feared his deep cover could be exposed at any time. His stomach clenched in trepidation. Despite a thick blanket wrapped around his shalwar kameez and his kufi cap, the icy cold cut through to the bone and his head thumped. A deep loathing for taking money from the Agency stuck in his throat, believing himself a prostitute. He had reluctantly agreed to the installation of a microchip, hidden in gel within the heel of his shoe, but as with so many couriers, he knew the penalty, if the Sheikh found out.

"Alaikum Salaam Wah. Allah u Akbar." The Sheikh gestured back. His long frame moved wearily, brown eyes glazed and sunken, no longer the charismatic figure once portrayed, his beard greyer than Mohammed remembered and full lips appearing anaemic. There were no illusions God was great, as the Sheikh exhorted so instinctively, or that it was Allah's work he did, even if some of his comrades convinced themselves otherwise. The Sheik's troubled thoughts masked a grievance. Being born into riches, as the scion of a fabulously wealthy family, yet subsequently abandoned by his father ate away at his psyche, driving him towards the violent pursuit of the Lesser Jihad. Living away from the male members of his family created a festering wound, which would last a lifetime.

Mohammed looked across at the plateau, planning an escape route. The encampment lay within a hollow with lightly-forested slopes on the ridge above shielding it from the worst of the winter weather. Snow-capped mountains towered like sentinels, no infrastructure allowed easy exit, only icy tracks. The ridge on the one side and the remnants of abandoned carts on the other formed a natural perimeter. Derelict villages in the vicinity appeared as witness to centuries of tribal conflict. All left the same ugly, decaying scar on the classical mountain landscape and none could offer sanctuary.

"You look tired." The Sheikh's tone etched compassion, incongruously for someone content to conspire in the catastrophic events, soon to create havoc on foreign soil.

"I'm exhausted." He sighed, an inner turmoil expressing itself in physical ailments. "The journey has been a struggle. I must be getting old."

The Sheikh nodded. "Aren't we both?"

A dreary mist hung limply over the valley, reflecting Mohammed's mood. "I don't think this winter climate is healthy, Sheikh." His voice cracked, shivering instinctively, as if someone had walked over his grave.

"The climate isn't meant to be healthy." The Sheikh had allowed the area to be infiltrated by an extremist form of Islam, maintaining a devotion to the religion, though blatantly deviating from the strict teachings of the Qu'ran, which called on men to treat one another as brothers. The area's rigid Taliban control had created a perfect breeding ground for the vulnerable and for his distorted and destructive brand of Jihad, the most divisive message of political Islam. Although his grievances may have been political, he intelligently articulated them in religious terms.

"Are we active on the American operation, Sheikh?" Mohammed knew the suffering it would cause and feared the great damage it would do to his faith and the good name of Islam.

"Of course." He replied abruptly.

"Why do we conspire with the Great Satan to do their dirty work?" Mohammed knew the Sheikh struggled to find peace within his heart, so inevitably he could never find it in the external world. His mystical teaching having taught him the reflexive universe always compelled the macrocosm to work through the microcosm of the human mind.

The Sheikh grimaced. "You're intelligent enough to know the answer."

"But I want to act in accordance with Sharia Law and the teachings of the Qu'ran?" Mohammed coughed persistently. Waking nightmares having been his brooding companion since he had sold his soul and become one of the CIA's recruits for their 'database' or as he would say in his language, 'al-Qaeda'.

The Sheikh shook his head, walking wearily alongside Mohammed. "We'll discuss it tomorrow."

"But I've things weighing heavily on my mind, Sheikh." He had lived a pretence in Germany, all intended as a false trail and evidence of a takfir methodology, so as not to draw attention to himself as a Jihadist within the House of Islam. It had taken him off the radar of the intelligence services, except for his Agency paymasters. No longer reconciled to being a good Muslim, he was permitted to deceive the infidel, even though he remained in awe of the Prophet's revelations.

The Sheikh turned to Mohammed. "I want the Egyptian present when we discuss these things."

Mohammed still found it strange he referred to Ayman Al Zawahiri as the Egyptian. It was his country of origin too, but no-one called him the Egyptian. "But the Law?" He persisted.

"What about the Law?"

"We can't go against the Law." Mohammed replied firmly. He had studied Carl Jung, whilst living in Germany, and was reminded of his famous observation 'He who looks outside, dreams; he who looks inside, awakes.' Yet he feared to look inside a diseased mind, deviated from its spiritual source, wandering in a barren wilderness.

"Don't recite the Law to me, Mohammed."

"But I worry about the course we follow, Sheikh." Mohammed craved an escape from a destiny which could eventually destroy him.

"The West will never understand the mentality of the suicide bombers." The Sheikh walked stiffly inside the largest house within the Pashtun fortress qala, with its typical large walled compound.

Mohammed's eyes followed the Sheikh. "But this operation grieves me." He failed to understand the strategy of attacking Americans on their soil, even if those with vested interests in positions of power connived in it. "It makes no sense to me."

Inside the largest room, the Sheikh reached for his chair, sitting down with a thud. "This can wait until morning, Mohammed."

"But it causes me pain and I need to sleep with a clear mind." He sat down next to the Sheikh, looking at the old tins of food, condensed milk and stale bread scattered on the table alongside him and puzzled at the life he had chosen. The room's bare concrete walls and matted floor hardly protected it from the weather, frost creating strange opaquely-patterned fantasies on the inside of the only window.

"We're all trying to escape the pain." The Sheikh looked at him with hollow eyes. "But we must push doubts to a place beyond ourselves, where ordinary living cannot reach them."

Mohammed sighed. "I'll fight for social equality, but I fear for the long-term damage to the name of Islam." He bowed his head before looking directly at the Sheikh. "I want some peace in my life and for my Muslim brothers."

The Sheikh nodded. "At one level, we all have this impulse to return to the peace and unity of the spirit. It's the source of all things of value, but life is full of compromises."

Sadness reflected in Mohammed's eyes. "I've spent my life with compromises."

"Do you worry about death, Mohammed?"

"Only the death of innocents." He replied, knowing he was not one of them.

"The nature of the world in which we live requires sacrifices and for now this is the Law." A hint of pragmatism echoed in the Sheikh's voice. "Soon we'll both return home and meet the Lords of Karma."

Mohammed took a deep breath. "But I'd like to correct some injustices before it's my time."

"Of course."

Mohammed reached across with his hand, touching his arm, leaving it there. "There'll be devastation for many of our brothers if we go ahead with the operation, Sheikh."

"Until the West change their policies and treat the life of a Muslim as valuable as that of an American, there can never be peace." The Sheikh's voice bristled with an energy, which had fuelled his life's work. "The idea that suicide bombers follow a spiritual urge to return home is beyond their comprehension."

Mohammed removed his hand. "I think you're missing the point." He stared defiantly at the Sheikh, wrestling with treacherous thoughts.

"I don't think so."

"Is this the last time we help your family's friends, Sheikh?"

"Are you questioning my motives?" The Sheikh asked angrily, lifting his head sharply.

"I'm just asking questions." Mohammed's voice cracked. He coughed violently, taking a handkerchief from his pocket and placing it to his mouth.

"When my time is at an end, you may have your way." The Sheikh squinted, looking into Mohammed's dark eyes. "Until that time, you can take refuge in your Sharia Law."

"When you mock me, Sheikh, you sound like the Egyptian." His loathing for his compatriot self-evident.

"What's your problem with him?"

Mohammed grunted. "He's intellectually bright, but he's a fanatic, scarred physically and emotionally by his imprisonment and torture at the hands of the Egyptian security forces."

The Sheikh's eyes narrowed. "Perhaps that's true, but I need fanatics and my people will listen to him because he tells them what they want to hear, whereas you burden them with something they want to deny." He lifted his hands. "This is your dilemma, Mohammed."

"I simply tell people the truth, Sheikh."

"But it's your truth and it doesn't mean it's everybody's truth." The Sheikh sneered. "There's a festering hole deep inside you, Mohammed, and it can never be filled."

"But I want what's best for my brothers."

The Sheikh shuffled uncomfortably in his chair, steely searching eyes looking at Mohammed. "Be careful not to confuse what's best for them with what's best for you."

Mohammed shrugged. "But what are your plans for al-Qaeda, Sheikh?"

"What do you mean by plans?"

Mohammed feared his impetuous nature would one day be the death of him. "That you do the bidding of your American friends in their secret agenda."

The Sheikh sighed. "What is this secret agenda?"

"It's their New World Order agenda." He replied. "On the dollar bill they call it Novus Ordo Secorum."

"What concerns you about this New World Order, Mohammed?"

"Their quest for the New Jerusalem, Sheikh."

"Not their policies?"

Mohammed shook his head. "Their policies are set out well enough in their public policy documents. The Middle East has oil and gas or they wouldn't be interested."

"But you take the American's dollars too, Mohammed."

Mohammed stiffened, recoiling for a moment, wondering if the Sheikh knew the extent of his Agency links. "I don't know what you mean." His voice faltered, but he lifted his shoulders with the mantle of indignity.

"You've always sought security from money, Mohammed. It's the classical motivation for someone brought up in poverty, but security never comes from the material world."

"But I'd never act against your interests, Sheikh."

"I want to believe you."

"But I can't pretend to be happy playing the stooge for your American friends."

The Sheikh folded his arms, eyes blazing. "Why do you call us stooges?"

"Because they plan this inside job for an agenda, which damages our interests and will cost hundreds of thousands of innocent Muslim lives."

"Are you frightened?" The Sheikh asked.

Mohammed shook his head. "No, but it simply doesn't make sense to me."

The Sheikh directed hollow eyes at him, searching for signs of betrayal. "Why don't you persuade the Egyptian it's a mistake?"

Mohammed stifled another cough in its infancy. "He'll never listen to me."

The Sheikh shrugged. "The payments have been made and the contract struck. It would be difficult to pull out now."

Mohammed groaned. "But all the Egyptian wants is revenge on the modern world, which has treated him so badly."

"But it happens to coincide with our plans, Mohammed."

"He's living in the past, Sheikh, poisoned by those events in Egypt years ago."

The Sheikh raised his hands. "Tell it to his face."

Mohammed looked nervously across at two heavily-bearded bodyguards, standing at the entrance to the room, blankets slung over their shoulders and a rifle strapped on top. "Sheikh, I can talk to you more candidly."

"Don't you like democracy?" He smiled crookedly.

Mohammed threw a strained smile back. "You're mocking me again."

The Sheikh shook his head. "There are times, Mohammed, when you think too much."

"Do you see yourself living this miserable existence forever?" Mohammed gestured with a movement of his hand at the paucity of the surroundings, bloated with the grim stench of poverty.

The Sheikh winced, holding his back. "I've lived in both worlds and the joy of life is in each of them, even if it's hidden in secret places."

'But what's the purpose of this collusion with the Americans, Sheikh?' Demons plagued Mohammed as he bridged the worlds of the East and West. He thought about the Ummah, the great brotherhood, and his deeply-felt urge to help his brothers.

"Can't you see the sacrifices we make will eventually lead to a world with Islamic values?"

"I want the same outcome, Sheikh, but not this way." His voice arched. He may have wanted freedom from the pain and sadness of the struggle, but knew the divine revelations of the Prophet were based on peace not conflict. His teacher taught him it also stood for the middle path and the goal of producing a moral man in the service of a just society.

One of the Sheikh's three wives arrived from an adjoining room, the hijab covering most of her face. He puzzled at the religious justification for this old tribal custom, as there was nothing in the Qu'ran relating to it. She took away the remnants of food, leaving a pitcher of water and some chai.

The Sheikh gestured towards the chai.

Mohammed wallowed in the feeling of warmth on his chest, as he drank it. He noticed a difference in the man he remembered in the Malawi Valley, in the foothills of the Spin Ghar mountains, where he had made his famous eight thousand word declaration. "Sheikh, I've never understood why Islamic clerics sustain their encouragement to love death more than life." He said. "It's not what the Qu'ran teaches."

"Our recruits sacrifice little when they offer their lives." The Sheikh stroked his greying beard. "The poorer the life here, the easier it is for them to choose glorious paradise."

Mohammed's face twisted. "But if we taught Tauhid, in its true meaning, the unity of all men, not just the Ummah, the Muslim brotherhood, we could transform the world." He reflected on the Sheikh's flawed interpretation of the Qu'ran, feeling he was beyond redemption, even if it explained his collusion with Americans and Jews.

"All in its time, Mohammed."

Mohammed shook his head. "But we must dispel the shadow of ignorance tainting Islamic ideology."

"And how do you propose we do it?"

"Knowledge can set us free." Mohammed replied. "It can shed light on the darker pathologies of the western nations."

"You're a mystical scholar, Mohammed, so you understand why our recruits feel an urge to re-unite with that part of themselves, which they've consciously forgotten."

"I suppose so."

The Sheikh sighed. "But you dwell too much on the spiritual and forget the practical nature of the real world."

"I understand your path, Sheikh, but I don't share your conviction about this American operation." A myriad of thoughts crossed his mind, twisting one way, then another, as he sat next to this wilful man, who still retained knowledge of the mystical Sufi teachings.

"If you could see the long-term outcome, Mohammed, you'd feel differently."

Mohammed envisaged an outcome with the stench of death in it, but he kept the thought to himself. "What about the Pashtuns and the innocent refugees who'll suffer from the destruction of their environment and way of life?" He knew eventually civilians would pay a price, as they inevitably poured out of the area in hordes, away from the lawless vacuum, but the Sheikh appeared oblivious to the consequences.

"But their children will be fed idealism by the teachers in the Madrassas, Mohammed, and the internet will become their information playground to spread the Islamic word."

Mohammed sighed, believing vulnerable young minds would be corrupted. "I worry about the role models available to these students of Islam and my karma in it all." He knew the Pashtuns, who lived in the border country, had originally supported al-Qaeda, but they would become disillusioned and he suspected Pakistan would eventually be brought into the maelstrom, with their ISI intelligence aiding the Taliban.

"Mohammed." He shouted starkly. "The repetitive pattern of the wheel of life may be obvious to you, but most of our recruits survive on blind faith and I don't respect them any less."

"But you're an educated man, Sheikh."

"The world masks truth except for those dedicated to mystical study, Mohammed." He shrugged. "But not everybody can follow that path."

"And which path do you tread, Sheikh?"

The Sheikh took a deep breath "I suppose at the beginning, some great spiritual truth resonated and inspired me."

"But has it deviated from its source?"

The Sheikh leaned back in his chair, briefly closing his eyes, recalling the mystical teachings offered to him as a privileged and wealthy student in the land of the two Mosques. "Perhaps the pain of the injustices I've witnessed has affected my beliefs."

"I fear for my soul, Sheikh." Mohammed knew memories had to be healed and replaced with inspiration, but he found it impossible to heal himself. Instead, his body cried out in pain and its agitated response became a constant reminder of the distance he had travelled from his soul's intended path. In the passage of time, he had become convinced his path in history was pre-destined and it led to a foreign land.

The Sheikh opened his eyes. "Each of us has the key to our salvation and follow different paths to redemption."

"But you have the same problem, Sheikh."

The Sheikh's face contorted. "Perhaps you're right."

"If so, we must both spend more time in meditation and devotion."

"You must do what you think is right, Mohammed." The Sheikh may have become adept at using his intellect and education to exploit and manipulate the weak-willed, but at a deeper level violence tainted his soul. He knew it was not the path of the Prophet.

"Where did it all go wrong, Sheikh?"

"Who knows the greater truth, Mohammed?" He replied, recalling how his path had begun innocently enough, waging jihad with the Mujahadeen, as freedom fighters against the Russians and bedding down with the Americans.

"Perhaps you listen too much to the Egyptian." Mohammed suspected the Sheikh's loathing of western values had begun at home, though the ideal to disrupt the decadent infidel civilization had taken years to nurture.

The Sheikh lifted himself in his chair. "The Egyptian may have created the desire within me to remove the western governments from the land of Mecca, but it doesn't mean it isn't right."

"But you're helping the same western governments?"

The Sheikh shrugged. "For the time being."

Mohammed rubbed his right hand across the back of his neck. "Islamic mysticism suggests knowledge without love is like the intellect without the heart."

"What does that mean?" The Sheikh feigned ignorance.

"Perhaps we should forgive the infidel, Sheikh, as our religion teaches us."

The Sheikh smiled wryly, knowing the classical tool of religion, the great divider of peoples, had often been used as an excuse for division. "But what about their historical treatment of Muslims?"

"It doesn't justify an action costing thousands of innocent lives, Sheikh."

"Don't play games, Mohammed."

"I'm not playing games, Sheikh." He softened his tone. "Someone once said that if God existed and cared for mankind, he would never have given us religion."

The Sheikh laughed, the comment resonating with him, knowing the great spiritual truths were almost always lost when mixed with religion. "My religion is important to me, but what I do is unrelated to my spiritual beliefs." It sounded hollow, even as he said it. Somewhere along his journey of life, he had been tempted into working for the Great Satan, at a time when both they and the CIA's database of recruits in Afghanistan, 'al-Qaeda', needed a common enemy.

"You surprise me, Sheikh."

"Why should it surprise you?" He hesitated long enough to throw Mohammed a stern glance. "The governing elite of the United States have become convinced the only way to ensure social cohesion within their country is to create terrorism as the phantom image to allow the contagion of fear to spread amongst their citizens."

Mohammed nodded. "They've even written it brazenly in one of their think-tank reports for anyone to read." He recited it. "By creating a fearful enemy, illusory or otherwise, and attacking the pacifists as unpatriotic, they create the necessary fervour and public support for a course of destruction and an erosion of civil liberties."

"I've read the documents, Mohammed." The Sheikh smiled. "You believe it's their fixation with this New World Order or the secret agenda, as you call it."

"Of course." Mohammed said. "Muslims will get the blame, even though as with many of the significant events of history, the truth is hidden secretly from the populace and re-written to the whims of its governing elite, the secret history."

"In time, the truth will emerge."

Mohammed grunted. "History will tell."

"Have faith, Mohammed."

Mohammed shook his head. "Even the Third Reich had similarities to this New World Order agenda, Goering having used identical words during the Nuremburg trials to excuse his part in the genocide." He felt a need to touch the Sheikh's soul before he committed to an action likely to prove divisive for Islam for a generation.

The Sheikh nodded. "I'm still puzzled at the ignorance on the part of the western population to the plans of their governments and their lack of shame."

"But the history of humankind is littered with the story of ignorance, Sheikh."

"But you're not ignorant, Mohammed."

"Maybe not." He sighed. "But we both know the intentions of the western governments, yet we help them."

The Sheikh stifled a yawn. "I'm tired and need sleep." He pointed towards a room adjoining the living room. "That's your room." He groaned as he moved. "Tomorrow morning we'll talk with the Egyptian in the next valley."

Mohammed shook his head. "I'd rather talk to you, Sheikh."

"I'm sorry, but it'll have to wait." The Sheikh replied, knowing he had another journey to make that night.

"Too bad." Mohammed whispered through gritted teeth.

"I've told you, Mohammed. You think too much."

"But you've studied the policy documents of the think-tanks of the American elite, the Defence Planning documents of Paul Wolfowitz, the 'Wolfowitz doctrine' for Middle East policy?" Mohammed looked at the Sheikh through sunken eyes, as cold as marble, and wondered if he knew about the one hundred thousand dollars he had accepted from the black ops department of the Agency, through the channel of the Pakistan Inter Services Intelligence, or the nature of his instructions.

The Sheikh stretched out, arching his back. "I've read the Project for the New American Century." He hesitated, turning towards Mohammed. "What they refer to as the need for a catastrophic event like a new Pearl Harbour for incursions into sovereign states, even reasoning why it should happen."

"It's their agenda, Sheikh." He said. "But why do we make it ours?"

"In time, you'll understand how it benefits us."

Mohammed sighed. "It's obvious they need to manipulate the minds of their citizens to increase their military budget, to engage in foreign wars for their strategic importance, and to erode the freedoms within their constitution."

"Of course, they'll introduce these measures immediately after our operation." The Sheikh said.

"Precisely."

"I understand." The Sheikh lifted his hands playfully, recalling the wording of the policy document. "They intend to intervene in sovereign states, calling for regime change in Iraq and for access to the Middle East for the oil and gas reserves."

"But if they're going to access the large oil and gas reserves in the Caspian Basin, they need Afghanistan." Mohammed's mouth opened and shut again. "How does that help us?"

"There's a greater benefit to us." The Sheikh said.

Mohammed stared at the Sheikh. "But it'll give them an excuse to declare war on our Muslim brothers."

"The dynamic created will help us recruit all over the world, with increased funding." The Sheikh's eyes widened. "And our brothers will turn back to religion"

"What about the carnage created within the shadow of these events?" Mohammed's tone etched concern. "Many Muslims will die in the aftermath."

The Sheikh sighed. "In death, there's a greater glory."

Mohammed looked at the Sheikh, feeling uneasy at the potential consequences of their actions. "They believe in their sacred geometry and the time of reckoning, when the world will look towards the ancient lands of Babylon." He recalled the prophecies of the Armageddon.

"But why should that bother us?"

Mohammed despaired at the darker side of the Sheikh's obsession. "But if you give them the excuse for an unjust war, they'll plunder our lands and loot the ancient relics from their resting places."

"I understand their beliefs and weaknesses." The Sheikh moved uncomfortably, taking water from the jug on the table.

"You mustn't give them an excuse for this devastation, Sheikh."

A pained expression crossed the Sheikh's face. "Sometimes chaos is needed to cleanse the world of its decadence." He hesitated. "And for now we need their money."

"But it's the mistake of a fanatic."

"You may be a friend and brother, Mohammed, but don't test our friendship."

"That's not my intention."

The Sheikh shrugged. "Then accept my decision, as all soldiers must, or we'll break down into anarchy."

"Theirs is a sham democracy, Sheikh, so let them do their own dirty work."

The Sheikh nodded. "Those with the vested interests are no different to the royal family in my country. The people with power, the shadow government, will always have power, regardless of who governs and what puppet is elected to do their bidding."

"Perhaps." Mohammed said quietly. "But do you really think the American people are gullible enough to believe these events are real and not manipulated in some way?"

"Mohammed, sometimes you're naïve." He smiled. "They'll believe it if it's repeated often enough and they control the media."

Mohammed grimaced. "So we'll be called terrorists, not freedom fighters."

"Does it matter?"

"It matters if our actions are condemned by the true scholars of Islam, who know it as a peaceful religion."

The Sheikh looked at him with pitiful eyes. "What's the United Nations definition of a war of freedom, Mohammed?"

Mohammed shrugged.

"The definition is stated as any struggle against foreign aggression. It's not terrorism, it's a war of freedom we began together and must finish together." The Sheikh moved his hands upwards. "Who do you think are the foreign aggressors in these incursions in the Middle East?"

"But by the same argument, Sheikh, we're getting involved in foreign aggression in the United States." Mohammed hesitated. "In our actions, we're no better than the Great Satan."

"Not if the invite comes from their government elite." The Sheikh replied firmly.

He sighed. "But they'll use it as an excuse to enslave our people, Sheikh."

"You may have the Prophet's name, Mohammed, but you're wrong." The Sheikh placed his hands on his knees before standing up stiffly and facing him, open-armed.

Mohammed reciprocated, embracing him as a brother, but his eyes avoided contact, shielding his thoughts and the nature of his double game. The US President's family could never be associated either with the Sheikh's capture or his assassination. In time it would fall to someone else, for he knew too many of the West's shadowy secrets and black operations and he would never be allowed to give evidence at any trial. He suspected the Sheikh knew it too, as he walked his precarious tightrope doing business with dangerous people of little conscience.

*   *   *

Evan observed his target carefully, having followed him for some time, and his night-time cover had been carefully selected. With the silencer attached to his L115A3 long-range sniper rifle, there was little chance of detection from the distance he could now remain away from his target. He had been the first to receive the prototype of the new rifle, before it went into general production. It weighed only 15 pounds, firing 8.59 millimetre rounds and he had quickly become proficient, aligning his target with precision, taking account of the wind tugging viciously at his jacket. He squeezed the trigger gently, like tickling his cat's stomach. The muffled sound of the shot hardly echoed, but through the magnified sights of the rifle he watched the man fall to the floor instantly, his companions diving for cover like butterflies with sore feet. The fact his target had been a colleague for some years, working as Communication Officers at GCHQ Cheltenham, before secondment to the Riverside offices of MI6, in Vauxhall, passed him by without guilt. His training had taught him to act professionally and detached and the man had talked. Wet jobs, where blood flowed, had become his speciality and a part of him enjoyed them.

Evan's athletic, confident appearance allowed him to mould into most environments, rich and poor alike, his pride demanding he wore contact lenses, strange blue ones. As with most recruits to the Foreign Office, he had a good command of languages, a pre-requisite for some of his postings, and a university education in information technology. His mastery of weapons was the legacy of Sandhurst officer training, long before he had been recruited by the Foreign Office for his special talents.

Now divorced, he resented the price he had to pay for his vocation, but craved the danger and adrenalin rush from the fire-fights encountered in troubled locations, all of which had fashioned a twisted perspective on life. The more personal skills and charm had always been used to good effect for the department, gaining trust easily, particularly enjoying female company, whether in business or for pleasure. Extensive in-house psychological training in gaining information from his contacts, and controlling them, had perfected his black art over many years.

His days of infiltrating student and anarchist movements may have passed, but his maturing years gave him other skills. He retained an important network of political contacts, many of whom lived near him in Pimlico, and all owed him favours for undertaking smears, spreading misinformation, or organizing break-ins, opening mail and arranging phone-taps. In any event, his mission in the Balkans completed, he quietly slipped away from his hiding place. By morning he was back at his desk dressed in his business suit, with no record of ever having left the country, looking to the whole world like a boring banker or stock or commodities trader in the City.

Back in the UK, some old-fashioned routine intelligence work was needed with individuals in sensitive positions. It was a day set aside for the sifting of paperwork, boring but necessary if he was to work his contacts in his adept manner, sometimes turning them. He would give a little classified information here and there, normally only that which a good investigator could discover, often taking the information away later or tainting it. Perhaps he would show them how a surveillance device had been secured to their premises, often taking it away in front of them, to reveal to them how he could be trusted, knowing another device was already in place elsewhere. It all gained the false trust, the currency he worked so well.

He had the more pleasant task of using a little charm to work the female Chair of the Parliamentary Committee on Security and Intelligence. Hardly a difficult challenge, but something he regarded as a perk of the job.

An appointment had been fitted into his schedule with a Muslim Agent, who he had turned, nothing of great priority at this stage, but all part of the long-term planning necessary for his work. As part of his debriefing, he gave him a CD containing terrorist material and arranged a liaison with a friend in Special Branch, who would help plant it at the premises of one of these good, patriotic Muslim boys in Leeds, whom he befriended in readiness for a future assignment. Clean skins with no record created less complication in the event the situation deteriorated, as they had no concept of how to escape the grid of paper-trail available to the intelligence services. He agreed to join him for the meeting with the Muslim leader, a teacher and youth leader. When the need arose, the Police could be instructed to act on intelligence and recover the CD at his home, threatening him with imprisonment, if he refused to cooperate. If his wife became pregnant, she could easily be arrested and threatened, if he failed to play the game.

The prospect of a lengthy prison sentence for them or their wives for merely being in possession of the material was normally sufficient to obtain maximum cooperation on any project. Protests they had never seen the material would fall on deaf years in difficult times. These matters were not even time-sensitive, so he didn't have to worry about the offence being statute-barred.

He organized a beacon-tracking security device to be placed in the vehicle of the Muslim Agent to record details of his conversations with any high-risk Muslim fanatics, if only to protect his back. This simple act of monitoring his activities would be sufficient for use in the blackmail to come. He would tape him at some stage for future record, but not yet, for it was all about timing and events would take a more dramatic course first.

On his desk, the tapes and mobile telephone transcripts of the Chair of the Parliamentary Committee on Security and Intelligence had to be studied in preparation for his forthcoming meeting with her. Similarly, the transcripts of the Muslim Agent he controlled in Leeds had been printed out for him, for every telephone call in the country was picked up at the listening station at Menwith Hill in Yorkshire. The echelon software could disseminate the calls in seconds, triggered by key words, and passed to GCHQ for analysis. He needed to check the e-mails of the subjects of his next assignment and their spending patterns. Even the so-called secure encryption systems were never completely secure, all having to pass first to GCHQ to collect a code before the encryption transmitted through the system. This break in the communication system gave the intelligence agencies complete control over every electronic communication in the country. He still puzzled at the ignorance of the public and how the extent of the Big Brother state remained secret in this modern internet-driven age. Everything was perfect for the covert actions necessary for the secret agenda, all legitimized by the taking of the Queen's shilling and compliant with the instructions of his paymaster, ultimately the British government, and a few powerful men controlling it.

CHAPTER TWO

More than 118 Fire-fighters and medics made witness statements referring to hearing the sounds of explosions and seeing flashes of light, as did over 100 first responders. One interviewee refers to hearing a series of deep below-ground explosions, then numerous explosions in the buildings upper floors before the first of the twin towers collapses symmetrically into its own footprint on the 11th September 2001. Another Fire-fighter in his statement relating to WTC 1 (pa-police reports 04.pdf page 6) states: "Suddenly there was another loud boom at the upper floors, then a series of smaller explosions which appeared to go completely around the building at the upper floors and another loud earth-shattering blast with a large fireball which blew out more debris."

One Fire-fighter referred to getting as far as the 24th Floor, before hearing a huge explosion that sounded like a bomb. It knocked off the lights and stalled the elevator. He stated he began to try and direct people down and about two minutes later there was another huge explosion like the first one. He was called to testify before the 9/11 Commission Committee, but walked out stating " . . . they were trying to twist my words and make the story fit what they wanted to hear." His testimony was not mentioned in their report.

Another Fire-fighter refers to " . . . the elevators exploding five minutes later (than the plane hits) and the lobby of the North Tower looked like a bomb went off." He referred to fires everywhere and also refers to another explosion in the building. He later states " . . . it just does not make sense." Another refers to hearing " . . . about ten explosions"

Mayor Guiliani confirmed the gas in the City had been turned off and any explosions were not gas related.

One tape refers " . . . I've got five patients involved in the secondary explosion at Tower One" and to " . . . we've got numerous people covered in dust from the secondary explosion" and also to " . . . we've got another explosion at the Tower." One Fire-fighter confirmed he had a warning the South Tower was coming down. Police and Construction Workers are heard on CNN, referring to WTC Building Seven, saying "Keep your eyes on that building . . . it's coming down . . . the building is about to blow up . . . (there'll be) flame and debris coming down."

One Lieutenant Fireman and former Auxiliary Police Officer explains. " . . . many other firemen know there were bombs in the building, but they're afraid for their jobs to admit it because 'higher ups' forbid discussion of this fact" and also to " . . . a gag order sent down the ranks" and also "there were definitely bombs in those buildings."

Many video downloads of witnesses confirm there were secondary explosions, including an ex-Air Force Medic who hears explosions and from a nearby radio hears the sound 'three two one' before the explosion.

After the attack, one witness uses his telephone and said he could "hear explosions below me." Similarly, another witness was going down after the attack and stated " . . . there was another explosion."

The Sheikh quietly left his qala fortress home in the middle of the night, travelling through the darkness in a pick-up truck to the next village for a clandestine meeting with the Egyptian. He struggled to keep the truck on the dirt-track road, deep ruts catching the wheels and pulling at the steering wheel, jarring his ageing body. Eventually, he arrived at his destination, exiting the truck painfully, holding his lower back and pulling his coat tighter, turning up the collar. In the corner of the front room of the old single-storey building, the intellectual, emaciated Ayman Al Zawahiri, the Egyptian, huddled in a corner, a thick blanket around his shoulders. The Sheikh acknowledged him, as the Egyptian looked across at his visitor hard-faced, unsmiling over thick-rimmed steel spectacles. His round, deeply-lined face, partially hidden by the white imamah around his head and the white beard framing it, still showed the painful signs of past torture. The smell of the invasive paraffin lamps irritated the Sheikh's nostrils, but he settled down cross-legged on floor cushions opposite the Egyptian.

"Wah Salaam Alaikum, Sheikh." The Egyptian smiled for the first time.

"Wah Alaikum Salaam." The Sheikh replied hurriedly, anxious to return to his compound for sleep. "The date?" He shifted himself on the cushions. "Have the Americans decided on the date?"

"It's the morning of the 11th September." He fumbled with some papers, before handing them to the Sheikh. "Here are the flight numbers and the airports."

The Sheikh perused the documents, before looking back to the Egyptian. "Is there anything else?"

He handed some additional documents to the Sheikh. "They've given the courier further information about the paper trail they want to create before the events begin."

The Sheikh looked at them carefully. "Good."

"Is he here?" The Egyptian asked, without referring to Mohammed.

"He's expecting a meeting tomorrow." The Sheikh grimaced, shifting his position again.

The Egyptian nodded. "Then we shouldn't disappoint him."

"Shall we tell him everything?" The Sheikh asked.

The Egyptian shook his head. "It's too dangerous." He looked across at the Sheikh. "If you want to keep the plans secret, be discreet."

"But he'll be organizing events from our side?"

The Egyptian gritted his teeth. "But you know the Americans must dispose of him at some stage, if they want to keep a lid on their involvement."

"Only much later."

The Egyptian lifted his blue, faded copy of the Qu'ran and waved it. "It's a loose end for them and they'll stop any trail leading back to them."

The Sheikh sighed. "I hope it's unnecessary, but you're right." He hesitated. "It's the way they work, which means my time will come too."

The Egyptian's face twisted. "Perhaps you're right, but you can play a different game."

"It'll not happen whilst the current President is in power." The Sheikh said.

The Egyptian pushed his spectacles further up his nose. "But you'll have to disappear after the events."

"Why should I disappear?" The Sheikh asked.

"If people think you're dead, they'll not look for you." He shrugged. "Otherwise everyone who knows there's a price on your head will search for you."

The Sheikh shook his head. "I hate the pretence."

The Egyptian pulled the blanket closer to his chest. "The more people who know the truth, the more difficult it'll become for you."

The Sheikh closed his eyes, as he thought for a moment. "It may be a good idea for someone to impersonate me on video and post it on the al Jazeera website."

The Egyptian smiled. "He'll have to look similar; not an obvious fake." He turned to the Sheikh. "But they'll analyze it in detail."

"I'll get a Taliban leader to announce your death and say he attended your funeral." The Sheikh said.

"And the events?"

"What about them?" The Egyptian looked quizzical.

The Sheikh took a deep breath. "Should we tell Mohammed about the secret technology being used by the Americans?"

The Egyptian shook his head. "It would be unwise."

"But it would give him more confidence about the mission's success."

"There are many reasons against it, Sheikh."

"You realize he's already asking questions."

"Is that important?' The Egyptian asked.

"He's not an ignorant man, of course."

The Egyptian grunted. "He's a foot soldier." He stood up slowly. "The less he knows the better for everyone."

The Sheikh stood up wearily, steadying himself. "I'll give it some thought by morning."

"But don't tell him about the real agenda." The Egyptian said. "It would be too dangerous." He opened the front door, stepping out into the night air.

The Sheikh nodded, opening the door of the truck. "He should know the events will dramatically increase recruitment."

"Such innocuous information will never satisfy him, Sheikh."

"I suppose so." He replied, closing the driver's door behind him.

*   *   *

The General ushered his most trusted and senior Colonel away from the main throng of the wealthy and famous at Bohemian Grove, Northern California. After passing numerous security cordons they sat on a bench under a large redwood tree. The drone of echoing voices wafted across the balmy evening air from the ceremonial events taking place close to the large bonfire with the image of a giant owl eerily standing as a sentinel across the glade.

"Only three people know the real purpose of your training, Colonel." The General said. "It's the most secret work you'll ever undertake for your country."

The Colonel nodded, aware of the honour bestowed upon him, having been introduced to two ex-Presidents and the current Vice President. He had no illusions about the bizarre ritual in which he had just participated, knowing it was intended to ensure compliance with strict confidentiality. Though his thirty year career had flourished after involvement in masonry-style rituals, the oath sworn that evening was more chilling than any he had given at his lodge. "I understand completely, General, and I'll do my duty."

This may have been the General's last task before retiring to an honourable and comfortable retirement, but he remained determined to do his duty too. "You'll report only to me, but as the Vice President has explained to you the events are critical to the long-term future of your country." He hesitated, turning furtively in both directions before looking steely-eyed at the Colonel. "We're all patriots here and sometimes difficult decisions have to be made to protect our country."

The Colonel brushed his hand across a balding head. His life and training had led him to this point. "I've given my oath freely that no word of the events will pass my lips, whatever the circumstances." He raised his shoulders. "You can rely on me, General."

"You do understand I can't discuss operational details with you yet." The General spoke softly.

"I'm trained to obey the orders of my superiors, General."

"So you've no questions?"

The Colonel sighed. "I've many questions, but I realize you'll tell me what I need to know when the time is right."

"Good."

The Colonel thought for a moment. "There is one thing, General." He took a deep breath. "What did the Vice President mean when he talked about significant sacrifices having to be made?"

The General shrugged. "Some loss of life is inevitable and I wouldn't wish to mislead you."

The Colonel nodded, knowing sometimes life and death decisions had to be made in the field of battle. "I understand."

The General placed his arm on the Colonel's shoulder. "I knew I could trust you, old friend."

"When will these events happen, General?"

"First, you'll be told about Operation Tripod in the next three weeks."

"But isn't that a simple War Games operation, related to a FEMA exercise?" The Colonel interrupted.

The General smiled quietly. "Of course, but it'll be the trigger for more dynamic events."

"How will I receive my final instructions?"

"All instructions will come direct from me personally." He hesitated, "We can't allow communications to be intercepted, so I'll meet you the night before and there must be no argument or question."

The Colonel shuddered, but knew there could be no turning back. He may have been used to accepting orders, but this operation had sinister and clandestine aspects to it, different to anything he had encountered before in the theatre of war. "I'll accept your orders, General, like a good soldier." He said firmly. "You wouldn't be using me unless you knew you could trust me."

"You've an elite group of flyers, Colonel, and you must emphasize the confidential nature of this operation, as part of the War Games."

"They've all been trained by me personally, General, and can be trusted to do whatever is necessary to ensure the success of the operation."

"Good." The General stood up, gesturing back to the main group.

The Colonel stood up alongside the General. "What about this secret technology?"

"There are many secret technologies, but what about it?"

"How many other people are aware of it?"

"A trusted few." The General hesitated. "People realize remote-control technology exists, but not the extent of it."

"But I've never heard of it being used in this way before?'

"Of course not." The General replied gruffly. "As with much of our secret technology, the public don't know the half of it." He turned away. "We don't want our enemies to be aware of our capacity to control events."

The Colonel nodded. "I understand."

"It's the same with the Pentagon's concept of full-spectrum dominance, Colonel." The General turned back and smiled. "People don't appreciate it means controlling space with weapons developed under the mask of missile defence."

"Have we developed these weapons, General?"

The General nodded. "We must protect our many satellites from enemies of the free world and billions have gone into development."

"Do you expect to keep all these technologies secret, General?"

"No-one will discover the truth." The General looked into his eyes. "It's why we're relying on our most trusted officers."

"What if I'm asked to report to a higher ranked officer, General?"

"I don't think you need worry about higher ranked officers." He smiled again. "There's promotion in the pipeline, all being well."

"So I'm not going to be thrown to the lions afterwards?"

"What makes you say that, Colonel?"

"It's happened in the past." The Colonel shrugged. "And matters may be out of your control, General."

"It'll not happen, Colonel. I've received confirmation that after the events in New York an order will come down from the Vice President himself." He placed his hand on the Colonel's shoulder. "Don't worry about being at risk because we look after our own."

"So you'll de-brief personally, General?"

"Of course."

They walked back towards a laughing noisy group. An Arab activist, whose name and wealthy family were well-known to Washington and Langley insiders introduced himself to the Colonel.

*   *   *

The wind whistled eerily from the plateau, slamming against the window of Mohammed's bedroom, the glass pane cracking sympathetically to its incessant beat. Ghost-like voices from the adjoining camp wafted across with the wind and pain pulsated through his body, denying him any respite or sleep. He wondered if his condition remained a mere chest infection or whether he had developed pneumonia, or perhaps succumbed to the endemic tuberculosis in these parts of Asia, some strains of which he knew had become drug-resistant. Dogs barked haphazardly outside and the distorted noise echoed relentlessly against the walls of his room. At one point, he heard the sound of an engine starting, driving out of the compound. Constantly cold, alone and enveloped in the darkness of this remote location, tortured thoughts allowed negativity to rise up in his consciousness. His was the classical case of a mind and body at war with each other, the mind taking precedence, so the body revolted. Morning brought some relief, coughing helping to clear the phlegm clogging his lungs during the night. He sought an escape from the role-play he had begun in the sham terrorist events about to take place, but his destiny loomed larger every day. For his part, the Sheikh sought sacrifices to create a false trail and lay blame which would incriminate al-Qaeda. Perhaps he should have been grateful to be flown out of the cauldron after playing his part in the subterfuge, though paradoxically he felt martyrdom would have been more acceptable, knowing the cataclysmic events would change the world forever and finally allow the Americans to directly confront and erode their rigid constitutional structure.

Soon after dawn he was summoned for breakfast, though it was mid-morning before he saw the Sheikh who invited him into the back of the pick-up truck with some of his bodyguards. They drove over the ridge and across shingle and dirt paths to a valley below, completely shorn of trees and hiding places. Heavy clouds rolled in as they reached a small village with basic huts for living quarters and he sat down shivering against one of the buildings. An old man offered him water and after a few minutes of respite, the Sheikh guided him towards a dingy building alongside the largest house in the village. The Sheikh, a white shawl around his head and shoulders, walked in ahead of him, slightly bowing his head to manoeuvre the low door frame, taking his position seated on cushions cross-legged in the far side of the room next to the Egyptian. Faded old mats covered the floor, though blankets made the sitting more comfortable, as they huddled close to each other in the cold. A glimmer of light intruded from the open entrance, where an old wooden door leaned wearily off its rusty hinges. Another trickle of light from a fading lantern in the centre of the room created strange shadows on the exposed walls and the unpleasant smell of paraffin hung heavily in the room, aggravating his chest condition. Mohammed looked at the smoke-stained ceilings of this barren room, its crumbling walls, the hanging door with its rusty hinges, so limp and useless, swinging noisily from time to time when the wind blew in its direction, and wondered in the moment what had led him to this place.

To the right of the Sheikh, the bespectacled Egyptian, looked at the visitor hard-faced and unsmiling through wary eyes. Mohammed stared back until he turned his attention to the file of papers on his lap, shuffling them into some form of order, and screwing his eyes to read them in the dimly-lit room. To his side, and on the floor, he noticed his worn copy of the Qu'ran, fanatically and faithfully carried. Mohammed pondered how the Egyptian epitomized the typical dour and unsmiling Jihadist.

He turned to the Sheikh. "When does it begin?" He asked, struggling to breathe in an atmosphere so deprived of oxygen and tainted with paraffin fumes.

"Soon. Inshallah." The Sheikh replied.

"How soon?" Mohammed sat down in this inauspicious little room, making himself comfortable, even though an old knee injury prevented him sitting cross-legged.

The Sheikh looked thoughtful. "The symbol of the golden dagger in a video to be released on a website will have an encrypted message secretly embedded in it. This will be the call for action."

"Have you told him my views?" Mohammed directed his eyes towards the Egyptian, his speech rasping, and he coughed harshly. He knew he needed antibiotics and wanted to return to Pakistan urgently.

The Sheikh folded his arms. "He knows, but he's with me, Mohammed."

"So it's the infidel's dirty work we do again, as we did with the Mujahadeen against the Russians?" He took a matted handkerchief from his pocket and blew his nose in the hope of eradicating the smell of paraffin from his nostrils.

"For the time being." The Sheikh replied, noticing the disdainful expression crossing Mohammed's face. "Life is full of compromises and for the time being politics and money dictate our future."

Mohammed puzzled at the Sheikh's pragmatic attitude. "So the hijacking is merely a diversion, a false flag operation as part of the cover-up to protect the American power-brokers." Some years had elapsed since he had been recruited to the cause, but his disillusion with it had become difficult to conceal, even if some instinct of self-protection allowed him to act the martyr.

The Sheikh shook his head. "Be careful, Mohammed."

"But you're making al-Qaeda the patsy, when it's an inside job?"

The Sheikh sighed. "Mohammed, why do you ask questions, when you already know the answers?"

He threw his hands up, looking injured. "Because I can't come to terms with what you want me to do."

"Why?" The Sheikh asked.

"Because Islam will come under siege and many Muslims will pay a heavy price for our actions." Mohammed's dark face creased, as empty sunken eyes, the soul in slumber, suddenly shone like beacons, their fire consuming him.

The Sheikh shrugged, unmoved. "Politics and crime, they're all the same."

Mohammed's eyes narrowed. "Politics is the dirtier game."

The Sheikh nodded. "But I need you onside over this."

Mohammed grunted. "I understand."

"The hijacking story may only be the cover, Mohammed, but it's crucial the others believe in the integrity of their martyrdom mission for the glory of Allah." The Sheikh hesitated. "The future of al-Q aeda is dependent upon it."

"I'd rather tell them the truth." Mohammed shook his head. "It's only right, if they're sacrificing their lives."

"No, Mohammed." The Sheikh frowned. "I can't risk the truth seeping out. Trust in Allah and the Prophet."

"I do, Sheikh, and I'm never frightened of the truth."

The Sheikh's eyes darted back. "Don't you understand?" He asked, pausing for a moment. "It may not be our doing, but this will inspire many soldiers to follow its idea for a generation. Zoroastrians, Christians and other Islamists will all join our crusade. The Americans will get their oil and gas, yet keep their people in fear."

Mohammed flinched, puzzled how a fundamentalist Sunni or Wahhabi like the Sheikh could belittle himself by associating with Shias, but the close associations with heretics, such as Jews and Americans were far worse in his eyes. He knew the Wahhabi's view of Islam was divisive, puritanical and violent, but it was not his vision. He turned to the Sheikh. "So it's an Islamic War you're provoking with the West to satisfy the whims of your American friends?"

"The divisions within the Muslim world have forged a scar in the psyche of Muslims for too long and this will help heal the wounds, Mohammed." The Sheikh could almost hear his old teacher's words as he spoke, recalling his old Palestinian theology teacher at the elite Jeddah private school he attended and wondered what he would say about his actions. He remained in awe of this zealous Sunni Muslim scholar who had first encouraged him to study the commentary on the Qu'ran by the fabled philosopher-poet, Sayyid Qutb, following his teacher to Afghanistan some years before to fight against the occupying Soviets.

Mohammed sighed. "I don't see it that way."

"But you do understand Jihad?" The Egyptian asked, his hungry eyes searching for an insight into Mohammed's soul. "We'll appeal to those who live mediocre lives, and whose families starve to feed the decadence of the West, with the promise of paradise for those who choose martyrdom. Hamdulillah." He raised both hands in the air in devotion, reminding Mohammed ironically of evangelical Christians.

"But the greater Jihad is the battle for our souls." Mohammed looked at the Egyptian, restraining a flash of temper. "Even the lesser Jihad must refer to a just war and I question the ideological basis upon which we justify this excursion."

"Is our cause not just?" The Egyptian asked through gritted teeth, almost by reflex, rubbing his hand against the back of his neck.

Mohammed tapped his thigh nervously, his eyes blazing. "You promote takfir, so Muslims who don't support your Jihad or don't do exactly what you tell them to do become kuffar and infidel and the legitimate targets of Jihad." His voice rose. "This makes you a fascist and no different to those you criticize in the West. It can't be right or just."

"You're kuffar." The Egyptian grunted, pointing his finger at him. "Mukaffir." He repeated angrily.

Mohammed sneered, but said nothing. He may have disliked him, but at least he was honest and if he had something to say, would say it to his face.

The Sheikh lifted his hand, looking sternly at the Egyptian. "Our way is right and it's just, but only the Prophet can pronounce Mukaffir."

"The US neo-cons operate from the same ideology." Mohammed said, his voice rasping. "You both believe the end justifies the means and want to frighten people into accepting our Jihad."

The Egyptian's eyes bulged and he pointed at Mohammed again. "You walk a crooked path." He shook his head. "Too many Muslims have abandoned Jihad for a love of worldly things."

"But in bringing the revelations of the Prophet to the people we must do it as directed by the divine revelations."

The Egyptian turned to the Sheikh. "How can you trust this rebellious man?" He hesitated. "I caution you, his heart is not sacred."

Mohammed shook his head. "I understand your doubts because I know the truth with the only beneficiaries being the greedy corporations of the West, like the Vice President's corporation and its subsidary, the defence contractor and the pipeline builders." He breathed heavily. "They'll make billions from the wars you provoke with the various defence and 'no-bid' pipeline contracts. They'll get their access to the oil and gas reserves in the Caspian Basin, the pipelines and their terminal ports at the Ocean. Even the Jews will benefit and the Americans will have their excuse for their incursions into Islamic countries for the next ten years." He began coughing violently again, placing his handkerchief to his mouth, noticing blood staining it.

"The world may be deteriorating into a sewer, Mohammed, but we'll benefit." The Egyptian picked up his Qu'ran again, clutching it against his chest.

Mohammed shook his head, putting the handkerchief away. "The world is responsive to the thoughts of its people. You're pushing the world into a downward spiral, rather than allowing it to aspire to a higher state and when you kill Muslim and non-Muslim, women and children, all in the name of Jihad, you gravely violate Sharia Law and the teachings of the Prophet."

The Egyptian's pallid face looked drawn "They'll see my vision and the clerics will follow my lead."

Mohammed looked to the Sheikh. "Why do you intercede in their wars?" He asked. "Few Muslims will accept the Egyptian's redundant vision in a modern society."

"You're wrong, Mohammed." The Egyptian replied dismissively. "Sacrifices have to be made."

The Sheikh lifted his left hand. "It'll not be us doing the killing, it'll be the Americans who will control the events."

Mohammed looked at the Sheikh with pitiful eyes. "You may want to keep the detail of the plans to yourself, but if I'm the leader of this group of soldiers, I think it's not unreasonable you explain everything to me."

"Either you follow orders like everyone else, Mohammed, or face the consequences." The Egyptian's voice strained menace, his spectacles quivering in rage.

Mohammed's voice still rasped. "The Taliban will never agree to the West's plans for the Caspian Basin, so it'll be an obstacle for them."

"I hear what you say." The Egyptian said, his face still contorting.

Mohammed placed his left hand over his forehead. "This is all about the secret government, shadowing the American puppet government and the elite financiers who control and lobby governments, lending money to all sides, as they always do." He feared the Egyptian, certain he worked to a different agenda to the Sheikh.

"Mohammed, you think too much." The Sheikh said.

"But there's a market in the Caspian Basin for about thirteen trillion dollars of oil and gas, Sheikh." Mohammed remained stone-faced.

"I know, Mohammed"

Mohammed's shoulders hunched. "But the Americans will be immune from any repercussions because they've not signed up to the International Criminal Court in The Hague and their government can safely ignore world opinion. It's our fellow Muslims and the eastern countries which will count the cost of our extravagance."

"You're telling us something we already know, Mohammed." The Sheikh's tone arched. "What's your point?"

Mohammed shrugged. "I'm certain you understand my position, Sheikh." His voice cracked. He hadn't slept properly for weeks and his time in the West had spoilt him. In the mountains, he struggled with the limited diet of buttered noodles, oats with goat's milk and occasionally a feast on scraps of lamb and samosas. Though he felt exhausted and in no mood for argument, a part of him preferred a blaze of glory to a slow disease-ridden death. He thought of the secretive existence he had chosen and the twelve months which had passed since he had last seen his family and children. There were some amongst them who wanted to depose the President in Pakistan and make the Islamic nuclear bomb available to this Wahhabi. He thought this would frighten the West, unless the fear of annihilation was part of their perverse strategy to control their population through the imposition of fear.

The Egyptian eyed Mohammed suspiciously. "We have our own agenda because the West will never understand militancy based on cultural conflict or ideology. Their materialistic attitudes could analyse the motives of a territorial conflict, but these events will have no conceivable goal."

Mohammed wondered sometimes if the Egyptian knew what he and the Sheikh knew. "And if the Muslim world offers the best of its men and sacrifices its sons to protect this ideology, will you be happy?"

"You miss the point." The Egyptian replied coldly. "This is not about sentiment, though blood-letting is sometimes necessary to clear away the old order of things. It's so written in the Qur'an and in this world of suffering there's poverty, old age, illness and death."

"But what about joy?" Mohammed asked.

The Egyptian shook his head. "Suffering is present even when enthralled in the midst of bliss, for when the factors which manifest pleasure and happiness dissipate, we immediately revert to the human condition and become distressed to some degree."

"You're a troubled soul." Mohammed glared at the Egyptian, barely able to conceal his contempt for his distorted interpretation of the Qu'ran.

The Egyptian pursed his lips. "Aren't we all?"

A pained expression crossed Mohammed's face. "But you must know the House of Islam will be used cynically to further a cause which has nothing to do with the teachings of the Prophet."

"Is that what you think?" The Egyptian asked.

Mohammed nodded. "I think you're working to the West's secret agenda."

"Enough." The Egyptian replied, the ferocity surprising even Mohammed. "You've sworn Bayat, the oath of loyalty to the Sheikh. Do you intend to break it?"

Mohammed recoiled, opening his mouth, but shutting it again quickly, his instinct for survival taking precedence. He needed to protect his position and play the role his paymasters demanded. "If it must be done, but it sticks in my craw, if I'm to be a scapegoat for the elite friends of the Sheikh's family."

"This is not done for them, but for the cause." The Sheikh scowled, knowing more than most the extent to which secret technology had been hidden from the people and the nature of the pin-point surveillance available to the intelligence community, with all telephone calls and e-mails flagged and stored for analysis by the software on intelligence computers. Even the new technology about to be used in the forthcoming events in the land of the Great Satan, would continue to be kept secret from the public. As with all secret technology, he knew it was often in use for years before they become aware of it. "We'll use the media outlets and websites to praise Muslims who leave their homes to fight Jihad. Their names will be written in gold in the green fields." He lifted his hands in the air.

Mohammed groaned. "Does the Qur'an say hundreds of thousands must die to achieve this ideology?"

"You shouldn't recite the words of the Prophet to me or question my motives." The Sheikh replied.

"Sometimes you're ignorant of our intentions, Mohammed." The Egyptian said.

"The torture has made you blind and perverse to the truth." Mohammed replied defiantly, wondering what the Egyptian was doing in his little poisoned world.

"And sometimes I wonder about your motives." The Egyptian replied equally firmly.

Mohammed thought carefully, inhaling a deep breath. "It's my motives, which make me sceptical of your plans." He sighed. "The intelligence community need to make their public more susceptible to radical solutions and foreign incursions."

"So what?" The Egyptian asked.

"How can it possibly help us?"

"Because it'll de-stabilize the West." The Egyptian replied, vitriol echoed in every cadence. "In time, the price of oil in the West will increase to a level which will squeeze them, jolting them from their decadent and deviant ways. We'll attack all the institutions of the capitalist countries in every way we can, including their financial institutions."

Mohammed shook his head. "They control too many countries for the price of oil to have a lasting effect. Every time a crisis happens, the western governments blame lack of funding for the military and the intelligence services and their budgets are massively increased again."

"I'm convinced things will change and this is only the beginning." The Sheikh said.

Mohammed turned to the Sheikh. "I don't see it."

The Sheikh groaned. "They'll exhaust their budgets in the next few years and in time the US dollar will cease to be the reserve world currency."

"But even if the dollar collapses as a consequence, it'll not stop the manipulation of weak Muslim governments." Mohammed moved his hands out, palms upwards.

"I think you're wrong, Mohammed." The Sheikh replied. "In time, Muslim governments will sympathize with al-Qaeda and listen to our voices."

"You'll see the path we tread, when you open yourself to the spiritual truth, Mohammed, as it's written by the Prophet." The Egyptian repeated his mantra.

Mohammed shifted uncomfortably. "I'll do what you ask of me, but don't think I'm an ignorant man or incapable of looking beyond the rhetoric and subterfuge."

The Egyptian pointed a shaking finger at him. "If you've reservations, Mohammed, we can call upon another soldier in one of the sleeper cells to take your place in this operation."

Mohammed blinked, wondering whether his honesty had placed him at risk. "I've already told you I'll do what you ask of me." He spoke more carefully. "You're not listening."

"Ziad Jarrah or Zacarias Moussaoui can take over the operation if you're not committed to it." The Sheikh looked directly at Mohammed, his expression unchanged.

"Well?" The Egyptian asked, sullenly, clenching a fist to his side.

"There's no need to involve them." Mohammed replied.

"You worry me." The Egyptian growled, looking across at the Sheikh.

"Enough." The Sheikh lifted his right hand. "He'll do it."

Mohammed's shoulders hunched again and an energetic silence filled the room. When the silence became too much, he spoke nervously. "I know the Americans have this secret technology they intend to use to effect the devastation, but how will it control the events?"

The Sheikh frowned openly, turning towards the Egyptian and back to Mohammed. "What secret technology?"

"Please don't treat me like a fool, Sheikh. I know you couldn't do this without the agents of the American government and someone has to control the complicated computerized flight management systems in the aircraft."

"Is that right?" The Sheikh asked.

Mohammed nodded. "It's absurd to think my people could do it, even if they're prepared to sacrifice themselves to leave the false trail."

The Sheikh grimaced. "When the time comes, you'll be told, but you must leave the detail to us for the time being."

Mohammed shook his head. "But how is your plan feasible when the Federal Aviation Administration's procedures are bound to be invoked when there's the slightest deviation in the flight-path."

"You must trust us, Mohammed." The Sheikh replied.

"But their systems of operation and military interventions can't be overridden." A puzzled expression crossed Mohammed's face. "If either the Transponder Code 7500 is entered or even if the transponder is simply switched off, the result will be the same. Fighter jets with sidewinder missiles will be scrambled into the skies within three minutes. The missiles have an eighteen mile radius and any hijacked aircraft will be blown away long before it can reach its intended target." He sighed heavily, almost pleading. "This is why I need to understand this secret technology, Sheikh."

"Who has told you about this secret technology, Mohammed?' The Egyptian asked.

"You forget I've a good contact in the Pakistan Intelligence Services, the ISI." He determined to protect his real source.

The Sheikh caught Mohammed's eye. "Don't forget I've my contacts within the same intelligence service and also within the CIA."

"I know." Mohammed replied.

"What happens to the aircraft isn't your problem, Mohammed." The Sheikh said firmly. "None of the military and government agencies will respond on the day. Steps have already been taken."

"You don't need to understand how this technology works to do your part." The Egyptian added.

Mohammed looked back at the Sheikh with watchful eyes. "But their F16 Falcons and F15 Eagles can be scrambled to intercept any hijacked aircraft heading for either New York or Washington."

"We know the strength of their military." The Sheikh replied.

Mohammed coughed painfully again, covering his mouth with his handkerchief, before looking across at the Sheikh. "But Andrews Air Base in Washington is just ten miles from the Pentagon. It has two squadrons with sidewinder missiles and boasts on its website it's there to protect the skies of their capital. They can scramble its jets within three minutes, so how can this new secret technology help the aircraft reach their targets?"

"The squadrons will not be scrambled, Mohammed." The Sheikh replied, emphasizing the negative.

The Egyptian rolled his eyes. "We can't tell you everything, but you'll be safe. Your job is to create the false trail, leaving the clues behind." He sighed. "I don't know why you create these issues when you'll be flown out immediately afterwards with the Sheikh's brother."

"What more do you want?" The Sheikh asked

"I want you to confide in me and involve me in the planning."

"But you must trust us." The Sheikh said.

"This mission is impossible, Sheikh." Mohammed raised his voice again.

The Sheikh lifted his head, staring at him. "I'm asking you to trust me."

Mohammed shrugged, aware of the Sheikh's eyes on him. "I do trust you like a brother, but I'm disappointed you don't trust me enough to tell me everything."

"Then it's an ego thing, Mohammed?" The Egyptian asked.

Mohammed shrugged again, but said nothing.

The Sheikh raised his voice. "You must understand, Mohammed, I've arranged for a number of my people to be trained at the Air War College in Montgomery, Alabama, and at Pensacola Naval Air Station, so everything is under control."

Mohammed gazed intensely at the Sheikh. "I want to understand, but I need information." He replied.

"You've all the information you need." The Sheikh's eyes narrowed.

"But Maguire Air Force Base in New Jersey has a similar capability to Andrews, but protecting New York." Mohammed said. "Even if they choose not to fly supersonic, one way or another any aircraft getting within ten miles of the targets is dead in the air, even if by some miracle they got that close." He paused for a moment. "Did you know there've been sixty seven intercepts of commercial aircraft already this year when they've only slightly deviated from their flight-paths; yet you're proposing aircraft will go to the Mid-West before taking a huge arc back towards New York and Washington and you believe the military will simply stand down and watch the events on television?"

The Sheikh nodded. "I understand your scepticism, but it'll be resolved." He grimaced. "You must learn to trust me, Mohammed."

"You ask too many questions." The Egyptian said.

"But they can even send one of their planes from Otis in Cape Cod, fly supersonic, and be in New York in ten minutes." Mohammed's voice cracked.

"True." The Sheikh replied calmly.

"I don't understand." Mohammed's eyes questioning.

"What are you afraid of?" The Sheikh asked.

"It's not that I'm afraid, Sheikh, but I want to give you important information, so you appreciate the risks."

"What do you want to tell me?"

"You know Norad's systems at Cheyenne Mountain are the most technologically advanced in the world and it's linked to the Pentagon's defence systems, which include a ground to air missile system." Mohammed spoke firmly. "They can pick up any aircraft which deviates from its flight-path within seconds, even if only by a matter of a few degrees."

"But you must listen to us, Mohammed." The Sheikh said, more firmly than before.

Mohammed shivered, softening his tone when it occurred to him in that moment he may have failed to appreciate the consequences of his belligerence. "I'm simply advising you that what you propose may be physically impossible."

"It's not, Mohammed." The Sheikh replied instantly.

"Can you at least tell me the plan for the Pentagon, Sheikh?"

"It's not possible." The Sheikh replied.

"But they'll have so much notice from the time of the deviation in the flight-path of the first commercial aircraft to take counter-measures long before any aircraft can close on the Pentagon?"

The Sheikh sighed, unmoved. "What makes you think it's an aircraft?"

"But.?" Mohammed hesitated.

The Sheikh sighed. "It's not dependant on any aircraft."

"I don't understand?"

"Why do you always ask questions, Mohammed?" The Sheikh's tone condescending. "I can't tell you any more about the plans for the Pentagon, but defence aircraft will be ordered to stand down."

"Is that what will happen?"

"The Vice President will control events through an operation called 'Operation Tripod'. The Sheikh looked at the Egyptian and back at Mohammed. "But now I've told you more than I intended."

"I don't think this is a good idea." The Egyptian interrupted.

The Sheikh grimaced. "Perhaps not." He turned back to Mohammed. "This operation will result in the military standing down."

"For the last time, you must trust the Sheikh on the detail." The Egyptian said.

The Sheikh shrugged.

"So there's nothing else I need to know?" Mohammed stood up wearily.

"Only that it's time for blowback." The Sheikh hesitated. "I need to know your people will do what is necessary."

"They'll do the job."

"Someone has to take responsibility for the psychological terror for the passengers to remain compliant, until the secret technology does its work."

Silence would have betrayed Mohammed's thoughts." He looked down and to the right, before recalling this signalled the action of someone telling a lie and blinked quickly. "My men know their duty."

"I need loyalty and no more squabbling." The Sheikh spoke with a tone of finality.

Mohammed nodded. "I'll not betray your trust."

The Sheikh stood up. "I want you to meet one of my commanders, Mustafa Abu al-Yazid, who controls operations in Afghanistan." He moved slowly out of the room, grimacing, and holding his right side, without looking back to see if Mohammed and the Egyptian followed.

Outside the Commander held a man, bare to the waist, showing the obvious signs of torture, wrists bound tightly behind him. His head, bloodied and bruised, hung limp-like. The Sheikh nodded and the AK-47 assault rifle, slung around his shoulder, slid down into the shooting position. The Commander removed the safety catch, cocking it, the rifle barrel pointing downwards at an angle towards the floor. He looked at the Sheikh.

The recruit looked up at the Sheikh briefly with pitiful eyes.

The Sheikh turned towards Mohammed. "This man has passed information to your friends in the Pakistan Inter-Services Intelligence about our acquisition of nuclear materials, so what would you suggest we do with him?"

"Is it something they didn't already know?" Mohammed asked, believing the whole scene was playing out for his benefit.

"Would that make a difference?" The Sheikh asked.

"It should, if he's one of our brothers, Sheikh." Mohammed replied.

The Sheikh ignored his plea, nodding to the Commander, who placed a hood over the recruit's head and lifting the rifle barrel. The sound of the bullet chamber sliding across echoed and the soldier's head dropped down to the floor, without protest. A brief volley of bullets and the poor man's soul released from its torment.

The Sheikh turned to Mohammed. "I must have loyalty above all else."

Mohammed shook his head, his distaste apparent. "I'm not sure I like what you've become, Sheikh."

The Sheikh shrugged. "Don't let our friendship end in the same way." He said coldly, before turning and walking away.

CHAPTER THREE

"Be conscious of Allah (God) and speak always the truth"—Qu'ran.

Mohammed Atta, the alleged chief hijacker, was referred to by one author as a double agent, secretly working for US Intelligence. The anti-terrorism programme, 'Able Danger', formed under the US Special Operations Command (SOCOM), revealed Atta was under surveillance by US military intelligence agents who had identified him as an al-Qaeda ringleader more than a year prior to his visit to the United States for flying lessons. The same author suggested Khalid Sheikh Mohammed and others were working to further an agenda originating out of Washington, strongly influenced by Tel Aviv, rather than out of some ill-defined Muslim hatred of the US. Although there is footage of Atta going through baggage control at Portland Airport on the morning of 9/11, there is no footage of him or any of the alleged terrorists getting on any of the four aircraft allegedly hijacked that day, despite the existence of CCTV cameras.

There is a recording of Mohammed Atta telephoning his father saying: "I'm in a whole lot of trouble. I think they're going to kill me."

The CEO of Odigo, the instant messaging service confirmed that two of its workers had received messages two hours before the events of 9/11 predicting the attack would happen.

October 2nd 2001—1,000 pages of legislation has been drafted, (allegedly in three weeks) and the Patriot Act is introduced into Congress and just over three weeks later President Bush signs legislation into law that gives the Federal Government dictatorial powers and severely, if not fatally, erodes individual liberties and rights under the US Constitution. On the 3rd October 2001 the Senate Judiciary Committee Chairman accuses the Bush administration of reneging on an agreement in relation to the bill and by the 9th October 2011 anthrax letters are sent to him and to the Senate Majority Leader, both Democrats. The same anthrax strain as is found at the Ames Research Centre, Iowa State University, though they are immediately instructed to destroy all their anthrax spores. Between November 12th 2001 and March 25th 2002 thirteen renowned microbiologists die, all but one are killed or murdered under unusual circumstances, including an astro-biologist with the Ames Research Centre—killed while jogging.

Shortly after the events of 9/11, five Israelis are arrested in a white van, after allegedly celebrating whilst filming the events. The van contains a large amount of cash and box-cutters. Sniffer dogs reportedly find traces of explosives in the van. They are held for 71 days, then released without charge and are allowed to return to Israel where three of them appear on television stating they were documenting the events, a comment suggesting a level of foreknowledge. All reports of this incident have since disappeared.

"It is a fact that high-rise buildings with much larger, hotter and longer-lasting fires have never collapsed."

"Once you eliminate the impossible, whatever remains, no matter how improbable, must be the truth." Arthur Conan Doyle.

Mohammed cautiously took note of the Sheikh's bodyguard for future reference, knowing he would only get one chance to carry out his instructions. Someone nicknamed Snake never took his eyes off the Sheikh or released his AK-47 assault rifle, often called a Kalashnikov after its inventor, Sergeant Kalashnikov, and the year of its first manufacture. It may have been heavier with less shooting power than the more modern MP7, but they were plentiful. Another old rusting Russian pick-up vehicle had arrived from the fortress qala in the next valley during the morning, its 0.50 calibre machine gun mounted on the back, and a bunker occupied by armed soldiers on the hill above, gave the Sheikh immediate protection. Mohammed knew the recent execution had been intended as a warning and if he showed his hand too soon the consequences could be fatal.

Back in the same austere and dingy room after lunch, they all sat in the same positions. Although Mohammed's handler had made reference to a secret technology, he had refused to elaborate and he needed to tread warily.

"Is the acquisition of the enriched uranium finalized?" Mohammed asked, swotting a fly flirting with him.

The Sheikh nodded. "Once the project is completed, we may use someone else to hide the A device."

"But I've organized it, Sheikh?" Mohammed asked, wondering if they suspected his Agency links.

"It's more important you concentrate on the American operation, Mohammed." The Sheikh hesitated. "We don't want distractions."

Mohammed's mouth dropped open, but he changed the subject. "I know the Americans want their pipeline deals through Europe, via Turkey and the Balkans and through Afghanistan and Pakistan, but there must be more to their complicity than these pipelines?" He looked first at the Sheikh, then the Egyptian.

The Sheikh grimaced. "You've too many questions, Mohammed."

"But I don't trust the Americans." He replied, scepticism in the tone.

The Sheikh sighed. "You don't have to trust them, Mohammed, but in life there's always a price to pay."

"But Muslims will pay in blood in the sleight of hand decisions made by the elite few, blindside of the American people." Mohammed coughed again, his condition aggravated by the fumes of two more paraffin lamps brought into the room.

"You must leave the planning to us, Mohammed." The Sheikh said.

Shadows criss-crossed the room and Mohammed again shifted uncomfortably, sitting on the floor with legs spread wide in front of him, his knees supported by clasped hands. "I don't want to be disrespectful, but there are flaws in the intelligence." He shivered, pulling a frayed, oddly-coloured blanket over his shoulder. At the entrance to the room, the door did nothing to protect him from the relentless cold wind, as it whistled across the plateau.

"I'm not going over old ground, Mohammed." The Sheikh said

"But Norad's reaction time, with the aid of the AWACS, will be seconds." He hesitated. "Are you sure this 'Operation Tripod' will work?"

"No more." The Sheikh closed his eyes.

"But I don't understand?" Mohammed asked.

The Sheikh opened his eyes. "I'm certain the military will stand down."

"Do I have to guess how events will be manipulated?"

The Sheikh grimaced, raising his voice. "Don't guess anything, just do what you're told."

Mohammed shrunk back against the wall.

"Unless it's new information, let's get on." The Sheikh's breathing agitated.

"Sheikh, wouldn't it be more believable if we flew out of New York, not Boston?" Mohammed hesitated. "It's critical our operatives believe in the integrity of their mission."

The Sheikh remained silent.

Mohammed sighed. "If the first aircraft are successful in New York, there'll be no doubt about what's happening and the military personnel will never stand down."

"I've told you the situation affecting the Pentagon is different and the critical intercept will not happen. It's been arranged." An impatient edge echoed in the Sheikh's tone. "And I've already told you more than you need to know."

"But I'm a professional and I've studied chapter seven of the FAA procedures in detail."

"No, No." The Sheikh replied angrily. "Please don't pursue this."

"What is it you're still not telling me?" Mohammed asked.

The Egyptian's face bulged. "You must do your duty if you want to leave this camp." He shouted. "You agreed to undertake this operation and must stop asking unnecessary questions." He nodded to the guards.

Mohammed heard the noise of the safety clicking off one of the rifles and the snap of the bullet chamber sliding, ready for action. His body stiffened instinctively.

"Stop!" The Sheikh raised his right hand. "He's our brother and we'll not turn on our friends."

Mohammed exhaled loudly. "Thank you, Sheikh."

"But you disappoint me, Mohammed, because I need you to follow orders."

"I do follow orders, Sheikh." He stuttered.

"Then do it." The Egyptian said.

The Sheikh leant back, speaking more softly. "It's important we restrict information, Mohammed, if only to protect the operation."

Mohammed heard a round pop out of the chamber and the safety catch click back, watching as the rifle slung back over the bodyguard's shoulder. "I understand."

The Sheikh nodded.

"You've met my family, Sheikh, and you know my children. On their sacred souls, any secret is safe with me."

The Sheikh sighed, leaning forward again, raising his finger. "If one word of it leaks out both you and your family will regret it." He gestured to the guards to leave the room.

The Egyptian looked at the Sheikh. "It's unwise."

The Sheikh nodded. "He's leading the group and knows the consequences for him and his family, if any information ekes out, even by accident."

"Don't trust this man." The Egyptian said firmly.

The Sheikh shook his head. "It may help him to understand the events on the 11th September." He looked at Mohammed. "He loves his children and wouldn't place their lives in jeopardy."

The Egyptian raised his hands. "It's a mistake."

The Sheikh ignored him, instead turning to Mohammed. "I'll tell you more on an oath on your children's lives, but if this is repeated, you'll regret it." His voice arched, echoing across the walls.

"I give you my oath, Sheikh, on my children's lives."

The Sheikh took a deep breath and turned to the Egyptian, then back to Mohammed. "First, the secret technology is similar to that used to fly an unmanned remote-control Global Hawk over the Atlantic last year. It's been installed in two Boeings." He hesitated. "It involves using a control beacon at the World Trade Centre and an AWAC aircraft to control the aircraft externally and take over the flight controls."

Mohammed nodded, surprised such technology remained hidden from the public. "So the instruments on the flight decks will be useless?"

"Correct." The Sheikh replied.

"What about the Washington flight?" Mohammed asked.

The Sheikh spoke quietly. "The aircraft heading towards Washington will have a particular significance and will be treated differently."

Mohammed sat back. "Interesting."

"This information is very sensitive and if it's divulged for any reason, we'll know the source." The Sheikh's eyes fixed on him.

"I appreciate you trusting me, Sheikh."

The Sheikh picked up a large bundle of documents at his side and handed them to Mohammed. "Now let's get on with the schedules and time-scales." He said. "I need you to study them."

Mohammed looked at them carefully. "These are American documents?"

"Of course." The Sheikh replied. "What do you expect?"

Mohammed directed his attention back to the documents. "It all looks achievable and I don't anticipate problems." He looked at one of the schedules, then at the Sheikh again. "But won't they pick up on the time I leave Portland and the fact I'll not arrive in time to catch the Boston flight the same morning?"

"Leave it to us to cover the gaps and we'll do the intelligence work." The Sheikh shifted his position. "Our American friends will come up with verification."

"Are you sure?"

"Just organize the mechanics on the ground."

The Egyptian turned towards Mohammed, placing his papers on the floor. "Your job is simple, the false trail. It's not our party, but we'll accept the invitation." He fumbled with his papers. "There are some things you don't know."

"I want to trust you, but I worry about the future for our people."

The Sheikh nodded. "It's better for us that the mafias of leadership and wealth in the West remain in power. They've no compunction against lying, cheating and killing to keep their hold on power and to create their own agenda of wars, oil and gas pipelines and the erosion of their constitution."

"But how does that help us?" Mohammed asked.

The Egyptian shook his head. "The removal of individual freedoms and civil liberties for the people of the West is good for all Muslims. Soon other structures of their decadent world will collapse including their financial institutions. Soon the inequality between the East and the West will seem as nothing." He said. "One day we'll control the West politically by weight of numbers."

"I understand." Mohammed said.

"Sometimes, you forget the company you keep." The Egyptian said. "The Sheikh first declared war on America in 1996, when no-one had heard of al-Qaeda, and you still question him." He hesitated, his body shaking. "Who do you think first incited Jihad and united the warlords, the mullahs and the chieftains?"

"You miss the point." Mohammed lifted his head, turning to the Sheikh. "At what point do we stop taking our instructions from the vested interests in the West?"

"Don't question my motives, Mohammed. I've shown you great forbearance." The Sheikh stroked his straggling beard, more grey than black nowadays, his once bulging cheeks now sallow and sunken, then looked at Mohammed. "I realize those in positions of power in the United States have their secret agenda." He chose his words carefully. "On this occasion it coincides with ours and they'll not react as normal." He winced in pain. In some spiritual sense, he needed pain as a penance, knowing if his soul suffered, then his body was bound to cry out in empathy. "If I say anything else, the secrecy and surprise are lost."

Mohammed nodded. "You've been frank with me and I can't ask for more."

"No you can't." The Sheikh pointed his finger at Mohammed. "Remember, I've worked as an Agency asset and I still have friends in high places."

Mohammed recoiled, feeling uneasy at the choice of words. "What are you suggesting?"

"Nothing yet."

"So how long are we going to work for your American friends, Sheikh?" He asked, realizing his impetuosity could one day destroy him.

The Sheikh shrugged pragmatically, glaring icily at Mohammed. "Only for as long as it suits me." He replied. "And what about you?"

Mohammed froze. "I don't know what you mean."

"Just as well."

Mohammed dropped his head, regretting the swiftness of his tongue. Even though the encampment was located close to the Pakistan/Afghanistan border, he knew he could only escape if the Sheikh allowed it. "I need you to confide in me, Sheikh."

"Of course you do."

"You must concentrate on one operation, but it's not the future of al-Qaeda." The Egyptian said.

The Sheikh smiled his crooked smile. "Are you with us, Mohammed?"

Mohammed took a deep breath. "I'll do my duty."

The Egyptian looked at Mohammed, speaking more softly. "An American Colonel, whose career involved clandestine operations, helpfully recited in his book some years ago that 'no-one has to direct an assassination, the active role is played secretly by permitting it to happen'. This is your clue." He raised his eyebrows. "The same author went on to suggest if a person asked himself who had the power to call off or reduce the usual security procedures, there you'd have the guilty parties."

Mohammed stood up, stretching aching limbs. "But what about the cover story?"

"What about it?" The Egyptian replied.

"The use of credit cards in our own names, the taking of a connecting flight with only minutes to spare, leaving flight manuals in Arabic in rented cars, even the driving licences have addresses such as the Pensacola Naval Base. It all appears so amateur."

"On this occasion, you must do as you're told." The Sheikh said firmly.

Mohammed felt disappointment. "Can I be candid with you about certain issues?"

The Sheikh sighed. "If you insist."

"First, my people have been described as inept pilots in little Cessna aircraft. Any investigator would know they can't undertake complicated manoeuvres or re-programme complicated flight management computer systems." He paused. "How will this be credible, even as a cover story?"

The Sheikh looked at the Egyptian, then back at Mohammed. "They'll believe it, if it's repeated enough."

Mohammed shook his head. "Eventually, the truth will come out."

The Sheikh shrugged. "If it does, it's a problem for the Americans, not us."

The Egyptian clutched his Qu'ran. "It's not that the American people are gullible; It's simply easier for them to accept the lie, when the truth frightens them."

"You must know how intelligence works. Mohammed. They control the media." The Sheikh said.

Mohammed grinned awkwardly. "I'm reluctant to be set up under another false flag operation, if it enhances the ability of the United States to implement all-out war or even black operations against Islamic nations."

The Egyptian groaned, a curse crossing his lips.

Mohammed sat back down, slumping back until he touched the wall behind him. "Your idealism has changed, Sheikh. I still remember the interview you did for CNN back in March 1997."

"I've not changed, but sometimes it's necessary to change strategy, Mohammed."

"I remember you criticized the Saudi Royal Family for being subservient to the United States, yet you do their dirty work." Mohammed hesitated. "Why?"

The Sheikh grimaced. "Because it suits al-Qaeda and we need images to inspire Muslims." He pointed to the water jug on the table and Mohammed dutifully poured a glass, passing it to him. The Sheikh drank it in one motion. "The image of burning and collapsing towers has an archetypal significance within the consciousness of the people of the West."

Something resonated with Mohammed. "But I fear the West will create wars against Muslim nations for the next generation."

The Sheikh nodded. "There are risks and sacrifices to be made."

"In that interview in 1997, Sheikh, you said the United States had set double standards, calling whoever fights against its injustices or dares to exercise freedom to speak out, a terrorist."

The Sheikh smiled. "You remember."

"I hate the egos of the Americans, Sheikh."

"It's an imperfect world and we must all find our place within it, Mohammed." The Sheikh hesitated. "Who do you think funds the Madrassas schools, where we recruit, changing the hearts and minds of Muslim children?"

Mohammed grunted.

The Sheikh wagged his finger. "Sometimes you must do evil to do good."

"I'm not sure I understand?"

"We must consider the larger picture, Mohammed." The Egyptian intervened. "Your friend, Mahmud Ahmad, the chief spy master in the Pakistan Inter-Services Intelligence, the ISI, told me the United States will invade Afghanistan by mid-October and they've already told the Taliban they'll invade unless they agree a pipeline deal."

Mohammed sighed. "I know the way the Americans work. If they're going into Afghanistan, they'll manipulate public opinion to do it."

"So whether we help them or not, it'll happen." The Egyptian replied.

The Sheikh grimaced. "The President of Pakistan will help the Americans because he thinks they'll stay loyal and support him, but he's a fool." He hesitated. "In time, he'll be ousted too."

"What are the American's long-term plans?" Mohammed asked.

"Do you really want to know?"

Mohammed nodded. "Of course."

The Sheikh opened both palms. "Hidden technology already exists, including such things as cold fusion, beam riding devices and zero point energy devices, all of which could dispense with any reliance on oil." He grunted, moving into a more comfortable position. "And I've heard some of the Operation Paperclip Nazi scientists brought over to the United States have developed red mercury vortex devices in Area 51 and have experimented with anti-gravity devices. Who knows how far this technology has been developed?"

Mohammed's eyes narrowed. "Then why don't they use these exotic energy devices, if they're cheaper?"

The Sheikh smiled. "The secret field of unified physics has moved on much further than the public are aware and we need to protect the assets of our Muslim brother nations by continuing the West's reliance on oil."

Mohammed shook his head. "But how long can they keep these devices secret?"

"For as long as possible." The Sheikh replied. "Some of these technologies have no carbon emissions and cost next to nothing if they invested in their development."

"Some of the technology stems from the Nazi's intention to be independent of foreign oil and so few really understood the extent of its development at that time." The Egyptian said.

"It's in our interests, Mohammed, to ensure there's no will to push investment into these things." The Sheikh said softly.

"But the energy crisis would end and there'd be increased wealth for everyone." The furrows on Mohammed's forehead tightened.

"It suits our Muslim brothers to keep their market in oil." The Sheikh said.

Mohammed shrugged. "So your elite friends with their vested interests retain their investments in the oil companies."

The Sheikh nodded politely.

"Without the West's reliance on oil, some of our brothers would have no assets with which to trade." The Egyptian said.

"I suppose it makes sense." Mohammed said.

"It's important they continue to rely on our oil or we'll go back to living in tents." The Sheikh said.

"But after the events in September, the western media will demonize you, Sheikh, and they'll hunt you down."

"In 1996 the Sudan offered to extradite me to the United States, but the then President turned down their offer. They've always warned me in advance of any incursions or bombing plans, so I'll maintain the liaison as long as it suits al-Qaeda."

"But for how long?" Mohammed asked.

"It suits us for the time being." The Egyptian replied.

The Sheikh looked at Mohammed with softer eyes. "The US President's family and those in the Carlyle Group, are not simply business partners, but close family friends. The Agency funded my family's construction company in the building of the cave complexes, which we use as part of our operations." The wind sent another icy blast into the room and the Sheikh shivered. "They'll airlift us to Pakistan when the Afghanistan invasion begins and find me a safe house there."

"I think it's a big mistake if you trust them because they change sides all the time." Mohammed shook his head. "Look at Saddam Hussein. One minute he's an ally in the Middle East and they supply weapons to him by the bucketful, then they complain about his weapons of mass destruction, which they supplied in the first place and still have the receipts."

The Sheikh nodded. "You're right, of course."

"But they're going to take him out and place his oil fields in the hands of the greedy American corporations and you'll give them the excuse."

The Sheikh smiled. "I know the monster who shares my bed, but for now he pays for the privilege."

"Sheikh, there'll come a time when you'll live your life in the shadows."

"I've not forgotten what they did with Noriega who only wanted to stop his money-laundering activities for the Agency's black ops department." The Sheikh replied.

Mohammed nodded. "When he tried to explain his connections with the Agency at his trial, the Judge wouldn't permit him to introduce any such evidence or the Agency's black operations."

The Sheikh smiled. "We both know the Americans intimately and the risks associated with any relationship with those in power."

"I hope I'm wrong, Sheikh."

"I'm under no illusions." The Sheikh said. "Any loyalty is temporary."

Mohammed grimaced. "But you're taking a grave risk."

"Maybe you're right."

Mohammed searched the Sheikh's eyes for the truth within his soul. "I still believe the operation's signature will be impossible to conceal."

"It's their problem."

"But this operation requires significant resources and it'll be obvious they're contrived events." Mohammed shrugged. "They'll never believe it's al-Qaeda's work."

"Khalid believes it." The Sheikh said.

Mohammed laughed a deep-throated laugh. "The egotistical one doesn't count. He can't see beyond personal glory, believing it's his great plan with no knowledge of your collusion."

"I've no reason to right his assumption." The Sheikh replied. "The western world is full of egos with no understanding of the spiritual concept of freedom, yet they still export their flawed ideologies."

"This is what I mean, Sheikh. They assume their democracy brings freedom, but in its trail money is power."

The Sheikh nodded. "But soon they'll live in a Police State with little freedom. Debt will follow the consumerism and the beneficiaries will be the international money lenders, as always."

"I've studied economics, Sheikh." Mohammed reminded him. "And they'll constrict the money supply which is the real cause of recessions with the perceived stock market crashes merely the symptoms."

"I've had a good education too, Mohammed." The Sheikh replied.

"But it's a trap and the people in the west are blind to its implications. Only the poor will suffer and the rich will get richer in the recession, which is bound to follow in the next decade."

The Sheikh nodded. "I think you're right."

"Then shouldn't we stop them importing their ideologies, Sheikh?"

"Muslims will eventually revert to a life based on spiritual values, Mohammed."

The Egyptian spoke calmly. "Perhaps the infidels will hate al-Qaeda with a passion, but our Muslim brothers will love us in equal degree, if only because we'll be doing to them what they've always done to us."

The Sheikh moved his arms out to the side. "You see, even the Egyptian agrees with me."

Mohammed smiled uncomfortably. "My concern is ending up with their New World Order full of unelected bureaucrats, living in a world governed by fascist dictatorships, beyond the rule of law. Organizations like the Bilderberger Group have no conscience for the innocent victims in their thousands who suffer from their decisions. They'll use recessions to argue for a one-world government, despite all the evidence it does not work, but it'll give them the excuse to mop up the assets of the weak and vulnerable."

"Mohammed, I've told you that you think too much." The Sheikh said. "If we do nothing, the world has its inevitable fascist environment, the model already existing in Europe and it'll spread to the Americas."

"I'll fight for our ideology, Sheikh, if it changes the course of history."

The Sheikh's eyes lit up. "Then fight with us, Mohammed. Help us change it."

Mohammed grunted. "I'm committed to this operation, Sheikh, so let's see what it brings."

The Egyptian nodded, placing his hands together. "In the course of time, I'm certain events will work in our favour."

"One thing you must remember, Mohammed." The Sheikh said, standing up and moving out of their cramped little room. "The Agency won't hesitate to hunt you down, if you divulge the clandestine nature of their involvement in these events."

"I'll not breach the confidence you've placed in me, Sheikh."

"You'd be a fool, Mohammed." The Sheikh turned and walked away, looking back for an instant. "And I don't think you're stupid." His faithful guards, who had waited patiently outside, followed him.

This was not the time for a move, nor did Mohammed's handler want action yet, for the events planned for the 11th September 2001 had to take their full course. Far too often, it was the assassin or prime perpetrator of events who would be the first to be eliminated to end the trail of investigation, so he understood the risks. It was the nature of the dirty game in which he had become embroiled and he had no illusions about the potential outcome. His soul would be lost if events followed their inexorable momentum, though redemption could yet be gained by disrupting the operation or squealing. An overwhelming urge from deep within his consciousness arose with a desire to save the lives of thousands of innocent people, but the carousel had begun its movement. One of the Sheikh's brothers in the United States would ensure its inevitable spiral, but he consoled himself that in the longer term he would change things. When he left the Sheikh's encampment that night he knew his destiny would take him back for a different purpose.

CHAPTER FOUR

"Enron had intimate contact with Taliban officials . . . Enron secretly employed active CIA Agents to carry out its dealings overseas . . . gaining information from the intelligence satellite project Echelon, (which eavesdrops on electronic communications throughout the world picking up key words or phrases), to land billions of lucrative contracts overseas . . . (Enron was, of course, a large contributor to the Presidential campaign of George W. Bush) . . . when Clinton was bombing bin Laden camps in Afghanistan in 1998, Enron was making payoffs to Taliban and bin Laden operatives to keep the pipeline project alive . . . and there is no way anyone could NOT have known of the Taliban and bin Laden connection at that time, especially Enron, who had CIA agents on its payroll." (National Enquirer).

Enron executive, Cliff Baxter, was murdered in January 2002 before he could speak about the dirty dealings in Texas. "Baxter's suicide was murder say top cops." (National Enquirer—4th March 2002). The Securities and Exchange Commission's offices were situate in Building Seven of the WTC and amongst the 3,000 to 4.000 files lost in its destruction were the files investigating Enron.

One of the purchasers of the World Trade Centre Lease in July 2001, (and insured it for considerably more than he paid for it), admitted in a TV interview that when Building Seven was on fire the decision was made to 'pull it'. It would normally take days to prepare the charges to demolish the building so it would collapse into its own footprint. It would have taken more than thirty men to place these charges with security cameras and foot patrols in the building. The same man was reported to be in the habit of having breakfast with his children each morning in the Windows of the World Restaurant more than 100 floors up in the North Tower, but did not do so on the morning of 9/11.

"Several discontinuities make no sense—hijackers having little flying experience—undoubtedly the 'hijackings' were a "parallel operation" . . . "as the consequences were anti-Islam and a 'catalyctic' event such as 'the new Pearl Harbour' referred to in the Policy for the New American Century, the Israelis had a positive reason to assist in doing it" . . ."19 Arabs and al-Qaeda did not have the expertise to demolish buildings." Said a veteran of 45 Marine Corps and a Military Insider in a TV interview.

"Evidence of the chemical signature of thermite incendiaries, nano thermite composites, have been found in the dust and steel samples and also of explosives in the dust samples."

"I'm due back at Andrews later this morning, but first I must take a position to the south, as part of this War Games Operation. It must remain top-secret and you've had your orders." The Colonel spoke firmly to the solitary occupant of Air Traffic Control at Otis in Cape Cod, feeling the need to explain both the reason for his return to his Andrews home base, ten miles from the Nation's Capital, and for taking off in the opposite direction first. It had been three weeks since his meeting with the General at Bohemian Grove, though his briefing the previous evening made it clear the task expected of him should anything go wrong. Although his involvement may only have been as back-up intervention and insurance, he still hoped it would not be necessary to take American lives.

"It's the General here. I've taken over the controls at Norad to oversee your mission." He said, once the Colonel was airborne.

"I understand, Sir." The Colonel replied, reassured by the General's direct control and involvement. He took his position at thirty five thousand feet south of New York, knowing an AWACS was five thousand feet above him to the north and a remote Global Hawk manoeuvred not far away.

"Flight 93 has had a problem. It's taken off forty minutes late from Newark, so it's time to do your duty, Colonel. Rely on your training and good luck."

"Sir" He replied by reflex, a sinking feeling stirring in the pit of his stomach.

"You should intercept over Pennsylvania, but once you've made contact, await my further orders, Colonel. Timing is everything."

"Yes, sir."

After a short time, the Colonel picked up the aircraft on his cockpit screen. "I have the aircraft in sight, General."

There was a short hesitation. "The order is to take out the aircraft, Colonel." The General said. "I repeat the order is to take out Flight 93. Confirm you understand the order."

Despite his combat training and a veteran of numerous engagements, the Colonel still found it difficult to come to terms with his orders, but he knew collateral damage happened in battle situations and difficult decisions sometimes had to be made. In any event, having committed to the action, there could be no turning back. "Confirm the order is to take out Flight 93, General."

"Correct." The General replied.

The Colonel fixed his instruments until a lock showed on his target on the screen in front of him. He engaged the missile, pressing the trigger, imagining it as a training exercise. "It's done, Sir." He said, watching as the missile hit its target, banking away from the subsequent explosion. "Back home to Andrews, Colonel." There was a pause. "You've done your duty, Colonel, but don't file any report until I'm with you shortly after midday."

"I'll be waiting, General." The Colonel banked his jet again, turning south towards Andrews. Tension in his body made him feel sick, but he manoeuvred his escape from the scene of devastation as quickly as possible, looking furtively around the skies.

*　　*　　*

"I'm not responsible for the recent 11th September attacks, nor am I surprised by them." The Sheikh sighed, having agreed to the newspaper interview, his first since the events in the United States had rocked the world. The statement was grammatically correct, though it may have been economical with the truth, for he had collaborated in the false flag operation, creating a false trail to enable attention to be deflected from those directly responsible. The extent of the links between his family and the dynasty ruling the United States, through institutions such as the Carlyle Group, was a matter of public record. He had worked long enough as an Agency asset to know the game and slumped back into a soft armchair, directing his gaze at his old acquaintance, the Editor of the Karachi-based newspaper, Ummat.

The Editor had travelled a long distance, through difficult terrain, to find the subject of his interview in the border country. He was grateful for the smell of pine, which wafted in the wind, as it disinfected the more pungent, dank smells associated with the lack of hygiene within the encampment and the unpleasant smell of animal and body odours. The Editor had tried to contact him at Bora Bora without success, eventually tracking him down to an isolated complex away from the majority of his recruits. In this tiny room, the Sheikh held court with the intention of placing the record straight for his Muslim friends, hoping he could negate the hysteria stirred up in the western press. Typically, an AK-47 Assault Rifle leaned against the Sheikh's chair, almost as a prop, as in the propaganda videos appearing on the Al Jazeera website. The young Editor was ambitious enough to believe he could demand editorial integrity, even if he was instructed to follow a particular bias in his reporting by those controlling and censoring much of the output of his newspaper.

He coughed nervously. "You know the United States Government has named al-Qaeda as the perpetrator of these terrorist attacks?" The Editor sat opposite the Sheikh with a tape recorder resting on the adjoining table, openly recording the detailed conversation. A notebook lay on his knees and he played neurotically with a pen in his right hand, screwing his eyes to concentrate his vision in difficult light in the small room, in such stark contrast to his mansion back in Karachi, with servants at his beck and call.

"Well they would, wouldn't they?" The Sheikh replied, disdain in his voice.

"Are they wrong?" The Editor asked.

"Certainly, they're wrong. I'm a Muslim and I try my best not to tell a lie, as the Qu'ran demands. I don't consider the killing of innocent women and children as an appreciable act. Islam strictly forbids it."

"Who is responsible?" The Editor asked.

"The United States is responsible for the oppression of the common people and for the death of those people, including the women and children, in the recent events. I can state this unequivocally and with all sincerity."

The Editor wrote the comments into his notebook, before looking up again. "Can I quote your exact words in my newspaper?"

"Of course, I don't fear the Americans." The Sheikh stroked his beard. "The ordinary citizens follow their leaders like sheep and will believe whatever they're told, even when intellectual and scientific analysis reveals their error."

"But don't you feel vulnerable to an attack from the United States?"

"The United States will do what they want to do and there's nothing I can do to stop them. They'll come into Afghanistan, but it'll be for the pipeline and the large gas and oil resources around the Caspian Basin, but not for me." He smiled his crooked smile. "Even if they suggest otherwise."

The Editor shook his head. "What do you mean?"

"The whole world will see for itself shortly, but they'll evacuate me first."

"Are you suggesting the September 11th attacks were intended only as an excuse for incursions into other sovereign states?"

He nodded. "The United States feigns democracy and this event will erode even more of the freedoms of their people and strip many of the protections of their constitution. It's their problem and you'll see the truth of my assertions in the actions of their government over the period of the next few months. It's all been pre-planned and their propaganda machines will make false statements to galvanize public opinion and to orchestrate the legislation and the war, which is bound to follow."

"If I publish these statements, the people of the West will never believe it." The Editor said.

"Probably not, but does that mean you shouldn't print it?" The Sheikh asked.

"Then why do you allow them to incriminate you?"

"Because they've promised us two things." The Sheikh replied.

"What are they?" The Editor asked.

The Sheikh leaned back in his chair. "First, a change in their position, so that US armed forces leave Saudi Arabia, though it's been agreed it may take up to two years to implement."

"And the second promise?" The Editor asked.

"I'll tell you on one condition." The Sheikh replied.

"What condition?"

"That you'll not publish it for one month."

"Why one month?' The Editor asked.

The Sheikh shifted in his chair. "Because there'll be an announcement by the United States government within one month and I don't want to prejudice it by a premature piece in your newspaper."

"Fair enough." The Editor replied. "I'll not even tell the proprietors."

The Sheikh nodded. "The second promise is a change in the US position in supporting a Palestinian State, something they've been reluctant to do."

"And they'll make that announcement within one month?" The Editor asked.

"The announcement is only days away, as you'll hear shortly." The Sheikh said.

The Editor hesitated. "I can publish this story once the announcement is made?"

"Of course." The Sheikh replied.

The Editor shuffled his papers, writing these things down. "So you're telling me that as a result of these events, the US government will change their position in supporting a Palestinian state almost immediately and they'll have their forces out of the Arabian peninsula within two years?"

The Sheikh nodded. "Correct." He looked at the Editor quizzically, pointing to a video. "Take that video and view it."

The Editor nodded.

"It's the suicide video of Abdulaziz al-Omari." The Sheikh said. "In the video, he wears a keffiyeh chequered headscarf, which as you know is worn almost exclusively by the Palestinians, and he stated all of these things in the video. I want you to promise you'll get it to Al Jazeera after the announcement. They'll show it for the world to see."

The Editor nodded. "I'll do it, but what if you're wrong?"

"History will confirm I'm right about all of these matters." The Sheikh replied.

"But even if the US government do these things, I suppose they'll never admit they've done it because of the events of 9/11." The Editor said.

"Of course not, but it's true." The Sheikh looked at the Editor carefully. "Even Hitler once said, the bigger the lie, the more likely it is to be believed. It's a sad, but true indictment of modern government."

"Are you comparing the United States government with Hitler's Nazi government?" The Editor asked, remaining in awe of the Sheikh.

"Not necessarily." The Sheikh replied. "But they want to carve up the world's resources through colonial wars of conquest and they'll erode democratic rights and freedoms in their own country to achieve it."

"Isn't that a problem for you?" The Editor asked.

"It's their problem, not mine." The Sheikh shifted painfully in his chair and winced as he moved.

"Do you hate the United States?" The Editor asked.

The Sheikh shrugged. "We're not hostile to the United States. We're simply against a system, which makes other nations slaves to them or forces them to mortgage their political and economic freedom."

The Editor wrote the statements down, even though the tape recorder continued to record the interview. He looked up again, carefully studying the expressions on the Sheikh's face, as if still uncertain whether to believe him. "Aren't you afraid of becoming isolated and incurring the wrath of the West?"

The Sheikh grinned, unmoved. "I face death every day and only in facing death can you live. It holds no fears for me." He adjusted himself painfully in his chair again. "The only reality at the core of our existence is spiritual in its essence and I've no fear of events in this material world."

The Editor had always taken kindly to this man, so reviled by the people of the West, and saw something deeper in the man, which perhaps others could not. "Why don't you let people see this part of yourself?"

The Sheikh laughed loudly. "So you think I need a public relations man do you?"

The Editor smiled faintly. "Not exactly."

The Sheikh turned away for a moment, as if looking inside himself, turning back and speaking quietly. "Are you genuinely surprised by the hysteria in the Western press?"

The Editor nodded. "Everyone is shocked by the events."

"That's the intention." The Sheikh lifted his hands in the air.

"I'd like to include everything you've told me, but perhaps it's not what the public or my proprietors demand."

"Will that stop you publishing the truth?" The Sheikh asked.

"I hope not, but tell me something about your life, Sheikh?" The Editor asked.

He shrugged. "Psychologists would have a field day if I told you about my life and they'd tell you the kidney problems I've had in the past were an expression of the toxic nature of old childhood memories and the like, so I think it's better I say nothing."

"What about the people you've killed?"

"What about them?"

"Do you realise it's wrong?"

"Not necessarily." He paused. "If I fight for the Americans against the Russians as freedom fighters, which I did, would the Americans argue it's wrong if I kill Russians?"

The Editor shook his head. "But it must do harm to you in some way?"

"Well, if I forgive myself, my body heals. It's simple from that point of view."

"But why can't you do it?" The Editor asked.

"Because it's my pain and I own it. I don't feel worthy enough to release it, so I choose the path of suffering instead."

"But that means pain stays with you."

"It's the way the Universe operates to balance itself." The Sheikh said, pragmatically.

For a moment, the Editor felt a strange affinity with this philosophical man of quite extraordinary charisma, but felt guilt for doing so. He knew he would never be able to print anything about this side of the man's nature. After all, this was a man who had been accused of cowardly and brutal acts of savagery towards innocent people with no compassion. Yet he spoke of spiritual matters and metaphysical things beyond the physical reality. He reverted to one of his rehearsed questions. "Will the recent events damage recruitment for al-Qaeda?"

The Sheikh smiled his lop-sided smile. "Quite the contrary." He replied. "Matters will escalate and the terror threat within the countries of the West will entirely be the responsibility of their governments."

"In what way?"

"Those at the highest level of government know all these things, but they need their citizens to remain in fear, as this will provide them with the public support for increased military spending and a complete erosion of civil liberties. It's all set out in their think-tank documents." He hesitated. "You should read them."

"And the American people?"

"What about the American people?" The Sheikh asked.

"Will they stand for this?" The Editor stammered his question.

"The government surveillance in the countries of the West will make them totalitarian Big Brother states. Eventually, even the financial institutions will suffer. All around them are illusions and lies, smoke-screens and mirrors."

The Editor leaned back, eyes widening, his hands dropping to his side until he grabbed his notebook, as it almost slipped from his lap. "What do you say is the part played by our government in Pakistan?"

He smiled. "It's a satellite for the United States, which is the reason the oil and gas pipelines will eventually feed into the ocean port of Karachi, so they'll continue to interfere with the internal politics in your country." He paused for a moment, "And I regret to say your country will suffer from the consequences."

The Editor shook his head. "I can't see my owners allowing me to write about our government in a way which may attract censorship."

The Sheikh sneered, his face distorting unnaturally. "If you have integrity, you'll print it anyway, before they find out." He paused, noticing the look of disbelief in the face of the Editor. "Within ten years your tribal areas bordering Afghanistan will be infiltrated by so many Islamic splinter groups, all under the protection of the Pakistan Taliban and motivated by anti-Americanism or class differences. You'll not recognize it."

"I'm not sure I understand the picture you paint?"

The Sheikh smiled. "It'll become the most important terrorist sanctuary in the world, with those in power protecting me."

The Editor sighed. "Maybe you're right."

The Sheikh nodded, but said nothing.

"So can you tell me more about the 9/11 atrocities, Sheikh?"

The Sheikh thought carefully before replying. "I must confess to being a CIA recruit in the past. I know how the events happened and the false flag operation, which accompanied it."

"So al-Qaeda didn't commit the atrocities?"

"I can assure you it wasn't al-Qaeda." He leaned back. "It would be impossible for us to have done it without help from the machinery of government and the military in the United States. You must look at who stands to gain from the events and examine the events which follow immediately afterwards, then ask the same question again."

"They say they've evidence of your involvement?"

The Sheikh chuckled. "And after everything I've said, you still believe them?"

"It's what others will say, Sheikh."

"Ask them to produce the evidence and examine it carefully, looking for corroboration of it." He smiled again. "Things are never what they seem."

"But I have to report the facts." The Editor said.

"Then report the facts about the events and what happened at the Pentagon, with no evidence of bodies and a hole, a mere sixteen feet in diameter, in the wall at the point of collision, an impossibility for a Boeing aircraft with a 46 feet height and two sixteen ton engines either side, which would have created huge holes to the side of the point of collision."

"So how did it happen?"

"I can't be sure, but could the hole in the Pentagon have matched the diameter of a missile or even a remote-controlled Global Hawk?" The Sheikh asked. "Isn't that the same type of dimensions?"

"The width of the impact area is around 65 feet, yet the wing-span of a Boeing is more than 124 feet" The Editor replied. "So you're probably right."

"I was not responsible for it, so I can't be sure, but there was no heat or smoke damage, as you saw with the Twin Towers and as you'd expect with a collision with an aircraft with more than 8000 tons of fuel on board." The Sheikh said. "I know some old Russian missiles were confiscated by the Americans on the fall of the old Soviet Union, so if you can find anyone who has forensically examined the evidence of debris at the scene you may find it matches the signature of one of them."

"I've seen photographs of the north-west wall before it collapsed and there don't appear to be engine holes either side of the main collision point." The Editor said.

"The problem is one of validation, as I'm sure they'd have collected and hidden all the evidence around the sites very quickly. Even the videos in the garages and shops around the vicinity of the Pentagon would have been called in as quickly as possible."

The Editor continued writing notes.

The Sheikh took some water, before settling back into his chair. "It's strange how these inexperienced pilots expertly flew a Boeing jet at 450 miles an hour and veered from its natural flight-path to avoid the side of the Pentagon it would have naturally targeted, where all the joint chiefs of staff would have been, to hit the re-enforced side."

The Editor nodded. "It does seem nonsense, if you accept the official line,. "

"All of this was done without leaving scorch marks on the lawns in front of the Pentagon and flying underneath their ground to air missile system. Quite a remarkable feat of piloting by any standards don't you think?" He hesitated, stroking his beard again, "Certainly for inexperienced pilots who couldn't fly little Cessna jets and I suspect even for the most experienced of pilots."

"But wasn't there American Airways livery on some of the wreckage there?" The Editor asked.

"There was also a C130 Military Cargo aircraft flying over the Pentagon on a similar flight-path at the same time." The Sheikh said. "They could easily have dropped this livery from the aircraft, but there's no way will anyone prove it, of course."

"But you know they'll not believe me." The Editor smiled awkwardly. "They'll say your evidence is tainted by your involvement with al-Qaeda."

"But what is al-Qaeda, other than literally the database of recruits, fighting initially with the Mujahadeen and created by the CIA." The Sheikh said. "It's simply metamorphosed into our wider al-Qaeda network."

"How can I corroborate this version of events?" The Editor asked.

"They've had time to set up their witnesses to confirm they've seen a planted black box somewhere in the Pentagon and the like, so it'll not be easy."

"What about facts?" The Editor asked.

"Check the facts and you'll discover that the aircraft allegedly being flown into the Pentagon went off radar for twenty eight minutes before the collision with the Pentagon." He lifted his hands. "That aircraft had to have landed somewhere in this time."

"It's unbelievable."

"That's your problem." The Sheikh replied. "As for me, I was lying in a hospital bed in Dubai, shortly before the events of 9/11." He hesitated. "I met the CIA Station Chief at the American Hospital."

The Editor stared at the Sheikh wide-eyed. "I suppose these things should be easy to corroborate."

"It's a matter for you because I've nothing to prove." The Sheikh said. "It became quite common knowledge within the intelligence community."

"I puzzle at the irony of that word 'community'." The Editor sat back, taking a deep breath. "Are you part of it, Sheikh?"

The Sheikh sneered. "Not in the way you think."

"Did you have any other visitors in Dubai?"

"Family members and prominent Saudis visited me, as well as officials within the Emirates."

"Can I check those things?" The Editor asked, needing corroboration to publish his piece.

"It can be corroborated easily enough."

The Editor stopped writing notes, his eyes glazed. "So what happens now?"

The Sheikh's eyebrows raised. "There's likely to be a fabrication of the evidence of the events."

"In what way?"

The Sheikh shrugged. "I doubt they'll produce the indestructible black boxes, or if they do belatedly, their content will be fabricated, as otherwise you'll hear pilots announcing they've lost control of their instruments."

"So what evidence will the Americans produce?" The Editor asked.

"At some stage, they'll produce some fabricated evidence incriminating me or al-Qaeda, perhaps recordings of air traffic control exchanges with alleged hijackers."

"So these recordings will be fake?" The Editor asked.

"If they were true, as with the black boxes, they'd release them immediately, but if anyone analyses the evidence honestly, they'll know al-Qaeda could never have been the perpetrators of these events, even if we did create the false trail."

"How will they fabricate the evidence?"

"Modern technology can create recordings easily." The Sheikh shrugged. "And look carefully at any videos confessing responsibility, for they'll certainly not be me, but some poor Arab actor doing it for the money or else an old video with the sound manipulated and out of sync."

The Editor nodded. "Will the Egyptian follow the same path as you?"

"If he has his way, he may take al-Qaeda down a different path, but his qualities are intellectual, not operational."

"What path would he take?" The Editor asked.

"He wants a more fundamental stance against the West, with Sharia Law in all Islamic States."

"Will the people in the West stand up against their governments?" The Editor asked.

The Sheikh shook his head. "Very few people in the West have the courage to take on their Establishment and, if they do, they'll become victims of the Big Brother State." He turned his palms upwards. "Their lives are too comfortable to rock the boat."

"Will any Western government stand up to the Americans?"

The Sheikh shook his head again. "They'd be isolated, financially and politically. It's out of the question."

"But they live in countries with democratic rights."

The Sheikh sneered. "The United States and European Union are untameable beasts, with fewer controls in place to prevent abuse by unelected commissioners. Their laws and regulations already erode many of their freedoms."

"But their constitutions?"

"They'll soon erode them further and the individual will be bludgeoned into submission, just as the European governments steamrollered their constitution through in the face of opposition from many of their citizens." The Sheikh sighed. "If that means spinning changes through without referenda they'll do it or they'll keep repeating the referenda until it's eventually passed, then it's too late to reverse it."

The Editor looked at his notes. "What's the West's purpose?"

"If you mean the events of 9/11, then look at the erosion of their constitution, the increase in the military budgets and their policies in the Middle East with regard to oil and gas."

"Can they be stopped?" The Editor asked.

The Sheikh shook his head. "There's no revolution in the West capable of preventing this relentless and inevitable march into totalitarianism and their New World Order."

"Doesn't that worry you?" The Editor asked.

"Fortunately, my concern is not the West."

"What will happen in this part of the world?" The Editor asked.

"The United States always intended to go into Afghanistan and planned for it, long before these events. They've war-gamed it as far back as 1997, according to one of their law professors, but this gives them their excuse."

The Editor moved his notes. "But this could have a profound effect on Pakistan."

"Not as much as in Afghanistan, where thousands of innocent men, women and children will perish with horrific deaths, with modern weapons annihilating a primitive people. The death toll will run into tens of thousands." The Sheikh grimaced, his face reddening. "How can close-range armaments in a poor country compete with smart bombs, destroying, maiming and incinerating indiscriminately?"

"How will this affect you?"

"The Taliban will turn to al-Qaeda for help." The Sheikh's voice cracked.

"And then?" The Editor asked.

"Iraq will be next, but not without a struggle, though not in the conventional sense because it's always been a divided country from its outset."

"But there's no al-Qaeda presence there?"

The Sheikh sneered. "They'll lie and say there's evidence of al-Qaeda there and of their complicity in the events of 9/11." The Sheikh sneered. "They'll make it up as they go along and they've no compunction about lying to get what they want."

"And Iran?"

"It's not going to accept a United States-controlled puppet government on its doorstep, so they'll develop their nuclear weapons, even supplying insurgents with small arms to fight the Americans."

The Editor hesitated as a man entered the room with some fruit and more water, which he placed on a table.

The Sheikh held out his hand towards his colleague. "Let me introduce you to Mustfa Abu al-Yazid. He'll take over events in Afghanistan when I leave."

The Editor stretched out his hand.

"Wah Salaam Alaikum."

"Alaikum Salaam Wah."

He turned back to the Sheikh. "What do the West hope to gain?"

The Sheikh gestured for the Editor to drink and eat. "You know the answer to your question."

"I suppose as the Caspian Basin has one of the biggest oil and gas reserves in the world, they need their pipeline." The Editor said.

"The big corporations, the defence firms, the oil companies and their subsidiaries will all make millions from the wars, which will please those who support the elite in power or have large stock options with these companies." He took some fruit, eating a small portion. "Check who stands to gain and observe the events."

The Editor's voice slowed. "But there's so much misinformation."

"They've whole departments within the intelligence communities devoted to misinformation." The Sheikh replied. "So it's difficult for the ordinary individual to establish the truth."

"Then what shall I write?"

"You'll soon be censored by your military government, so publish what you can, as it may be your last opportunity to write the truth, though eventually your military dictatorship will fall."

The Editor nodded. "But what about you?"

'I'm a risk to the West, but the current President will protect me, for as long as he remains in power." He grimaced. "Afterwards, it's a different matter." The Sheikh stood up, stretching tired limbs. "I'll not be in Afghanistan when the real fighting starts. The intelligence agencies will help me to avoid capture." He smiled. "They wouldn't want me to embarrass them at a trial, would they?"

"Perhaps you underestimate their loyalties." The Editor suggested.

The Sheikh nodded. "They're experts in the black arts of the double game and there's a risk they'll want closure at some time."

The Editor stood up alongside the Sheikh, offering his hand. "And if they do?"

The Sheikh shrugged. "If they do, I'm an obvious and necessary target, but it'll not happen for some time yet."

"Does it worry you?"

"The path I've taken is fraught with danger, but if it's your destiny, you take it as part of life's journey."

"But don't you live in fear of recriminations?"

The Sheikh walked away, then turned back to face the Editor. "I fear for the future of this planet, if the West is allowed to create a world in its image, but not for myself."

"But the reality is you'll spend your life in hiding." The Editor said.

"Perhaps it'll give me the time and discipline to explore the inner worlds, as my spiritual teacher taught me." The Sheikh smiled. "The people of the West will discover a different reality facing them in the years ahead."

CHAPTER FIVE

15th August 2001—officials at a Flight School in Minnesota report to the FBI that Zacorias Moussaoui, a French-born man of Moroccan descent, had enquired about flight lessons for a Boeing 747, which he wanted to fly, but not to land or take off. He had no previous training in flying even small aircraft. Between four to six calls were made to the FBI, before they returned the call.

17th August 2001—Moussaoui is arrested on immigration charges and an agent warns he was planning to fly something into the World Trade Centre. FBI agents request a FISA warrant to search his laptop computer. It is known factually that Headquarters deny this request.

24th May 2002—Intelligence reports reveal FBI agent, Coleen Rowley, had accused a supervisor in Washington, David Frasca, of altering her request for a warrant for Moussaoui before the 11th September 2001 attacks. She suggested Frasca was later promoted as a direct consequence. This mirrored the subsequent promotion given to the intelligence officer in the United Kingdom, who agreed to "sex up" the report on weapons of mass destruction in Iraq, at the behest of the British government, and was subsequently promoted to Head of MI6, the British Overseas Secret Intelligence Service.

"The planning of the events was technically and organizationally a master achievement. To hijack four huge airplanes within a few minutes and within an hour to drive them into their targets with complicated flight manoeuvres! This is unthinkable without years-long support from the secret apparatus of the state and industry"—Andreas von Bulow—former Secretary of State of Defence and former Minister of Research and Technology—6ᵗʰ May 2006—"The official story is so inadequate and far-fetched that there must be another one."

Prior to the 9/11 events, the intelligence budget in the U.S. was $26.7 billion, but by 2008 that budget had almost doubled.

An F.B.I. Agent, (one of only a handful of native Arabic speakers in the Agency), confirmed at the time of the bombings of U.S.S. Cole that a Senate Intelligence Committee member told him that the White House could not have al-Qaeda linked to the attack. The Agent also confirmed that the events of 9/11 could have been avoided.

"World Trade Centre Building Seven exhibits none of the characteristics of a building destroyed by fire, which would normally include a slow onset with large visible deformations, a symmetrical collapse which follows the path of least resistance, (laws of conservation of momentum would cause a falling to the side most damaged by the fire) and evidence of a fire temperature capable of softening steel."

"I fear I may be assassinated soon." John O'Rourke stared moodily out of the window at the gloomy weather outside, before pacing his penthouse apartment in Berkeley Square, near Piccadilly, in the heart of the City. He waited for a response, but none came. He had a penchant for the dramatic, since his days in the priesthood, but this time his feelings had been reasoned to a conclusion anyone might reach in similar circumstances. "This isn't irrational, as I've information which certain individuals and institutions of government would do anything to prevent becoming public." He hesitated, stopped pacing and sat on the leather sofa. "It might be a faked suicide or a death by an induced heart attack, or even some obscure accident, but you'll know the truth. I know too much." He blurted into a strained silence, staring at Nadia wide-eyed, helpless, but again she refused to respond. Despite being fifty years old, he still took pride in his clean-cut, well-turned-out appearance and he retained a boyish charm, looking and feeling much younger. In his refined way, with his starched and privileged upbringing, this was the nearest he would ever get to making a genuine plea for help, though he never realized the plea had been made to the wrong person.

"You're becoming paranoid." She replied eventually. "And I don't like you talking this way." She shielded moistening eyes, knowing it was no mere paranoia, for reasons which he would have been completely unaware.

"I'm not, Nad."

She groaned. "Please John, it upsets me."

"I need to make something clear." Despite the wisps of grey peppered into his hair, John appeared wilfully ignorant of the ageing process or how attractive she still found him. "My beliefs would never permit me to commit suicide." He spoke as a true Catholic, his deep voice honed from the pulpit many years before.

"I understand, John, but concentrate on the positives."

"I try." His voice cracked.

Nadia took a deep breath and stood over him. "You forget I've known you for many years, your battles with the Establishment, your history as a defrocked priest, but mostly your work as a prize-winning journalist."

John looked away, a part of him felt vulnerable, but as always she lifted his spirits. "Nad." He turned back. "This time I think the whole of the Establishment machinery could topple down and overwhelm me."

"You'll be fine, John." She said softly. "You've always written uncompromising articles and books, yet you're still here to tell the tale."

A naivety in his character, when it came to women, meant he failed to pick up on the doubt in her voice and, as always, found it difficult to understand deceit in others. "But there are so many things I still want to do with my life."

"Are you sure you're not over-reacting?" She asked, politely.

"Not this time." He replied, no hint of uncertainty in his voice.

She sighed, wondering if this was the time to tell him the truth, even if it meant leaving him and never returning, but something held her back. "I'll protect you any way I can, John."

He gestured for her to sit alongside him. "I don't know what I'd do without you, Nad."

She raised her hand, rejecting the invite, wondering how she found herself in this predicament. "I've things to do, John."

"But I need you, Nad."

"Give me a moment, whilst I fix this." She took a tissue from its box on the coffee table and dried her tears, pretending eye make-up had run. Although subtle lines had written their life story on his face, she was strangely more attracted to John than ever. It annoyed her that men could age so well, while women suffered under the same process, but she knew only too well how life contained many injustices.

"I've been given crucial information, Nad." He looked at her approvingly, the willowy figure and sultry looks still pleased and aroused him, even if he could not tell her.

"Leave it there, John." She said. "This isn't your fight." She could manipulate most men, but not the one she loved more than any other, her happiness having been eroded by events impacting on her feelings.

He sighed. "But I don't know what to do."

"Why do you need to do anything?" She asked, wanting to retain her secrets, but sensing there was nothing hidden at the deepest level of her being, which would not be revealed to the deepest level of his.

"I need to talk through the issues with someone I trust." He gestured again with his hand for her to sit next to him.

"Is the great John O'Rourke admitting he's human?" She asked, sarcastically, moving to the sofa, stretching and leaning towards him, her figure more pronounced by the pose, but John gave no indication of appreciation. At one level, this incensed her. If it were not for another more sinister agenda, she would have been long gone, if only to protect her sanity.

"You know me better than anyone, Nad, but don't mock me." He sounded hurt.

"I know, but I couldn't resist it." She didn't think she was meant to live alone and felt more isolated than if she had chosen to live by herself. John's failure to consummate their relationship in recent years still puzzled her, as she still lusted after him, even if she pretended otherwise. The haunting memories of a more youthful passion stirred her and living with him did nothing to lessen the lonely dark nights when time turned back on itself, before rushing forward again in playful caricature. She may have been placed there for sinister reasons, but with the passage of time she had found it impossible not to fall in love with him and it caused heartache.

"What do you think I should do?" He asked, pulling back instinctively. He had been afraid to commit to her and a sexual relationship in those circumstances was too painful.

"You'd better tell me the problem." She said coldly, recoiling at the unconscious body movement away. The guilt she felt after succumbing to a sexual liaison with John's Editor didn't help and though she excused it as against her will, she could never actually remember telling him to stop. Only recalling the revulsion and guilt afterwards, for which she punished herself and living with John was part of it. There was another reason for guilt, something she could never excuse and these negative memories manifested themselves as repeating patterns of self-punishing behaviour.

"This piece I've been working on started innocently enough, but seems to have developed a life of its own." He said, distracted by her movements.

"But normally that's a good sign, isn't it?" She asked, still feeling the sexual attraction when close to him. Betrayal was a cloak he had worn before, so she kept her darker side from him, even if it worked against their relationship at some deeper level, subconsciously maintaining an invisible barrier between them. There were times she wanted to confess her indiscretions, so she could give all of herself to him again, but she knew it was too late, so kept it back in a little black box in her brain. In the meantime, guilt acted as one of the links in the chain which bound her to him, more even than love.

"It's not the accuracy of the piece that's the problem." He sighed. "More the impact it would have on the vested interests if I publish it."

She nodded. "And why should that bother you?"

"I suppose I'm frightened of the consequences of not being around for my children."

"But you're not around for your children anyway." She said sharply.

He recoiled. "That's unfair and not like you."

She grimaced. "Sorry. I was trying to be flippant, but it wasn't funny."

"I've so few friends I can really trust with this stuff."

She felt guilty again and looked away. "I don't believe the Establishment or those with vested interests see you as a threat." She turned back. "They're too arrogant and you're small change."

"Doesn't that make it easier for them?" He asked, hesitating momentarily. "If they can assassinate or incriminate Presidents and leaders of states with complete immunity, then I'm an easy target."

"You keep saying it, but you've no evidence of these things." She said, exasperation echoing.

"But organizations like the Committee of 300, and the corporate entities which support them financially, thrive on spiritual wickedness and JFK, Bobby Kennedy, Nixon, William Colby and others all refused to follow their line, crossing them once too often. The same problem existed with Bhutto in Pakistan and Aldo Moro in Italy, all had to be eliminated."

"But surely they wouldn't take chances on being caught?" She asked.

"In some circumstances, they use organized criminal gangs to do their dirty work. In others, highly trained black operation units with sophisticated equipment are used. They control governments and manipulate assassinations all around the world, creating cover stories to protect the clandestine nature of their work." He looked up. "It's the secret history."

"What's secret about it?"

"Leaders die in suspicious circumstances if they cross the shadowy vindictive figures holding the reins of power, manipulating world affairs to suit their needs."

"I don't want to be rude, but you're of no significance, John." She sighed. "I think you're making more of this than you should."

"It's the ordinary man, who frightens them." He moved from the sofa, picking up his blue blazer from the back of a chair, slipping effortlessly into it. He felt comfortable wearing it and needed confidence at a time when doubts seeped into his psyche. His mystical training in the priesthood had taught him the Universe threw back at you precisely what you thought about and felt the most, so to be confident, he needed to assume it first and to avoid fear he had to assume courage.

"Maybe you're right." She said.

He turned to her again. "Secret organizations like the Bilderberger Group, whose hand-picked members include politicians, bankers and multi-millionaire businessmen, dictate all the politically significant events from their highly secret meetings. Nothing happens in the world without passing through them first." He stretched his arms above his head and sighed. "All the future Presidents and Prime Ministers are vetted at these meetings, before they're allowed to fight for office."

She shook her head. "I still don't believe they'd kill you, John. It would draw attention to everything you've championed."

"Maybe." He shrugged.

"Besides, despite the threats, they never actually harmed you when you published the copies of the Gnostic scrolls which your uncle, the Cardinal, had taken from the Vatican vaults."

"But I fear they'll do it this time." He spoke slowly, the morose tone so untypical of him, even if he could be as dry as a Martini.

Moving towards the table, she grabbed her handbag, walking towards the mirror in the hall. Taking her Yves St Laurent colour stick, she stared into the mirror and placed the colour under her eyes, rubbing it in with a delicate finger movement, pressing it into the light wrinkles and dark shadows, which had begun to appear on her face. She played with her hair, like an artist with a swish of paint here and there, studying her work carefully afterwards. Feeling fragile and vulnerable, she yearned for approval and if it came from making love to John, she was determined to have him one last time.

She turned around and walked towards John, looking at him directly and grabbing his arm, shook it. "I want you to stop this negative attitude and look at the world more positively. Do you understand?" She waited for a response, but none came. "You're normally so positive. I don't know what's got into you."

He nodded and pulled his arm away from her. "You're right, but I can incriminate too many powerful people, the shadow government behind the scenes, which uses the intelligence black arts, dictating foreign policy." He took a deep breath. "And I'm sure there's a large file on me at Special Branch and with the intelligence services."

"So what are you going to do about it?" She asked.

"I don't know yet, but you can't fight fire with fire." He replied. "The energy is too destructive."

"So you're going to turn the other cheek?"

"You know me better than that." He raised his voice. "But I'll not stand by and allow government terrorism to exploit ordinary people. It's no different to allowing terrorists to do their dirty work." He clenched his fist. "Someone has to make a stand."

She groaned. "And I suppose it has to be you?"

"If need be."

"John. Sometimes you're so stupid."

His eyebrows lifted, his mouth dropping open. "All I'm saying is that government agencies feign to abhor terrorism, yet they use the same tactics to control the people, only professing legitimacy."

She raised her hands in the air, turning her back on him, as he reverted to his time in the pulpit. "You're not preaching to me again, are you?"

"I suppose so."

"Then stop talking about it and do something about it." She turned to square up to him, hands on hips. "You're a journalist, remember?"

"What should I write?"

"Tell the truth as you always embrace with such enthusiasm." She sat down again, speaking more softly. "And if you want my help with research or in compiling articles, then ask me."

He nodded, hesitating for a reason he could not fathom. At one level, he knew something had changed, but consciously resisted the need to know by detaching himself from the emotional connection, even if he retained genuine affection for Nadia. His odd girlfriends were suspicious of the arrangement and rarely lasted, which pleased her, as otherwise the bargain she had made with herself would have been unfair. "Then help me, Nad."

She nodded and sighed.

"Good." He smiled, oblivious to any distress he caused, striving with apparent ease to remain immune from her considerable attractions. Ironically, a discipline he had miserably failed to master during his earlier years as a young priest, which had led to his painful departure from the corridors of the Catholic Church.

She took a deep breath, wanting to ask questions without being obviously curious. "What do you want me to do?"

"Some of the information in my possession will destroy the faith the people in the US have in their government, which they still arrogantly believe is the perfect model for democracy."

"So much so they insist on exporting it." She interrupted.

He hesitated. "What does your brother do in New York, Nad?"

She shielded her eyes, but he hardly noticed. "He's some sort of businessman." She lied.

He took a small notebook from the inside pocket of his blazer, sat down on the sofa and wrote some notes, before turning to her again. "The reality for Americans is they'll never accept they live in a Police State, as a consequence of the Patriot and Homeland Security Acts, with their constitution eroded by a calculated course of events."

"They're just frightened and don't know what else to do." She said.

"But even the wealthy in positions of power know it can all be taken from them by the manipulators of events."

She began clearing up his clutter. "You underestimate the American people."

"Perhaps."

"So what's this information you suggest is critical?" She turned to him. "If it only relates to events in the US, how can that affect your safety here?"

He laughed. "The Americans believe they're the world's police force and geographical boundaries don't stop them."

She smiled. "Maybe."

He moved across to his desk, unlocked it, and took out a detailed manuscript, throwing it on the coffee table with a thud. "Read this."

She picked it up, sitting back on the sofa, scanning the first page. It was what she needed. "This isn't exactly bedtime reading, so summarise it for me and I'll go through it later when I've more time."

He looked out the window. "You'll find incontrovertible evidence of the collusion of the U.S. Administration in the 9/11 events." He turned and pointed to the manuscript. "I've detailed precisely how they did it with the secret technology, something they deny exists, though promising they'll develop."

"What secret technology?"

"It's all in there."

"So you already have all the material you need?"

"I need tangible corroborating evidence before I can publish it."

She nodded, involuntarily. "So you're not raising any issues about British Intelligence?"

He looked at her with a puzzled expression. "What do you mean?"

She sighed, surprised at his naivety. "Nothing in particular."

He dismissed the fleeting thoughts entering his head, before disappearing into the ether. "I've information about high-ranking government officials who want to come out of the closet, but the U.S. government will suppress it."

"Is that in here?" She pointed to the manuscript.

"I must be careful, as they've no scruples about taking lives, if officials break rank."

"John, it's a matter for you, of course, but I'm tired of you talking about these things, then doing nothing."

"But if I'm right, they'll kill me."

"If you're right and it's too dangerous, ignore the material and get a life." She said firmly.

"You may be right, but the truth must come out and it's not in my nature to walk away." He hesitated. "There's already considerable internet material and books coming out all of the time on different aspects of these shadowy events. Just look at the number of hits YouTube gets on 9/11 items."

She shrugged, hating the way he made such a virtue of truth. "Then you've made your choice."

"I suppose so, but there are high profile characters speaking out. You only have to look at the Scholars for Truth movement, the Architects and Engineers for 9/11 Truth and many others."

"But why don't you let them do the dirty work, as they have the benefit of safety in numbers?" A puzzled expression crossed her face.

He shook his head. "All academics must stand up to be counted, but they know nothing of the secret technology behind these events."

"And you say you do?"

"Sure."

"Do you intend to share this material?" She fidgeted on the sofa.

"Perhaps."

She tapped her fingers on the side of the sofa. "But others must have access to the same material, John." She looked into his eyes. "If you're right, the intelligence agencies will monitor all the e-mails and telephone calls of these people, including you."

"Of course."

She nodded involuntarily again. "How would you propose to contact these people, without placing yourself in the firing line?"

"I'm probably already in the firing line, but it's a chance I must take, even if I don't quite know where to start."

She sighed noisily. "Why must you always play the hero, John?"

"It's not just me, Nad, but a growing number of people know the truth and once the information reaches the critical mass, the momentum will be unstoppable."

She stretched out, taking all the seating area on the sofa, deliberately seeking the most provocative position. "Pretend I'm your Editor and tell me what you'd write."

He turned to face her. "I know how the aircraft were driven into the Twin Towers and I've collated some interesting information about the events at the Pentagon."

"And if the Editor asks for corroboration?"

"There are missing parts of the events, but I've been promised the corroboration."

She adjusted herself into a more demure position. "What if I tell you it can't be published?"

"I understand the need for corroboration for credibility, otherwise it'll be ignored as a conspiracy theory."

"Perhaps that's all it is."

His jaw tightened and posture stiffened. "You know better than to believe I'd pursue a conspiracy theory, unless completely convinced of its authenticity."

She smiled, knowing it would offend him. "You're so predictable, John. I thought you'd mellow with age, but no chance."

"It's not funny, Nad." His face flushed. "A lot of people died because of decisions by faceless bureaucrats who control events with immunity." An inescapable sadness reflected in his eyes and, for the first time, she could touch the priest, which remained in him, palpable and obvious.

Her expression captured the same sadness, her heart reaching out for him, before it was too late. "Leave this story alone, John." She said, feeling empathy in the moment.

His weakness had always been women, but he still failed to appreciate Nadia's clear message. "My life must have meaning, even if that involves sacrifice." He looked through her. "It's what I believe."

She knew the game the way the cards fell. "Have you ever thought of the other people in your life?" She waited for a response, but none came. "Me, for example."

He shook his head. "You're strong, Nad. I've never had doubts about your ability to cope, whatever happens."

"Then your children." Her eyes misted over. "Don't you want to see them get married and have your grandchildren?"

He stared at her, but said nothing.

"Have you thought about your duty to them, John?" She asked, more forcefully.

"Am I being that selfish, Nad?"

"There are times you're too principled and too honest." She allowed her head to drop onto his chest naturally, hiding her eyes and heart from him, thinking private thoughts without intrusion. "If you're right about this information, leave it to someone with a reputation to carve because I've got a bad feeling about it."

"You know my philosophy. I must cleanse my world, taking responsibility for all the events in it, only then does it become a better place for my actions and a better place for my children."

"Oh God." She spoke softly into his chest, hiding her fears and guilt.

He lifted her head, cupping it in his hands, so his eyes met hers briefly without flinching. She blinked, pulling her face back down again. "Don't you see?" He asked.

"I don't see anything."

He stroked her hair gently. "If we all take this responsibility, the world might be a better place."

She groaned, feeling John was too good for this world. "I know you were a priest, but you lose me."

He smiled, releasing his grip. "I think you understand, Nad."

"No I don't, John."

He wanted to help her with her demons and painful memories, but something inside made him feel it was his fault. "If this information has been passed to me, it becomes my responsibility to deal with it. Ultimately, I make my decisions from the source of spirit and follow my heart."

"Oh God. There you go again." She sat up.

"Nad. Don't close your heart." He said firmly. "There are no limitations on what can be achieved if we follow our bliss."

"Look John. I don't pretend to understand this stuff about the outer world reflecting the inner world, as you always preach, nor do I have your knowledge of comparative religions or spirituality, but I really don't want to know about it." She stood up, walking away from the sofa, unable to face up to the metaphysical parallel universe he sometimes inhabited.

"But you should, Nad, and one day you'll be forced into doing it."

"No. No." She replied firmly, knowing her knowledge of the world had been tainted by a different experience.

"Don't you see, Nad?" He waited until she turned to face him. "Most people make choices and decisions stemming from their past memories, not from inspiration, which is a spiritual source."

She shook her head. "Why do you still have this urge to save me?" She asked, without waiting for a response. "I've gone beyond saving." Her eyes expressed the truth, even if John remained ignorant of it.

"I don't believe it." He stood up, reaching out for her, his arms moving around her waist and resting his head on her shoulders. The fragrance from her body, reminded him of past passion, but he felt a need to step back.

"You're within my sphere of influence and to some degree I must take responsibility for you too."

Her face reddened. "Bloody Christians. Why do you always want to save someone?" Her eyes opened wide. "Why can't you convert to Buddhism or something and learn about the Middle Path?"

He laughed instinctively and loudly. "You're magic, Nad."

"I've no wish to be magic, I'm just trying to be pragmatic, John."

"But you must be whatever you are, Nad."

"I know what I am, John, but do you?"

He nodded. "Being born in the West, my karma is a western one."

She groaned, but said nothing.

"I'm sure the Buddhists are trying to bring peace to the world in their own way too."

She rolled her eyes, looking up again, her voice reflecting exasperation. "There you go again, missing the point."

He smiled. "Why are you so reluctant to search within yourself, Nad?"

"John, you're so blind about so many things, intellectualizing everything means you miss so much and you should do things naturally, but too much of your life is spent away from your heart and up in your head."

"What do you mean?" He protested, even if something resonated, recognizing the personal flaw in his character.

"Live down here, not up in the heavens."

He shrugged. "It's the priest in me, I suppose."

"I think you're right." She nodded. "You refuse to change, even when the world tumbles to its destruction around you."

"But it doesn't have to tumble into oblivion, Nad." He said. "We can change it."

"And how would you propose to do that miracle?" She asked cynically.

He smiled. "If you don't like the way the world is leaning, help me change it."

She groaned. "But how can one person make a difference?"

"Do you really believe what you're saying, Nad?"

"I do." She replied instantly and firmly.

"Well, I don't and I can't." He said, equally firmly.

She shook her head. "Oh God." She muttered under her breath, barely audible.

He smiled again, walking in circles nervously around the room, collecting his thoughts. It infuriated her.

She ignored the movement, returning to the sofa, closing her eyes and leaning back, as if in meditation, placing the palms of her hands over her face. "I'm concerned about you." She said quietly, taking her hands away.

"I'll take precautions." He took a deep breath. "I've placed information in a sealed envelope and passed it to my lawyer for safe-keeping, in the event anything untoward should happen."

She felt vulnerable, even to John's innocent eyes. "That's total nonsense." She allowed her head to drop into her hands again. "If what you say is right, it'll not make the slightest difference."

"What do you mean?" He asked.

"How will that protect you?" She lifted her hands.

"I'm under no illusions about these dark forces, ruling the world from the shadows." He said.

"Oh God, there you go again." She lifted her eyes upwards and her head moved up with them, then raising her hands, so they covered her ears, restraining an urge to scream. "Dark bloody forces! Jesus, where did I dig you up?"

He laughed loudly at her irreverence.

For a few minutes neither of them spoke. Eventually, she dropped her hands, opening her eyes, regaining her composure and remembering her mission. "Sorry. That was going too far."

"No. You're probably right."

"Lets' be constructive." She spoke assertively. "Tell me what other evidence you have?"

"I've evidence of the 3.5 billion dollars awarded to Pakistan, in the summer of 2003, still being used to fund terrorism and destabilise Afghanistan, even if most passed to individual personnel within their military and government."

"So what?" She asked. "People are not interested in foreign policy and whether other countries destroy themselves and it's no great secret. People are only concerned about events directly impacting upon them."

He shook his head. "People are concerned about the deaths of hundreds of thousands of innocent people around the world."

She looked up. "John, you don't know me at all." She spoke starkly, prompted from a deep desire to confess her involvement in the events, which would soon affect him, but she held back.

He recoiled. "Then why am I talking to you?

"Tell me why you're talking to me John?"

He thought for a moment. "I suppose it's because I care about you and I think you care about me."

She turned away, fighting off a tear. It was the closest he had come to saying he loved her still and her heart ached. "John, you must believe me when I tell you I'm beyond redemption. I don't want you thinking about me anymore."

"But I do."

She threw her arms upwards, as if in tantrum. "Why do you have to say these things now?" She asked without turning back.

"What do you mean 'now'?"

She sighed. "Nothing."

He felt there was something, but could not catch the thought in his head long enough to remember it. "It's because I care about you and I wanted you to know the course I've set."

She took a deep breath, turning to face him. "So you'll not turn back?"

"No. I can't." He replied.

"So what's next?"

"I'm afraid that if the Americans or their intelligence partners in the U.K. don't eliminate me in this country, it'll happen during my travels, perhaps Pakistan."

"Why Pakistan?" She asked about the country of her birth.

"I do work there for my Editor from time to time and the President in Pakistan and their military intelligence, the ISI, were always used as another arm of the CIA and the National Security Agency. The country is being destabilised and they need to target another leader in a country they must control, if the pipeline planned from the Caspian Sea for its oil and gas reserves is to have its planned port of embarkation in Karachi."

"Do you think this is what it's all about?" She asked.

"It's part of the globalisation, the control of the population, of oil and gas and part of the secret agenda of the shadow governments."

"At least, they'd never get away with assassination in this country, John." She shielded her face, feeling vulnerable in the moment, certain her part in a betrayal etched itself too obviously in her face.

He noticed nothing unusual, nor would he, because he still loved her and it had always been his weakness. "Don't be naïve, Nad."

"John, you're the one being naive. You seem to think everyone has the same moral standards as you."

"Perhaps you're right." He nodded. "Some people are unconsciously programmed about what's right and wrong and no amount of logical arguments or hard work can change their thought patterns."

Nadia grabbed his arm. "You do know you can always trust me, John?"

"Of course, Nad." He replied. "It would never enter my mind that I couldn't trust you."

She looked thoughtful, afraid to catch his eyes. "Good."

"I don't know what I'd do if you weren't in my life, Nad." He said. "I always used to preach about the intervention of the imagination to re-programme people's minds, especially if an image was so compelling, it would affect behavioural patterns."

She shook her head. "John, you still don't understand most people's nature."

"What do you mean?"

She sighed. "So few people are capable of changing the patterns of their behaviour or are even motivated to try." She looked quizzical. "Don't you see?"

"Sorry." He replied instinctively, in denial.

Her hands shot up in the air again, uttering a stifled scream. "I don't want you to be sorry. I want you to be real."

"Why do I upset you so much?" John asked, shaking his head.

"I don't know." She lied.

"I need your counsel on these things." He said, a pleading schoolboy innocence in his voice.

She closed her eyes for a moment; then opened them. "If you really want my counsel, avoid a violent undemocratic country like Pakistan; it's dangerous, especially in the tribal areas."

He sighed. "But even in this country it's certainly not safe, Nad."

She shook her head. "Don't take unnecessary chances, John. You've friends in this country and they'll protect you." She moved away, walking to the bathroom, finding some respite, leaning against the sky-blue tiles for a few moments, taking some tissues to dry her eyes. Betrayal did not come naturally to her, especially as she still cared for him and she needed a few moments to regain her composure before returning to the open-plan lounge, decorated by her in minimalist fashion with John's passive compliance. He insisted in leaving papers all over the place and it annoyed her, so in return she left knickers and clothes on the back of chairs and placed pots of flowers to clutter his living space. She needed to remind him she was there and existed in a silly game of marking each other's territory, which had no winner and succeeded only in suffocating each of them.

When she returned to the room, he followed her movements carefully. "You know initially no-one wanted to believe me about Group 13, the Clinic and the ex-SAS assassination units when I published articles about them."

"I remember." She replied.

"They accused me of diluting the integrity of journalists generally and of factual weaknesses in my pieces. Their propaganda and use of misinformation through their friends in the media is subtle, but very effective." He looked up to check Nadia was paying attention.

"I'm listening." She flashed an awkward smile at him.

"It was the same with the Permindex Corporation, one of the previous sub-contracted assassination organizations of British Intelligence. There was a great outcry when, all those years ago, I outlined their relocation to the Bahamas in the deal with Meyer Lansky, the bagman for the Mafia, and their subsequent transformation to Intertel. Now all this information is in the public arena." He placed his head in his hands. "I still don't know how I got away with it."

She longed to hold him, but resisted the urge. "If they didn't harm you then, you've no reason to believe anything has changed."

He lifted his head, looking at her carefully. "My Editor, George, tells me he's been under pressure from the major shareholders to curtail my contributions to the newspaper. His job is on the line if he supports any further articles on the subject of 9/11."

"Why do you listen to that man?" She asked, an emotional charge in the question.

"I don't know why you dislike him so much when he's always been loyal to me."

Her eyes looked upwards and she grunted, stifling an instinctive comment.

He ignored the obvious. "I've been too close to the truth and certain influential people are worried. I've even been approached from someone on the House Security and Intelligence Select Committee, but I think she's being monitored. I'll have to be careful." He avoided mentioning she was the Chair of the Committee, as if part of him remained wary.

She could see vulnerability in his eyes. "And who is that?"

"I'll tell you after I've seen her and have the information."

She shook her head. "Have you thought of forgetting this stuff and learning to live life?"

"I've told you why that's impossible."

"But you could live comfortably abroad in the sun without any of this aggravation." She looked doleful. "Money has never been important to you, anyway."

"It would destroy me." He whispered, as if needing to convince himself.

"You need to leave this cloak and dagger stuff to younger men."

He shot a grimaced glance in her direction. "You may as well ask me have I ever thought of not breathing." He said. "It would betray everything honest and decent in my life." He hesitated. "And I couldn't live with myself."

"It's an option you owe to your two children." She said, as a last throw of the dice if she was to avoid compromising him.

"That's below the belt." He raised his voice. "Poor David Kelly wanted to settle for a simple life, but look what happened to him in the end."

"What happened to him?"

"They wouldn't let him go quietly." John replied. "All he wanted to do was tell the truth about the absence of weapons of mass destruction in Iraq, a truth the government aggressively denied at the time." He took a deep breath. "Subsequent events have proved him to be an honest and conscionable man, who had merely told the truth as he saw it, but was pilloried for it, then killed."

"But he killed himself, didn't he?"

He sneered. "Does someone commit suicide only a couple of months before a daughter is about to get married and leave an upbeat message to a friend in the pub cribbage team that he was looking forward to the game the following Wednesday?"

"It does sound suspicious." She agreed. "Didn't the two ambulance personnel, a man and a woman, give a press conference about it?"

He nodded. "They stated that after forty years of experience between them attending at suicide scenes, including where people had cut their wrists, they were both convinced David Kelly hadn't died in the location where they'd found him or from the injury they witnessed."

"So what are you saying?"

"I'm just giving you the facts." He replied. "Most people recall the pruning knife allegedly used to commit suicide had no fingerprints on it, but there were a further five items on the body and at the scene which also didn't have fingerprints on them."

She shook her head. "I didn't know."

"There were no fingerprints on the packet of pills, a mobile phone, his watch or a water bottle found near his body."

"But why do you find it necessary to fight every injustice, John?"

"It's not just me." He took a deep breath. "Someone has written a book suggesting he was killed to silence his criticism of the grounds for going to war in Iraq." He fixed steely eyes on her. "A distinguished American colleague, who met Kelly at a Foreign Office conference, agreed he'd been murdered."

She shivered. "It upsets me to think about it."

"We can't bury our heads in the sand." He persisted. "A Liberal Democrat M.P. was initially refused access to classified information."

"It makes me feel uncomfortable." She looked away.

"On the same morning he allegedly killed himself, he had booked a return ticket to Iraq." He hesitated, until she looked back. "Why would he have done that if he had the slightest intention of killing himself?"

"You're right."

"The evidence doesn't stop there." He shrugged, turning his hands over. "A helicopter hired by Thames Valley Police mysteriously landed at the scene of Kelly's death ninety minutes after his body was discovered, stayed there for five minutes before leaving, either depositing or collecting something or someone."

"It's sad." She said, tears welling up.

He moved to comfort her, but she pushed him away. "But these are facts, Nad."

She lifted herself up, pushing her right palm out. "You upset me, John."

"But I wanted to warn you if events turn out badly." He softened the tone.

"I'll cope." She dried her eyes with the back of her hand. "I always do."

"The last thing I wanted was to distress you." He hesitated. "I didn't want you to think it was paranoia on my part either." He reached out, placing his hand on her shoulder.

She turned away for a moment, took a deep breath, and turned back. "One day you'll understand that I love you."

He wanted to believe her, looking directly into her eyes, fatally failing to notice the shadows hidden in their depths. "In my way Nad, I love you too, but love takes many forms."

"I understand only too well." She said.

"Sometimes I wonder if you understand my feelings, Nad?"

She shook her head. "Perhaps not." She steeled herself. "Now let's resolve your immediate problems." She took a deep breath. "What else do the authorities know?"

"For starters, they know a former Deputy Director of the F.B.I. with specific responsibility for counter-terrorism talked to someone." He sighed. "They know I'm moving too close to the truth."

"What's happened to this man?" She asked.

He shrugged. "He's been silenced, but the conversation may have been taped."

"What did he say?"

"After complaining he was getting no co-operation from the State Department who blocked his investigations into the bombing of the U.S.S. Cole in the Yemen at every step, some of his information passed to British Intelligence." He looked upwards, as if inspiration could be gained from the heavens. "He was too clever for his own good and decided to resign, believing he could quietly retire, but he was offered and took the post of Head of Security at the World Trade Centre immediately before 9/11." He turned to her. "But he obviously couldn't escape the claws of the Establishment."

She shivered. "As I said, I don't want to think about it."

"The Western governments have secret plans to create a New World Order, a global fascist society, which will control our lives and gradually erode all our basic freedoms. They needed some significant events to justify the controls they want to put in place, creating the events to ensure the public clamour for security." He started pacing again. "The ordinary citizen won't even notice these restrictions until it's too late to do anything about it."

"What's this got to do with the events of 9/11?"

He smiled. "They needed it to pursue their secret agenda. They had to attack the American constitution first, because it's a written constitution, whereas the British constitution is unwritten, more flexible and easier to manipulate." He took a deep breath. "Of course, they needed their excuse to go into Afghanistan and Iraq and without those events they could never have gained the public support needed to undertake another war against a defenceless nation."

"Do you believe all this, John?"

"Of course I do." He replied. "You only have to examine the analogies with Hitler and the engineered events of the thirties. Do you remember your history lessons?"

"It wasn't exactly my favourite subject."

He felt compelled to recite a quotation, as a comparison between old and new politics. "An evil exists that threatens every man, woman and child of this great nation. We must take steps to ensure our domestic security and protect our homeland."

"Sounds like the President." She said, instinctively.

"It does, but it was Hitler when he announced the creation of the Gestapo and the erosion of freedoms in Germany. Hitler's armies may have been defeated and destroyed on a physical level, but the higher fascist energies which created the Third Reich are still alive and flourishing destructively behind the scenes of every significant event."

A shiver ran down her spine. "But John, you can't compare the two regimes." She hesitated. "And the death of a Deputy Director of the F.B.I. may have just been coincidence."

"You know I don't believe in coincidence." Furrows etched deeply into his forehead. "I met the Deputy Director once. He wanted to tell me something and I agreed to meet him a second time."

"You did?"

He nodded. "But he died during the events of 9/11, before the second meeting could take place."

"Do you have any clues about what he wanted to tell you?"

"None whatsoever, but if the authorities thought he was talking, they'd have been unhappy about it."

She shook her head. "Yet if someone does their beckoning, John, they'll reward them." She hesitated. "Isn't there a lesson for you there?"

"Like the man who sexed up the weapons of mass destruction report to justify the incursion into Iraq subsequently getting promotion to the top job?"

She nodded. "Precisely."

"Sometimes I think you really don't know me at all, Nad."

She sighed heavily. "I think I know you well enough."

"The US Congress allocated forty billion dollars to fund the so-called 'War on Terrorism' immediately after 9/11, just as those in control of the events always intended."

She sat down heavily on the sofa. "Didn't the US President ignorantly refer to it as a crusade, until he was advised of the significance of that word to Muslims?"

"As always he did what he was told afterwards."

"So you're going to publish and be damned?"

"At some point, I must." He said.

She stretched her arms above her head. "Well, you've a faith which believes the essence of the soul, is indestructible and immortal, so that must be a consolation to you."

He nodded. "The priest, which remains part of me, insists I follow a certain course, irrespective of the dangers." He looked at her and for a moment thought he noticed something close to pity in her eyes.

"You're such a fool sometimes, John."

"Perhaps, but terrorism is vile and pitiless, with no compunction about maiming innocent women and children. State terrorism is no different and if I die fighting for what I believe, then I'll be happy." He looked at her again, but she turned away. "Do you understand?"

She shook her head and turned back. "No. I can't pretend I do."

"It's what I am."

"Why has it always got to be you, John?"

"Because this information has passed to me and it becomes my responsibility when I see the events being orchestrated by the shadow governments."

She screwed her eyes. "But you have a distorted view of humanity and not everyone is like you"

He shrugged. "I suppose I want you to help me, as there's a part of me which believes I can't do this on my own."

She laughed, scornfully. "I don't believe it. The great John O'Rourke is asking for help."

"Now you're mocking me again."

"I couldn't help myself." Normally, she would do anything for him, but it was too late now. She had been dragged into a complex world of subterfuge, from which she couldn't escape, unless a deal could be struck. If there was a time to seduce John, she thought, it was now or never. She moved off the sofa and walked towards the dining chair, placing one foot on the rung of the chair, hoisting her skirt, mimicking an adjustment to a stocking to ensure he had a tantalizing view of her white panties, teasing him to the point of distraction.

"What are you doing?" His mouth gaped open, eyes fixed on her, touching that darker side of lust, which had been his downfall in the past.

She started undoing the buttons on her blouse, slipping it off and tossing it blatantly on the floor. "I don't like this." She watched unashamedly, as he drooled. "John, your mouth is open."

He closed his mouth. "Nad." He called her name with pleading eyes, breathing in the possibilities. "This isn't fair."

"She looked at him directly. "Do you want me?"

He sighed, afraid to answer honestly.

"Have you missed me?" She asked, unzipping her skirt and watching it drop to the floor, revealing more of that firm unblemished body he still lusted after.

He recalled her nubile slender body so well. "You know I've always wanted you, but that was never the problem, was it?"

"What was the problem?" She asked, pulling her bra, then her panties off completely, bending over as she did so, before throwing them across the floor and turning to face him, stark naked.

He moved towards her, arms open. "Didn't you realize the problem?"

She shook her head. "Of course I don't know the problem?"

"The problem was that sexually I could never trust myself with you."

"You never told me." She replied.

"Because it was my problem, Nad, not yours."

"What do you mean?"

"I was addicted to your body and wanted to pay homage to it every day."

She shook her head. "But why should that be a problem?"

He smiled. "It reminded me of difficult times as a priest. I was obsessive about sex and I couldn't stop myself then, just as I can't stop myself now."

"I don't understand?"

"As a good catholic, I believed abstention from sex was the answer because when you get defrocked for having a sexual addiction, you have a serious problem." He looked at her, expecting a response, but none came. "I tried to stay away from you. I thought it was better for both of us and although I missed the sex, I felt differently, almost at peace, as if my addiction to your body was somehow under control."

"Why didn't you discuss it with me?" A look of torment crossed her face, realizing her choices may have been different if she had known. "You're such a fool, John, because you should have realized I love you."

He shrugged, feeling uncomfortable at the opening of his heart. "The Catholic Church gives you a fair share of guilt for almost anything a normal person would enjoy." He looked pitiful. "I may have been a priest, but I'm no different to anyone else."

She looked at him, tugging at his clothes in an urgency to be one with him again. She felt damp in anticipation, moving to the bedroom, wanting to enjoy the closeness without the uncomfortable floor underneath her, pulling him with her, taking complete control, barely allowing him time to do anything. The athletic longing of her body took all the action necessary, following naturally and reciprocally with his still youthful body. It was as if they had never been apart, but when the unity of feeling had dissipated, the decisions she had to make became more difficult than ever. Her eyes filled with anguished questions and deep sadness, which he noticed, but dismissed, as his love for her had always masked the truth. She had so many questions, which a paralyzed heart could never answer. There may have been a little leap of expectation with the intimacy, but she would now have to endure the pain, as she realized it was too late for any redemption and there could be no turning back from the course she had set herself.

CHAPTER SIX

"In an age when all the grand ideas have lost credibility, FEAR of a phantom enemy is all the politicians have left to maintain their power"—The Power of Nightmares (BBC Panorama programme subsequently mysteriously shelved).

"In the early 1970's, Dick Cheney, (Chief of Staff under Gerald Ford) and Secretary of Defence Donald Rumsfeld claimed that reconciliation with the Soviets was impossible because they were hiding weapons of mass destruction, (WMD's), and a generation of nuclear submarines, which were undetectable by current technology. The CIA at the time called it a complete fiction and it ultimately proved false. Nevertheless, trillions of dollars were spent on the biggest peacetime military build-up in US history during the subsequent Reagan administration"—The Power of Nightmares.

"Governments have always used 'false flag' terror operations to get support for wars on their enemies . . . . (knowing) a state of 'false' war only serves as an excuse for domestic tyranny."

"The history of the strategy of tension . . . shows how violence is drip-fed to a public that comes to crave security—and real leaders are kept above suspicion—it's why States use false flag operations."

In relation to the 9/11 Commission, is it possible the Secretary of Defence could give three different explanations of what he was doing on the morning of 9/11 or that the first he knew about the twin towers being hit was being told by his Secretary that she had seen it on television, with eye witness testimony to the contrary being ignored? Is it possible that the man in charge of the military saw the first Tower being hit on television, then went into a meeting where he remained unaware of what was happening for the next forty minutes? Is it possible that the FAA did not inform the military that the fourth aeroplane had appeared to have been hijacked, contrary to both common sense and the word of several FAA employees? Is it possible that the Report fails to mention—even in a footnote—that the most serious allegations made public by FBI whistleblower Colleen Rowley? Is it possible that they can ignore so much evidence from fire-fighters in relation to their compelling evidence about the sound of many explosions and their reference to it appearing as a controlled demolition? Is it possible or believable that despite the most advanced technology in the world available to them, military aircraft were sent out to the East when all the dangers were obviously and clearly to the West and to the North, all this despite evidence that there were sixty seven intercepts of commercial aircraft which had only slightly deviated from their flight-paths in the nine months prior to the events of the 11th September 2001 without any such difficulty. Is it really coincidence that the War Games Operation Tripod and the FEMA operation in New York were set up for the 11th September 2001?

Nadia looked across at John, sprawled across her bed asleep. His face still looked boyish after a recent haircut, his mouth typically open as he slept. They had made love all night, like passionate young lovers again, barely able to tear themselves apart, his appetite never sated, but she sobbed quietly, tears dripping unashamedly onto the pillow. She could only give him a brief moment of respite and her heart ached at the thought of her betrayal. A meeting pencilled in her diary would settle matters, but until then she intended to gather as much information as possible as a bargaining tool. In a paradoxical way, she thought she could still help John, perhaps even save his life, rationalizing her position, wanting to enjoy the moment, yet knowing the consequences and the inevitable end to the relationship. If she could kill for him and solve all the problems by doing it, she wouldn't hesitate. She was certain of it, enjoying none of his scruples, nor seeking the responsibility they brought. In a recurring nightmare, she had seen him threatened, looking down on a scene with a gun in her hand, pointing it at a man barely recognizable in the shadows. It haunted her and she determined to ask her handler for a hand-gun, in the event it was a glimpse or remote viewing of some dangerous future event. In some ways, she felt John would welcome a release from the sorrows and imperfections of this world, but she wanted no part in it.

They had dragged themselves out of bed for lunch in a familiar quiet restaurant, near Maidenhead, bordering a pretty section of the River Thames, by a lock in the river, where boats backed up waiting for their turn to pass. It reminded her of past romantic dinners, laughter and more instinctive times, before intrigue crept into their relationship uninvited, like a cancer taking hold of something perfect and changing it to something imperfect and ugly, only much too late to stop the disease spreading its fatality. Last night may have been a mistake, she thought, but in some masochistic way she needed it.

Something drew John's attention to a large black car, with partly tinted windows, pulling up about fifty yards behind him, at a point in the road where no building or other reason existed for it to stop. As they got out of his car, no-one alighted from that vehicle.

"That's strange." He said quietly.

"What's strange?" She asked, turning her head and squinting in the sun.

"Nothing really." He hesitated. "It's just that black car has stopped back there and no-one has got out. I had the impression it had been following us."

She placed her hand above her eyes, shielding them from the sun, before turning back to the front. "I'm sure it's your imagination." She said, without facing him, moving into the restaurant ahead of John. "You've been worrying about your safety and it's bound to have an effect on you."

"Perhaps." He pointed to a table on the restaurant patio by the side of the river, checking he could still observe the car. "Shall we sit here?"

She nodded. "It's private and no-one can listen to our conversation."

A cool breeze swept across from the river, so the outside tables remained empty, providing the solitude their meeting demanded, yet allowing them to observe the boats navigating the lock. For her part, Nadia needed respite from the tortured thoughts plaguing her. Small birds, singing in the branches of the trees competed for attention with the ducks in the river, a short distance from their table, all oblivious to the strange people sharing their territory and to the events unfolding around them. Silver service dining in the better locations was an indulgence to which she had become accustomed, even if her income and lifestyle could hardly justify the cost, so she supplemented her income. Their table rested in the quietest part of the patio area to the side of a weeping cherry tree, conveniently shielded by the tree from the worst of the breeze. The waft of the kitchen aromas, garlic and herbs mingling with fresh ingredients as they cooked, crept pleasantly across to their table, stimulating the appetite.

"Are you feeling more positive?" She asked, sitting down first at the table, distracting him from his attention to the car. "You seem more cheerful, away from the grief these problems have been causing you."

He sat down opposite her, his face stained with dark lines from insufficient sleep. "The grief still follows me around, but I wanted to warn you I was undertaking something which had risks associated with it."

"But you've always taken risks, John. It's you." She understood him perfectly.

"Because I believe life is an illusion, created by the archetypal thoughts of humanity."

"Then if you're right, you've nothing to fear, whatever happens to you, except an escape from that illusion."

He smiled and wagged his finger. "You're absolutely right, of course. Sometimes I think you're not listening when I talk about mystical philosophy, but I must remember not to underestimate you."

"What information can you share with me?" She moved the cutlery, stretching her arm across the table, placing her hand on his arm and leaving it there. "Now that you've asked for my help."

"Are we back to the piece I'm writing, already?" His eyebrows raised. "I've only just sat down."

She squeezed his arm. "I thought this was the purpose of lunch."

He nodded. "I need to collate a large amount of material as background, some of which is in the public arena."

"That should make it easier."

"I intend to gather the major corroborating stuff myself, but if you could compile some of the background material and liaise with the various writers already going public, it would help."

"Where are you going to look for the corroborating material?"

"Various sources, but I've an important meeting coming up with this person on the Security and Intelligence Committee."

"Tell me about it?" She asked impatiently.

"When I've something tangible I'll tell you." He replied.

"Then what about this new technology?" She asked, stopping only as the menus arrived.

John ordered some wine and sat back, food menu in hand, taking a deep breath with a heave of his chest. "I feel better already."

"I'm pleased." She offered a genuine smile.

He leaned across the table, as if someone might hear. "I've sent the information about this new technology to one of the figures involved in the Architects and Engineers for 9/11 Truth campaign in the U.S. and invited comments." He took another deep breath, feeling a surge of well-being. "As soon as I know anything, I'll discuss it with you, if you're still certain you want to get involved."

She hid her disappointment. "So you've already divulged this information about the secret technology to someone else?"

"Two people."

"What did they say?" She asked.

"They appear not to have been too surprised."

"But it means they acknowledge the possibility that their own government have been responsible for the death of their citizens." She sounded quizzical.

"They've done it before at Pearl Harbour."

"Are you referring to that report, 'The Project for the New American Century'?"

John nodded. "The Report confirmed the need for a new Pearl Harbour to justify foreign incursions into sovereign states and the need for this massive additional military budget and since 9/11 they've had it."

"Have they achieved it?" She asked.

"In 2002, after the events of September 2001, the military budget was increased substantially to almost 350 billion dollars, with significant rises since."

"I'm not really surprised." She said.

"It's monstrous, Nad." He said. "There are too many deluded people, acting in ignorance of the secret agenda, wading into events on the back of either patriotism or religion, without realising they're being manipulated, like pawns in a larger game beyond their comprehension."

"I'm sure you're right." She released her hand from his arm and sat back, crossing her legs demurely. At one level, she wanted to still be there for him, whatever the price. Yet she had found herself involved in intrigue, which had overwhelmed her, taking her on a course of its own volition, the momentum impossible to stop. How she could possibly consider betraying the man she had loved more than any other still puzzled her.

He relaxed into his chair, looking at the movement of a boat through the lock. Taking out half-moon spectacles and balancing them on the end of his nose, he looked at the menu again, making the choices in his mind, before closing it.

"What about the interview with the former German Defence Minister after the comments he made in 'Der Tagesspiegel'?"

He nodded and smiled. "You do remember the things I tell you."

"I remember the article and, of course, I speak German."

He hesitated, while a waiter, dressed in a blue apron with white stripes, served the chilled Chardonnay they had ordered, offering the cork to him before pouring two large glasses, placing the ice bucket on an adjoining side table. When he had left, John resumed the conversation.

"You're right about the article. It's never been translated into English, but the essence of what he said was that for sixty decisive minutes both the military and intelligence services allowed fighter planes to remain on the ground, contrary to normal procedures, effectively standing down on the Vice President's orders."

"It had a resonance of truth." She touched his arm again and hoped he would reciprocate, but something still held him back. "The report also suggested that for hijackers briefly trained on little Cessna jets to hijack four large aircraft with complicated computer-management systems, all within a few minutes, and within another hour or so, to drive them into their targets with complicated flight manoeuvres was unthinkable."

He raised his index finger on his right hand. "The article made an important proviso, saying it would be impossible without years of support from the secret apparatus of the state and industry." He smiled approvingly. "You have a good memory for these things."

She nodded, offering a smile. "I just want to help you."

He took out his notepad from the inside pocket of his blazer and studied detailed jottings, then placed it on the table. "I had a telephone conversation with a pilot of an A300 Airbus, who had been in the Control Tower at Kennedy Airport at the time of the hijacking, but before I could undertake a detailed interview he had died, his aircraft mysteriously brought down in New Jersey, only weeks after 9/11."

"But didn't they suggest that particular aircraft was brought down when the rudder came off, by apparent excessive use?"

"Well they would wouldn't they?" He replied.

"If you've no evidence to the contrary, John, don't give people the opportunity to challenge your work by raising issues incapable of being proved."

"Maybe it was coincidence and again maybe not. Either way, it was convenient for those doing the cover-up, but I accept it would be better to keep the piece relevant to provable matters, rather than conjecture."

She sipped her wine. "You've always told me to give people facts, not opinions and coincidences, so you can't be put down as a conspiracy theorist."

"Yes, the facts."

"Isn't there an internet film called 'Loose Change', which sets out all the facts and figures surrounding the events?" She asked.

He nodded. "I've looked at it, but I've more incriminating evidence than the facts portrayed on that film, though some of the facts outlined are interesting enough and hard to refute."

"What evidence?"

He took another deep breath. "You know we're supposed to believe a highly-trained and sophisticated terrorist, takes a risk by taking a connecting flight from Portland only minutes before it's due to take off, reaching Boston only minutes before the hijacked plane takes off."

"I've seen the video of him." She interrupted.

"You've probably seen the video of him going through baggage control at Portland because they've never shown him at Boston, though everyone assumes it." He poured another glass for himself, topping Nadia's glass at the same time.

"I didn't know."

"No-one realizes the truth." He shook his head. "They allege this same man leaves amateurish clues behind as to his and his colleagues' identities and intentions. Even the names on the official passenger lists don't contain the alleged hijackers, many of whom have subsequently been found to be very much alive."

"It sounds provocative material." She sipped her wine.

"Why do you think the original passenger list was not immediately released, but strangely the names of the alleged hijackers were released very quickly?"

"I suppose there's always a reason." She replied.

He grunted. "As it happens, I've got the passenger manifests of all the aircraft involved in the events."

She looked up from reading her menu. "I still find it impossible to believe a total of eight pilots allow themselves to be overwhelmed by terrorists carrying no weapons other than paper-cutters, especially as there were judo champions, rugby players and weightlifters amongst the passengers on Flight 93?"

"You're right."

"And what about the missing black boxes?" She asked.

"What do you mean?"

"Shouldn't you be concentrating on these idiosyncrasies in the evidence?"

"You're probably right." He replied. "None of the pilots managed to get an alert to the FAA, despite the transponder codes being available throughout the aircraft, not only from the flight deck."

"It makes no sense."

He nodded. "How convenient this is for the secret government."

"Obviously, you believe there are reasons why no alerts were recorded?"

"I know exactly why there were no alerts and it has nothing to do with the terrorists." He replied.

"Tell me why?"

"It's part of the way it was planned and implemented, with the war games Operation Tripod intended to confuse, enabling the military to be stood down."

"As a man of principle, I know you'll do what you think is right, no matter the consequence." She said, deciding on a course of action of her own.

He sensed something about her manner or a nuance in the words, which did not sit right. "I still need more tangible evidence."

"I understand." She said, knowing her need to live an uncomplicated life contradicted the reality. The same waiter arrived, taking their order, refilling the wine glasses at the same time.

"I've brought the tape of my interview with the former Head of the German domestic intelligence service." He tapped his bulging pocket.

She wasn't listening, having retreated into a place within herself, an internal world free from the complications of the existence she had created.

"Nad, are you alright?" He asked.

She lifted her head high, jerking into life, recalling the question. "Yes, the tape."

"This must be boring you, Nad."

"Of course not, John." She touched his hand, removing it as the waiter arrived with the first course, taking her napkin and placing it neatly on her lap.

The waiter placed their first course on the table and left. He tasted the first mouthful and licked his lips. "I need to use some of the material on the tape to establish the amount of planning, precision and resources needed for the attacks, which could only have been achieved with the support of a state intelligence organization."

She savoured her food, before looking across at him. "Surely this is only circumstantial evidence?"

"You're right."

"But I've told you I'll help with this work?"

"I'm not sure you appreciate what I'm dragging you into because I'm certain it's going to be dangerous."

"The great benefit of freelancing, John, is that it's not particularly time-sensitive, so I can give you my time easily." She said firmly. "And I'm determined to help you, whatever the risks."

He nodded. "But I don't want you to get hurt, do don't place yourself in any dangerous situations."

She smiled, one of those brief fake smiles, but he didn't notice. "It's not a problem for me, so what can I do?"

"You can start by looking at the copy letters allegedly left behind by the hijackers. They don't ring true to me."

"What exactly do you want me to do with them?" She asked.

"You're a Muslim, study them and tell me whether they could have been written by a fanatical terrorist, fundamentally believing the pillars of Islam."

She took a mouthful of food, quickly swallowing it. "I've a psychologist friend who can help with profiling, if that's what you need, but all of this is conjecture and circumstantial again."

"But I need as much background information as you can gather."

"My brother lives in New York, so if you need research done there or even by my extended family in Pakistan, they'll offer assistance."

He neatly took his napkin, wiping the side of his mouth. "I'm a little concerned about any communications with Pakistan. It's too much of a satellite arm of the CIA, but perhaps your brother in New York can help if you're careful about what you say in communications with him."

"It shouldn't be a problem, just tell me what you need."

He heard only what he wanted to hear, closing his mind to the rest. "Listen to this." He took a small tape recorder from his blazer pocket, placing a tape inside it, and lowering the volume until it would only be audible to them.

She sipped the last of her wine and John dutifully picked up the wine bottle from the ice bucket, pouring another glass, before placing the napkin back over the top of the bottle with the panache of someone comfortable doing it. She leaned over to listen to the taped interview. She wanted an escape from her little arcane world, but even though ideas streamed into her consciousness, she concentrated on the tape, remembering as much as possible. For some minutes, neither of them said anything, simply listening to the tape and finishing their first course. John finished first, flicking the pages of his notebook, taking his pen from the top pocket of his blazer and writing notes, stopping the tape briefly as the waiter came to their table to clear away the first course. Lifting his finger he brought Nadia's attention to the black car still parked in the distance.

He called the waiter's attention to it, pointing to the car. "Do you know if anyone from that car has entered the restaurant?"

The waiter looked across, shaking his head. "I don't think so, but I can't be sure." He looked back at John. "Would you like me to ask in the restaurant?"

He shook his head, waving him away. "Thanks, but no need."

He started the tape again, stopping it, as he noticed a movement in the corner of his eye, looking up in time to see the black car turn and move away.

"It's going away." He said, pointing to the car again.

"I hope it makes you feel safer." She said.

"Not necessarily, but it's odd."

He played the rest of the tape, before turning to Nadia. "Can your brother get the details of the flight-path of the two aircraft, which hit the World Trade Centre Towers and find out if they passed over the nuclear power installations at Indian Point?"

"Why do you need to know?" She asked.

"Terrorists desperate to cause the greatest damage to the United States would look for a better and easier target, such as the nuclear power station, if death and destruction was the real aim."

She nodded. "I'd never thought of it, but I'm sure my brother will help."

"Can he get me the flight-path of the aircraft which allegedly hit the Pentagon?" He asked. "It would help."

"Why do you need it?" She asked.

"Because I'm puzzled by the complex manoeuvre to veer around the Pentagon at great speed away from its natural flight-path, then hitting the side away from the obvious and natural target of the Defence Secretary and the Military Joint Chiefs."

"Didn't some Boeing engineers say the manoeuvre was impossible even with the most experienced of pilots?" Nadia asked.

He nodded. "It did all this, somehow flying at 450 miles per hour with great technical ability, underneath the radar and defence systems, yet not scorching the grass in front of the Pentagon before the collision."

At that moment, the waiter arrived with their main course, neatly laying it in front of them and replenishing their glasses. "I can get the flight-path for you." She swallowed the first mouthful of her food quickly. "But my brother may ask why I need it."

"Tell him you don't know."

"Can I tell him about the nuclear facility?"

"You can tell him whatever you like." He hesitated. "I don't like secrets."

She closed her eyes, retreating back into that place where she felt comfortable and away from an aching heart. Lingering deep within her psyche, an idea surfaced as an answer to her problems and in the moment it made sense to her, even if the solution involved further betrayal, though she hid her thoughts in that little black box in her brain, almost as second nature. She knew John would never understand the mechanics of deception or the darker side to human nature, so alien was it to him.

"You're miles away." John said, oblivious to her thoughts.

She opened her eyes, dragging herself back to the present. "Sorry, this place is so peaceful."

He looked around. "I understand completely."

She sighed. "I get the feeling you don't think the Pentagon was hit by one of the Boeings?"

He nodded. "I'm convinced the Boeing was diverted elsewhere."

"So you think something else hit the Pentagon?"

"Correct." John replied.

"That's interesting." She tilted her head, but changed the subject. "Back in the apartment, you talked about the lessons of history?"

He smiled. "I was telling you people never learn the lessons of history."

"What lessons in particular?"

John took some food, talking before he had quite finished eating it. "Some of the actions of Nazi politicians have similarities to the actions of current politicians, yet people forget the lessons."

"What do you mean precisely?" She leaned forward.

"Well, the day after Hitler burnt down the Reichstag, blaming and later executing an innocent man, he invoked Article 48 of the Weimar Constitution, allowing civil liberties to be suspended in Germany. The decree was stated to be for the protection of the people and the homeland, just like the basis behind the Patriot Acts and the Homeland Security Act in the United States today."

"European history was never my best subject, but didn't they also censor the press?"

"It was considerably more than the mere abolition of a free press, but of course the CIA has gone on record as saying they own the media in the United States, so they don't have to abolish it."

"Remind me what happened in Germany?" She asked.

He placed the cutlery down on the table. "All freedom of speech and rights of assembly and association disappeared overnight; even the rights to privacy on postal and electronic communications went in an instant." He looked at her. "Does it ring any bells?"

She shivered and a glazed look crossed. "Oh God."

He nodded. "Yes. I still pray to him in difficult times."

"That's not what I mean." She said. "I'm genuinely interested."

"In Germany, there was no protection against unlawful searches and seizures, even eroding the rights of certain individuals to own property. Everyone puzzled as to how quickly these things were invoked."

She shook her head. "That's spooky."

"In comparison, consider how quickly over 1000 pages of the Patriot Act were brought into the statute book. It was approved by Congress only three weeks after the events of 9/11, and do you have any idea how long it takes to draft complicated legislation?"

"I've no idea, but I guess it takes a long time." She replied.

"It's obvious it was written long before the events of 9/11. If so, what does it tell you about the events themselves?"

She nodded compliantly. "Are people so gullible they can't see these things?"

"Quite the contrary." He placed his hand on her thigh under the table, unaware of the feelings it generated. The first thing to go in their relationship had been laughter and the second had been touch. "The truth is that people want to trust their governments."

"Not anymore." Her voice gravelled.

"The alternative makes them uncomfortable and in the security of their homes people don't want to believe their worlds could change so dramatically. It frightens them." He looked sorrowful. "It's this fear, which gives the shadow governments the control over the people and allows them to implement their secret agendas."

She flushed, staring blankly ahead. At that moment, she vowed she would no longer sacrifice herself to the frozen lakes of this static relationship. There was no growth in it and as the only certainty in life was that it changes, something had to change. She stirred herself away from her thoughts. "People deserve better, but you always told me if everyone understood the spiritual essence of what they are, they could take the fear from their lives and face the truth."

"It's what I believe." He hesitated. "If we expand our consciousness without fear, the world expands as a consequence."

For a brief moment she had an urge to confess everything, but something held her back. "How do you face truth, John?"

"I embrace it." He replied instinctively, failing to notice the edge in her voice.

She looked away, gathering her thoughts again. His reply reinforced the course of action she had now determined to follow, knowing she could no longer live in the painful vacuum. "Really?"

"The world would be a better place if the finer virtues were fixed in people's minds, but I acknowledge it's an imperfect world."

She smiled and nodded.

The waiter cleared dishes from the table, leaving them to savour the remainder of the wine, the old man's orgasm, he remembered someone once saying. "I've contacted the American lawyer, who brought the suit for damages against the US President and other administration officials for allowing 9/11 to happen and for using the Sheikh as a scapegoat."

"I'd never heard of him, the action for damages or reference to the Sheikh being used in the events, only that he was responsible for them." She leaned across the table.

"There's no reason you would." He took her hand. "The late Robin Cook indicated to some members of the press and in the article he wrote one month before he died that 'al-Qaeda' was simply a CIA creation, in effect the 'database' of CIA recruits initially fighting with the Mujahadeen against the Russians."

"I find this fascinating." She placed her free hand on top of his hand, sandwiching it between her hands.

He stuttered briefly. "I. I can fax the questions I need to ask him direct to your brother, if he's happy to contact the lawyer and tape the interview."

"No problem." She nodded.

"In particular, Nad, I want to know what documents he has in his possession which can prove either the US President or one or more members of his administration were complicit in the attacks, as he claims."

"Anything else?" She asked.

"I need as much information as possible on this 'Operation Tripod'."

"The operation which resulted in the military standing down?" She asked.

He nodded. "It's the operation name for the war games and FEMA event organized by the administration for 9/11."

She sat unmoved. "Politics is such a dirty game."

"Intelligence work is certainly a dirty game, Nad."

She swallowed hard, but played the game like a professional. "I'd prefer to have nothing to do with it." She took her hand away. "I hate these people."

"The US intelligence picked up internet messages with their echelon software, such as 'tomorrow is zero hour' and 'the match is about to begin', yet they did nothing and instead later suggested they were in the process of translating them from the Arabic when the events occurred."

She nodded involuntarily. "Extraordinary."

"The Director of the National Security Agency admitted this before Congress, though he said they intercept more than two million electronic communications an hour from their satellites and listening posts around the world." He sighed. "Of course, this includes one at Menwith Hill in Yorkshire linking with GCHQ Cheltenham."

"So what happened to those intercepts?" She asked, rubbing her arms with her hands, as a chill breeze swept across from the river.

"They must have been suspicious because they were translated almost immediately." He took a last sip of the wine. "I was told they only do that if they believe they come from al-Qaeda."

"I'll telephone this lawyer in the States and ask him to expect the fax." She said. "But are you sure he'll cooperate?"

"Unless he's bound by some form of client privilege, I've reason to believe he'll help us." He busied himself, writing notes. "My concern is simple. I'm just one man against a group of immensely powerful people. They've proved they've no qualms about killing thousands of innocent civilians, including thousands of women and children in both Afghanistan and Iraq, even if you ignore the victims in the Twin Towers." A sour expression crossed his face. "I'm obviously dispensable."

"I hope that's not your epitaph."

"That's cheerful, Nad."

"I'm being pragmatic." She said. "My brother told me the Mayor of San Francisco made a statement immediately after 9/11 to the effect his security personnel had warned him the day before 9/11 not to fly by air on a scheduled trip from San Francisco to New York the next day. This was reported in the San Francisco Chronicle at the time."

He nodded. "It was widely reported afterwards." He leant back in the chair, stretching his arms. "Newsweek in the States did a report saying high-ranking Defence Department and Pentagon officials had also been advised to cancel travel plans for the morning of 9/11 for security reasons."

"Didn't they try to backtrack later and withdraw some of these comments."

He sneered. "Someone must have had a visit from the men in black suits."

"Quite possibly."

He took the notebook from the table and placed it in the inside pocket of his blazer. "I've things to do, so we'd better leave."

"No problem."

"Can you get your brother to verify the facts involving Goldman Sachs and their alleged contacts within Mossad, as they apparently had an absentee rate in excess of fifty per cent on 9/11."

She shivered again. "I'm sure they'd circulated a memo the day before advising employees to stay away from government buildings the following day."

"Sure." She said. "I'll ask him."

He raised his index finger. "One other thing." He hesitated. "A Mossad expert reported that on the 7th September 2001, the CIA received a message sent by the Mossad's Station Chief in Washington warning of the imminent possibility of a massive terrorist attack, but they ignored it."

"I'll ask my brother about it."

"Even the Israeli Prime Minister has subsequently leaked confirmation that the CIA was warned of these events, so if your brother could collect any information about it, it would be extremely useful."

She smiled. "My brother knows a number of influential people in New York and he'll know where to find this information."

"Good."

She leaned across the table again. "I can recall him telling me Mossad agents were on the roof of Building Seven videoing the first plane hitting the North Tower, so they must have known it was going to happen."

"You've never mentioned that to me before." He said. "Though I'd heard something similar about a white van being seen with Israelis celebrating. Perhaps it was the same people because they were subsequently arrested, but released some time later."

She screwed up her face. "I must have forgotten about it until now."

"Didn't another Jewish company relocate immediately before 9/11?" He asked. "Your brother may recall it."

"It should be easy enough for him, but they're the sort of questions and enquiries which may draw attention to your research." She hesitated. "Isn't that dangerous?"

He shrugged. "I'm not sure how I can avoid it, but the sooner I publish my work, the less risk for everyone involved and the heat will gradually reduce."

"Of course, they may not think it's significant or even that you're important enough to worry about you." She said.

"Maybe they're right." He replied. "They're taking more chances now than they've ever done, as if they're untouchable. Perhaps this boldness is the weakness which will allow us to get at the truth."

"Perhaps it's something to do with this fixation about the date of December 2012 and some significance associated with it?"

"It could be, but I'm still surprised by the chances they're taking." He replied.

"I do hope you know what you're doing, John." Her eyes narrowed. "I'm worried about you."

"Nad, we've been there already." He said. "Perhaps they think they're immune or else there's a scarier and more sinister version of events."

"And what's that?" She asked nervously.

He smiled. "This could all be leading up to some contrived catastrophic event which will change our world forever and 9/11 was merely a stepping stone on its path."

"I'm not sure what you mean." She said. "Are you suggesting something even more catastrophic than the 9/11 events?" She hesitated. "Now that really is scary."

"When I've got all the evidence and the facts, you'll be the first to know, but that's exactly what I'm saying." He stood erect, chin up. "We've already sleepwalked into a real Big Brother world bereft of real freedoms, with torture justified in typical Orwellian language from those in positions of power. It may already be too late to call foul."

"It's grotesque." She said. "They're even using political, religious and sexual correctness as a newspeak to tell us what we can and cannot say."

"They now tell us how to think, as well as how to speak, but they can't be underestimated. The extent of their surveillance techniques would surprise most people. There are secret technologies considerably more advanced than anything you hear about from the media. In the States, they cleverly use emotive words to disguise their intent and play on the minds of the weak-willed."

"I'm sure you're right." She recalled her field of expertise and its relevance. "If the government is allowed to get away with the genetic engineering of foods and the introduction of chemicals into the water supplies, they'll quickly generate a feeble, weak-willed population."

"I'd forgotten, Nad, you were a staunch opponent of the introduction of genetically-modified foods and had written a number of articles."

"I interviewed some leading scientists in the field, all of whom had significant reservations about the validity of published studies on the subject and told me the real problem is the irrevocable damage to people's DNA as a consequence of it."

"What's the world coming to Nad?"

"It's leading to something quite dramatic, John. I'm sure of it."

"Even the Patriot Act is using an expression to mean something completely different from its content, inferring you're not a patriot if you don't agree with the erosion of freedom contained within it and that it's unpatriotic to challenge these things or the events of 9/11." His eyes contained many unanswered questions. "It's all very convenient for them, of course."

She rose from the table, her thoughts elsewhere.

He looked across at her. "Are you alright?"

"Sorry. I was miles away."

"Can I give you a penny for your thoughts?"

She smiled. "They're worth far more than that."

He ignored the quip, returning to his subject. He had the mercurial knack of being able to do two things at the same time and never lose his place in the conversation. "Soon we'll be back to the thirties with children encouraged to inform on parents and neighbours on neighbours."

"But it's so difficult for the individual to do anything about it when they're fighting against the state and establishment machine." She sighed. "This is what worries me."

"It worries me too, Nad." He took her hand, as they moved away from the patio and out of the restaurant. "And we're back to the lessons of history, once again being created by repetition and misinformation, rather than truth." He took a deep breath. "Herman Goering famously said something on the subject at the Nuremburg trials."

"I think you're about to remind me again."

He smiled. "All the Nazis did is what all countries and governments do. They inform their citizens they're being attacked and place them in fear, then attack the pacifists for being unpatriotic. In the end, the citizens clamour for the protection and security the state offers them."

"It's before my time and I hadn't heard it." She said, her face reflecting her concern at the pain he would soon endure.

"It was before my time too, unless you've forgotten."

She smiled. "Are you sure?"

They walked onto the road outside and began crossing to their car. "Did you know none of the pilots gave the procedural 7500 code over the transponder for a hijacking?" He asked.

She nodded. "I think you told me."

"It's unbelievable that none of the stewards or pilots in any of the planes could enter the code." He turned to her. "I don't believe in coincidence and there has to be a reason."

She felt uneasy for some reason. "Then what's its significance?"

"My research reveals the reason." John leaned towards her and whispered, looking around furtively. "It's impossible to believe the pilots and their crew could forget their training to alert ground control. The hijackers couldn't have prevented it, so there had to be another explanation."

"You'll end up making me paranoid." She looked sideways, mimicking John's actions. "If you know the reason, share it with the world."

"I need more corroborative evidence first, Nad."

"That makes sense, John."

"I also believe the United Airlines plane brought down in Pennsylvania was purposely brought down by an American F16 fighter jet."

"But why?" She asked.

"Because it took off late and could not take down its original target." He replied. "I believe I know its intended target."

She shook her head. "So they shot down their own aircraft?"

"I know it's provocative and it'll be difficult for people to accept."

"Why would they do it?" She asked again.

"I'll tell you when I've got the evidence, not before."

"But why can't you tell me?" She asked, looking up in time to see the black car with the tinted windows, quickly accelerating and bearing down on them.

"Look out." John screamed, noticing the car at the same time, pushing her to one side out of the line of the car, before diving to the other side to avoid its path. He remembered his journalistic training and caught the number plate before it sped away out of sight.

She stood up, brushing herself down, shaking and walked across to John. "Jesus Christ. What was all that about?"

"It's alright, you can just call me John." He joked.

She shrugged. "It's not funny, John."

He reached out, pulling her into his arms and holding her for a few moments. "I've got the number plate, but if my guess is right it'll lead us nowhere."

"What do you mean?" She asked. "Surely, if you report it to the Police, they'll track it down."

"Now you're being naive Nad." He said. "This is the work of the intelligence services or contractors working for them." He took a deep breath, releasing her. "I've seen their dirty work before."

She shook her head. "Let me write down the registration number?" She took out a diary and a pen from her handbag and John recited it. Strange thoughts gyrated in her mind. "Now I'm more determined than ever to help you, John."

"I think it's just a warning, Nad."

"You could have fooled me."

"I'm getting close, too close." He sighed, a deep resonating sigh.

She leant across, placing her head on his shoulder. "I'm really frightened."

"You'll be fine." He stroked her hair. "What were we talking about, Nad?"

"God knows."

"Probably, but I'm pretty good at remembering too." He smiled again.

She lifted her head. "Doesn't anything frighten you?"

"Sometimes, Nad, but I've told you, this was only a warning." He replied. "I'm sure of it."

"John, I think you were talking about the aircraft brought down over Pennsylvania and the transponder codes being inoperative."

He took a deep breath. "I'd forgotten."

"So what was the reason the United Airlines flight was brought down?" She asked.

"It had taken off late, too late to reach its intended target before fighter jets had arrived over New York."

"And its target?"

"Building Seven, adjacent to the Twin Towers."

"It makes sense." She nodded. "They'd have needed to destroy any evidence there."

"It's the same with the black boxes. They were fire-proof, shock-proof and supposedly indestructible, yet were never produced at the time, despite all the valuable data it would have possessed."

"So what would they have revealed?" She asked.

"In all likelihood, the pilots reciting that something had gone wrong and they'd lost control of their flight instruments."

"So we're back to the new technology?"

"Sure." He replied. "They couldn't have someone listening to the voices recorded in the black boxes and working out the obvious."

"And if they fabricate them?"

"No-one would believe it if they suddenly turned up now." John said.

"But it took more than five years after the events, long after his capture, for the alleged confession from Khalid Sheikh Mohammed to seep out of Guantanamo." She said. "Yet many people still believe it."

He looked across at Nadia, failing to notice the rapid movement in her eyes. "Unfortunately, many people will continue to believe it."

She stared ahead. "Yet my brother told me he was tortured and water-boarded so many times."

"But they used the evidence from the torture much sooner." He said.

"In what way?" She asked, intrigued.

"In due time, Nad." He replied. "They destroyed all the tapes of the interrogation during those incidents of torture, but they'd have been nowhere nearer the truth, after so many incidents of torture, than before any torture had taken place."

"Is that what you believe?"

"It's been proven that the problem with torture is there's no certainty as to the truth of the confessions." He walked across to the car with her. "Every experienced interrogator knows there may be some truth in what is said and some untruth and no way to tell them apart. Governments who really want to get at the truth don't use it. The problem is that when faced with the pain, a victim will tell the interrogator anything they want to hear, just to stop it."

"Then why did they do it?" She asked.

He opened the car door for her and moved to the other side, settling into the driver's seat, hunching over the steering wheel, his mouth dry. "They were left with few alternatives because of the perverse ideology of the people at the heart of the US administration."

"I'm not sure I understand?"

He shrugged. "They wanted to invade Iraq, yet they could find no facts or operational evidence to support a relationship between Saddam Hussein and al-Qaeda, so what could they do?"

"I think people realize that now, John."

He groaned, leaning back in the seat. "I hate the lies, but they used the amateurish weapons of mass destruction dossier to try and establish evidence of a connection with al-Qaeda to justify their actions and do what they always intended to do."

She placed her hand on John's arm. "It's such a nonsense."

He moved his right hand to clasp her hand. "But they needed something to place before the 9/11 Commission and they had nothing. They could soften up those sitting on the Commission and place their own people there, but they still needed some evidence."

She moved her head close to John, without even realizing she was doing it. "So they tortured people to get the so-called evidence?"

He moved his hand to the steering wheel. "Of course, torture is evil." He said. "But it also destroys the possibility of knowing the truth with any certainty."

"So it's only now the real truth is emerging." She lifted herself upright.

"Precisely." His face twisted angrily, hating injustice with a passion bordering on psychosis. "We already know they falsified the evidence of weapons of mass destruction, but there had to be a connection to the events of 9/11 to justify the invasion of Iraq." He looked across at her. "Torture was the only way they could create the al-Qaeda link and a justification for the war."

"But who was responsible for all of this?" She asked.

"It was the Vice President's brief to justify the false intelligence."

She nodded. "I remember reading that a quarter of the footnotes of the 9/11 Commission Report came from so-called intelligence gleaned from the abuse of al-Qaeda prisoners and torture."

"If you think about it." He said. "Having already gone into Afghanistan on a false premise, the major part of the basis and justification for the War in Iraq and the mass killing of a hundred thousand people or more, many innocent women and children, was a lie, tortured out of someone."

"It's immoral." She said firmly.

"Sure." He replied instantly. "But the whole 9/11 thing is based on a lie. This is why they needed Khalid Sheikh Mohammed as one of the fall guys, though the man was by reputation so boastful and arrogant, it would have been much easier to manipulate his ego, without the need for torture at Guantanamo."

"Was he an important figure?"

He shook his head. "He wanted to believe he was an important figure, but he was insignificant in the scheme of things, simply being played like a violin from both sides; al-Qaeda and the intelligence officers of the American administration."

She felt sick inside, knowing her complicity with the intelligence community would create equal havoc in its time and she feigned distress.

His human frailty took him away from the place where secret thoughts could be discerned. "There are important prisoners in many of the other ghost prisons around the world, Nad."

"They could lock you up too, John, if you're not careful." She grimaced.

"Who knows what they'll do to cover up their grubby participation in these events."

"So do you think they'll arrest you if you publish this material?" She asked.

He lifted his eyebrows, doleful eyes penetrating her soul. "I don't honestly know the answer to the question."

She sighed, wondering if the solution she had pondered so seriously in the restaurant would work. "I wouldn't want to live in a world without you, John." The tone surprised even her and if she could not be with him, she still wanted to protect him.

He looked up, eyes bright and alert. "That's a sweet thing to say."

She smiled awkwardly again, turning her face away, before looking up coyly. "It's the truth."

There was a silence. "You're a good friend, Nad." He said. "And I've so much affection for you."

She groaned. "Please don't, John."

His face contorted, puzzled. "What's wrong?"

"Nothing." She replied calmly, controlling her emotions before they exposed the truth and it was too late. "Tell me more about your research, if you need me to help you."

"I don't know what else you want to know." He said.

"The more you tell me, the easier it is for me to help."

He nodded. "I've been told about a proposal, referred to as 'Home Run' by one researcher. It was resurrected for use for the first time in the events of 9/11."

"What do you mean resurrected?" She asked.

"Well, in 1959, it was placed before the then administration and it proposed flying an aircraft by remote control into a high-rise building in Miami and blame it on Castro, as an excuse to invade Cuba."

"And I suppose remote-control technology has moved on in the last fifty years?"

He nodded. "If they find out the full extent of my knowledge, I'm certain they'll try and suppress it."

"And who are these faceless bureaucrats?" She frowned.

"Who knows exactly." He replied. "But one of their options is to eliminate me, before anything can be published. It's what they do, but the trick is to publish it before they find out, then there'd be no purpose in it, as all it would do is draw attention to my work."

She groaned. "Then you must publish this material soon."

He stared at her, slowly shaking his head. "It's easy to say, but much more difficult to do. Many people know the flaws in their government's position, but I'm one of the few on the outside who knows precisely how they organised all of the events and the technology they used, with al-Qaeda simply undertaking the false flag operation, as the scapegoat."

She nodded. "It's frightening, John.2

"But I know it's an inside job, Nad, and I intend to prove it."

Her head dropped. "It's not the way it's presented by the government-controlled media."

He failed to appreciate the subtleties and nuances in her tone or body language, fulfilling only his psychological need to unburden himself, passing on some of the responsibility he carried. "This knowledge is dangerous and from their point of view the solution may be a lethal one, before I can publish the truth."

"Don't talk like this John."

"But the evidence is so compelling they may not use their usual methods of misinformation to discredit me." A vulnerable expression crossed his face. "But I definitely need your help."

"I've told you I'll help." She lied, allowing the words to come out, knowing the expression on his face would haunt her. "Do you think the incident with the car means they know about the material in your possession?"

"Probably."

"Then it's too late already." She said. "Unless." She stopped immediately.

"Unless what?"

"Nothing." She made a movement of her right hand, dismissively. "Just a thought."

CHAPTER SEVEN

Dr David Kelly, one of the world's leading experts in biological and chemical weapons, was hounded after famously speaking to Andrew Gilligan of the BBC, indicating he was of the view there were no weapons of mass destruction in Iraq and that the government was purposely sexing up the Iraq dossier to justify an excuse for war. He was subsequently found to be correct.

The government appointee and Inquiry Chairman astonishingly and secretly classified unpublished medical and scientific records relating to Dr Kelly's death, to prevent its publication, for 70 years—including the post mortem report and photographs of his body—without any apparent legal precedent for doing so. Liberal Democrat M.P. Norman Baker, who has written a book on the affair, has had his application for access to the classified documents denied under Section 41 of the Freedom of Information Act. He is appealing the decision and is part of the Coalition Government in the UK.

Furthermore, the cause of death was allowed to be registered on the death certificate some five weeks before the Inquiry had been completed, unsigned by a Doctor or Coroner, and wrongly reciting there had been an inquest on August 14 2003. The Public Inquiry, therefore, reaching a pre-determined conclusion some five weeks before it ended. The government used the obscure Section 17a of the Coroners Act to replace an Inquest, which has never been held, with a Public

Inquiry, despite the fact that unlike an Inquest, the Inquiry would not have the power to hear evidence under oath, to subpoena witnesses, to call a jury or be able to aggressively cross-examine witnesses. This section of the Coroners Act has only ever been used three times before and on each of those occasions it involved multiple deaths. The wording on the death certificate is ambiguous in that it should state precisely the place of death, but it states only 'found dead' at Harrowdon Hill.

A number of leading doctors are certain Dr Kelly did not die in the way described and believe Dr Kelly could not have bled to death, as alleged, from the wounds to the ulnar artery. This corroborates the two ambulance personnel, with over 40 years experience of attending suicides, who gave a press conference indicating they were convinced Dr Kelly did not die at that location, as there was insufficient blood on Kelly or at the scene, the first Police Officer at the scene agreeing. It has emerged from a Freedom of Information request that a police helicopter with heat-seeking equipment flew over the place where Kelly allegedly died on the night he disappeared, July 18, 2003, at 2.30 a.m. and did not detect his body.

It is now apparent that the pruning knife used in the alleged suicide, had no fingerprints on it, nor on four other items found at the scene. A US Air Force officer who served with Dr Kelly in Iraq, confirmed Dr Kelly had an injury to his right elbow, which meant he was unable to use his right hand, even for basic tasks such as cutting up food. She had offered to attend the Inquiry, but was not called. She also confirmed he had difficulty swallowing pills. Even an experienced clinical pharmacologist, has confirmed he informed Thames Police he believed Dr Kelly's death may not have been murder as Dr Kelly could not have swallowed more than a safe dose of two co-proxamol tablets because there was so little in his system after death.

The Police removed wallpaper at Dr Kelly's home, apparently sweeping for listening devices, just hours before his death was discovered, during which time Dr Kelly's family were asked to wait in the garden. Even colleagues at the Ministry of Defence were apparently warned off attending his funeral.

The Police search operation for Kelly's body was called "Operation Mason" and it started even before he had been reported missing. A close relative of Kelly, Wendy Wearmouth, has stated she found it incredibly unlikely he would have committed suicide, as it would have been totally against his whole way of being. On February 27th 2002, Kelly tells British Diplomat, David Broucher, during a conference in Geneva that if Iraq is invaded, he would probably be found dead in the woods.

She took hold of the Prime Minister's right arm firmly, as he talked to a local New Labour dignitary at a pre-function drinks party. He may have been a cabinet colleague, but she needed an opportunity to collar him without the strong-armed publicity and spin machine around to protect him. She could not resist it, placing herself between him and the Special Branch Protection Officers, stationed on the other side of the mahogany-panelled room, so elegantly decorated with red velvet curtains and crystal chandeliers. The chit-chat buzz from loud-mouthed politicians within the room allowed her as private a discussion as possible, so alienated had he become from his colleagues and the grass roots in the party, particularly those colleagues who cared.

She thought of her lofty ambitions and the enthusiasm for the principles of New Labour when first elected, against all odds, even the polls, recalling the elation at being in a position to make a difference and be of service to the people. They were genuine feelings and aspirations, but it had all turned sour in the months and years that followed. Her feelings of isolation had become exaggerated in the passage of time and she felt drained by her lonely and ultimately unsuccessful attempts to retain the party as one of principle to the point where she had considered carefully whether she could in all conscience remain in the Cabinet. As the political party had been such a powerful influence in her life, she could never leave it, but the chance to be more vocal from the backbenches and from an influential committee had become more attractive with the passing of time. Already she had been demoted in the Cabinet hierarchy, summoned to Cabinet rarely with limited input when it became necessary for the photo-shoot, the female presence and the spin.

The Prime Minister turned around to face her, his smile melting, furrows evident in his face. "What is it, Lynne?" He asked frostily.

"I want to talk to you about this War."

"Does it have to be now?"

"It's the only chance I'll get, as you know perfectly well."

"If you must." He relented grudgingly.

"You do realise by joining this illegal war against Iraq, the whole of the Middle East will be de-stabilised?" Lynne was one of the original Babes, as the large intake of female M.P.'s were so famously caricatured by the tabloid press at that time, much to her annoyance.

He screwed his face unpleasantly. "Not now."

She shook her head. "And you've distorted the truth about the weapons of mass destruction."

The boyish smile evaporated, a hardened expression taking its place. "There was an evil dictator in power who needed to be overthrown."

"So it's about regime-change then?" She brushed back her short-cropped mousey hair with her right hand and it lodged neatly back on her shoulders. Her beige two-piece jacket and skirt fitted around a still-youthful body, an expensive handbag accessory hooked over her shoulder, locking into her left elbow.

"Not exactly, but significant threats existed, of which you're unaware."

"Tell me and if they're real, I'll support you."

"These are intelligence issues, which can't be discussed in these circumstances in this environment." He looked away. "You'll just have to trust me."

"Have you considered the increased terror-threat, which is an inevitable consequence of your decision?" Her eyes narrowed. "I've spoken to other members of the Cabinet and I know there are serious dissenters, so this decision is all down to you."

He looked at her, moving his hands in front of him. "If you didn't go along with the decision, you had an alternative." He flushed. "It's necessary to join our allies, if we're to retain our place at the top table of nations."

"But I wasn't part of the Cabinet when that decision was made."

"I'm sorry, but I couldn't remember."

"You're playing politics with people's lives." Emotion crept into her voice. "I've talked to someone in intelligence and they suggest at least two thousand Muslims in the UK alone will become radicalized because of your decision. They'll now be monitoring sleeper cells on a daily basis as a consequence." Her eyes widened. "It'll take a generation to recover."

He shook his head. "We had no alternative other than to pursue this course of action and you must trust our judgment." He said. "It's the least I expect of cabinet colleagues in a situation where conventions of Parliament apply."

"What specific conventions?" She asked.

"Collective responsibility of Cabinet to start." He replied instantly. "If you didn't agree to this course, then the honourable thing to do was resign your position in Cabinet after the decision was made." He looked at her quizzically. "This remains your prerogative, of course."

She ignored the suggestion. "But did you honestly believe there were still weapons of mass destruction in Iraq when weapons inspectors' reports indicated there were none of any consequence?"

He spoke through gritted teeth. "Our intelligence suggested they remained a threat."

"Those intelligence reports were being manipulated and sexed up, to use your language, and you know it." Her voice raised and cracked.

"Are you prepared to trust us on this or not?"

She shook her head, but said nothing

"If you're not, then there are serious consequences." He pursed his lips. "Do you understand?"

She made no attempt to disguise the pain on her face or the horror she felt at the immense loss of life. "That's a cop-out to prevent further enquiry."

He hesitated. "Are you sure you want to do this?"

"I must."

"I ask you again, if you've any ambition, don't isolate yourself because I'm bound to mention this to my cabinet colleagues." His eyes bulged, face reddening, as he pointed a finger at her, raising his voice to a dangerously-public level. "Enough is enough, our course has been set in stone and there's no way we can turn back, it's too late."

"We must get out of this disaster?" She asked, the tone echoed sadness.

"Of course not." He replied harshly. "It would show weakness and indecision. Government is not run in that way and there's nothing you can say, which will change the course we're all committed to follow. We must be in this for the long term." He hesitated. "It's called Politics." He turned away, moving towards some other guests, attempting to smile, but its falseness creating an ugly caricature instead.

Despite attracting the attention of others in the room, she pursued him, her anger physical and palpable. She placed her arm on his shoulder, forcing him to turn back towards her. "Your argument is primitive and inarticulate, if you're suggesting terrorists in Iraq or a regime like Saddam's could have the capacity to attack us with weapons of mass destruction, it's bullshit."

"You're making a big mistake." He looked around furtively, uncomfortable with the attention the argument created, a number of people stopping private conversations and turning to face them.

She noticed the attention too, but too late for concern. "If anything, all you've done is increase the threat of terror on the streets of Britain and allow al-Qaeda into Iraq, a country where they've had no presence whatsoever." Her eyes never left his. "Iraq has had nothing to do with the events of 9/11, so why do you do it?"

"The threat is already there, as you'll see in due course."

"What do you mean?"

"Nothing." He stared at her with fiery eyes, hardened and immune to the truth, as if some bubble protected him from the reality of his position. "I warn you, young lady. Stop right now or you'll regret it." He turned away immediately.

"Are you threatening me now?" She moved around to face him again.

He set his chin firmly, but said nothing.

"What are you going to do?" She hesitated. "Set your dogs on me, as you did with poor David Kelly and the BBC?" She knew as soon as she had said it that the comment was unwise, but it was too late now.

He turned towards her menacingly, an ugly expression distorting his face. "You'll regret that comment."

She sighed, already aware her stance would alienate her from her most senior colleagues. "It saddens me how politics now reflects the human condition, isolated from the goodness in the world."

"If we didn't have politicians, there'd be anarchy young lady." He said through gritted teeth. "You should be glad there are politicians prepared to make difficult decisions, which make the ordinary citizen safe in their bed at night." He gave her a twisted look. "They'll thank us for the actions we've taken and you should show a little gratitude."

"I can't stay in the government, if you persist with this dangerous liaison with the Americans."

"It's perfectly obvious you can't stay in government." He said. "Your actions have consequences and you've made your choice." He looked at her with steely eyes. "I'll expect your letter of resignation in the morning."

She nodded. "You'll have it, but don't think it's going to shut me up."

"If it doesn't, then someone at the Whip's office should explain to you the damage you'll do to the party by your extravagance."

"This isn't a decision I've taken lightly and I understand perfectly well what I'm doing. I can live with it, but can you?"

For a moment, she recoiled at his physical movement towards her, as he appeared to be having great difficulty in restraining himself. For the first time, she saw fear in his eyes. It was at that moment, she realised this was not the man she once knew and admired as a friendly and inspiring leader, before power had overwhelmed and consumed him. It was as if someone else had taken over his body and was using him as a vehicle for power, so different from the man she revered within her political party those few years ago.

"I've nothing more to say to you." He said coldly.

She aimed one final salvo, before he could move away. "Be careful this doesn't become New Labour's legacy because the consequences of your decision will involve the blood of thousands of innocent victims." Her eyes moistened and turning away, she took a handkerchief from her handbag, attempting to hide her distress.

"It's clear to me you don't understand the difficult decisions, which must be made in government and obviously you're not ready to make them." He directed his comments to her back.

She twisted around to face him again, but he had already turned away, brushing past another guest, angrily moving towards the function room, where the Special Branch minders relaxing at the door, stiffened to attention.

She followed him relentlessly. "We're increasing the terror threat by dividing the Muslims in this country. It's inevitable the boundaries of this dispute will stretch beyond the Middle East and you must see it." She raised her voice, determined he should hear what needed to be said, failing to understand the dangerous instincts driving the man she had once respected. "Or worse still, perhaps you do see it and have a different agenda."

He turned around briefly, but said nothing, though the expression on his face menaced.

What she had not realised, and could never have known at that time, was the extent to which her outburst would place her life in serious jeopardy.

She had always been told by her father to box with her two feet on the ground, but she had ignored his advice. It was a fatal mistake, for which there would be a price to pay, but someone had to stand up for what was right, whatever the consequences. "I suspect the events of 9/11 may not exactly be what they appear to be either."

He still ignored her, so she spoke more loudly, a newspaper hack paying particular attention to the now public exchange, making rushed notes in a small notebook, a smile broadening on his face at his good fortune. "The problem the public must confront is how four aircraft with crews trained in detecting and avoiding hijacking attempts could all be taken at the same time by a handful of men using box-cutters and flown so precisely and expertly into targets, whilst simultaneously evading the complex defences of the US military on its own territory."

She waited for a response, but though he faltered in his walk, no reply came, so she continued unashamedly. "How could they do this if they only had rudimentary flying skills, as the reports suggest?" Without thinking of the consequences, she persisted. "You do realise more people are questioning whether these aircraft were captured by remote-control electronic technology, similar to that used by the Global Hawks."

This time he did turn around, his expression grim. "You're a fool." He said. "You're isolated and will become more so."

"What's that supposed to mean?" She asked. "If I'm to be threatened, then do it in front of all these witnesses."

"You're walking a dangerous path, young lady."

"Is that what you think?" She asked, oblivious of the threat.

He turned away, walking towards the toilets, the Special Branch officers in tow.

She took one last swipe at him, an emotional volley, which would come back to haunt her. "Perhaps the real question is whether you're going to do something similar in this country to gain public support for unpopular measures?"

She noticed he lifted his head and take a deep breath, but if he had wanted to say something, he resisted the urge, neatly stepping into the gents toilet, giving her no further attention.

*   *   *

Some weeks had elapsed since Lynne's angry conversation with the Prime Minister and John agreed to meet her, at her request. She felt alone in the face of an unseen, but very real enemy and needed an ally. For his part, John had never been able to track down the perpetrators of the events outside the restaurant, but for reasons which he did not yet comprehend, there had been no repeat.

The unusual venue of the remote and quaint Mid Wales town of Hay-on-Wye had been chosen because John had been attending as a speaker at the Literary Festival the previous day. As always with the Festival, it was Spring Bank Holiday, when so many visitors descended on the town, not just for the Festival, but to browse the old second-hand bookshops, which littered the town. If she was being observed, she hoped their meeting may have been viewed as accidental, though it could hardly be said to be a quiet location at this time of the year. The bookshops and restaurants were overflowing and hordes of cars had convoyed along the banks of the River Wye to reach their destination. It may have been Spring Bank Holiday, but there was no hint of summer on this windy cloudy day and most of the visitors still wore winter coats to fend off the chill.

John had arranged for the Manager's first-floor office at the Hay Cinema Bookshop to be made available and uninterrupted for an hour, though its glass-panelled door and frontage made it a far from clandestine meeting place. More than half an hour had elapsed and still no sign of her. As an impatient man, he found it impossible to sit down and do nothing, so spent the time browsing the old books in the upper section of the Manager's office and the old framed photographs of Hay and the Cinema hanging limply behind the Manager's desk. They revealed a flavour of the agricultural town in its heyday many years before. At one point, he stepped outside to peruse some musty old books on mystical subjects in the middle section of the first floor. Mysticism had been a driving influence in his life since his days in the priesthood before allegations of heresy and sexual deviancy raised against him. It was a more pleasant way to use the waiting time efficiently, rather than allow his increasing aggravation at the delay disturb his demeanour.

A slim-line and gaunt version of the lady he remembered eventually arrived, nervously sitting down opposite him, furtively looking around the office and back through the door at the rows of old shelving top-heavy with books on any subject imaginable. She wore a dark jacket with white pinstripes over a buttoned up white blouse, carrying a Louis Vuitton handbag and a small black folio case. She lit a cigarette and chain-smoked throughout the discussions, shaking intermittently. He did not have the heart to remind her that here in Wales they had already brought in the ban on smoking in public places, ahead of England. There were many people in the town feigning intellectual interest or simply wanting to be part of what President Clinton once famously described as the Woodstock of the Mind and they crammed into the small confines of the bookshop, making secrecy impossible, if that was intended by the Chair of the influential Parliamentary Committee on Intelligence and Security.

He waited patiently for her to talk, fiddling nervously with correspondence and old books lying haphazardly on the desk in front of him. At one point he sneezed, caused either by the dusty old books or Lynne's smoking.

Eventually, after a silence, she took a deep breath. "I'm being ostracized by my party, but other things are happening, which are more sinister. I expected the Prime Minister to isolate me for my views on Iraq and the excuses used for the War, but I didn't expect the other things."

"What other things?" He asked.

She trembled visibly. "I'm being made the subject of the same type of dirty tricks, as those who oppose the government in the United States. We all know Valerie Plame was vindictively exposed as a CIA agent, simply because her diplomat husband, Joseph Wilson, dared to criticize the US President's manipulation of the facts of Saddam's weapons of mass destruction."

He nodded. "I remember the case."

"It was particularly galling for Wilson, especially as he thought he'd proved without any doubt, after a visit to Nigeria, Iraq had not been trying to acquire yellowcake uranium."

"Sure."

She sighed. "Someone I trust has told me to be very careful, as there could be threats to my life."

"But you are the Chair of the Parliamentary Committee on Security and Intelligence?" He said quizzically.

She groaned and looked down. "I took the position after my resignation from Cabinet and a meeting with the Whips. It was a way to pay me off and keep my mouth shut because they didn't want me criticizing from the backbenches of the House of Commons." She looked morose, dark circles under her eyes ageing her. "I'd criticized the Prime Minister in public and had become frightened, so I thought this would be the safe route."

"I'm sorry." He sat back, giving her time to speak her piece.

She looked up with pleading eyes. "I never thought it would come to this."

"What can I do?" He asked.

"I'm not sure." She sighed. "Everyone seems immune to the rule of law, but I've heard from a very good source you already have significant information about the events of 9/11 and you're not easily intimidated?" She looked directly into his eyes.

He screwed up his face. "That's worrying."

"What do you mean?"

"If you know about my research, how many others do too?"

"Well, what do you know?" She asked impatiently.

"I'm a little reluctant to say too much at this stage." He replied, not wanting to bare his soul or research yet. His instinct was not to trust politicians, though her reputation for integrity went before her.

"If you don't confide in me, I can't trust you with the information in my possession." She huffed. "It's got to work both ways."

He hesitated, but made a judgment to test the water and divulge a little of his evidence. "I've information about the use of new technology in the events of 9/11 and I've a source providing me with documentary proof of the complicity of government officials in the events."

She nodded. "Then you need to be careful too, as no-one in government in the United States will allow action to be taken against the powerful vested interests there."

"But Lewis "Scooter" Libby has received a two and a half year prison sentence for obstruction of justice and perjury, after Richard Armitage had implicated him."

She laughed sardonically. "Do you really think he'll ever serve one day of that sentence?"

He shrugged. "Perhaps not."

"It'll either be commuted or he'll be pardoned by the US President at the end of his term." She looked at him intently. "Watch this space."

He nodded. "You're probably right."

She sighed. "I fear something will happen to me in the same way as David Kelly."

His eyes widened, having shared similar thoughts. "Are you suggesting what happened to David Kelly wasn't suicide?"

"I'm not saying anything yet, but I don't believe David Kelly died in the place where he was found or from the cut to the ulnar vein in his wrist. He'd broken the rules and dared speak against the government, so they released the dogs on him."

"You surprise me." His eyebrows raised. "But it's reassuring that a Chair of an important Parliamentary Committee questions these things." He hesitated. "I thought I was becoming paranoid thinking these things."

She looked up sharply. "Why?"

"We all have doubts." He replied.

"You must have heard the press conference when the two ambulance personnel indicated they didn't believe it possible he could have died where they found him or that he died from the cut to his wrist, as alleged."

"But the Inquiry?" He played devil's advocate, even though he shared her suspicions.

"In Westminster, everyone rumoured and joked they had the Judge, though his reputation was that of an honourable man, so it was impossible to prove it one way or the other." She hesitated, staring at him. "Look, I'm a mother and I know a father would never be so insensitive as to kill himself just two months before one of his daughters was due to get married. It makes no sense."

"Do you blame the Prime Minister?" He asked.

"He'd always have someone between him and the smoking gun, so there's no way you could place it on his doorstep, even if he was involved." She shook her head. "Whatever else I think of him, he's not a fool."

John sat quietly for a moment. "I assume he and the MI6 man responsible for sexing up the Weapons of Mass Destruction dossier were upset at Kelly?"

"Of course." She replied. "They did a great disservice to the British Intelligence Services by sexing up that dossier. Normally, this is not what they do, but the clue is in the subsequent promotion of the same intelligence man who did it."

He nodded. "I understand the way it works."

"Do you realise there were no fingerprints on the knife he allegedly used to kill himself?" She asked.

He smiled awkwardly, taking a deep breath. "Nor on several other items found on him or at the scene, but you'll never prove it wasn't suicide and, in fairness, his wife believes he killed himself."

"You're right." She said. "I must express these views as an individual, not as Chair of the Committee because they aren't official views and you can't quote me on it." She hesitated. "I may have to deny it, if you do."

"I know the score and I'll not quote you on anything without your permission."

"Good." She nodded. "You've a reputation for placing integrity before a good story."

"But if they can dispose of Kelly, then what about you?" He looked directly at her. "Are you safe?"

Her head dropped. "I'm being followed on foot and by a car with darkened windows, which is stationed outside my home every night. Whenever I look out of my window, the headlights are switched on and off. At one stage, a hearse was parked outside my house, but when I went towards the vehicle to talk to them, they drove off quickly."

He nodded again. "They call it heavy harassing surveillance, but normally it's intended only to intimidate." He smiled. "I've had it myself."

"Then you understand it's scary."

"If it's any consolation, it's normally a first warning, so you're probably safe for the time being, but have you asked your contacts within the intelligence community or contacted the Police?"

"Of course." She nodded. "My intelligence friends deny any knowledge of it and when I've called the Police, the cars disappear by the time they arrive. I can't get near enough to take a photograph of the registration plates." Her eyes looked heavy. "It's almost as if they listen to my telephone calls." She took a deep breath. "It's got to the stage where I think the Police believe I'm just a neurotic lonely woman."

"They probably do listen to your telephone calls." He replied. "And even if you could get the registration number, it's unlikely there'll be any official record of it."

She shivered. "I suppose the intelligence people would deny any knowledge of it, wouldn't they?"

"Of course they would." He recalled his experiences of surveillance. "If your telephone is compromised, the moment you telephone the Police they'd know immediately and move any incriminating evidence away from the scene."

"But what can I do?" Her voice cracked noticeably.

"Ignore it." He said, tempted to say more, but erring on the side of caution.

"It's easy to say, but not so easy to do." Her eyes showed fear. "It's intimidating and having a detrimental effect on me."

His heart went out to her, recognizing her pain. "I understand, but what can I do to help?"

She sat back, staring at the ceiling, then back at him. "I don't know."

"If you want me to publish anything, I'll need to tape this interview." He tried to focus her attention.

She nodded, but said nothing.

"If you want to start, I need to know if this interview is on the record?" He asked, tilting back in the chair.

"I suppose so." She stuttered, searching her handbag for another cigarette, lighting it expertly and quickly.

He slid a small tape recorder onto the desk in front of her and switched it on. "When you're ready."

She took a deep drag on her cigarette. "I need to get the Prime Minister out of government or else I'll suffer the same fate as Kelly."

"What would you like me to do?" He asked sympathetically. "You do understand I may have to disclose any information you give me in this interview."

She recoiled nervously. "This tape could place me in grave danger."

He nodded. "Perhaps."

"So are you prepared to hold onto it until I give you written authority to use it?" An edge of suspicion intonated in her question.

He hesitated, recognizing her doubts, but realising he was no worse off by accepting the pre-conditions than not having the interview at all. "I'll do what you say, but I could never get any piece past my Editor without some corroboration of this material."

She rose from the chair, positioned on the other side of the desk from him, and circled the room, before settling back into the same chair. After crossing her legs, she pulled down the hem on her skirt below her knees, distracting him. "You must appreciate that if you break your promise, it could be my death warrant?"

"I've never broken my promise before and I'll not do it now." He replied firmly. "I'm sure you know my reputation or you wouldn't be here."

She stared ahead, biting her lip. "I suppose I must trust your judgment, though my instinct is only to give you evidence on strict condition it doesn't link me directly as the source."

He thought for a moment, facial muscles straining. "Well either way, I'll not do anything without your permission first."

She sighed. "One way or another, I'm resigned to doing what must be done, whatever the price."

He noticed the sorrow and pain in her eyes. "If you make it a condition I don't mention your name I'll honour it, but you must know the importance for a journalist of proving his sources." He paused. "At least to his Editor."

She nodded.

He shrugged. "It makes it easier to get the piece published in the first place."

"But do you appreciate the consequences for me?" She asked, her voice cracking again.

"Of course." His voice was naturally low, but he tried to project reassurance. From his time in the priesthood, he had recognised the signs of someone on the edge and knew Lynne was close to breaking point.

She looked troubled. "I'm going to trust you, but please protect me."

He nodded. "I promise I'll do everything I can to protect you." He had the ability to look into the eyes of people and distinguish those who lived from those who merely existed, though when he became emotionally involved it was a skill which deserted him. He knew so few showed the expression of what he would call wondrous consciousness.

She searched for an ash-tray to place the remains of her cigarette, eventually moving towards the rubbish bin, pressing the cigarette end firmly against the side of the bin and placing it inside, before sitting back down. "I fear their propaganda machine will do what the intelligence service may not have the balls to do itself." She said. "Even Members of Parliament or Chairs of Parliamentary Committees are not immune."

"I've told you I'm an honourable man, so I'll do whatever I can to protect you."

She thought for a moment, squirming slightly in her chair, and took a deep breath. "I believe you."

"Good." He smiled. "Take your time."

She took another deep breath. "You'll probably recall the Northwoods Project of the late fifties, when the United States government intended to crash a drone plane into one of their buildings in Miami and blame it on Fidel Castro?"

"Most people have heard of it since it was widely reported after the events of 9/11." He replied.

She nodded. "This was intended as a way of gaining public support and justification for an invasion of Cuba."

"I remember details of the project were released under their Freedom of Information Act."

She lit another cigarette, taking a deep drag before continuing. "Anyway, I've intelligence which suggests this operation was resurrected for the events of 9/11."

He leaned back into his chair, feeling cold. "It coincides with research information in my possession, but unless you have some serious evidence to support the allegation, no-one is going to believe the government would murder thousands of their citizens in such a blatant way."

"But I do have the evidence." She said stoically, her body stiffening. "Besides, they've done it before with Pearl Harbour, so what's the difference?"

He leant forward, placing his elbows on the desk. As an investigative journalist he had to take a studied and disciplined approach to the analysis of any new evidence. "I might want to talk to you again about Pearl Harbour."

"The Pearl Harbour evidence has always been there." She said. "The purple machine they'd developed, which had cracked the Japanese military codes, but they needed an excuse to get into the war."

John nodded. "As J. Edgar Hoover famously said, 'the individual is handicapped by coming face to face with a conspiracy so monstrous he can't believe it exists.' And 9/11 is no different."

"Even Roosevelt admitted in 1942 that he was perfectly willing to tell any untruths if it meant winning the war."

She looked away, then back at him. "I'll give you an article written by a friend of mine about Pearl Harbour and he clearly proves the government had cracked the Japanese military codes with this machine and by sending the aircraft carriers away from Pearl Harbour they were effectively inviting an attack to get America into the war."

"But this is old hat." John replied. "I'm really looking for some unequivocal proof, rather than conjecture, in relation to the 9/11 events to support my investigations about what really happened on that day."

She cleared her throat, speaking frostily. "I don't deal with conjecture."

He smiled. "But you're a politician."

She nodded, smiling nervously. "I suppose you've a point, but I've a sworn statement from someone who worked on the secret technology which made it all possible." She hesitated. "A technology the United States government unsurprisingly deny exists, though they freely promise they'll develop it in the future, which they can promise with certainty if they've already developed it."

"Who gave you the sworn statement?" He asked.

"A friend." She replied.

"Have you shown it to anyone else?"

She nodded. "I've discussed it with a colleague who is Chair of the Counter-Terrorism Sub-Committee in the House."

He tried to suppress concern, but instead journalistic instincts stirred. "Are you talking about the remote-control technology, which drove the planes to crash into the Twin Towers and possibly the Pentagon?"

"I guessed you knew." She replied.

He nodded. "My sources told me how it happened, but I'd been waiting for more tangible proof and some corroboration, as otherwise my Editor won't publish any piece on the subject. He's made it clear to me on more than one occasion when I've made repeated attempts to get this stuff into print."

She relaxed. "The events involving the Pentagon are slightly different and there's a significance relating to the events surrounding the plane which crashed in Pennsylvania."

"Flight 93?" He asked.

"Yes."

"I'm interested in Flight 93, but first tell me about this sworn document." He lifted himself up in the chair. "Do you have it with you?"

She placed the black folio case on the desk in front of her with a thump, unzipping it and taking out the notarized statement, before handing it to him. "You'll even find details of the unmanned Global Hawk flights prior to 9/11 all there, including the one over New York with the AWACS on the 11th September 2001."

Leaning across the desk, he took the statement from her, reading it slowly, eyes widening. He stood up, walking away from the desk, moving in a circular fashion around the room, as was his habit when concentrating. After a few minutes, he sat down again, placing the statement and the information on the Global Hawks and the AWACS on the desk in front of him.

"What do you think?" She asked.

He looked at her, more focused than before. "It's what I expected. There've been so many cover-ups on so many issues. I spoke to a reporter on BBC Newsnight, who had been given a copy of an F.B.I. document, which revealed how some of their agents were investigating the Sheikh's brother, who was the President, Treasurer and U.S. Director of the World Assembly of Muslim Youth."

She nodded. "I saw the programme myself."

"So you know this investigation related to National Security and this organization had been suspected of funding terrorism, including the al-Qaeda network. Another of the Sheikh's brothers was suspected of complicity in the affairs and significantly, he lived just two blocks from the house where four of the alleged hijackers, who were named by the FBI, are said to have stayed."

She began to relax and stifled a chuckle. "Surprisingly close to the CIA Headquarters in Langley, Virginia, too." She looked at him carefully. "Of course, he was shepherded out of the country after the 9/11 events when all other flights had been grounded."

"How do they get away with these things?" John asked.

She fidgeted in her seat. "It all stinks, doesn't it?"

"Politics is a dirty game." He said, forgetting for the moment he was talking to a politician.

"It's not why I went into politics." She said firmly, stiffening in the process.

He looked into her eyes. "No offence intended, but no politician holding high office dares to tell the whole truth about situations much of the time."

"Then it's a dagger through the heart of democracy."

"I agree completely." He watched her demeanour soften, even smiling. "Yet when the US President arranges for bin Laden's brother and his entourage to be flown out of the country after the events of 9/11, at a time when all other planes, domestic and international, were grounded, he seems to get away with it."

"People want security and are frightened by the alternatives." She said.

"You must wonder at the haste to get them out, but few do."

She rose from the chair, turning her back on him, looking out to the shelves of old second-hand books and the customers jostling, before turning back. "If I speak off the record, with the tape off, can I trust your confidentiality?"

At that moment, the Manager intruded apologizing for the interruption, but taking something from her drawer and leaving the room again. Lynne walked around the room again, looking at some of the books in the Manager's office.

He smelt a waft of Chanel No 19, his favourite perfume, but could not work out if it was from the Manager or from Lynne. She turned back to face him again and he looked directly into her eyes. "I give you my word. I was trained as a priest and you can trust me, but I'll need hard evidence if I'm to assist you or publish anything."

She smiled. "Sorry, but weren't you a defrocked priest?"

He laughed a deep-bellied laugh. "I see your point. It's not exactly reassuring is it?"

"I'm placing my life in your hands, though if this material is true, I'm probably dead already." She smiled quirkily, as if uncertain whether to laugh or cry.

He returned the smile, recalling the paranoid language he had used with Nadia and amused to hear someone else talk in the same fashion. "You must trust me because I'm very much on your side." He hesitated. "I share the same fears and the same demons."

"Everyone I know thinks I'm crazy." She said, surprised at the empathy she invoked.

He grimaced. "But that sounds like you've already spoken to other people about it?"

"Only people I trust."

John grunted, but said nothing.

"So do you think that was a mistake?" She asked quizzically.

He didn't respond, as there could be only one response and it would not help her. Instead, he moved around the desk, placing his hand on her shoulder. "I understand your position completely. I've been pursuing my investigations along similar lines."

"I know."

"How do you know?" He asked.

"A friend in the intelligence community suggested I contact you."

"Oh Shit." He said, forgetting his company "If he works in intelligence, that's worrying. It's a dark art and I don't trust anybody there because they're all dealing with smoke and mirrors, working constantly in the shadows."

"I trust this guy or I wouldn't have come to see you."

"Perhaps I'm being paranoid." He shook his head, recalling other events in his career. "I've often wondered whether I'd become yet another victim of some unfortunate accident, but I always take steps to protect myself by ensuring certain documents are secure and dealt with in the event something unforeseen should happen to me."

"How do you make them secure?" She asked.

"I've a good lawyer and instructions are left for documents to be made public and released immediately into the public arena in the event of any unfortunate accident, which may befall me. A domain is purchased and material for the website already set up and the funds are immediately available to cover optimization of the site and marketing it."

"That's an interesting idea."

"I've even copied it in code to more than 100,000 people, so that much of the material will be released automatically on linked sites, if anything should happen to me." He hesitated. "Perhaps you should do the same, if you've a lawyer you can trust."

"I hadn't thought about contacting my lawyer, but he seems to do land transactions only, so I'm not sure he can help."

"Is there anyone else?"

"I've only spoken to the man in intelligence." She paused. "He's given me useful information, so I've begun to trust him."

"But that's what they do."

She grimaced, deep lines on her face highlighted. "What do you mean?"

"They give you worthless information until you trust them."

"But he was the one who told me the U.S. Government had given visas to al-Qaeda operatives for terrorist training by the CIA, before being returned to Afghanistan and Iraq. I've been given certain documents, which prove it." She hesitated. "Why would he do that if he was working me?"

He tilted his head. "I'm not sure talking to someone in the intelligence community was a good idea. Their loyalty is normally only to their paymasters, but I don't want to jump to conclusions yet."

"But I trust this man." She placed her hand inside the black folio file and produced a memory stick. "He also gave me something else."

"What's that?"

She handed the memory stick to him. "He gave me this material too."

"What's in it?" He asked.

"Just download the material and look at it and make your judgment afterwards."

"Very well, but can I meet him?"

"Maybe I can arrange it, but I'd have to speak to him first, of course."

He nodded. "Naturally."

"If you're sure you want the responsibility, I can pass other documents to you, but I don't have them with me today."

"But you're an M.P. and the Chair of the Security and Intelligence Committee. Wouldn't they be safer with you?"

"If you're a student of history, you may recall one female M.P. being arrested under the infamous Regulation 18b at the beginning of the Second World War when she dared to speak out against the banking organisations and companies pushing the countries into war. She was imprisoned for several years, even though a judge and jury had found her not guilty of any criminal offences." She hesitated. "So tell me, do you really think they're safe with me?"

"I see your point." He watched her eyes grow sad and realized she could not handle the responsibility.

She sighed again. "Besides, I know more about the extent of surveillance in this country than the ordinary citizen and I'm certain they're not safe with me."

"Well. You know more than most, so I'll rely on your judgement."

"My days of believing in fairy tales have long past." She placed her trembling hand on his forearm.

"Are you sure you're alright?" He asked, instinctively, as a priest would.

She took a deep breath. "I've already been warned to back off, but you're right. If you took these documents, your life would be in grave danger too, but maybe you're stronger than me."

"It's not a problem." He said.

"But it should be."

"What do you mean?" John asked, nervously.

"The Americans are vindictive and if they thought you were getting too close, they'd draft a secret indictment and go for extradition."

"On what charge?"

"They'd conjure up something and once you were in the United States, it would be difficult to get you out."

"At least I'd be able to get publicity for the information in my possession." He felt uneasy, but he smiled for her.

"I shouldn't really ask you to do this for me." She took a deep breath. "I've this real foreboding that my time in this world is limited. It's why I asked to meet you as far away from London as possible. This surveillance thing is getting to me and I honestly don't feel I can cope with it anymore."

He nodded. "I suspected as much when you first contacted me."

"I can't take it any longer." Her voice cracked again.

He reverted to his priest mode. "You realise the greatest service you can do for your soul development is to be your enemy. Just imagine the worst and expect the best."

"I'm not sure I understand. You'll have to explain it to me when I'm more amenable."

"Sure."

"In the meantime, I've got some other documents I want to pass to you too."

"What other documents?" He asked impatiently.

"Not yet." She replied. "I feel as if I'm on the verge of a nervous breakdown and the stress of all this is unbearable. I'd always thought I was strong, but I feel vulnerable and I've recently become aware of my limitations, even taking anti-depressants, which I vowed I would never do because of their known side-effects."

"Don't beat yourself up over this." He moved and sat on the edge of the desk near her.

She shook her head. "I've been getting strange telephone calls in the middle of the night, disrupting my sleep patterns."

"Have you answered them?"

"No-one is ever on the line and I've struggled to get back to sleep." She exhaled deeply, blowing out her cheeks. "This has been going on for weeks now. All the telephones start ringing, but there's never anybody there."

"It's part of the warning." He replied.

"I've felt isolated and afraid to discuss it with anyone." She said. "The person I've contacted in intelligence told me not to tell anybody, but I must or I'll go mad."

"I'll share the stress with you." He took her hand, squeezing it.

She squeezed back and looked up at him. "I had to speak to someone."

He listened, drawing from his past experience as a priest many years ago. "I know."

"What should I do?" She asked, her hand still trembling.

"I've never feared death because you can't live life to the full unless you've overcome this fear. Death is an illusion, a strong one, but nevertheless it's illusory. It's one of the spiritual paradoxes, as from a certain point of view it isn't death, but birth to a more expansive reality and birth is really a death to that same reality."

Her head dropped. "That's too deep for me."

He laughed, watching her carefully. Although her body was in front of him, her mind was somewhere else, his words untouched, even though at some level it was what she needed to hear. "The essence of what we are fundamentally is immortal and indestructible. Even physicists can now establish energy cannot be destroyed, only transmuted into another form. It's a mystical experience when you completely accept the inevitability of death without fear. It's what Christians are taught. From that point onwards, you can live your life completely and fully without the restrictions and limitations imposed by fear."

She looked into his eyes and placed both hands around his waist, pulling herself closer to him and squeezed, burying her head into his chest. "I'm not sure I understand what you mean."

"I was offering you the freedom of knowledge."

Even if she did not quite understand the reason, she felt secure with him and more relaxed than for months. "I think you're a good man and I wish I had time to get to know you better." Her manicured voice leaked unfiltered raw emotion and a need for love and intimacy.

He recognized it, having witnessed many dramas and role-play at times of stress in the course of many years as a priest, then as a journalist. He'd played the part of a victim himself in relationship dramas, even though he knew it was a stereotype behaviour pattern. It was nothing to do with education, more to do with need and the eyeing up of potential candidates for the supporting role in the drama. In these circumstances, he had come to realize all other faults are willingly overlooked and the self-deception sustained. Nevertheless, in this instance he recognized this was no mere drama or role-play, but she was genuinely in fear and desperately needed some reassurance and semblance of balance in her life.

"What do you want me to do exactly?" He asked, lifting her head up gently with his hands.

She stepped back for a moment, releasing her grip, taking a deep breath again. "I was given certain documents by a loyal intelligence officer. As I had a unique position, initially on the House Foreign Affairs Committee and more recently as Chair of the Committee on Security and Intelligence, he felt I could exert influence on the Government, but I've failed. He knew I'd fallen out with the Prime Minister and my position on the Parliamentary Committees had been a poor substitute for a place in Cabinet." She stared ahead, eyes glazed, lost in a world she struggled to comprehend.

"What did he expect you to do?" He asked.

She looked up again, eyes clearer, taking a deep breath. "He wanted me to use parliamentary privilege to raise questions in the House at the weekly Prime Minister's Questions, but as you know you must give notice and this caused serious problems. Every time I thought I could ask a relevant question, I was ambushed or a door would close or the Speaker simply ignored me. In truth, I began to have cold feet. It didn't help that the same intelligence officer has since disappeared on an assignment in the Balkans and I fear the worst for him." She groaned, shivering noticeably again, before lighting another cigarette with some difficulty and taking a deep drag.

He waited patiently until she was ready to talk again, saying nothing.

"The intelligence officer warned me this could happen, but he had such courage, incriminating certain people close to the Prime Minister, but he told me the Prime Minister would always create a buffer of bodies between him and any direct evidence." She sighed. "But he had a view on his culpability."

"What do you think happened to this other intelligence officer in the Balkans?" He asked.

"I don't know." She placed her head in her hands. "He told me one of his colleagues may be given a contract to terminate him or else they would sub-contract the work to outside contractors."

"How can you be sure the man you've confided in isn't the same man who would have handled such a contract?" He asked the obvious question.

"But he was his friend." She sounded offended.

He nodded, not pursuing it. "So what exactly do you want me to do?"

She looked up and, through the fear, fire still somehow stirred. "You must bring this information into the public arena."

"Of course, if it's possible."

"But your reputation suggests you're the one person who can do it. If not, all is lost and my time has been wasted."

He smiled. "I can probably get this material out there, one way or another, but so could you if you wanted."

"I can't do anything at the moment." She shook her head. "Getting out of bed is difficult enough and I can't even face opening my mail."

"I guessed as much."

"I must be close to cracking up."

He looked at her with sympathetic eyes. "I'm sorry." He thought for a moment. "I need to see all your documents and I must have your written authority when you're ready to move on it."

She opened the black folio case again, taking out a bundle of documents, which had been tied in red tape, handing them to him. "Perhaps these documents will help to start."

He took and studied the documents carefully, which included another sworn affidavit, various memoranda and copy e-mails and a dossier marked in blue handwriting 'Home Run'. After a cursory glance through the material, he looked at her and smiled. "Although I've amassed evidence pointing the finger at the U.S. Government, I needed this sort of corroboration for credibility. It's very helpful and unequivocal." He shuffled the documents into some form of order.

She nodded. "I've done what I can within the confines of my position, and I began rattling some cages, but I don't feel I can do anymore. In truth, I need help to do this work or otherwise the rule of law will be eroded and our freedoms and civil liberties unnecessarily restricted."

He pointed to the affidavit. "Are you convinced this is how the 9/11 events happened?"

She looked directly into his eyes. "The intelligence officer who gave me these documents believed it and he's probably paid a price for it with his life."

He returned his attention to the documents.

She waited until he had finished reading them. "When I took these documents, I didn't realise it was a poisoned chalice." She studied him carefully. "Are you prepared to take them, knowing the dangers associated with them?"

He recalled his many battles shedding light on the deception and injustices created by the Establishment and fighting for the underdog. "I like a challenge and how could I refuse you?"

"Thank you." She sighed, her head dropping again.

He took out the notebook he always kept for such occasions and jotted down some notes. "I'll take this material and try to bring it into the public domain, but I'd like to involve you in the process in some way. I think it'll be beneficial in the long term."

"You're not frightened?" She asked, hardly waiting for a reply. "I've felt so alone, especially since the intelligence officer disappeared in the Balkans, even when I've been in the hustle and bustle of the City and Parliament."

"I do know the feeling." He said softly, compassion in his eyes. "But you must search for that part of yourself which is intrinsically sacred and it'll give you the peace that passeth all understanding."

She smiled a genuine smile for the first time. "I see you're still a priest." Her voice sounded stronger.

John laughed. "I may have been a defrocked priest, but I was still a priest."

"Does it change the way you live your life?" She asked.

"I live my life knowing the essence of what we are is ageless, timeless and immortal, so the worst that can happen to me is they kill the bodily shell I occupy for a miniscule of time."

"So you know what I'm talking about?" Her voice echoed through a maze of confusion.

He recognized it, as he had been there before. "Of course."

"No-one else has any idea of what I'm going through." She lifted her head and body upright and took a deep breath.

"It's only at times of crisis do people discover the essence of what or who they are. It's why so many people only find the spiritual part of themselves after nervous breakdowns or crises of one sort or another." He talked with confidence, hoping it would transmit to her. "If it's any consolation Marcus Aurelius once said what we do in this life ripples through eternity." He smiled again. "I believe it."

She reciprocated the smile. "And, of course, it was Nietske who famously said what doesn't kill you makes you stronger."

"Then we'd better keep you alive, hadn't we?" The words came easily even if he may not have realised how difficult the reality might be.

"Are you still religious?" She asked, showing a sudden interest in his spiritual philosophy.

"Not religious at all, more spiritual in an unorthodox sort of way." He replied. "I suppose you could call me a heretic because the Church would and did, but I follow only the vibration and resonance of truth, as I feel it, but in the process I'm now utterly free of catholic dogma."

She moved towards him, placing her head against his chest again. "Are you married?" She asked, out of context.

He stepped back, his eyes widening. "Why?"

"Don't be shocked." She rested her head against him again.

"I'm just surprised at the manner in which you ask."

She chuckled. "It's just that I could do with a close physical relationship right now."

He laughed, his old-fashioned belly laugh.

She raised her head and smiled again.

"I'm divorced." He said, laughter subsiding for a moment. "But you should realise you're talking to someone who has always had a serious problem with sexual relationships, even when I was in the priesthood, so I'm not sure I'm the right man for you."

"Shame." She replied.

"Perhaps we should go somewhere with more privacy and see how things develop." He said brazenly, unable to resist the patterns of behaviour, which had caused so many of his past problems.

"Perhaps." She said. "I want to tell you something else, now that I trust you."

"What's that?" He asked, intrigued.

"It's important, but I don't want people around when I tell you."

"Sounds interesting?"

"It's something the intelligence officer told me before his last posting, though I've no evidence of it yet."

He still retained a child's attitude to secrets and mysteries. In the meantime, his mind spiralled with the prospect of intimacy. "We'll never get into any of the hotels in Hay this weekend or any privacy, so why don't we go to Crickhowell." His eyebrows raised. "It's not far and I know the lady who owns the Bear Hotel." He held back a mischievous smile with difficulty. "And there's an annexe with four-poster beds, if we want to stay the night."

She nodded. "If you know the way, I'll follow." She held out her hand wilfully and he took it willingly.

CHAPTER EIGHT

7th September 2001—U.S. Department of State:

"American citizens may be the target of a terrorist threat from extremist groups with links to Osama bin Laden's al-Qaeda organization . . . . As always, we take this information seriously . . . . and remain on heightened alert."

Prior to the events of 9.11: "The United States threatened the Taliban with a military overthrow and the return of the King in exile, if, inter alia, a pipeline deal could not be negotiated."

Post 9/11—An International Law Professor Boyle: ". the war against Afghanistan has been war-gamed by the Pentagon going back to 1997 . . ."

Statement on the proposed "Cordoba House" Mosque near Ground Zero—Newt Gingrich: "There should be no mosque . . . . so long as there are no churches or synagogues in Saudi Arabia . . . . it is a test of the timidity, passivity and historic ignorance of American elites . . . . Cordoba House is a deliberately insulting term . . . . in Islamic symbolic terms means Islamic rule in the West . . . . every Islamist in the world recognizes Cordoba as a symbol of Islamic conquest (originally in Cordoba, Spain) . . . . No Christian or Jew can even enter Mecca. And they lecture us on tolerance, . . . (yet) if they were serious about religious tolerance, they would be imploring the Saudis, as fellow Muslims, to immediately open

**up Mecca to all and immediately announce their intention to
allow non-Muslim houses of worship in the Kingdom . . . .
and be willing to lead such a campaign . . . . America is
experiencing an Islamist cultural-political offensive designed
to undermine and destroy our civilization. Sadly, too many
of our elites are the willing apologists for those who would
destroy them if they could.,"**

What can you tell me, which isn't already in the public domain?"
George, the Editor, asked John. He shuffled papers on his
antique desk, pushing away an empty cup of coffee in a
beleaguered attempt to clear space. He lifted gold-rimmed spectacles back
on to the bridge of his once-broken nose and swept stray hair back from his
forehead across a thinning scalp, slipping back into the comfort of his chair
with the thud of a man overweight and unhealthy. Perspiration saturated
his forehead and dripped into bushy eyebrows. He stroked a greying, out
of fashion moustache away from his upper lip, before folding his arms,
wondering how he could cajole information he needed out of John.
"Tell me, John, how would you convince our readers that the American
government was complicit in the events of 9/11 and what evidence you've
obtained to support it, which is not already in the public arena?"

"You're such a cynic, George." John replied. "The tone of your question
defies the possibility I'm right." He sat comfortably opposite him in an old
split leather chair, placing a case on the floor to the side. Various framed
photographs of celebrities and staff hung on the wood-panelling behind the
Editor's desk, noticing one photograph of him with George and, strangely,
even one of Nadia with George. Background noise from the main floor of
the office meant each of them had to raise their voices naturally.

"It's my job to be cynical, John."

"I'd like to protect my sources for the time being, for reasons of their
personal safety." John took out a folder from his case on the floor and
placed it on the desk in front of him. "Before you read these documents,
all of which are copies and not originals, I require certain assurances." He
held back the material downloaded from the memory stick, keeping it in
reserve.

"What reassurances?" George unfolded his arms, touching the two days
of stubble on his chin. "And where are the originals?"

"First, you must promise you'll not disclose my sources or release these documents without my prior written agreement." John trusted him, though something under the surface made him feel uneasy and triggered the need for these assurances.

"And the originals?"

"They're in a safe place for now."

"If the piece is to be published, I need the source and the evidence, John." He said. "You know the score."

"I'll not show you anything without your promise, George." He sighed. "It's up to you because I'll only reveal the whereabouts of the original documents when the time is right and not before."

"But I may not be able to publish anything, if I have to give this type of assurance or you don't cooperate." George replied, happy to play hardball in circumstances where he had a different agenda. Besides, he had already promised someone else all the documents and information received and he had no intention of placing his position at risk.

"If that's the case, so be it, but I need to protect my source, whose life may be in grave danger." John said firmly. "I'll not give you anything without your promise first."

George nodded, feeling cornered. "Very well, I'll give the assurances for now, but in the long-term it's another matter. You must know I'll need corroboration of any one source or some evidence supporting it." He leaned forward, his chair creaking under the transfer of his considerable weight, feeling no dishonour at the deceptive nature of his reassurance.

"I understand your position, so you can read the documents on strict condition they remain confidential until I get the permission of my source to make them public."

A junior member of staff knocked, entering the room with two cups of coffee, before removing the empty cup abandoned on George's desk. She smiled and left quickly. George watched her carefully, sipping his coffee. "Agreed." He opened the folder to read the documents inside, without even looking at John, perusing them with an Editor's eye.

"After you've read those documents, can we take a walk into the car park before we discuss their content?" John asked.

"Is this absolutely necessary, John?" He sounded unconvinced. "Do you think this office is bugged?"

"Have you swept it recently?"

"No, but why should I?"

"Your links with me for a start."

George scoffed. "Really?"

"Patronize me, George." John picked up his case and pointed to the folder. "Bring your folder and the copy documents."

"If you insist, but I'm not into this cloak and dagger stuff." His knees creaked as he lifted himself out of his chair with difficulty, exhaling a deep breath. He took one large final gulp of coffee and gathered up the documents, placing them back into the folder and following him out of his office. They took the lift down to the car park, finding a quiet location, away from the main thoroughfare. Their voices echoed eerily, only adding to John's paranoia, but his instinct suggested caution and he needed to protect Lynne.

"I'm getting too old for this, John." George may have respected him as a journalist, but felt he owed him nothing and had never understood the nature of his character, so different in temperament from his own. He guessed John never knew about his relationship with Nadia, for it had never been mentioned and he remained cordial.

"I need these discussions to remain strictly confidential for the time being, in view of their sensitivity. No tapes or notes yet." He placed his hand on George's arm.

George breathed heavily, looking more bedraggled than usual. "Agreed, but if you want to publish your piece, then I'll need something more substantial."

"I'll give you as much notice as possible, but in return will you promise to publish it, once you've had the complete piece with all the evidence in support?"

"I must get permission from the owners to publish anything provocative, John, as you must know."

"I appreciate you'll be placed under considerable pressure to bury it, if your proprietors get a whiff of the piece beforehand."

"So you want me to place my job on the line." He grunted, having no intention of doing so.

"You've got the material in there." He pointed to the folder. "I'm talking about my life and the life of one of my sources in particular, which are rather more important than your job."

George lifted the folder and shook it, wondering how vaguely he could answer. "I can understand its sensitivity." He said. "Your piece had better be good and it needs to be well-sourced. If it is, then I'll do what I can to publish, provided I have no restrictions placed on me by my bosses in the meantime." His evasive reply gave him the caveat to prevent its publication, should he deem necessary, though he remained an old fashioned paper man at heart and loved a good story as much as anyone.

"There are those within the US government machine who have no principles and believe they're above the rule of law. Their vindictiveness is epitomized by their exposure of Valerie Plame as a CIA Agent because of her diplomat husband's criticisms on Iraq." John looked around nervously. "I'm doing far worse than her husband ever did. I'm blaming them for the genocide of 9/11, so what do you think is likely to happen to me?"

"If that's the case, you're placing my life is in jeopardy too, so it's in my interests to ensure confidentiality." He jostled words with John, for this was his art.

"You understand this means no telephone discussions." He said. "I don't want to be another suicide victim."

"What happens after publication?" George asked.

"It can't be in anyone's interests to do anything after publication." John raised his hands. "What would be the purpose?" He asked. "The horse would already have bolted and if anything happened to me, it would only draw attention to my work and an even bigger scoop for you."

"I hope you're right."

"As a matter of principle, this material should be revealed to the public if only for the purpose of retaining confidence in democratic government."

Principles were not things George traded in, but he jousted with him. "Now I've only had a cursory glance at the documents, but I'll need to go through the piece you write carefully."

"Do you doubt the validity of the documents?"

George lifted his head, unable to hold John's attention, looking away again. "You've known me for almost twenty years, so don't get paranoid on me. I'm a friend." His heart was heavy as the words poured out, for he knew a true friend would never betray him, as he had done with Nadia and the words sounded hollow, even as he said them. "My audio memory is stronger than my visual memory, so I want to hear how you intend to run the piece."

John sighed. "Sure, I'll outline it, but you must understand my nervousness."

"Of course I do, but if you'd rather not go into the detail now, so be it." George said, lifting his hands in the air. "But you came to me.

"Well, as you can see from the material in there, many of the alleged skyjackers were granted visas by the U.S., which were issued out of the consular office in Jeddah, where as you will know the CIA has a strong presence."

"Yes. I noted it."

"The article will be simple, dealing only in concrete facts. No dramatics. I'll leave that to you and you can title the piece, as usual. The last forty years has seen technology improved out of all recognition in the area of remote-controlled aircraft. It's logical that remote-control technology has been substantially improved since the fifties."

"But what facts?" George asked.

"I wanted to start with reference to the Northwoods Project and what we know about the improved technology since that time. I can prove there has been a programme of configuring remotely-controlled fighter aircraft since 1959. For example, an unmanned Global Hawk flew across the Atlantic in April 2000 and a year later it flew from Edwards Air Base in California to Edinburgh Air Base in South Australia. I'm convinced it played a significant part in the events, but I can't give you all my information yet, but I know precisely how they did it."

George shook his head. "The piece has potential, but I must have more information and evidence, if I'm to help you."

John sighed. "Very well, but I'm investigating whether it was a Global Hawk, which collided with the Pentagon, or whether it was one of the confiscated Russian missiles being used to deflect attention from the real culprit." He stopped to observe George's response.

"Are you suggesting it was not the hijacked plane which collided with the Pentagon?" George asked.

"I'll revert to you with confirmation of all of these facts as soon as I have the corroboration I'm seeking, but either of these possibilities would explain why there was a hole only sixteen feet high at the point of collision, if you look at the photographs of the wall before it collapsed or more likely demolished." He pointed to the folder again. "You'll see from the photographs, there's no evidence whatsoever of any impact damage where a Boeing's two six-ton engines either side would have left their imprint on the building and a Boeing is 46 feet high. It explains why the remnants and debris at the scene are more in keeping with either the dimensions of a Global Hawk or one of the confiscated Russian missiles, taken at the time of the breakdown of the Soviet Union." He hesitated, looking intensely at George. "It certainly could not have been the Boeing which collided with the Pentagon and this is why the debris was cleared up away from prying eyes and forensic examination immediately afterwards and all the CCTV in the neighbourhood gathered up within minutes."

"So you don't think the debris was a Boeing?" George asked.

"I can't be sure yet, but there was a military cargo plane on a crossing flight-path and I'm investigating it at present."

"I'll need to examine the evidence if I'm to publish it." George said, cynicism in the tone.

He pointed to another piece of evidence. "It's also the reason why it flew at more than 450 miles per hour and veered around the side of the Pentagon, which would have been its natural target and its more direct flight path, to the side of the Pentagon away from where the Defence Secretary and Joint Chiefs of Staff were occupying their offices and hit the newly reinforced side. All of this without leaving a scorch mark on the lawn outside the building, yet underneath their defence ground to air missile system. You'll note the statement of a senior and experienced flight captain, which suggests that he could not have manoeuvred a Boeing in that way and a Boeing engineer who states it would be impossible." John looked at his Editor quizzically.

"There are more questions than answers, if it really happened this way." George talked like a typical Editor. "And what about the technology referred to in the affidavit and sworn statements?" He pointed to them.

"George." He sighed. "Everyone knows Norad has the most advanced technology at Cheyenne Mountain and much of it is secret. It's already documented, so if you add the technology referred to in the affidavit and the sworn statements, you know exactly how they manipulated the events of 9/11."

George used a handkerchief to mop perspiration dripping down the side of his face. "But hasn't the US President made some comment since the events stating they're developing this technology to which you refer? He groaned, looking directly at John. "Wouldn't this suggest they haven't perfected it yet?"

"Well he would wouldn't he?" John shrugged. "They always develop the secret technology long before the existence of it is made public."

"I suppose so." George sounded cynical still.

"It's typical government spin and misinformation." John said. "If you look closely at the documents in the folder, you'll note one of the notarized documents refers to the technology having already been developed. I can even tell you how they guided the planes to the Twin Towers, using Building Seven as the homing beacon and the control centre for the events.

It was conveniently the site of the CIA headquarters in New York and it's the reason it had to be demolished, despite it not being hit by any aircraft or debris after the events."

"But I'll need more factual detail in the piece." George said, trying to accumulate more information.

John's face strained. "I can produce other evidence I've researched myself, but I can't tell you everything yet." He groaned. "You must trust me."

George nodded, but persisted. "Give me an example?"

John shrugged again. "If you're not interested in the piece, tell me and I'm sure another Editor will be interested?"

George's voice raised. "No No. I'm very interested, but I must protect you, if I'm to publish the piece." He placed his hand on John's arm. "Give me a little more."

John felt instinctively nervous. "Nadia's brother seems to be well-connected and he's told her Mossad had agents videoing the first plane as it hit the North Tower and others celebrating in a white van nearby were arrested, yet released later despite the white van containing evidence of explosives. Those on top of Building Seven were found not to have visas. Yet they were allowed to leave the country without questioning by the security forces, just as a number of the Sheikh's family were allowed to leave from Logan International Airport when all other aircraft, international and domestic, were grounded." He raised his hands. "It doesn't make sense George."

"Did Nadia give you this information?" George asked coldly.

"She's been helping me with the research, that's all."

"And is that it?" He asked.

John shook his head, feeling discouraged. "An article in Quill Magazine back in February 1998 outlined the extent of the development of this remote-control technology. Just think about it for a minute." He hesitated. "Wouldn't it explain why they haven't found or disclosed the black box material, yet they conveniently find a paper passport of one of the alleged hijackers some blocks from the Twin Towers, which conveniently escapes the fireball." He looked at George with eager eyes. "Give some credit to your reader's intelligence."

George moved his hand to John's shoulder. "Remember, I'm on your side, John, but I need more corroborating evidence."

"I've more facts and been promised further documentary information by my source, but you'll only get them when I can do it without placing my source in danger." His eyes widened. "You must trust me on some things, in the same way I must trust you with my safety. It must work both ways."

George shook his head. "But you haven't told me your sources or how you came into possession of this documentation?"

"You know I can't do that yet, as I must protect her." A dour expression masked his concerns. "I don't understand why you're so cynical when even a former chief of British Airways mentioned early in 2001 that the Global Hawk technology could be used to take over flight controls in the event of hijacking."

"Mm. So your source is a woman." George smiled smugly.

"You mustn't even mention that to anyone without my permission." John said firmly, projecting his voice to a level reflecting the demand.

"Alright, Alright, but do I know her?"

"Well you'll certainly know of her, but don't press me on this right now." John's stern expression tightened.

"Calm down." He turned his palms downwards and flagged them. "Ring me and say you're ready to talk and I'll know what you mean. Until that time, be careful."

John left hurriedly, without returning to the office. He felt uneasy about the discussions, without understanding the reason, dismissing the thoughts and filing them away in a box somewhere in his brain. There were things he needed to do and an important meeting had been diarized, requiring his urgent attention.

John rushed down Piccadilly, trying to catch the attention of a cab to avoid being late for his meeting with Lynne. A hurried breakfast repeated on him, bringing its taste into his parched mouth. He took some chewing-gum from his pocket to disguise it, but needed to drink some water, if he could find a vendor and the time. He had twenty minutes, so no need to use his cell-phone yet. A childish excitement stirred, even his pulse raced, at the thought of meeting her again and memories revived in his imagination. Yet he had a sense something was wrong, a gut feeling in what he knew to be the region of the ganglion of spiritual nerves around the solar plexus area. Over the years, he had learnt to trust this feeling rather than anything logical stemming from the working of his brain. He knew instinct derived from a spiritual source, which was far more reliable than logic. Eventually, he arrived at Hyde Park and walked up and down the crescent-shaped path, bordering the lake, with no sign of her. Traffic noise droned in the background, though the smell of the park air refreshed his senses and he took a deep breath, filling his lungs with energy. He scrutinized the area with trained eyes, knowing safety was paramount, but the environment appeared sterile enough. A group of happy children played noisily, running around excitedly with a freedom impossible in London's stark streets. He noticed a number of people of different sexes walking dogs, but all of them walking at pace and moving too quickly away for danger. A couple hugged and kissed on a bench nearby, but it looked real and lustful, not pretence. Someone else carrying a newspaper and walking slowly had to be watched, but he seemed nondescript. He knew suspicious characters came in all sizes and ages and in many different guises, but in the meeting of the eyes he could always sense real danger.

He wallowed in the warmth the sun brought to his body this beautiful summer's day, so far removed from the nightmare scenarios he had played out in the lonely dark nights. The innocent sounds of playful children screeching and laughing embraced the gardens around him and when the sun shone it was easier to escape the harsher aspects of life and for a moment he daydreamed. If situations were thrust at him, he reasoned he could accept them, as if they were destined and choice did not arise. At another level, he knew everyone had choices and things happening to him now were a direct result of thoughts, actions and events from the past.

Soon he spotted Lynne, walking towards him carrying a yellow folder and an envelope, taped across the top with thick tape. Over her shoulder she carried her Louis Vuitton handbag. She wore a loud yellow two piece suit and a blouse with frills and lace at the top. There was no doubt he found her attractive, though he wondered why his first thoughts were always physical ones when it came to women. He felt awkward and slightly embarrassed when he noticed a tallish athletic middle-aged man obviously accompanying her. As he drew closer, he noticed gaunt features on his face, his eyes sunken. At first glance, he thought it reflected a life surrendered in some way and his face etched with stress lines, eyes carrying the pain of betrayal, something with which he was familiar.

She offered her cheek for a kiss, appearing more relaxed than previously. "Meeting you in London like this is probably asking for trouble, but I needed to see you."

"And I wanted to see you too." He silently moved towards her, kissing her on both cheeks.

She gestured to the man. "This is Evan, the intelligence man who agreed to meet you. He suggests public areas such as this are as good a place as any to meet, so I've bowed to his experience in clandestine matters."

She paused while he offered his hand in greeting and John reciprocated as a courtesy. "He's been of great help to me since his colleague went missing in the Balkans." She moved her glance from John to Evan and back again.

John smiled politely, recalling her explanation about the disappearance of the other intelligence officer after providing her with information. He turned towards Evan. There was something about him, which made him suspicious, though the fact he worked in the intelligence arena of deception and double games was enough. The fact the meeting place had been his suggestion made him even more nervous.

"So you're the famous John O'Rourke." Evan said.

John looked directly into his eyes, trying to assess body language and demeanour. "So what's your job in the intelligence service, domestic or foreign?" He asked, noting he refused any sustained eye contact.

Lynne intervened. "John." She said firmly. "You can't ask him questions of that nature."

He turned to her. "But you've already told me he works for the intelligence service, so what's the problem?"

Evan held his right hand up, turning towards her. "It's alright." He said. "I understand his suspicions, as his vocation is little different from mine."

"I find myself in a difficult situation because I want to protect Lynne." John said. "If it means upsetting people, I'm not afraid to do it."

"I'm as fond of her as you are, please believe me." He replied.

Lynne lifted the envelope in her possession, handing it to John. "Evan has given me this envelope and risked his career, his pension and even prosecution under the Official Secrets Act to do it." John took the envelope. "I'm grateful to him for agreeing to meet you because he's taking grave risks."

"If that's the case, I apologize." John said. "Perhaps it's wrong for me to be so suspicious, but you must understand my position."

Evan nodded. "It's perfectly understandable and I don't get offended by cynicism. Some things I see in the course of my duty place such trivial niceties into perspective."

A chord was being played out of tune and echoed something within his psyche, but he thought perhaps his experience of the dirty and dangerous intelligence world may have tainted his senses. "What's in the envelope?" He asked Lynne, the rising tone of an investigative journalist apparent.

Evan answered the question, even if it had not been directed at him. "You'll find a tape of an interview with someone you may know. The memory stick additionally contains collated further information and evidence which may be useful to you in your research."

"Who did the interview?" He asked, still abrasive.

"A Deputy Director of the FBI, formerly in charge of counter-terrorism."

"Do you mean the late Deputy Director?" John asked.

Evan nodded. "The interview took place prior to the events of 9/11, so you may find it useful."

John raised his eyebrows. "I didn't think he did interviews."

"A document in there also confirms the location of one of the American Global Hawk aircraft at the time of 9/11." He smiled. "Though I gain the impression you may already have it."

"This is the remote-controlled aircraft, which can fly up to 65,000 feet and stay in the air for almost a day and a half." John replied.

Evan nodded, pointing to the envelope. "Well done." He smiled. "It also has a range of 12,000 nautical miles, but you'll see from documents in that envelope, one of them was in the air above New York, then in the vicinity of Washington, during the 9/11 events."

"Hmm." John viewed him with greater respect, though he seemed too open for the usual intelligence services candidate, but he had been wrong in his judgments of people before.

"There's one other thing I should mention, but you'll find no evidence of it in the envelope."

"And what's that?" John asked impatiently.

"You may recall the New York Times quoting the US President as saying that a new technology would be developed allowing air traffic controllers to take over and land hijacked planes by remote control in the future."

"I remember it well." John said, biting his lip, intending to listen rather than give out information.

"I've gathered evidence in relation to the technology." Evan said.

"That's interesting." John said.

"The technology already exists, of course." Evan said. "I'd been posted to Fort Meade, near Baltimore, Maryland, working for the United States National Security Agency, when this information became available to me." He hesitated, looking at Lynne. "I've been posted there at least four times."

John's mouth dropped open, hardly believing a man trained in intelligence work, subject to psychological vetting could divulge this information so readily. "Didn't Lufthansa change the unit on the Boeings they acquired when they became aware of the existence of this technology?"

Evan recoiled. "You've done your research well."

"Perhaps we should discuss these things in more detail when you've more time?" John asked, more in hope than expectation.

"Perhaps." Evan said. "One final thing you need to know." He hesitated again. "Your apartment and car are both bugged and they're tracking your cell-phone. All your e-mails are intercepted and examined carefully, even your travel patterns and credit card receipts are all being analysed from the Grid."

"How do you know these things?" John asked nervously.

"I know." He replied with conviction. "So you'll have to be more careful if you want to keep your research private."

"Is this the echelon software?" John asked.

Evan smiled again. "They've had software for years which can trace your location even when your mobile is switched off and they've created a large file on you already." He replied. "People in the intelligence community know that with the microchip on GPS telephones they can tune in and listen to conversations taking place in the vicinity of the telephone even when the mobile is not being used."

John stepped back for a moment. Although he had been in this position before, it still took him by surprise. "So how do you stop it?"

He shrugged. "Take the battery out and go out into a field and hope it's a windy day."

He nodded in his direction. "Thank you for the warning, but you'll have to take great care too or you may find yourself a victim for passing this material to me."

"Frankly, they're so busy countering terrorism and monitoring radical Muslims that they're missing almost everything else." He sighed. "The Russian activities, for example, are back up to Cold War levels, with large numbers of officers posing as diplomats and trade officials in London and their aircraft probe our air space once again, even their nuclear submarines test our sonar defences."

"You sound upset?"

"I am."

John wondered if this explained Evan acting out of line. "Are they a real threat still?"

"They have the capability to undertake assassinations on our soil and we should be worried." His eyes caught John. "So much for Regnum Defende?"

"I'm sorry?" Lynne queried.

"Their motto, Lynne." John smiled, knowing his latin. "The Defence of the Realm."

Lynne nodded. "You sound quite exasperated by it all, Evan."

Evan looked towards Lynne. "Just a little."

"Are you intending to resign over it?" She asked, before John had time to ask the same question.

He shook his head. "Remember what I told you, Lynne, watch your back." He replied, the tone firm and sinister. "Your position in the House won't protect you and you've created powerful enemies."

Lynne grimaced, but said nothing.

"Good to meet you Mr O'Rourke." Evan said and in a moment, he had turned and walked briskly away.

"What was that all about?" John asked.

Lynne appeared more relaxed. "He told me there's a surveillance team monitoring my movements, my e-mails and telephone calls too."

"Yet you seem more relaxed than when we last met."

She nodded. "You helped."

"I'm pleased I could help."

She lifted herself up. "I tried to face death in the eye and imagined the worst scenario and it took away my fear of it. Shortly afterwards, I spoke to a terminally-ill friend who told me he didn't fear death, as you could die only once, so it was pointless dying a hundred times beforehand. He told me the trick was to live in the moment, one day at a time."

He smiled. "Sounds like sensible advice." For a moment, there was silence, a comfortable silence and he leaned towards her. "I like being with you, just with you, no agendas." He touched her arm. "Do you know what I mean?"

She laughed, a laugh which started from the stomach, and she pulled him closer. "You mustn't make me feel like a teenager again."

"Why not?"

"I've too much on my mind." She replied. "Catch me when I can relax in the evening."

A faint smile crossed his lips. "No problem."

"Tonight for example."

"It's a date." He nodded. "Now tell me a little more about Evan and this material?"

"He has downloaded a statement from a CIA operative confirming they were not going to capture the Sheikh." She replied. "If he came into their hands, they would have to kill him first, as he knew too much and could spill the beans on the President and the Vice President with his links to the Agency."

"The material from the memory stick came from a special source." She said.

"Sure, but how did you get hold of it?"

"Someone working for our cousins across the water gave it to him and he passed it to me with instructions to use it as I saw fit." She took a deep breath. "He told me at some stage they'd have to kill the Sheikh, but not under the current Presidency. At a later stage, they'd either get one of their Muslim agents to do it or it'll fall to the next President to organize the task."

"But why?"

"John." She said firmly. "You surprise me sometimes by your naivety. You must know it suits the US to have their bogeyman and he's not everything he appears to be."

"Right."

She smiled. "Of course, their corporations need to be in Iraq and Afghanistan too."

He nodded. "I understand."

"What else do you need to know?"

He thought for a moment, before looking at her. "What about this man Evan?" He hesitated. "I can't quite make him out."

She turned away, without answering, as if still weighing up the merits of divulging too much, but after few seconds turned back. "He's a friend of the person who disappeared in the Balkans and he simply wanted to warn me. He knew about you and wanted me to have this envelope." She pointed to it and the folder. "Once you've taken these documents, there's nothing to be gained by harming me." She smiled. "I've no other information or evidence which could possibly interest them."

"What about plain vindictiveness or as a message to others?"

"I never thought of you as a cynic, John."

"Years of journalistic experience have made me cynical." They turned and walked slowly along the path together. "What else did you learn from him?"

"Well, as you now know, they're monitoring you too." She looked earnestly at him. "Does it worry you?"

"It's nothing new, but, like all people, in a perfect world I'd prefer not to be involved in the complexities arising from this type of surveillance." He hesitated. "You always worry in the event they plant evidence and you get incarcerated for your troubles."

She nodded. "Yet if no-one makes a fuss or stands up to be counted, governments and the powerbrokers will literally get away with murder."

"You're right, of course." He replied. "You sound like me."

She hooked her arm around his and leaned towards him again. "So what will you do?"

"I'll talk to my editor again and supply him with any additional information necessary for him to run the story."

She frowned. "I think you'll have to be careful about him."

He stopped abruptly, turning towards her. "What do you mean?"

"I don't know anything for sure, but I've gained the impression there've been meetings between someone from the intelligence community and your editor friend. I wasn't sure of the position, so I didn't know whether to mention it to you because I didn't want you to end up paranoid too."

He shook his head, shoulders hunching, and the furrows in his forehead tightened. "How sure are you about this information?"

"Not enough to be certain." She replied.

He shook his head "I've known him for years and trusted him. I've also left an envelope containing incriminating evidence with him."

"Sorry, but I thought I should tell you."

"What do you suggest I do about it?"

"Why don't you try and retrieve the envelope and observe how he reacts."

"It's in my nature to confront him, if there's any doubt about his integrity." His face lost its previous sparkle.

"Then it's your call, but I'd have thought subtlety may be more appropriate first, wouldn't you?" She said.

"If I've a fault, it's impetuosity."

"Then don't make instant decisions." She looked at him with genuine affection, lifting her hand to stroke the side of his face.

He felt warm at her touch. "That feels good."

She smiled, looking more attractive for it. "You'll know if the envelope has been opened by your editor presumably."

"I'll have to meet him and take it one step at a time." He pointed to the yellow folder. "What's in there?"

She handed it to him. "Some of these documents are intelligence reports, which came into my hands as Chair of the Parliamentary Committee on Security and Intelligence in the House. They outline intelligence views about the technology Evan has mentioned." She took a deep breath. "There's even reference to the way in which it works and some copy e-mails and memos, which show the cover-up."

He took the folder, placing the envelope inside it for safe-keeping. "You realise you're taking a big chance and you're in breach of the Official Secrets Act by doing this, as is Evan?"

"I know." She replied. "But I feel good about it and the risk of being prosecuted is the least of my worries." She pointed to the folder. "There's also some information in there about the Sheikh, which you should find interesting." She looked furtive. "He's definitely a CIA asset."

"Does the technology relate only to the Boeings that collided with the Twin Towers?"

She nodded. "Not all the Boeings have the technology, but definitely the ones involved in the events of 9/11." She said. "But you'll have to follow up on this stuff yourself."

"I'm grateful." He said, a serious expression crossing his face.

She shook her head. "No, I'm grateful to you." She said. "You've taken a risk by involving yourself on my account and I appreciate it."

"It's been my pleasure." He laughed. "Literally."

She laughed too and squeezed his arm. After a few moments she pointed to the folder again. "By the way, I've placed Evan's telephone number inside the folder, as he has more information, which he may be prepared to discuss with you, if he trusts you."

"What's that?"

"He must tell you." She said. "I suggested he speak to you today, but he seemed reluctant to say any more at the moment."

"It sounds interesting, but does he know you're giving me his telephone number?"

"No." She replied. "So let's hope he trusts you."

He nodded. "Frankly, I'm always suspicious of intelligence people living in a world full of deception and subterfuge. It's alien to my nature and they play too many double games, often playing one side against the other." He hesitated. "Tell me honestly, do you trust him?"

Furrows tightened in her face and she thought for a moment, before replying. "I suppose I do, but there are no guarantees with these people, as you'll know too well, and I wouldn't necessarily put my life in his hands."

He separated himself from her momentarily, opening the folder, walking slowly, scrutinizing the content and enclosures carefully, before closing the folder again."

"What do you think?" She asked.

"Interesting stuff." He took the envelope out of the folder next, considering its content, before turning back to her. "There's reference to a US government employee in here and an affidavit about his work. Do you think it would be a good idea to contact him?" He placed the envelope back in the folder and placed the folder under his arm.

"You'll have to be careful, if you do." She replied.

"What about Evan?"

"To a degree I trust him, even if I wouldn't put my life on it." She replied. "I knew his colleague very well and trusted him completely, which is why I put his telephone number in the folder, but I suggest you don't say too much until you're sure. You'll have to use someone else's telephone if you choose to ring him, so it's not traceable to you." She turned her face up to the sun and took another deep breath. "It's good to be alive on days like this."

He nodded.

She turned back to him. "It's a great relief to get rid of all this stuff." She said. "I've felt so much more relaxed since I discussed these things with you."

"And have you thought about the information I gave you in Crickhowell?" She asked.

"Do you mean the information about the events in London on the 7th July 2005?" He looked quizzical.

She nodded.

"I'm still researching some of the information you mentioned, for corroboration reasons because if it happened as you suggest, then British Intelligence have managed to undertake the events in a more sophisticated way than achieved by the Americans."

"Be careful please." She said. 'This is dangerous information and our intelligence services are more subtle and perhaps more experienced at covering these things up."

He nodded. "Of course I'll be careful." He looked at her with a lover's eyes. "Are you sure you don't have time for lunch?"

"Sadly, no." She released her grip on John's arm and adjusted her jacket. "I've a meeting in the House, which I can't miss, but definitely dinner tonight."

"Shall I ring you or pick you up?"

She smiled. "You've got my card, with my address on it, so just call around and pick me up. I'm sceptical about telephone calls, especially if they're monitoring me, as Evan suggests."

He placed his arms around her shoulders, squeezing her. "Just take care of yourself."

She gently pushed him away, as she looked over her shoulder. "Tonight."

"Well, tonight then?"

She smiled again, more broadly, before turning. "I'll look forward to it."

He watched as she walked away, waving as she glanced back over her shoulder to look at him and he turned to walk in the opposite direction. Some feeling in the pit of his stomach forced him to stop and turn back. As he did, he noticed two people wearing hooded jackets near her, about one hundred yards from him. One of them grabbed her and the other thrust something towards her, before grabbing her handbag. He heard her scream, but everything appeared to happen in slow motion, as if he could not believe the events his eyes were witnessing. They fled quickly, as she slumped to the ground, before he ran towards her. He heard a young couple nearest to her shout at the men and the male ran after them, whilst the female knelt down to attend to Lynne, but turned away, screaming at high pitch. Her boyfriend stopped in his tracks, turning back at the sound of her scream, at that point more concerned with her than chasing the two assailants.

When John reached Lynne, it was too late. Her face was ashen and pained. As he bent down to cradle her, he noticed blood seeping through her clothes at the point of her midriff. He noticed the two men in the distance jumping into a car waiting for them at a nearby exit. The girl's boyfriend had returned to the scene, breathlessly comforting her. After a minute or two, when a crowd had morbidly congregated, the man telephoned the Police and turned to John. "How can they do this, just for a handbag?"

He placed her head back on the ground gently, shaking his head, standing up and turning to the young man. "I don't think it was just for the handbag." He said, a sickening feeling overwhelming him, taking him to a desolate place he had visited before and knew well. He desperately wanted to turn back time, but the vagaries of fate refused him, instead leaving another emotional scar seared deeply into his consciousness. In that moment, he determined to do whatever became necessary to right a grave injustice. "Do your worst." He murmured under his breath.

CHAPTER NINE

When all international and domestic flights were grounded after the events of 9/11, one flight only was allowed to pick up passengers at various points in the U.S. and fly out of the country. Amongst the passengers picked up and escorted out of the country were members of the bin Laden family and their 'associates'.

Of the names of the skyjackers supplied by the F.B.I. within forty-eight hours of the events of 9/11, none were listed on the passengers' manifest on their respective flights and many were subsequently found to be very much alive.

Despite the failure to initially locate or produce the black boxes of the various aircraft, allegedly indestructible, the authorities do find, (some blocks from the twin towers), a 'paper' passport purportedly belonging to one of the hijackers, which had miraculously escaped the fireball.

When told of the second attack on the Twin Towers by his Chief of Staff, the President does not act surprised and the Chief of Staff acts like he is delivering a progress report to which he knows there'll be no immediate response, even though he knew there were other hijacked planes in the air. Neither does the secret service try to take the President away from danger, as they are trained to do, unless they knew he

**was not the target and not in any danger. The Chief of Staff
steps back without asking for a decision and the President,
the Commander in Chief of the military, stays a further
twenty minutes.**

John dragged Nadia, under protest, to a friend's apartment in the same
block, without explanation, taking her into a small study for privacy,
giving her time only to gather personal items in a shoulder bag and a
separate large handbag, both slung over her shoulder. The room had two
functioning chairs, a desk with a computer on it and a printer underneath
and little else. Brash blue and white wallpaper on the walls closed in on
him, making the room appear small and a roller blind, partly closed, shed
strange shadows into the room, with little light. The odour of stale tobacco
hung unpleasantly in the air and the allergy John suffered from the effects
of smoke started to make his eyes water. He needed to free himself from
the shackles bolted to him by the possession of this dangerous information
and his mind spiralled into overload at the thought of the recent events.
At a logical level, he questioned the merits and wisdom of challenging the
Establishment again, but on every other level he knew he could never allow
Lynne's death to be in vain.

"It definitely looks like it's my turn next." John said coldly, staring
at Nadia. He placed his briefcase down at the side of the computer table
and explained the detailed circumstances of Lynne's death. "If they felt
a need to eliminate her, a much higher profile figure than me, then why
stop at her. I'm an easier target and everything she knew, I know." He
took a deep breath. "I know you're going to feel uneasy about the idea
of surveillance in our apartment, but I've been told, quite unequivocally,
they're bugging both the apartment and my car, which is why I've dragged
you over here."

She shook her head, sat down and moved towards him, placing her
arms around him, resting her head against his chest. Though she had taken
certain steps to reduce the risks, she fully understood the real danger he
faced. "I'm so sorry."

He felt her shiver against his body. "My concern now is to protect
you."

She looked up. "I'm more worried about you." She said. "Can't you do
a deal with these people, if only for my sake?"

"A deal?" He asked, arching his tone.

"You must do whatever is necessary, John, but my advice would be to meet these people and negotiate with them."

"Really?" The rising tone reflected his disappointment. "You want me to capitulate to these faceless bureaucrats?"

She shielded her eyes. "You've always explained the way these people work and it's an option for you."

He sighed. "Sometimes, I think you don't know me at all."

Releasing himself from her embrace, he settled back into one of the chairs in the room. It felt strangely comfortable and an irresistible feeling of tiredness washed over him, but he needed to generate energy, as there was little time. "These people are invisible." He said. "They're the secret government, controlling world events through the media, including selecting friendly governments and various shadowy front organizations. Even the banking system conveniently ties us all into this Matrix, but unlike a group such as the Mafia, there's no figurehead. Many of these people in positions of considerable power are faceless, rarely courting publicity."

"I do understand, John, but you look exhausted and in no mood to do anything or even think straight right now." She looked at him with genuine affection.

His shoulders hunched and he nodded. "I've been questioned by Police Officers for hours and they insisted on taking a Witness Statement immediately, despite offering to go there first thing in the morning. It didn't help that after dealing with a Detective Superintendent initially they insisted a young copper, still wet behind the ears, should take the Witness Statement. It took an eternity and it's drained me."

"It's understandable." She replied,

"They wanted to know if Lynne had given me anything or said anything of significance, but fortunately I had deposited the documents in the boot of my car before the Police interviewed me, so I denied it."

"What file?" She asked, her head lifting.

"Amongst other things, I've been given a tape by an intelligence officer, who was friendly with Lynne and I need to make some notes." He spoke carelessly, perhaps from tiredness or from negative thoughts intruding like some uninvited guest at a party.

She looked thoughtful, taking his hand in hers. "Please let me help you."

"This time, I do need help."

"Where's the tape?" She asked.

"It's in my pocket." He replied instantly.

She hovered around, showing enthusiasm when he had none. "If you're going to listen to the tape, let's do it together." She said. "I can help you."

Tiredness never allowed for the implications of candour and he took the tape from his blazer pocket, taking a tape recorder from his briefcase before placing it on the computer table. He placed the tape in the recorder, switching it on. The Deputy Director's voice came across clearly, and the voice of someone he did not immediately recognize. A British accent, more precisely a Welsh accent came across. It had to be Evan he thought.

"It's weeks away, but they still do nothing." The Deputy Director's voice sounded strangely artificial on the tape.

"What do you mean?" The second voice, Evan, asked, appearing more distant than the first, as if he was further away from the microphone.

"The President knows there'll be a spectacular and knows it somehow involves the hijacking of aircraft or some attack from the air. The intelligence is clear, but they do nothing."

"Who's behind it?" Evan asked.

"His State Department blocked my investigation into the Sheikh and the al-Qaeda connection to the attack on the USS Cole in the Yemen, so it's not difficult to guess, though the President is merely a puppet, only exercising power at the behest of those controlling him."

"So are you saying there's a link between the U.S. Government and the Sheikh?" Evan asked.

"I'm convinced he remains a covert CIA asset, as he's always been, and is being protected and will continue to be protected by this President, provided he doesn't rock the boat."

"So he's not the renegade who hates America, as he's portrayed?" There was a pause and he appeared to answer his own question. "I didn't think so."

A groan on the tape triggered the Deputy Director's voice again. "This has the stamp of the black ops department set up by the President's father when he was Director of the CIA. It's attached to the Air Force Intelligence office at Langley, but they'll feed this official line to the media who'll do their bidding, without asking too many questions. It's all part of the game. They're not answerable to anyone and they're funded by a combination of drug money, previously laundered in Panama, until Noriega stopped playing the game, and also funded by the oil cartels."

"This is a serious allegation." Evan asked. "Do you have the evidence?"

"Of course it's a serious allegation and I can't go public yet, but wait and see. It's July 2001, remember the date and what I've told you."

"I'll remember."

"If the whispers in intelligence circles are accurate, then I guarantee within six months the world will know what the higher echelons of power already know."

"What have you done about it?"

"What can I do?" There was a pause on the tape. "I'm talking to you and placing my career at risk and possibly being prosecuted or worse." There was a pause again, before the same voice continued. "I've badgered my superiors to the point where they want me to resign my position. They say it's untenable and I'm certain there are al-Qaeda operatives already in place in this country and a department within the CIA keeping certain information back from the FBI."

"But isn't there an Agency watchdog who'll report on this in due course?"

"That's the point." He replied. "'In due course' means years in the future and the present Director will be long gone and will be protected anyway because he's done what he's been instructed to do. They'll try to suppress any report, but even if it does come out, they'll protect their man; they always do."

"Will you resign?

"Probably." There was a slight pause again. "But I'll tell you something else, which is obvious from my investigations and the information I've analysed. There'll be an excuse to go into Afghanistan by October."

"I think I know the answer, but I'll ask the question anyway." Evan asked. "Why Afghanistan?"

"Why do you think?" The reply came, the same voice answering the question. "The oil and gas reserves around the Caspian Basin are the third largest in the world. There'll be an oil pipeline through Afghanistan and eventually down through Pakistan to the port of Karachi. They'll be looking for a pipeline through the Balkans too, but they must control these countries first."

"How do they propose to do it?" Evan asked.

"As you know, overseas development funds are often used to control a country financially and on the ground, even creating puppets in government."

There was a pause on the tape for about half a minute. A bright-eyed Nadia squeezed John's hand firmly. The sound of papers being shuffled could be heard on the tape, then the Deputy Director's voice again.

"Here's a copy of one of my memos. You'll see I've even gone over the heads of the Director, talking to the Secretary of State, but for some reason the Administration doesn't want to know."

"What do they hope to gain by being passive at a time of clear and present danger?" Evan asked.

There was hesitation. "Something is up and it's big."

"What do you think it is?" Evan asked.

"I'm convinced they intend to use some impending event to crystallize public opinion into following their secret agenda. They'll say the rules of the game have changed, or something similar, to erode freedoms and do things they can't get away with now." There was a short pause again. "Perhaps more control over the people and the erosion of the liberty of the individual, currently protected by the Constitution. It'll undoubtedly result in an increase in the Defence budget and military spending for this agenda."

"An incursion into Afghanistan or Iraq perhaps?" Evan asked.

"Probably both, but Afghanistan is the initial priority."

"But surely the people wouldn't allow it to happen?"

"It depends on the gravity of the situation. I'm genuinely frightened about the prospect of these events, as should the American people. The government will manipulate events so that it'll appear as if the ordinary citizen is clamouring for action, not the government, and they're indulging public opinion."

"But there's no public will for conflict after Vietnam or for the erosion of personal freedoms for that matter." Evan's voice said.

"Something will happen to change the perception in the minds of ordinary Americans. I'm certain of it." Again there was a short pause on the tape. "I know they've already begun drawing up some very restrictive legislation, which in the normal course of events would be unpalatable to the American people and would never get through either Congress or the Senate."

"What type of legislation?"

"They're compartmentalising the stuff, so I can't be sure, but I'm certain they'll attempt to erode the Constitution in some way."

"It must be a serious event, but what are you anticipating?" Evan asked.

"From the intelligence I've seen, it'll involve a hijacking and the sacrifice of American lives." There was a slight pause. "It doesn't quite make sense to me because there are failsafe systems in place, which should prevent any hijacking having the remotest possibility of success, so I don't quite understand how it'll happen."

"Is this reflecting the policy document drafted by the Under Secretary for Defence, the Policy for the New American Century?"

"I guess so."

"So you're suggesting a Government would sacrifice the lives of their people simply for the opportunity to impose greater controls and to limit their freedoms and increase the military budget?" Evan's voice sounded surprised and had raised his voice.

"It goes much further. I'm certain they intend to use it as an excuse to make incursions into other sovereign states and take control of them to protect the oil and gas, just as the policy document suggested."

"Do you have any evidence I can pass to someone over the water?" Evan asked. "I can give you whatever guarantees you require so you're not incriminated in any way."

"I wouldn't have brought you here without it, but I insist you don't divulge the source of the information." His voice took on a harsh edge. "I've a family to consider and you'd be placing me at risk."

"I promise." Evan said. "I can initially refer to the Wolfowitz policy document, if necessary."

Again silence on the tape, then the sound of papers being shuffled, before the sound of Evan's voice could be heard again. "I'm a family man too and I understand your position and will do all I can to protect you."

John spoke over the tape. "I thought he was divorced."

The tape continued, the Deputy Director talking. "You know I'm dead if you divulge this stuff in any way which could point the finger at me, so you don't have permission to quote me." He hesitated. "I'm looking for a quiet retirement and this interview is only to be used if something unforeseen happens to me in the near future." After the sound of more papers being moved, he continued. "Here it is. You'll see the ultimatum given to the Taliban last week by my government." The Deputy Director's voice tailed off.

"Hmm, I can understand your concerns." Evan said.

"Good."

"Though surely this can't be just for the oil and gas?" Evan asked.

"There's an even greater irony."

"And what's that?" Evan's voice echoed.

"I believe they've begun development on revolutionary technologies, which could do away with the world's reliance on oil and gas altogether, but there are vested interests, which will prevent its full development at present. It's being blocked."

"Why?" Evan asked.

The Deputy Director's laugh was audible on the tape. "How could the US administration, particularly the President and the Vice President, so tied up with its ownership and links with oil companies and its connections through the Carlyle Group and its family ties with Saudi Arabia, cut its own throat?"

"Tell me about this new technology?" Evan sounded curious.

"There's one which uses a magnetic energy field and anti-gravity devices and its cost would be minimal. Similarly, in Area 51 they've reversed alien technology to develop Element 115, using 115 protons to create enormous energy. There'll be no energy crisis in thirty years' time, even if it may be a few years before it's perfected, unless further funds are made available. Even the captured Nazi scientists as part of Operation Paperclip continued their research on the development of spin polarization, the properties of vacuum flux and Zero Point Energy, especially the technology used on the Bell, 'dei Glocke."

"Then why don't they invest the funds?" Evan asked.

"There are too many vested interests."

"And the one that's ready for use?" Evan asked.

"Fusion."

"A nuclear reactor?"

"You're thinking of nuclear fission, but I'm talking about cold fusion." The Deputy Director chuckled. "Nuclear fission splits atoms whereas this technology is clean energy, using fusion to squeeze atoms together under enormous pressures and temperatures until they fuse, releasing huge quantities of energy." There was a pause. "With cold fusion, the only resource you need to create it is water."

"I'm not technical." Evan said.

"There are many secret developments in the field of energy technology and free energy is available, including using sea water, red mercury vortexes and much more than you can imagine." There was a short pause. "The world could change for the better and there'd be greater wealth for everyone, if the technology was only released and developed, but all are kept top secret and curtailed for reasons of vested interests."

"Why do they suppress it?" Evan asked.

"Oil and gas of course." There was a grunt on the tape. "There's so much technology being suppressed, but one project uses magnetic fields to create energy and another uses special type of lasers, mimicking the reactions which take place in the Sun. More importantly, it has the effect of creating more energy than the amount of power initially placed into the reactor."

"And it's clean?" Evan asked.

"It's the ultimate energy source. No carbon, limitless, safe and secure. The atoms used would be hydrogen atoms from sea water."

"How much investment would be needed?" Evan asked.

"About ten billion internationally." There was a hesitation on the tape before the Deputy Director continued. "That's nothing compared to what they spend on weapons of war, a small fraction of the country's annual military budget." There was another longer pause for perhaps two minutes until the Deputy Director's spoke again. "I had to investigate the deaths of the passengers on the TWA 800 flight which crashed soon after take-off from New York. The autopsy on the victims frightened me, the blood in the veins of the passengers had gelled and their brains turned to mush. I had to suppress the truth."

"What was the truth?" Evan asked.

"The aircraft flew too close to the Brookhaven Naval Research Station and caught an experiment with a Moesbaur high-frequency gamma-ray beam device."

"And that is what caused these effects on the victims?"

"Yes, but there's so much the public don't know. They're blind to it all and although many have heard of Area 51 and secret experiments, they've very little knowledge of what is really going on."

"So what do these people in power really want?"

"To control the population and maintain a centralization of power controlled by the elite. There's even a mind-control project called Project Monarch, in which they use an IBM 2020 chip. I don't want to be a part of it and I need to get out, if I'm to retain my sanity. I want a life with my family, before it's too late." There was another pause and the sound of papers shuffling again. "Take these documents."

"Is this why they were pressing for identity cards in the UK, so they can control the population?" Evan asked.

"Well, it's been proved they'll not protect the UK from terrorist attack or from criminals, despite the propaganda. A European Commission Report prepared for your former Labour Home Secretary and other Home Affairs Ministers in Europe has stated as much, but they need their databases for the control they seek."

"It's the New World Order stuff again." Evan said.

"Exactly."

"And they're not too fussy about the control of their databases from past experience." Evan commented wryly.

"They're fussy for everyone else, but not themselves."

"Sure."

There was another long pause before the Deputy Director's voice could be heard again. "It even suits them at this stage to send out an environmental message and this allows them to increase taxes and further control the people through the tax and banking systems. If these banking systems are ever at risk, they'll mortgage the country to protect the system. Somewhere down the line, one of their men will even get a Nobel Prize for awareness of the environment, when the true motives and the secret agenda will be hidden."

"And the new technology would presumably help the environment?"

"It would do away with the energy crisis and there'd be no anxiety in the future about the supply of limitless clean energy. I know this for a fact." In any

"And you've evidence?" Evan asked.

"Yes, I've got evidence. This planet can take care of itself, if the technology is released, and there's enough abundance within this planet to accommodate everyone's ambitions."

"But presumably there's no political will to do it?"

"That's the problem. We could abolish poverty within a generation, but this would take away the central control and they don't want abundance for everyone, as people would have more time to think and they'd rather people work hard until they drop, beyond the current pensionable age if at all possible."

"It's why George Orwell, a Labour politician, referred to the thought police in his novel 1984?"

"We're already seeing it in place with political correctness and so on."

John and Nadia listened to a sigh on the tape, glancing at each other, before the Deputy Director continued. "There'll be relocation of some of the bigger oil and defence companies to the oil-rich friendly middle-east countries if the flak gets too much, as part of this New World Order agenda obsessing those at the top."

"How certain are you about these things?" Evan asked.

"I've worked for the FBI for many years and understand the situation more than most, but I can't fight the Establishment anymore. It's impossible, so it's time for me to retire and spend more time with my family. The new Director of the FBI has made it easy for me to get out."

"Sometimes the films in Hollywood are nearer the truth than people understand, but by fictionalizing it, they hope to trivialize the progress genuinely made into these fields of research." There was a hesitation. "Too many statesmen are stained with blood and oil."

"So what about your future?"

"They want me to go quietly and have offered me a post as Chief of Security at the Twin Towers in New York."

Nadia shivered as she listened to the tape and John squeezed her hand.

Back on the tape, Evan asked another question. "Are you going to take it?" "Probably. I'm just banging my head against a brick wall in my present position and they'll push me out if I don't take it."

At that point the tape stopped. John looked at Nadia, who took her hand away and stared blankly ahead.

"What do you think?" He asked.

She roused herself, shaking her head. "The state of the world right now is sad."

"But it's the state that's always existed, except people never knew the truth."

"Most still don't." She said.

"You're right, but the internet has revolutionized communications and although it works for them, it can also work against them."

"What are you going to do about it?" She asked.

"I'll do what needs to be done, but for starters I need a meeting with Lynne's intelligence friend again."

"Can you trust him?" She asked.

"How can I be certain?"

"You can't."

"Then I should start from a position of not trusting him, but what have I got to lose?" He reached down at the side of the computer table and picked up his briefcase, taking a large envelope from inside. "I want you to take this envelope and hand it to my lawyer, Julian, tomorrow. It contains copies of all the evidence, including the sources and the piece I've written."

"And you trust me with this material?" Nadia sounded surprised.

John raised his eyebrows. "Of course." He said. "It'll protect my back for the time being because Julian has got a website ready to go live if something happens to me and he'll optimize the site for high ranking on the search engines."

"Sure." She replied, bright-eyed, restraining her enthusiasm.

"I'll give Julian the original tape myself after I've typed out a transcript." He held out the heavily-sealed envelope, thick tape around it, with no hesitation.

She snatched the envelope from his grasp hurriedly and starkly. He looked at her strangely for a moment.

"I just want to help you." She said, regretting her abrupt action.

"I understand." He replied, resignation in the tone.

"I still worry about you." She said. "There are so many people who care about you, including your two lovely daughters." She stretched an arm out to him. "And you have me."

His eyes dampened, voice cracking. "I worry about the impact these events could have on my two daughters. They're still so young."

"Your daughters are adaptable. They'll be fine."

He shrugged. "But what else can I do?" He looked at her with doleful eyes.

"Why do you always need to get involved?" She asked.

"But what if everyone thought that way, especially after what you've heard on the tape."

She sighed, slipping the envelope into her shoulder bag, which she had taken from her shoulder for the purpose. "I can't just sit back and let you sacrifice yourself all the time."

"So what can you do?" He asked.

She hesitated before speaking. "Well for starters, it may be better if I move out." She said. "I'm a distraction you can do without and I'd prefer not to live where everything is being monitored. It's not right."

John groaned. "I'm used to living with you and I don't want to go back to living on my own."

"It's painful for me when I see you suffering." She said. "I'll still help you, but I can't watch you slowly destroy yourself and it'll only be for a short time."

He stiffened, watching as she stood up and moved towards the door.

"Don't talk to George, please." He said, opening the study door, remembering what Lynne had said.

She stopped dead in her tracks and turned around. "What's the problem with him?"

"I've reason to doubt whether he's playing the white man."

"What do you mean?" She stiffened.

"I'll find out soon, but something was said by Lynne, which I have to explore." He replied.

She huffed, turned back and started to walk through to the living area of the apartment.

"Wait." John said, before she could exit the room completely. But she didn't and couldn't, a different course already set.

*   *   *

The lights had been dimmed and Mohammed sat comfortably and anonymously in a private drawing room of a small yet sumptuously decorated hotel near the beach in Ajman in the United Arab Emirates. It remained a safe haven, even in the post 9/11 environment, and certainly less conspicuous than the more up-market areas of neighbouring Sharjah and Dubai, just a few miles down the coast, so it was the perfect setting for his low-profile meeting with the CIA Station Chief in the United Arab Emirates. The world had changed as time had passed since the events of 9/11 and this more remote part of the UAE was one of the few places he could still remain anonymous.

Mohammed wore the standard Kandura, sometimes called the Disha Dasha in the UAE and the Thob in Saudia Arabia. This long white robe covered him from the shoulders to the feet. With the typical Egile head-dress covering most of his head, he was hardly identifiable or different from so many Arabs in this affluent corner of the world. He was quite certain no-one would recognize him and he enjoyed roaming freely in an environment with anonymity; so much safer than his home country of Egypt or even Pakistan.

He fed beads from one hand to the other in a spiritual ritual of penance. He could not eat or drink, as it was daylight in the holy month of Ramadan and forbidden and he acknowledged the spiritual discipline. Still amused by his death, as the leader of the terrorist events during the 9/11 atrocity, he mingled amongst the rich and affluent with complete immunity.

The Station Chief wore white casual trousers, black shoes and a short-sleeved blue shirt, with a pen and a mobile telephone wedged into its pocket. He carried a small black briefcase and his bespectacled appearance was best described as nondescript; ideal for his profession. He could easily have passed for an estate agent with all the property development in this part of the world. A large percentage of the big cranes of the world had been situated in the UAE at one stage, as testimony to the rapid property development away from its hitherto reliance on oil. The ambition to create the highest building in the world, a short distance down the coast in Dubai, was part of the business plan. Even the Vice President's old corporation would eventually relocate to this area, as the expatriate population gradually increased.

"The time has come for the Sheikh to be eliminated." The Station Chief spoke coldly, but unequivocally. "But you understand we can't be responsible for it?"

Mohammed's face creased sullenly and his heart sank. He knew it was his death warrant too, for it would be impossible, even for him, to assassinate the Sheikh and walk away alive. His guards, his constant companions, had insulated him too well for escape, even if he managed the assassination in the first place.

"I suspect this means you want me out of the way too?"

The Station Chief's silence created its own reply.

"Am I an embarrassment to you like the Sheikh?"

The Station Chief smiled. "Not necessarily." He replied. "We can always explain away any sightings and you're not as high-profile as the Sheikh." He opened his case "Besides, we built your cover and what's in a name."

"But it'll be my death warrant."

"That's for you to organize, but you're not a problem for us or perceived as any threat."

The words sounded empty to Mohammed. "But if I'm to kill the Sheikh, I'm a dead man already."

"You agreed to the contract a long time ago and got paid a considerable advance for it, except we wanted it on hold until a more appropriate time." He hesitated, refusing any eye contact. "We're just calling in the contract now." He took out some documents from the case, looking at them. "You'll get the 25 million dollars on his head as a bonus and it'll be passed to your family, as previously agreed. That's a promise cast in stone."

"I'll want the final half of the original contract price in a bank account first." Mohammed played the game in the only way he knew.

"It can probably be arranged, if we know you're straight."

"So why the Sheikh now?" He asked.

"There are reasons?"

"You've been protecting him for years, even taking him out of the firing line in Afghanistan when you went in there with all guns blazing."

The Station Chief sat back, his shoulders hunched, wondering how to reply. "He's not doing what he's told and my people don't take kindly to double-crossing. His family has tried to reason with him without success and he seems determined to destabilise Pakistan, trying to organise regime-change."

"So that's it."

He nodded. "Musharraf was our man and the Sheikh has caused major complications for us there."

"But you're always organizing clandestine regime-change." He paused. "What's the difference?"

"You know the difference." He replied. "We'll not tolerate rogue agents."

Mohammed shook his head. "But you can take him out easily with a smart bomb from distance." He moved his hands out. "You know exactly where he is and how to locate him, so you don't need me to do it."

"Too much risk of civilian collateral damage." He hesitated. "In any event, there can be no mistakes this time and I've told you we can't be seen to be responsible. Besides, he knows too much and it'll be on the net if there's a mistake whereas if a Muslim does it, there's no connection with the Agency or the United States."

Mohammed looked scornful. "Do you ever get your hands dirty?" He asked a rhetorical question, which demanded no answer, nor did it get one, but he pressed him. "How do you sleep at night?"

He grunted. "I don't always sleep at night, but our business is a dirty business and somebody has to do it, if there's to be some stability in the world and our citizens protected."

"The World Police Force again."

"But it's a safer world because of it." He said. "It's how we all reconcile what we do."

Mohammed sneered. "Is that what you convince yourself?"

The Station Chief's tone changed. "Are you going to honour the contract or not?"

For a few seconds there was silence, before Mohammed nodded. "I've always known it was likely to be me in the end, but as I've said I want the final half of the contract money up front for my family beforehand." He shrugged. "It's only fair, bearing in mind I'll not be around to ensure you honour the contract."

"Don't you trust me?"

"Not particularly, but that's not the point."

"Then what's the point?"

"I need the certainty that my family will be taken care of and this is the only way I know to be sure."

"There'll be other opportunities to take care of your family."

Mohammed sneered. "We both know my chances of walking away from this are minimal." He raised his eyebrows. "And if I fail and die in the process, would you still pay the contract?" He paused, but there was no response. "It's not unreasonable I should want my family protected in that event."

The Station Chief grunted, but said nothing.

"My elder son needs to go to University and what I'm doing is giving a better life for him and my family." He tried to catch the eyes of the Station Chief. "Perhaps you don't understand my motives."

It resonated, even within the cold heart of the Station Chief. "Quite the contrary, I understand completely." He replied. "I'm motivated the same way."

"Well, you've got my bank account details, so let me know when the monies are deposited and I'll make my preparations." He hesitated, turning his head to the side. "And my farewells."

"Very well." He said. "The funds will be there, within the week, after I've authorised it with Langley." The Station Chief knew no risk of double-cross existed, as Mohammed was already dead according to official records and it was easy to kill a dead man without a trace of identity, even if they did not want to do it themselves. He felt comfortable talking to him. In some strange way, he liked him, perhaps it was his surprising honesty in a world where few were who they appeared to be, even if it did not stretch to being conscionable in the conventional sense.

"I'll contact the Sheikh and tell him I want to see him, so as soon as the funds are in place, I'll go. Either he or I will be dead within a month or more likely, both of us."

"Very well, the balance of funds will be paid to your family's account within the week on the strict undertaking you'll carry out the contract?"

"You people like to refer to contract, almost as if you're afraid to use the word kill." Mohammed smiled wryly. "Can't you tell it as it is?"

"You're right, but its habit." He replied. "When anyone recording conversations could incriminate you, it's easier to use a word which could be construed with another meaning." He shrugged. "Being evasive is a necessary part of our stock-in-trade."

He understood perfectly. "It's why others always do your dirty work for you."

"Sure, but somebody has to co-ordinate it at some level."

"And if I fail, you could save yourself the bonus."

"I respect you, Mohammed, and I like you, so you can be certain I'll make sure your family has whatever it's owed."

Mohammed nodded. "I can't ask for anything more." He sighed. "I suppose if it wasn't me, it would be somebody else."

The Station Chief calmly handed over the documents he had taken from his case. "These documents will help with the information you'll need." He closed the briefcase, before turning to him. "One final thing; this operation must remain a black covert operation."

Mohammed nodded again, standing up alongside him and holding out his hand, which the Station Chief took immediately. "I wouldn't have expected anything else, so I suspect this will be our last time meeting."

"I wish you good luck and I do hope you can return to your family." The Station Chief hardly waited for a response, turning and walking briskly out of the room and the Hotel. Anyone witnessing the meeting would have assumed a standard business meeting was taking place, even in the low-profile area of Ajman, rather than the Marina or the Burj Al Arab in Dubai.

*   *   *

John placed his briefcase and laptop case on the floor, as he fumbled for the key to unlock the front door of his apartment the following day, but the door opened with the weight of his hand. He tried to recall whether he had closed the door properly before leaving, but as he walked into the apartment, the cause was self-evident. The living room had been ransacked, though something was not right about the crime scene. The television and DVD Recorder remained in their place and had not been stolen, despite their greater second hand value, but his computer and fax machine, both of which could easily be traced back to the burglary, had gone. It dawned on him there could only be one obvious explanation and a gnawing feeling in the pit of his stomach made him realise it had begun. This was no simple burglary. He knew at some stage he would be targeted and felt dim he had not taken better precautions. Though his mind spiralled with many thoughts, there could be no turning back from this point of conflict, so no purpose in half measures.

Although he had deposited Lynne's yellow file in his briefcase, he double-checked to be certain, breathing a sigh of relief when they remained lodged in the same compartment he had placed them earlier in the day. Nevertheless, he was reassured he had given the envelope to Nadia. Inside the apartment, he noticed his bureau had been damaged and lay open. All his research work and working papers in relation to the events of 9/11 had disappeared. His mind raced with thoughts about the duplication of this paperwork and as most remained on his laptop, with some copies in his briefcase, he realized most of the hard copy could be easily duplicated. On the telephone display he noticed a number of withheld telephone calls yet no messages and guessed they had easily been able to check the apartment was empty this way. He telephoned Nadia to explain the events and she crossed her fingers, as she reassured him the sealed envelope with the information and evidence for Julian remained in her possession and again promised it would be passed to him in accordance with his instructions.

CHAPTER TEN

9th September 2001: A foreign intelligence service intercepts a telephone call (and passes the information to the CIA) from bin Laden to his stepmother: "In two days you're going to hear big news and you're not going to hear from me for a while."

10th September 2001:

National Security Agency intercepts recorded, but not acted on:

" . . . the match is about to begin" . . . "tomorrow is zero hour".

In a programme about the alleged conspiracy theories involving the events of 9/11 the BBC ignore many factual matters. They also state that there were no casualties when WTC Building Seven collapsed, but a Master Special Officer of the Secret Service died when the building came down.

It was the BBC who first reported that WTC Building Seven had collapsed, twenty minutes before it actually did. The announcement was made with the building still smoking behind the person making the announcement. Google was compelled to remove the video from their various Servers minutes after it appeared. The obvious question is who had told the BBC it was collapsing and who quickly covered up the recording afterwards?

An officer of the New York Fire Dept. was close to Building Seven when it collapsed and agreed there was no reason for it to fall down as it did.

"The FEMA investigation is a half-baked farce . . . . and may have already been commandeered by political forces whose primary interests, to put it mildly, lie far afield of full disclosure . . . . and the crucial forensic evidence (which should have been examined at the scene, as with any crime scene, let alone the crime of the century) is on a slow boat to China"—Editor of Fire Engineering—"the structural damage from the planes and the explosive ignition of jet fuel in itself were not enough to bring down the Towers" Fire Engineering—January 2002.

Hugo Bachman—PhD. Professor Emeritus and former Chairman of the Dept of Structural Dynamics and Earthquake Engineering—Swiss Federal Institute of Technology—"In my opinion, the building WTC Seven was, with great probability, professionally demolished"—Tages Anzelger Article—9th September 2006.

"A localized failure in a steel-framed building like WTC Seven cannot cause a catastrophic collapse like a house of cards without a simultaneous and patterned loss of several of its columns at key locations within the building"—Ramal Obeid—Structural Engineer, U.C. Berkeley.

Danny Jowenko—an expert in controlled demolitions for twenty seven years—" . . . it starts from below . . . they have simply blown away columns. " "This is a controlled demolition—a team of experts did this . . . this is professional work without any doubt."

Jim Marrs in his book 'The Terror Conspiracy' states: "The totality of the information available today can only lead to two inescapable conclusions: either the highest leadership of

the United States is composed of imbeciles and incompetent blunderers or they are criminally negligent accessories to the crimes, if not worse."

Clandestine meetings had become an unfortunate, but necessary safeguard for John, knowing the grave risks involved, whatever precautions he took and it went with the territory. He needed information from Evan, even if it increased the danger. It may have been summer, but the evening air was cold and damp, a depressing drizzle sweeping across London, enveloping the stars and hiding them from view. John turned up the collar on his navy blue Boss overcoat, as the chill wind reminded him of the vagaries of the British summer, grey clouds sagging onto the sad streets of London, turning them into the loneliest of places. Traffic noisily shunted by and though it was not quite dark, the lights from the windows of the Hotel had begun to cast eerie shadows in the twilight. He may not have been cold, but he shivered as he waited at the side of one of London's more fashionable hotels, feeling like some pimp supervising a high-class hooker stalking the City searching for the big payday. There were too many paparazzi around for his liking, but it was not his choice of meeting place and he hardly noticed as Evan appeared from somewhere behind him.

"How are you coping with recent events, John?" He asked quietly.

He turned to face him, noticing immediately the strong smell of alcohol. "Lynne's death is still difficult to accept." He took a deep breath. "How do people conspire to kill someone in this civilized world?"

Evan's face appeared sombre, his eyes tired, but he was the wrong person to ask such a rhetorical question. "People think these things only happen in third world dictatorships." He shook his head. "But sadly it happens all the time, though on most occasions it's covered up or passed off as heart attacks, suicides or accidents." He spoke with a conviction stemming from first-hand knowledge.

"Well you and I both know her death was not the random mugging portrayed by the media." John gave him a knowing look.

He shrugged. "I agree with you completely."

"So, what are you going to do about it?" He asked, raising his voice.

Evan shook his head. "For now, nothing."

"Nothing?"

Evan sighed. "People in positions of power are vindictive and they'll do anything to protect their place at the top table." He took John's arm, gesturing towards a taxi rank. "When I move, I must be absolutely certain I'll have the necessary support."

John nodded, but said nothing.

Evan threw him a hard-faced look. "My friend who disappeared in the Balkans, tried to move too quickly, but I can't make the same mistake."

"So why did you choose so conspicuous a meeting place?"

"The more public the better." He turned to John. "It suggests I've nothing to hide."

"So are we likely to be observed?"

"I can't be sure." He looked into John's eyes. "You don't appear to understand how things work in the intelligence field. I need to make the meeting place public and lodge a report openly thereafter, explaining a genuine reason for the meeting."

"What genuine reason do you mean?"

"Perhaps to warn you off."

John sneered, his face twisting. "For all I know, you could be gathering information or you could be playing both sides."

Evan smiled, before clearing his throat. "Of course, I could and it could look that way to my paymasters, but you'll just have to make a judgment."

"Where are we going?" John asked.

"To my Club."

John raised his eyebrows. "Are you mad?"

"Trust me."

The words sounded hollow. "That'll be like Epsom on Derby Day. How can we talk freely there?"

"This way, it's better for me and better for you, as it's all out in the open with nothing to hide, so no-one will suspect anything." He smiled. "I also happen to know there are no surveillance devices at the Club."

"Where's your Club?"

"It's the Oriental Club at Stratford House, Stratford Place, off Oxford Street."

He thought for a moment, looking directly at Evan, realizing he had little choice, if he was to gather the information he needed. "You know best."

Evan hailed a taxi. Soon they arrived at the Oriental Club, situated in an old three-storey building with Grecian-styled architecture and the traditional triangular facade at the top, a union flag standing proudly on its roof. It may have been reserved for the starched brigade of the diplomatic service and the higher echelons of aristocratic society, but it was impossible not to be impressed by the classically-designed nature of the building itself. Stewards ensured the appropriate protocols were followed and John signed the register, though feebly using his middle name as his surname, as if somehow it made a difference. It reassured him and made him less vulnerable in a foolish way. He stopped to look at the rules of the club, which outlined the history and noted the qualifications for membership, with one such historical rule making reference to employment by the East India Company. He looked up at the portraits of the Duke of Wellington and Clive of India and walked past the staircase leading from the lobby to the First Floor bedrooms, before following Evan to the Library.

After ordering two double gin and tonics and settling into a quiet corner of the Library area, John sat back into his leather lounge chair, surveying the room as surreptitiously as could be reasonably possible in such circumstances. Thick velvet curtains framed the windows and the marble pillars and high ceilings gave the room an ambience of affluence and decadence. He understood the obvious appeal and no doubt subsidized room rates for members allowed it to thrive in this location. Subtle lighting highlighted what appeared to be original paintings adorning the walls, with another of its recited First President, the Duke of Wellington.

"What do you want to know?" Evan asked softly, in the slight Welsh lilt he retained, despite years away from his homeland.

"Well, I've read the yellow file and considered the contents of the envelope you gave Lynne."

"And the tape?"

"Of course." John replied. "I've listened to the tape, but more than that I believe I know precisely how and why the events of 9/11 happened, but I need more firm evidence if I'm to be believed."

"So how did it happen?"

"First, I need to establish credibility and believability because people will not want to accept the truth without overwhelming evidence. Without that evidence, my piece will be dismissed by the intelligence-controlled media, as you know, even if I could get it out there in the first place."

"Understandable."

John took a sip of his gin and tonic. "I don't want to be left stranded, being left only with a remote website, as my only avenue of publication."

Evan lifted his glass, sipping his gin and tonic, smiling innocently. "I guess you realised it was me on the tape with the Deputy Director?"

"I recognized the Welsh accent." John replied. "The trace remains distinctive."

Evan smiled. "I suppose so."

"Did you know I was burgled yesterday? He asked.

"I didn't, but I can't say I'm surprised."

John shook his head. "I find it difficult to believe you people do this sort of thing." He said. "Is it the governments which are at fault or is it you intelligence people?"

"Not people like me." He sat back in his chair. "I'm insignificant in the scheme of things."

"Then who is it?"

"It's the financiers, the media barons and the elite aristocrats who make the big decisions." Evan shrugged. "They're the ones with the real power, the people in the shadows who the public never see. They control what governments are appointed and what they do whilst they're in power, holding sensitive information against all the politicians in case they get out of line."

"How do they control them?"

"Perhaps a little blackmail or if that doesn't work, they eliminate them ruthlessly." He replied. "You've seen the perfect examples in the recent history of the U.S. with the Kennedys, Nixon and even Clinton with his womanizing, which is nothing unusual, but none of it would have become public if it were not for other external events." He took another drink. "It normally never does."

He shook his head wearily. "Yet you still work in this dirty business?"

Evan sighed, leaning forward in his chair. "It's not easy."

"Then why do you remain in a service, which you say isn't easy."

He shrugged. "When I was first recruited as an undergraduate at Aberystwyth University, I had ideals as to the integrity of the service and of government. In time you learn the truth, but by the time you find out it's often too late to do anything about it." He hesitated as looked around the room. "If you want to preserve your place in the sun, you don't rock the boat, because you risk losing your job, your pension or even imprisonment for breach of the Official Secrets Act if you do." He looked straight at John. "Most find it easier to take a pragmatic approach to their profession."

"So why are you rocking the boat now, by divulging these things to me?" He asked the obvious question.

Evan looked away again, his mind wandering to some other place, before turning back. "The answer is I don't know, but this government has deliberately misled Parliament and the public, even members of the Cabinet, and in doing so, they've compromised the security services."

"Is that the only reason?"

"I genuinely didn't know what would happen to Lynne and I liked her." Evan's eyes focused on John again. "More than that, we were lovers for a time."

John recoiled for a moment. "Lovers?" He pulled himself up in his chair.

Evan nodded. "I would never have stood back and allowed her to be placed at risk." He took another drink and looked back at John. "We had a lot in common."

"When did it end?" John asked, naively looking for some reassurance he was not her lover at the same time.

He smiled. "It finished before you."

"So you knew about us?"

"It was hardly a secret?"

"Fair enough" He relaxed back in his chair.

"Before these events, I'd already been disillusioned after the disappearance of a good friend in the Balkans, but I would still have been reluctant to pass on information." He allowed his mind to wander, then took a deep breath. "But now the position has changed and I'll do whatever is necessary to help you. I owe that to Lynne's memory, if only for a limited period."

"Why?" John asked.

"It's obvious isn't it?" He hesitated. "I'm not going to be around for any length of time."

John thought for a moment. "I liked her too, so we're in a similar position."

"Good." Evan fidgeted uncomfortably in his chair. "Now what do you want to know?"

"I really need more tangible facts and evidence, so I can quote these things in my piece and make it credible"

"Where do you want me to start?"

"Can we start by recapping on the events, perhaps starting with the Pentagon?" John asked. "I still don't know whether an unmanned Global Hawk was unleashed on the Pentagon or one of the Russian missiles confiscated at the end of the Cold War and the break-up of the Soviet Union."

"Why do you think it was a Global Hawk?" Evan asked.

"Because the hole in the wall before it collapsed was only sixteen feet high, which is the same dimensions as a Global Hawk and there were no holes where each of the six ton engines of a Boeing would have hit the wall."

"Is that what you think happened?" Evan asked.

John grimaced, unhappy at the sparring. "I've information an old Russian missile may have been used, but I can't write my piece until I know which alternative is correct?"

"What's your guess?" Evan asked.

"Whatever it was, it flew around the Pentagon too sharply for a Boeing and underneath the ground to air missile system at about 450 miles per hour."

"You're right about it not being a Boeing." Evan said.

"So was it a Global Hawk or a missile?" John asked.

"The information in my possession suggests it was an old Russian missile confiscated when the Soviet Union broke up, so that if things went wrong, responsibility could easily be passed to a rogue state or terrorist with no manifest on the missile suggesting it was American-built."

John's eyes opened wide. "Can you provide me any evidence?"

"Not at present, but as you know it wasn't picked up by the normal military or civilian radar systems because they planned to fly it underneath another aircraft coming in to land at the Ronald Reagan airport in Washington." Evan hesitated. "This is why it came around the Pentagon away from the natural flight-path if it had been the Boeing."

"What else can you tell me?"

"It's your call." Evan said. "What do you want to know?"

"For starters, how did they deliver the missile?"

"Probably a submarine in the Atlantic."

"Are there Air Traffic Control Radar images available in the infrastructure of the Pentagon?"

"Yes."

"So what are you saying?"

"It's simple." Evan replied. "Any commercial airliner within 200 miles of D.C., which changes its course, or turns off its transponder, would have been intercepted at supersonic speeds within minutes. Andrews Air Base could have quickly scrambled the F15 and F16's fighter jets they had at the time of 9/11 in under three minutes and they both carried Sidewinder missiles with a eighteen mile radius."

"They boasted as much on their website at the time, but what I really want to know is why those aircraft, based just ten miles or so from the Pentagon, were in the skies only after the Pentagon was hit and one hour 45 minutes after the first flight had deviated from its flight-path?" John asked.

Evan shrugged. "Because they weren't meant to be there any earlier."

"But how did they get away with it when Andrews also claimed on their website at the time they had combat units at the highest state of readiness?"

"The same way they've always got away with it." He replied. "Look at the lessons of history."

John nodded. "So nothing could hit the Pentagon, unless it's allowed to happen?"

"Of course not." He replied. "The leads are in the file and the envelope I gave Lynne." Evan sighed. "Do you still have them or did they go in the burglary?"

"I've kept them with me the whole time."

"Then follow the leads." Evan said. "The surface to air guns with rotating turrets at the Pentagon failed to fire and you can guess the reason."

"So you don't think it was a Global Hawk?" John asked.

He shook his head. "I can't be sure, of course, because they've covered it up so well, but the evidence of the limited area of impact damage to the front of the Pentagon plus the evidence of what witnesses saw and heard means it was either missile damage or a Global Hawk." He took a sip of his drink. "Of course, the lack of any evidence of bodies or bodily parts, even the evidence of witnesses who refer to the whistling noise prior to impact and what they refer to as a small aircraft, all suggest it was either a remote-control Global Hawk or more likely the missile."

"So what's happened to the bodies on the Boeing?" John asked.

"Probably in a landfill somewhere, most certainly unidentifiable now."

"But what about evidence I need for my piece?"

"Well for a start, you can always refer to the manifest showing a Global Hawk missing and I'll try and gather some evidence about the Russian missile."

"But that would mean they killed all the occupants of the plane or diverted it and, if so, there must have been a huge number of people in the cover-up?"

Evan nodded. "I suspect that's where the al-Qaeda connection comes in. If the people in the plane were eliminated, it would have been by the persons they thought were the terrorists. Effectively, they would have employed these people to play the part of terrorist hijackers, as contractors, to do their dirty work."

John shook his head. "How do you know these things?"

"You just have to look at the passenger manifest for the aircraft which allegedly crashed into the Pentagon." Evan smiled. "You'll find a significant proportion of the passengers were military personnel. Much more than would normally be on such a plane and it doesn't make sense."

"As someone who works in the intelligence community, what's your view of al-Qaeda?"

"It doesn't exist as an organisation as such, but it's a nebulous random group of rival factions lumped together to scare the ill-informed." Evan replied. "It's the remnants of the database of CIA recruits who with the Mujahadeen fought the Russians, at the behest of the Americans." He studied John carefully. "But you know that already."

"But what about the Sheikh?"

"The Sheikh was definitely a CIA asset, but he's being protected at present and has a safe house in Pakistan whenever he needs it."

"Is he alive?"

"I guess he's still alive, probably in Pakistan." Evan hesitated. "They're more concerned about the brains behind al-Qaeda, the Egyptian. He's the reluctant asset following the Company line only whilst the Sheikh controls him."

John hesitated, as a member walked past the table. "But they must have taken such risks to cover up the whole event." He said. "How did they manage to keep the operation clean?"

Evan smiled weakly. "Partly by compartmentalization, but I suspect they felt they were unlikely to ever have the same number of people at the head of the institutions of power ever again." He replied. "They'd infiltrated all the agencies of government and even had a majority in Congress to protect them against a Nixon scenario."

John took another sip of his gin and tonic and leant back. "Even so, it's difficult to imagine a government committing such an atrocity and killing so many innocent people."

"Even as an intelligence officer, it's difficult to imagine, so the ordinary citizen will find it impossible to believe without a weight of evidence." Evan said. "And I'd spoken to the Deputy Director before the event and looked at the intelligence information."

"So you've reached a reasoned conclusion?"

"I can analyse evidence as well as anyone and I'm convinced it doesn't add up any other way."

John shifted in his chair. "Can you help me prove it?"

Evan shook his head. "I can only pass on bits of information, as I gather it." He replied. "I can only point you in the right direction and give you the best advice."

"Advice?" He asked. "But what I need is evidence and facts."

"I understand."

"What about the way they controlled the two planes which hit the Twin Towers?" John asked. "How does this remote control technology work and at what point did they take over the flight controls?"

"You've seen the envelope and the file." He replied. "I know top secret remote-control technology exists and it's capable of taking over the controls of certain Boeing aircraft, including the two Boeings involved in the 9/11 events, but of course the technology has never been made public."

"But the US President made a speech saying they would develop this technology, so it could never happen again." John said.

"Of course, he could say it with confidence because he knew it already existed."

"Is some sort of beacon and control centre necessary for its operation?" John asked, voice arching.

"Sure."

"What about Building Seven?" John asked.

"It had the beacon." Evan lowered his voice, as a steward passed. "You've got the evidence in your file revealing a Global Hawk positioned at 60,000 feet above New York on the morning of 9/11."

John nodded. "I thought as much."

"All it needed was a point on the ground with Building Seven, which is why that building, the Command Control Centre, had to be destroyed."

"It was, of course, the CIA Headquarters in New York." John said.

"Sure."

"So it had to be destroyed?"

"Yes."

"I suppose they couldn't risk human error?"

"I'm convinced this technology was used to take over the flight-management computers on the aircraft." Evan replied. "That way, no risk of mismanagement of the operation could occur or mistakes in piloting by someone with too much courage and no sense, or even some hijacker having cold feet at the last moment."

John's face strained with tiredness, his eyes heavy and slightly bloodshot. "It also explains why hijackers who couldn't fly little Cessna jets didn't have to take over the complex flight management computer systems." He said. "You mentioned previously you'd spoken to someone at Lufthansa. Is this why they took this technology out of their Boeings and put their own in its place?"

"Of course." Evan replied. "They didn't want the U.S. having the capability of taking over one of their planes."

"So you're convinced the American government was complicit with the terrorists, stage-managing all of the 9/11 events?"

"No doubt." Evan pushed his hair back from his forehead. "At one level, you have to admire their audacity and balls."

John shook his head, but said nothing.

Evan looked around furtively, before leaning towards John. "For whatever reason, Mossad knew and the Israeli Prime Minister, Ariel Sharon, leaked information proving he had warned the CIA and the US President." He hesitated, looking around again. "But there's always so much smoke and mirrors with Mossad, like all the intelligence agencies, so you can't be sure they're not playing a double game."

"Did MI6 know in advance?"

Evan spoke quietly. "In your file, there's a copy of the communication showing that my department, within MI6, and also the German BND had both been aware of the events in advance, but they ignored warnings, as did their intelligence agencies."

"What does that mean?"

"The only explanation is that the events were meant to happen and they needed to facilitate them. In fact, there's some evidence Mossad had infiltrated an al-Qaeda cell within the US, but the Americans obviously allowed the events to happen."

"Would they have known about the Mossad link?" John asked.

"Of course." Evan replied. "They've got an office at Langley and the Americans were using the al-Qaeda operatives for the false flag operation, probably training them at one of their air bases, most likely Pensacola."

"It explains why some of the alleged hijackers had driving licences with the Pensacola Air Base as their address and why they all had their visas granted so easily?"

"Sure." Evan finished his gin and tonic quickly, raising his hand to order another.

So, it all went to plan." John said, declining an invitation to have another drink.

"There were a few hitches." Evan tilted his head one way, then the other. "At one stage, a flight attendant on the American Airlines flight, which subsequently hit the Twin Towers, called to her control centre and raised the alarm at least twenty minutes before the first event, but still the military stood down."

"Why?"

"Because everything which happened that day was meant to happen." He lifted his hands in the air. "Even when the flight over Shanksville, Pennsylvania, went wrong with the forty minutes delay in take-off, they still dealt with it using plan B to prevent the truth leaking out."

"In what way?" John asked.

"Let's just say that having taken off forty minutes late, it couldn't hit its original target, as there would have been military jets in place by that time." He turned to John. "And it couldn't be allowed to land, so it had to be taken out."

"How?"

Evan took a deep breath. "There was a fighter in the sky to cover such an eventuality and it just took it out."

John shook his head. "But couldn't they have crashed it by remote control, as with the New York flights?"

"Not possible." Evan smiled. "They needed a beacon and that was arranged elsewhere, not over Pennsylvania."

"So what was its original target?"

"Probably WTC Building Seven." Evan replied.

John nodded. "And the authorities would have us believe Flight 93 dropped off the radar, despite the United States having the most advanced technology in the world?"

"Of course." Evan replied. "But people are frightened by the alternative, John."

"But what was the purpose of all these events?"

"It's obvious by the subsequent events, isn't it?"

"What do you mean?" John asked.

"I don't believe you're that naïve, John."

"Imagine I am, Evan."

He smiled. "It resulted in the consolidation and expansion of government and executive power, the erosion of civil rights, the increase of the military and security budget and the protection of the oil and gas in the Middle East by incursion into sovereign states." He paused for breath. "All of this was planned with precision beforehand."

"And the vested interests needed all of these things for their secret agenda." John said.

Evan took a deep gulp of his second gin and tonic, almost finishing it. "That's about right."

"What conclusion should I reach for my piece?"

"You don't need to be Brain of Britain to work out the obvious conclusions, especially if you remember the pipeline deal which went through in 2002."

"What I don't understand is why no-one has put all the facts together?" John asked.

Evan smiled. "The Homeland Security Department and the Patriot Act have done their intended work and created greater powers and a huge increase in resources towards security and the military. They were intended to suppress freedom of expression and restrict human rights and they've succeeded."

"People of character and courage will still speak out."

"The Truthers are already out there."

"What?" John asked.

"The Movement For 9/11 Truth and Engineers and Architects for 9/11 Truth and Scholars for Truth and many more, though they're all being monitored by the intelligence agencies." He hesitated. "They call them Truthers."

"But won't they try to discredit them?" John asked.

"Why don't you speak to them?"

"Perhaps I should."

Evan nodded. "There's an architect from San Francisco doing a tour of the United Kingdom shortly and he'll be discussing the engineering and architectural anomalies in the events relating to the buildings."

"I'll contact him."

"He'll provide you with factual evidence which should satisfy you as to the impossibility of the events happening in the way the US government portrays them."

"Do you have his contact details?"

"Google his website." Evan sat back in his chair. "Those in government are still frightened of the adoption of the Johannesburg principles on human rights and freedom of expression, which states quite clearly that any restriction on freedom of expression can only be imposed if there is an imminent threat."

John sneered. "I suppose they'll argue semantics on what imminent means."

"Of course."

John took a deep breath. "Given the history of how useful acts of terror have been in enhancing state power, it would be inevitable an unscrupulous government would eventually orchestrate events to create such an act when the need arose."

Evan smiled. "Now you're becoming cynical, John."

John nodded. "My friend, Nadia, mentioned something about Mossad agents on the roof of Building Seven videoing the first plane hitting the North Tower."

"I'll make some enquiries on it and get back to you." He looked around again. "It's strange how your friend has so much information."

"She has a brother in New York who told her apparently."

"If you give me his name, I'll look into it."

John wrote down his name in his diary without thinking twice, ripping out the page and passing it to him.

"This meeting will have to be short or they'll question it." Evan took the last remnants of his gin and tonic in one large gulp. "I'll do a report of the meeting, but it'll state that I've asked you to back off from the story and mention the incentives I've offered." Evan hesitated, as other members moved closer to their table, sitting down in chairs, no more than a metre away.

"I understand." John finished his drink. "But what incentives?"

Evan's voice lowered in tone. "Do you want a gong or would the security of a million pounds shut you up?"

"Are you serious?" John's eyes bulged wide.

"It's easy enough to organise, if you wanted to be compliant."

John flushed, perspiration dripping down the side of his forehead. "You can arrange it?"

"Probably."

"What about prosecutions for those powerful people who engineered these events?"

Evan shook his head. "No. No. No. You know better than that."

"But it would be right and fair."

"They're never going to prosecute anyone." He replied. "The Americans haven't even signed up to the International Criminal Court in The Hague, so these people have immunity and they've too much power. If they prosecute one, they'll blow the whistle on the others all the way to the top. It could never happen."

John nodded. "I suspected as much."

"So what do you want me to say in my report?"

John shook his head. "You already know I'm not interested in money or rewards."

Evan watched as a steward moved towards the adjoining table, serving drinks and moving away again. "It's what I expected, but you'll have to be extremely careful."

John moved his glass across the table, as he manoeuvred away from his chair. "I still can't come to terms with the number of people involved in the cover-up."

"But it's mainly military and they're trained in secrecy and obeying orders."

"But how could they organise the demolition of such enormous buildings and cover up the evidence?" John asked, as they walked out of the library together.

Evan leaned towards him, whispering. "Whoever is involved will be too scared to say anything, even if the engineering evidence will eventually become clearer."

"But how do you cover up the demolition of a 47 storey steel-framed building, which wasn't hit by any aircraft?"

Evan grunted. "They had to demolish it in the aftermath to destroy any incriminating evidence, especially as the United Airlines flight had been delayed leaving the airport."

"Perhaps there was another reason the building was destroyed, relating to the other offices in the building." John said.

Evan nodded. "If it was used for controlling the events, they had to pull it."

John kept his voice low. "You do realise the Twin Towers and Building Seven were the first steel-framed buildings in history ever to be destroyed by fire, if you accept the government's version of events." He hesitated. "And, as you say, Building Seven was not even hit by any aircraft."

"I hear what you say, but they'll discredit and smear anyone who doesn't follow the government line." Evan still spoke softly. "Even if a team of experienced architects say it's impossible."

"What about the chances you're taking in talking to me, Evan?"

Evan shrugged. "There's evidence existing as to the use of an incendiary explosive to demolish the Twin Towers. It'll be in the dust analysis."

"What incendiary?" John asked.

"Thermite." He replied quietly. "There's ample evidence of its use because of its unmistakable chemical signature."

"Isn't that a game changer?" John asked. "Surely, it proves there was an expertly-controlled demolition of the building."

"No more." Evan placed his finger to his mouth.

John looked around furtively, shaking his head again. "I've spoken to some experts and they confirm there's no engineering reason why Building Seven was affected by the destruction of the Twin Towers, if it wasn't hit by any aircraft."

Evan shook his head. "Not now."

"But they tell me the black smoke from the fire shows there was little oxygen in the fire for it to spread and the fires would have been extinguished by the sprinklers, even if fire-fighters couldn't reach the fire quickly."

"I know, I know" Evan said.

"Do you suggest I talk to anyone in particular about this evidence, if only to prove an expert point?" He asked.

Evan thought for a moment, before leaning towards him again. "Talk to the Editor of Fire Engineering Magazine in the States. He called it a farce, as until that date no protected steel-framed building in history had ever collapsed due to fire. The building was designed to cope with 160 miles per hour winds and even an aircraft colliding with it at 600 miles per hour."

"Is that why the government didn't allow forensic examination of the debris?" John asked.

"Because it would have revealed the steel had been shredded into small pieces and the chemical residue of iron oxide and sulphur oxide would have been present." Evan replied.

"I think I've read a piece from this Editor of the Fire Magazine."

Evan nodded. "He's gone on record publicly as saying that at its worst fire could only have bent low-carbon steel, not shredded it into small pieces."

"It may not be enough, but it's more difficult to attack an expert witness." John said, collecting his coat from the lobby of the club.

"But they'll get their own expert witnesses to contradict it, so you'll need more than circumstantial or expert opinion evidence to take on the might of these powerbrokers, John."

"I understand." John said. "Do you fancy sharing a taxi?"

"I'm staying here tonight."

John nodded.

"I may be able to give you further evidence, but not tonight." Evan whispered. "I need to protect my position first or I'll end up the same way as my colleague." He looked around. "It's too dangerous at the moment."

"What further evidence?" John asked impatiently.

Evan screwed his face, rolling his eyes. "I can't tell you anything else for now, it's too sensitive."

"Anything will help." John said.

"I must go now." Evan pointed back inside the Club.

"What should I do next?" John asked.

Evan thought for a moment. "Eventually, you'll need someone to come out of the woodwork and confess to some complicity in these events."

"But how do I do that?"

Evan shrugged. "Many people have died in mysterious circumstances simply to cover up the truth."

"Really?"

"More than you can imagine." Evan said. "So they'd have to be brave individuals to fight these men with the vested interests in positions of power."

"I've always known the Establishment and organizations like the infamous Bilderberger Group control the media, the police and many other powerful organisations."

Evan nodded. "We shouldn't be discussing too much here, John."

John moved out of the front door and tried to hail a taxi without success and turned back to Evan in the doorway. "I still can't get my head around the enormity of these atrocities."

Evan sneered. "But how else could they get the public support for the invasion of Afghanistan?"

John nodded.

Evan returned to the lobby, asking the Steward to ring for a taxi, then turned back to stand by John's side on the pavement outside the club. "Did you know a decision on the invasion had already been made by the US President in an Executive Order in July 2001, as an ultimatum had been given to the Taliban to agree to the pipeline for gas and oil through Afghanistan or else they would invade by the following October?"

"I didn't know." He replied. "What about the corroboration for this secret technology."

Evan looked over his shoulder and back to John. "The people who work on this technology are either dead or controlled making it impossible to speak to you." He said. "Many of these people know if they assist you or divulge any evidence, they're most certainly dead, as may be members of their family." He shivered. "You really have no idea of the pressures under which they're living on a day to day basis."

"But where do they develop this technology?" John asked.

"Most of the advanced technology is worked on at Area 51, of course." Evan said. "It's why they're so sensitive to any breaches of security and why strange occurrences, such as sky-wakes are evidenced in its vicinity."

"But how do they have this hold over them?" John asked.

"There's so much you don't know and I don't want to complicate a task which is difficult enough already. Evan replied. "The affidavit will have to do for the time being."

"Where is this man now?" John asked.

"I've tried to contact this man since, but I think they've literally pulled the plug on him." Evan replied. "It's a dangerous path I'm treading too."

"So the only answer is for me to find from someone at the highest level of government or the intelligence services and hope they'll put their life in my hands."

"They'd be admitting complicity themselves." He said. "You'd be better believing in miracles."

"I suppose so."

"And if you go to the States, you'll be arrested under the Patriot Act or the powers of the Homeland Security legislation and hung out to dry."

"For doing what?" John asked.

"Evidence is likely to be fabricated and you could end up rotting away in a prison like Noriega or end up the victim of another haphazard mugging." He said.

"But I must go there at some point."

Evan shook his head. "Take my word for it, it'll be a mistake." He raised his voice. "Don't go to the United States."

"But I can't just do nothing."

Evan took hold of John's hand. "A CIA witness recently gave evidence in the Courts in London openly admitting the Supreme Court in the US can authorise them to lawfully kidnap someone in another sovereign state and bring that person back to the US to face their justice."

"I read about it."

"Remember the Patriot Act makes the U.S. almost a Police State now and freedom of speech is hugely curtailed since their constitution was eroded." Evan released his grip on John's arm. "Unlike Britain, the Justices are political appointees in the States, so do you really think a trip to the States is advisable?"

John sighed. "Perhaps not."

"Even the four Bank employees in London were extradited to the U.S. using terrorism legislation, even though none of the allegations were terrorist-related offences."

"But if I'm to pursue this matter, it's time to be pro-active and I'm determined to bring it into the open." Tension showed in John's face.

"Sow the seeds and publish what you have already." Evan said. "It's a start and if you don't get sued for defamation or get prosecuted, then it's a validation."

"What if I do get sued or prosecuted?"

"You'll get your publicity." Evan pushed his hands out. "But they've got nothing to gain by doing anything after you've published your material, except draw attention to it."

"What about you?" He asked.

"What about me?"

"Well, what are you going to do now?"

Evan looked around again. "I'm going to take a short trip over the Channel for a while because they'll know what I've been doing very shortly and there are few places to hide."

"What will you do there?"

"I'll take some precautions and when the time is right, I'll come out of the closet, but it'll cost me my job and pension or worse."

"How will I get hold of you to collect the other information you promised me?" John asked.

"I'll get the material to you one way or another." He said. "If I can find some additional information about the plane which crashed in Pennsylvania, I'll get it to you."

"Thanks."

"As you know, I'm sure the plans went awry when it took off more than forty minutes late from Newark."

"And the passengers?"

"The passengers may have tried to overwhelm the hijackers, but by this time the two planes had already crashed into the Twin Towers and they could no longer justify watching this aircraft flying south, delayed from its intended flight time." Evan replied. "But I wouldn't believe the recordings of the mobile telephones."

"So what do you think happened?" John asked.

"The mobile telephones would not have worked in the aircraft at that time and at that height, so they were recorded afterwards and if you amplify the recordings, one of them can even be heard at the end saying something like 'well done'."

"But why did they have to destroy it?" John asked.

"If the passengers on Flight 93 had overwhelmed the terrorists, they'd have been faced with live hijackers who could have spilt the beans." Evan smiled. "Either way, it would have spoilt the whole plan and the game would have been up."

"And presumably because the flight had been delayed, there would have been fighter jets over New York and Washington by this time?" John asked.

"I'm sure they needed to shoot it down to protect the whole operation." He replied. "High level officials became involved in the normal intelligence activity of compartmentalization to restrict knowledge." He lowered his voice. "It's what happens."

John's mouth opened and quickly shut again. "If you genuinely believe they shot their own aircraft out of the sky, then any sustainable evidence to prove it would help my piece."

"I'm sure of it, but why not get someone over there to take some witness statements."

"What about the original lists of passengers?" John asked.

"I can get you copies of the manifest easily enough, but the original list of passengers handed out by the FBI didn't have many of these so-called hijackers."

"That's what I understood."

Evan nodded. "Half of those subsequently accused have been found to be very much alive and not involved in terrorism whatsoever."

"So what do you suggest I do by way of evidence-gathering?" A frustrated edge echoed.

"Why don't you explore the evidence to prove that mobile cell calls could not at that time be made at an altitude of more than 8000 feet?" Evan asked.

"Is that right?" He grunted, tilting his head. "I'm still struggling to comprehend why they felt the need to take such drastic action against Flight 93?"

Evan allowed a faint smile to cross his face. "They'd have been left with no alternative if you think about it for a moment." He stared at John. "Its mission may not have been Washington at all, as I've explained, but it was still 150 miles north-west of Washington and I'm sure the original plan involved hiding the evidence in Building Seven."

"So what happened?" John asked.

"As the delay caused it to fail in its primary objective, it could never have been picked up by the beacon, due to its distance from the control centre, so they had to do something."

"So perhaps the alleged hijackers were involved in some sort of incident in the air by this time."

"Think about it, John." Evan replied. "It was already way behind its schedule, so this aircraft would have been confronted by other military aircraft in the air and plan B had to be implemented."

"And Plan B?" John asked.

"They couldn't allow the aircraft to land." Evan said firmly.

"I can see that it would have caused problems."

Evan felt a squall of rain hit his face and looked up at the sky. "Once the aircraft couldn't be used for its original target, it had to be destroyed."

John thought for a moment. "I suppose the live hijackers on board may have been an embarrassment, perhaps leading to a different view of events after questioning?"

"Exactly."

"So how could they take the chance?" John asked a rhetorical question.

"For certain." Evan replied.

John moved back a few feet under the cover of the doorway of the club and Evan moved alongside. "More than any other aircraft, they had the sort of passengers on board who could easily have overwhelmed hijackers armed only with paper-cutters." John said.

Evan nodded. "And any fracas on the flight-deck would only have involved, at worst, a minor blip on the control of the aircraft; perhaps a drop of 1000 feet whilst it took place."

"I suppose it could not explain a crash."

"You're getting the picture." Evan said.

"And it certainly wouldn't have been in the interests of the hijackers to crash the plane in Shanksville." John said.

"Precisely."

John shook his head. "It would explain why the debris was scattered over a distance of eight miles, so didn't resemble a normal crash site with large parts of fuselage and body parts all within a short distance."

"It looks that way, but I need more evidence before reaching any conclusions and I can't promise anything."

"If you do gather additional evidence, how long will it take?"

"I've told you, I can't promise anything because I'm breaking ranks." Evan looked at the taxi arriving, then back to John. "You must understand they control me financially and although I'm divorced, like you I've a child to consider too and I'd like to support my family. They know the death of my colleague is intended to be a deterrent to anyone thinking of freelancing or breaching the Official Secrets Act."

"I understand." John said. "You've given me more information than I could realistically expect, so watch your back."

Evan patted his left arm gently. "I've taken a risk, but felt compelled to do it."

John walked towards the taxi. "Park Lane." He said, entering the taxi, raising his hand to acknowledge Evan, as it moved away.

*   *   *

The call to prayers was compelling, touching the deepest part of Mohammed's soul and raising his spirit to a level which transcended logic or rationale. It must have been a past life memory, which triggered the emotions, as he could recall feeling the same way even as a young child when he would not have understood its spiritual significance. Endorphins sent out from the brain lifted his heart to the point of ecstasy. The message of comradeship, of purpose and of validation of Islam was intoxicating in its message of a fraternity of faith and the global Ummah or brotherhood and the rapture within his heart of being one with the Prophet. He knew only Muslims could defeat the divisions created by deviant Islam, which flouted the basic tenets of the teachings of Mohammed in the need for harmony, for tolerance and for compassion. Yet he could never reconcile the Sheikh's alliances with Jews, even American Jews.

Mohammed spent more time at prayer this particular Friday and more time in penance, feeding the beads between his hands frenetically. It was only in the shadow of death did his heavy heart realize the extent to which he longed to live and watch his children thrive, but his course was inevitably set.

By the time he had travelled to the rugged country bordering Pakistan and Afghanistan, his mind was single-focused on its last unique purpose. He felt the Sheikh had become a man of flimsy spiritual values, still not fully appreciating the virtues of healing the rifts between Muslims. In sharing his bed with odd bed-fellows, and Jews were strange bed-fellows, he believed the Sheikh a heretic, so determined to carry out his instructions without remorse.

The Sheikh had moved to another remote mountain village outpost, living in a walled house with friends and guards to the side of a ridge of trees shielding the house from the worst of the weather, now that the first blast of winter was about to cast its cold shadow again and a low mist shrouded the hills in the distance. Eventually, Mohammed met him, carrying his AK-47 assault rifle, as always, with trusted guards hovering around him.

"Wah Salaam Alaikum, Sheikh." He said, gesturing with his hands against his forehead and heart. The Sheikh gestured back. About half a dozen of his guards followed suit. Mohammed observed the numbers at the house and tried to put his old friend at ease.

The Sheikh walked up to him fearlessly. "I had your message, but what brings you here, Mohammed?"

"The UAE Station Chief wanted me to speak to you about the political vacuum in Pakistan." He replied. "He hoped you'd listen to reason and avoid any criticism of the regime, especially as your brothers hope to influence you to change your course."

"Is that right?" The Sheikh asked, the tone unnerving Mohammed.

"I'm just the messenger." Mohammed replied quickly.

The Sheikh smiled. "And what if I'm not open to persuasion?"

Mohammed rubbed his hands together. "What do you mean?"

"I think you know what I mean." The Sheikh opened up his arms and offered an embrace, which he accepted without hesitation.

Mohammed felt ill at ease, knowing the way controllers worked and it had already occurred to him that it may not suit the Americans if he was to be found alive in the same way as the others. He was not naïve enough to believe he had been sent on this errand solely for the purpose suggested by a diligent intelligence officer. "Don't you trust me, Sheikh?" He asked, nervously.

"Why should I?" The Sheikh fenced with him.

"Because I've always counselled you honestly, even if I've never been one of your lackeys." He chose his words carefully.

"It's not you I mistrust, but the Agency." The Sheikh replied. "It's as fickle as the wind."

"What can I say, Sheikh?"

He looked directly into his eyes and smiled. "You're just the sort of person to be sent to do their dirty work and, frankly, I've been expecting someone."

Mohammed shook his head. "I don't think you understand my purpose."

"Perhaps I'm wrong." The Sheikh said. "But the Agency is already setting up its connections with the future leaders of Pakistan under the guise of democracy. Perhaps they've forgotten about the loose ends."

Mohammed felt a foreboding, but ignored it. "Maybe they still need the army." He said. "You'll have to be careful, Sheikh."

The Sheikh grunted, but said nothing.

"Sometimes you hear only the words and not the spirit behind them, Sheikh."

"I hear everything, but let's talk as friends for a time." The Sheikh smiled. "Why don't we talk about old times?"

"I'd like that." Mohammed replied, relaxing a little.

"We can amuse ourselves by discussing the events of 9/11 and wonder at how the American government got away with it all in the face of such overwhelming and obvious contradictions." He smiled again. "Even you didn't believe it was possible, Mohammed." He turned to him. "Do you remember?"

Mohammed smiled back spontaneously, for the majority of people had been so patently gullible. "Sure." He turned his hands out. "They say the definition of a conspiracy theory is a theory not backed up by the evidence. If so, the only conspiracy theory is the one put out by the U.S. government."

"You're right, of course." The Sheikh grimaced. "The weight of evidence clearly pointed to an inside job." He looked unwell and when he moved it was like an old man, bones creaking, movements slow and cumbersome. "Even with the manipulated anthrax scare, soon after the events of 9/11, they seem to have got away with it all."

Mohammed nodded. "Despite a number of scientists confirming the concentrated anthrax could only have been manufactured at a United States military facility, as it was too concentrated to be Russian anthrax or anything terrorists could access."

The Sheikh smiled again. "You would have thought the American people would see the clue when it emerged that the President and his entourage had been taking the anti-anthrax medication, Cipro, a month before the scare."

"It's no surprise there was never an indictment for it." Mohammed said.

The Sheikh took a deep breath. "Did you know a considerable number of the scientists, who confirmed the military source of the anthrax, died in mysterious circumstances shortly afterwards?"

Mohammed nodded. "Why don't their people see the truth?"

"You shouldn't be surprised, Mohammed." He replied, wincing. "The media will only publish the government line. It's why Muslims refer to the United States as the Great Satan."

"Yet we've taken their money and been on their payroll, so what does it make us?" Mohammed asked.

The Sheikh looked intensely at him. "Prostitutes I suppose." He said starkly, out of character.

Mohammed shivered, as if someone had walked over his grave again. "You're right." He walked towards the main house within the walled encampment, keeping to the slow pace of the Sheikh. "But what if we've got a higher motive?"

"Really?" The Sheikh turned to him.

"Does that absolve us of responsibility for our actions?" Mohammed asked.

The Sheikh shrugged. "It's a tainted world and we're all imperfect souls."

Mohammed continued to walk towards the house until the Sheikh deviated on the path, turning towards an area where some of his men were undergoing training. He recognized the Commander, from the brutal execution of a Muslim brother on his last visit. His stomach knotted and he felt uneasy. "Do you think all the contradictory evidence of the events of 9/11 will eventually emerge or will we always be the bad guys?" He wondered if this was his opportunity, but hesitated knowing by the time he took out his hidden handgun he may only get one shot off and would be brutally dealt with instantly by the bodyguards who still hovered around the Sheikh. The hesitation was his final mistake.

"Maybe one day, but not yet." The Sheikh stroked his beard and looked at Mohammed with sorrowful eyes.

"What about ordinary people, Sheikh?" His voice cracked.

"If the ruling classes are purged from time to time, it's good for the ordinary people." He replied. "The powerful elite families believe they're immune and treat the American people as idiots, but events may change their minds."

"What events?" Mohammed asked, growing more nervous and agitated, his voice sounding hesitant and movements less fluid.

"My friend, I'm afraid you'll never know."

A soldier with an AK-47 rifle emerged from the front of the training group and the Sheikh nodded to him. He adjusted his belt of bullets, cocking the rifle and removing its safety catch before sliding the bullet chamber.

The sound cut Mohammed like a knife. "What are you doing?" He asked, even if he already knew the answer. He stood still, involuntarily, looking sad and defeated, his body shaking out of control in the moment. Incongruously, his mind remained active and many thoughts raced into his head, mainly anguished unanswered questions. As always the intelligence officer was playing both sides against the middle in traditional fashion and now it was his turn, as with so many double agents, to pay the piper. He searched for the handgun beneath his clothing and wondered if he had enough time to reach for it, but fumbled and the moment was lost.

Mohammed felt the barrel of the Sheikh's AK-47 prod him in the ribs. "Don't even think about it."

"You asked what I was doing." The Sheikh said.

"It seems unimportant now." Mohammed stammered.

"The answer is simple." The Sheikh said. "I'm doing the dirty work of the Americans again." A soulful expression crossed his face. "You forget I've been working for the CIA since 1986 and I've friends in high places, so you simply can't be allowed to turn up unannounced." He shrugged. "They worry about the loose ends."

Mohammed nodded, rooted to the spot. He looked around for an escape, but realised the futility of his position, making one final plea, an agonised expression staining his face. "I didn't think you'd kill old friends too?" He looked at the Sheikh pitifully, his eyes hollow. "They're making Muslims kill Muslims." He hesitated. "Don't you see?"

"I understand completely." He replied.

"What about my family?"

"I promise I'll look after them and your children will get the education you craved." Some compassion resonated in his voice and Mohammed believed him. "You deserve at least that old friend."

"Then this is it?" His voice cracked again, but mustering courage, not wanting to die a coward's death, which seemed important to him in the moment.

"Mohammed." The Sheikh said. "I know they instructed you to kill me, but it's you they really need to take out of the picture and I'm surprised you didn't see it?" His voice softened and he looked at the soldier and nodded. The soldier took aim, looking at the Sheikh for the final instruction.

"Wait." Mohammed said, lifting his hand.

"But they can't have you turning up unannounced, Mohammed." The Sheikh said. "It would let the cat out of the bag about the real 9/11 events." He hesitated as if he wanted an answer, but Mohammed could not respond, his mind remained in a vortex preparing for a transition to another world. "You're supposed to be dead, but you're a liability to them."

Mohammed took a deep breath, it occurred to him it was his last, and took a last twisted look at the Sheikh. "As I suspected all along, you've always been working for the secret agenda of the western governments." The thought of the futility of his actions remained the overwhelming idea etched in his mind. "But the people followed you and believed in you, not realizing you were a quisling working for the American elite."

"You worked for the Americans too and took their money." The Sheikh said. "You're as much a whore as I am, Mohammed."

"But." Mohammed managed a second breath and wanted to say something of consequence. For a split second, he saw an image of his family in his mind's eye. He prayed for one more opportunity to see them, but knew it could never be. There was fear, but not a fear of death itself, more the uncertainty of the ending and the doubts of a wasted lifetime's beliefs. It was as if in the instant, he had a revelation about what was true and what was important in the scheme of things, more a recognition of his soul's purpose in this lifetime and how he had deviated from it, but he wondered why it came too late for redemption. "What about you, Sheikh?" He looked directly into his eyes. "You'll be the next."

"Time will be my assassin and he's breathing heavily over my shoulder." The Sheikh said starkly. "I know it'll be my turn one day and I've no illusions about it."

"Are you going to pull the trigger, Sheikh, or are you going to leave it to others again?" He reached a point of no fear or doubts, just a return home.

"Does it matter?" He asked.

"If you don't know the answer, I can't tell you." He replied, being closer to his soul than the Sheikh at that moment and strangely seeing things with a greater clarity in his final moments.

His head dropped and he slumped to his knees. "I'm ready, Sheikh." He tilted towards the ground as if in prayer and in his own way it was a final act of submission to his God.

The Sheikh nodded again to the soldier. The last thing Mohammed felt was the thud of a bullet, then nothing, not even pain, as his spirit departed from his body, in a final sweet release.

CHAPTER ELEVEN

The Times of London—3rd September 2001:

"On September 3rd the Federal Aviation Authority made an emergency ruling to prevent Mr (Salman) Rushdie from flying unless airlines complied with strict and costly security measures. Mr Rushdie told The Times that the airlines would not upgrade their security."

A hugely decorated officer with inside knowledge of military protocol has declared 9/11 was an Inside Job. He has stated that it is apparent to him the massive military exercises that took place on 9/11 were intentionally staged to confuse civil defences.

Another quote refers to " . . . if a stand down order were given it would probably have to come from as high as the Vice President." Other video evidence, including that of the Secretary of Transportation, who was in the White House relates a young man telling the Vice President when Flight 77 was fifty miles, then thirty miles from Washington, then ten miles away. He asked the VP, "Do the orders still stand?" The Vice President turned to him, stating "Of course the orders still stand. Have you heard anything to the contrary?"

Fire induced collapse is organic with a gradual degradation and results in a toppling over chaotically due to organic weakness caused by fire and it has totally different characteristics from an explosion, which implodes and collapses vertically and

symmetrically into its own footprint. Fire does not cause 90,000 tons of concrete and steel to vapourize into dust, nor 47 core columns to fail, nor would fire eject concrete and lumps of steel out of the building, many hitting buildings across the street and some six hundred feet away. Gravity alone cannot explain the speed and distance of these steel ejections, nor can it explain how seven hundred bone fragments, each half inch long, were found on top of a nearby skyscraper.

A Structural Engineer states—"The prevailing (official) theory would have us believe that each of the Twin Towers inexplicably collapsed upon itself crushing all 287 massive columns on each floor while maintaining a free-fall speed as if the 100,000 tons or more of supporting steel framework (and five inches of reinforced concrete on each floor) did not exist."

I t's been a long time." George said, as Nadia settled into a cushioned, brocade-edged chair opposite him in the quiet lounge of a popular hotel in Central London. Designer sunglasses perched precariously on her elfish nose. She adjusted them expertly, looking intently at this unattractive man. They may have been indoors, but she needed an artificial barrier to shield her from the prying eyes of the man she despised. They sat in one of the quieter corners of the room, so no-one would pass directly across them as they entered or left and her chair touched heavily-lined curtains behind her.

"How have you been?" A smug expression, the sort only gained from carnal knowledge, crept across every pore in his face, like some poisonous ivy, as he recalled the previous intimacy.

She shook her head, feeling his eyes penetrating her clothing, undressing her again. It sickened her, but she determined not to be a victim again and beneath the sunglasses she adopted an assessing squint, scrutinizing her unsuspecting prey. She had purposely chosen a public venue for a meeting to avoid unpleasantness, though she would have preferred to have avoided all contact with a man she detested. Although she found him repulsive, the meeting was necessary to carry through her plans, whatever the personal cost.

"I'm not here for pleasantries." A harsh edge reflected in the tone. "I need to put a proposal to you and I believe this is in John's interests or I wouldn't be here."

"Why should I help you?" He asked coldly, beads of perspiration dripping from his forehead.

A waiter dressed in black blazer and pin-striped trousers attended the table, inviting an order. She ordered coffee, but George needed a gin and tonic, having become dependent on a stiff drink to carry him through a stress-laden life.

When the waiter left, she leant forward across the white-clothed table, pulling the sunglasses down on her nose, so she could observe him squirm. "Perhaps you don't understand my position." She lowered her voice. "If I need to tell John what happened when you raped me, I'll do it."

He sneered. "It's a bit late for that now my dear, don't you think?" He leaned back in his chair cockily. "Anyway, what have you got to gain by such a frank confession at this late stage?" He paused again, as if wanting to milk the moment, convinced he had nothing to fear in the threat. "John will blame you at some level and will wonder why you didn't tell him earlier, if it were true."

"Maybe." She said, with a confidence which surprised him.

"Anyway, my recollection is you consented to that little episode."

"It was little and you know I didn't consent." She said coldly and sarcastically, determined to savour her revenge.

"Do you think John is going to believe you and, even if he did, it would be the death-knell for your relationship.

The waiter returned with a tray, depositing the coffee, milk and sugar on the table, then turning to George, placed the glass of gin, ice rattling, on the table, placing a small amount of tonic in the glass before placing the tonic bottle to its side, before moving away.

She turned to George again. "I've already decided to end our relationship and move out of the apartment, but there are things I intend to do first." She still felt revulsion at the memory of their past encounter, but took a deep breath. "Now it's time for me to tell you some brutal facts." She sat back. "I was recruited by MI6 some considerable time ago, as there are many advantages for a Muslim working in predominantly Muslim countries without drawing attention to myself and I've the perfect cover as a journalist." She smiled. "Journalists are supposed to ask lots of questions."

"Why are you telling me now?" He asked, strangely fascinated.

"Be patient." She poured milk into her coffee, adding a little sugar, stirring the cup and taking a sip to taste, before slipping the cup back into its saucer.

"I assume John has no idea?" He asked, more subdued.

She smiled again, taking satisfaction at his change of demeanour. "Of course not, but I've had to complete intelligence reports on my relationship." She took a large sip of coffee. "It's not my finest hour."

He shook his head. "I don't believe it."

She sneered. "Even the meeting when you raped me was only undertaken because I was instructed to find out how much information you had in your possession." She shrugged. "My report at that time logged your rape and I underwent a medical examination to establish the rape and my injuries. I gave a detailed signed Witness Statement to my handler for recent complaint purposes." She hesitated, revelling for a moment in the palpable discomfort of her victim. "Don't pretend you're immune from prosecution, as I could still use the intelligence log, the witness statement and the medical report, which revealed obvious signs of violence, as evidence of immediate complaint and forced sexual intercourse."

"It's too late for that and anyway I'll say you consented." He said dismissively, moving uncomfortably in his chair.

She smiled. "Rape is not an offence which is bound by time limitations or constraints and the medical report establishes forced sexual contact. My handler has told me he'll support a complaint, if I decide to make it. I can explain away the delay because I was trying to salvage a relationship which has since floundered." She looked across at him, his face etching a sad picture and his mouth dropped open. "If you divulge anything about this meeting or anything I tell you, I promise you with everything that's sacred to me, I'll pursue the complaint."

He slumped forward in his chair, his face ashen. "I still don't believe you." He stammered with little conviction. "I know you and you'll never do it."

"You never knew me." She said firmly.

He sat back, shaking his head. "I still don't believe it."

"It gets worse." She said. "I also have evidence of your complicity with the intelligence community and reports you've filed about John. I've got the copies in my possession, signed by you." Her eyes narrowed. "Do you want me to show them to him?" She asked.

He shifted in his chair once again, his complexion drawn, and took a handkerchief out of his pocket to mop his brow. "You wouldn't do it."

She unzipped her bag and took out documents. "Here's a copy of the medical report for you." She pointed to the second bundle of documents. "And here are copies of the intelligence reports you've filed." She dumped them on the table. "Do you recognize the signatures?" He snatched them and began reading. "You can keep them." She said. "They're only copies, of course, not the originals."

He looked up from reading the reports. "I still don't believe you'd do this. You've nothing to gain."

"What about revenge, an old-fashioned motive." She said, coldly.

"Not after all this time."

"Do you really think I'd tell you about my links with the intelligence service, if I was the slightest bit concerned about what you could do to hurt me?"

His head dropped. "You're just bluffing."

She sneered again. "Don't be absurd." She said. "What have I got to lose now the relationship with John is over and will never be resurrected?"

"But you'll never give evidence against me on an allegation of rape?"

She nodded. "I promise you, I'll not hesitate to give evidence against you."

"A jury would never believe you after all this time."

She scoffed, unable to resist a little ridicule. "Even if you managed to persuade a jury of your innocence, you'd have a trial hanging over your head for months. My handler has told me he'll have a word with the Crown Prosecution Service and ask them to make an application for a remand in custody. As you know, it's one of the few offences where there's no presumption in favour of bail, so you'll have to take your chances."

His eyes bulged in their sockets. "Are you blackmailing me?"

"Let's say I'm telling you the facts."

"So what do you want?" His voice cracked. "You could just file the complaint without any need to discuss it with me, unless you want something." His experience as an Editor and journalist kicked in.

She nodded. "It's simple." She said. "I've been given a cast-iron assurance by my brother that provided I recover all original and copy documents John has in his possession in relation to the events of 9/11, which includes the documents you presently hold, then no harm will come to him from the Langley side."

He raised his bushy eyebrows. "But how can you trust these people?" He looked at her with disdain. "They'd blackmail their mother, if there was a benefit for them in it."

She nodded. "Maybe, but I've enough information to cause problems if they don't keep their promises. Besides, my brother in New York has a friend who does contract work for Mossad and he's confirmed the deal." She took a sip of her coffee. "I'm satisfied John will be left alone."

"And your brother trusts someone working for Mossad?"

"My brother has a colleague who has infiltrated an al-Qaeda cell in New York, so they wouldn't say it, unless it was true." She said candidly, though belatedly regretting the candour.

He sighed. "You must be confident, if you're telling me this stuff, but what if I was to tell my connections about your brother?"

She laughed loudly. "I'm confident you'll find good reason not to do it. In any event, it's just your word against mine." She sipped the last of her coffee and looked across at George, still feeling ill at ease in his company.

"So how am I supposed to do this?"

"I want the original documents today."

"What now?"

She nodded. "I'll go back to your office with you now." She said. "You must give me all of the documents, including John's piece, though that's less critical. If you try to double-cross, or keep copies of any of the documents, then they'll contract out the problem." She placed her elbows on the table, placing her hands together. "I don't think that would be a good idea. Do you?"

He grunted, but did not reply

"These people won't discuss the matter with you reasonably, as I'm doing."

"You really want me to go to my office right now?" His voice reflected resignation.

"Of course. I've told you. Now." She placed emphasis on the last word.

He shook his head. "I didn't realise you were such a hard bitch."

She laughed again, taking pleasure in his discomfort. "I told you that you didn't know me."

"Obviously not."

"Life has made me this way". She said coldly, standing up from the table and gathering her handbag. "Shall we go?"

*   *   *

Within twenty four hours, Nadia was in New York, discussing events with her brother. Not even jet-lag would allow her the peaceful sleep she craved, but more than anything she needed redemption. She hated her brother's apartment, low down in the block, so you could hear a constant traffic drone, even the sound of neighbours arguing through paper-thin walls.

"I need you to speak to my man here about what your friend John is doing." Her brother said, brazenly. He was a swarthy man in his early forties, bespectacled and well-groomed, who could have passed for a Jew, Arab or an Asian. In fact, the perfect recruit for his vocation.

She shook her head. "I've done enough talking to intelligence people, but I want to protect John or I wouldn't be here." She gave her brother a fierce glance. "You promised if I passed these documents to you, no harm will come to him and I've kept my part of the bargain." She raised her voice. "You keep your part or you'll never see me again and you'll cease to be my brother."

He raised both hands in the air palms downwards. "Be calm." He hesitated, surprised by his sister's firmness. "The deal will be honoured, but they just want a full report."

Her eyes blazed. "Don't you dare backtrack or you'll regret it." She said. "You promise me now they'll not harm him."

He nodded. "Of course not, but I can't speak for British intelligence because they'll not be bound by Langley promises."

She groaned. "This is semantics and I acted in good faith."

"Nadia, you're being naïve."

"What are you going to do about it?" A forlorn expression masked her face.

"I don't know, but if I explain your assistance in this matter, I'm sure they'll persuade London to hold off on your man."

"What do you mean, 'if'?" She asked.

"Nothing, just an expression."

"Then just do it, or there'll be a serious falling out between us." She said. "You're not going to play your intelligence games with me."

"Don't worry, Nad."

She looked steely-eyed. "You must help me or in my eyes you'll not be my brother."

"There are books being written and conspiracy theorists coming out of the woodwork everywhere, so I'm sure they'll do me a favour." He looked directly into Nadia's eyes. "But if they asked you to do a favour in return, would you do it?"

She sighed loudly, stamping her foot on the floor. "Not again."

"Just this once."

"I know the game, but you mustn't play me this way."

"I 'm not, Nad."

"I'm not a fool." She said. "I've been down this road before and I'm out of their clutches forever." She placed the palm of her left hand on the back of her neck, rubbing it, walking around in a circle before facing him again. "They've fucked up my life already and I need to get away from them, so don't drag me back in."

He nodded. "But they need female operatives with linguistic skills, who blend easily into middle-eastern and far-eastern countries, so from their point of view, you're too good an asset to lose."

"This is not what I want." She sat down heavily on the sofa. "I'm your sister and I'm asking you for help please."

"They'll look after you sis, as they've looked after me." He spoke stoically, as if pitching for a sales job.

"You can't be serious." Her eyes widened, nostrils flaring.

"But what are you intending to do here if you want to live?" He asked. "The United States is not the easiest place to live with no money."

Her jaw tightened. "For the last time, I'm telling you not to do this."

"All I'm asking is what are you intending to do?"

She shrugged. "For starters, have a holiday away from the stress I've endured in London, dealing with intelligence freaks." She hesitated. "At this moment, it's one day at a time and you're not going to make me think differently."

"But after your holiday?"

"Go home and start all over again. If I did stay and they gave me my green card, as they promised, I'd want to write." She looked directly at him. "One thing is for sure, I'm not getting involved in intelligence work ever again."

"It's not so easy to get the right jobs in journalism over here."

"I'm your sister and you want to place me at risk again." She shook her head. "I can't believe it."

"You misunderstand me." He said softly.

"This is a dangerous time with intelligence people killing each other on everyone else's territory and all the rules are out of the window." She glared at him. "Don't you dare place me back in the firing line."

He shrugged. "Well think about it and we'll talk about it tomorrow. If John has no immunity in the U.K, you might want to consider it."

"I'll sort out the London end myself." She said.

"Well you'd better act quickly, as they may call on him tomorrow unannounced." He said.

"Then I want him out of there." She moved towards the telephone, but he stopped her, placing her gently back onto the sofa. "If you do that, you'll place my life in jeopardy, so hold back on it for now."

"No." She reached for the telephone. "You may be my brother, but I don't trust you anymore."

He restrained her gently. "Listen to me." He sat down on the sofa alongside her. "You may place John's life in greater danger and there are other matters you need to know about him and his investigations."

She shook her head. "There's nothing you could say, which would prevent me helping a man I've loved more than any other and to my dying day I'll regret ever listening to you."

*   *   *

Evan walked towards the apartment block, taking safeguards to protect against surveillance and clutching a folder tightly, as if his life depended on it. He had decided to freelance on the side and there were risks. In his world, he knew there was no such thing as complete protection against surveillance because it was a contradiction in terms, but he had an electric device in his other hand. Once inside, he took the lift to the penthouse floor and rang the doorbell.

John answered bare-footed, wearing boxer shorts and a tee shirt. He had reading spectacles on the end of his nose, which almost fell off when he saw him. "I didn't expect to see you tonight."

Evan placed his right index finger to his mouth with a "ssh" and pointed inside the apartment. John ushered him inside with a flowing gesture of his left hand, but said nothing, as instructed. The electrical device had a red and green light on it and as it neared the telephone junction box on the wall, it emitted a strong buzzing sound and the red light became bright. Evan took a screwdriver out of his coat pocket and unscrewed the box and with a gentle pull removed the surveillance device from the socket, disabling it in the process. He held it in the air, as if in triumph before fixing the junction box back into its original position. John observed patiently and quietly as Evan checked the rest of the apartment with his machine, then watched as he dismantled the light fitting in the lounge, pulling a miniature camera from its fitting, within the ceiling rose, smiling as he held it. He completed his sweep of the apartment, seemingly satisfied and walked back into the living room.

"Don't you have a girl who lives here with you?" He asked.

"She's left a note saying something had cropped up and had to visit her brother in New York." John replied. "So you're safe to talk freely."

Evan shrugged, tilting his head. "Really."

"Yes. I'm on my own."

"Just as well." He looked around the room, stationing himself at the window "It's time to give you more information, whilst there's still time." He looked drained, his face gaunt with bloodshot eyes in need of restorative sleep. "I've held back some information for reasons of self-preservation, but I must pass it to you before it's too late."

"What information?" John asked.

"There are dark forces controlling events, even here in the U.K. Although the United States is viewed as the Great Satan in the eyes of Muslims, the Americans learnt their dirty trade from us."

John looked at the clock on the mantelpiece, noting it was almost midnight. Evan moved from the window and sat down with the thump of a tired man, placing his folder alongside him.

"Can I get you something?" John asked.

"I'd love a gin and tonic."

John nodded, slipping into the bedroom to put on a dressing gown and afterwards into the kitchen to make the gin and tonic. He knew Evan used alcohol to combat stress and needed it, as a drug addict needs his fix, before properly functioning again. As a former priest, he often analysed behavioural patterns and knew Evan was running away from the truth about some aspect of his life and without confronting it he could never escape his demons or achieve salvation. This analysis should have allowed him to reach a different judgment of his character.

"What's made you take the risk of coming to see me in the middle of the night?" John offered the gin and tonic.

Evan took a deep breath and sighed; a long silence followed before he spoke. "You know, of course, that there's American government complicity in the events of 9/11."

John nodded. "The evidence is overwhelming."

Evan smiled quirkily, a disingenuous sort of smile. "Yet you believe the events of 7th July 2005 in London are genuine terrorist atrocities?"

John's body straightened, his attention focused. "Are you suggesting otherwise?"

Evan took a sip of his gin and tonic, before replying. "I'm going to tell you something, which may have grave consequences for me. It's equally shocking and as in the United States no-one will want to believe it." He turned to John. "They'd rather believe the lie."

John sat down next to Evan. "What are you telling me?"

Evan took another deep breath. "It's the reason they needed to silence Lynne, as she had the same information I'm now passing to you."

John shifted his position.

"For her, it was something closer to home than the 9/11 events." Evan said.

John felt uncomfortable for some reason. "What frightened them?"

"She had wanted to reveal certain information to her Select Committee in open session in Parliament, where she could rely on privilege to avoid any action in the civil courts, whether defamation or otherwise."

"I'm listening."

Evan nodded. "She felt the publicity the statement would attract would provide her with a level of protection."

John shivered. "She told me she had considered raising questions at Prime Minister's Question Time, but was always ambushed every time she tried."

"She told me the same thing." Evan said. "But this information may place you in greater jeopardy, John."

John nodded. "I understand, but it's a familiar experience for me and it goes with the territory."

Evan took another drink, before turning to John again. "You mustn't let the authorities know you've received this information." He hesitated. "It's far too sensitive."

"I'll have to do my best"

"If the truth is known, there'll never be any confidence in politicians or the intelligence services ever again."

John sneered. "I don't think there's much confidence in politicians at present, do you?"

"But they'll kill to protect their positions and justify it as in the public's best interests." He reached for the folder by his side. "They always do."

John stretched out on the sofa. Any natural intuitive doubts harboured towards Evan had proved inaccurate and it led him to feel more comfortable in his presence. For his part, he accepted the risks and his training as a priest had made him philosophical about the illusory nature of life. "If you want me to give you permission to divulge these things, knowing the risks, then I'm telling you go ahead."

"Very well." Evan shuffled the documents in the folder. "I've evidence in here, which explains a project to lure innocent Muslims into an assignment in which they would become victims of an atrocity almost as appalling as 9/11." He handed it to John. "It beggars belief a government or intelligence organization would be capable of undertaking it." He looked at John with anxious eyes, pleading for redemption. "If I wasn't already in this game, I wouldn't believe it."

John had seen this vulnerable side to people many times and recognized in it the deeper needs and impulses from the soul. Though he had escaped his former life as a priest, he still picked up on a person's finer qualities, even if he often missed their darker side completely. "Your selfless actions will ultimately become your redemption, Evan." He placed his hand on his arm.

"Do you think so?" Evan asked, relaxing and leaning back.

"Perhaps your conscience requires you to pass on this information if you're to be at peace, Evan." John's boyish attitude to morality misinterpreted character.

Evan sighed. "You're a good man."

John shook his head. "Life should be a question of service, to God and to man."

Evan grunted.

"It gives me peace to sleep at night." John clicked into clichéd priest mode briefly, stumbling like a schizophrenic from priest to journalist.

"I'm not into the religion thing." Evan said.

"Neither am I." John smiled.

"But you were a priest?" Evan's voice arched.

John smiled again. "I believe in spirituality, but not the idea that one creed or religion is superior to another or that you need a church or religion as an intermediary to reach God. Such an idea is anathema to me and only an ignorant man or a bigot could believe such a concept." He sat up. "It's the development of character which counts and the harmonisation of our actions with the essence of the universal spirit of which we're all a part."

Evan looked bemused. "That's too much for me."

"In my experience, there's a unity in all things, whether you view them as a priest or a humanist." John said, the priest never far from the surface.

Evan shook his head, taking the folder and handing it to John. "Look at the memoranda and documents in there before I tell you what happened on the 7ᵗʰ July 2005 in London." He leaned back.

John took the folder, intrigued, perusing its content carefully. After reading the first document, he looked up at Evan. "Is this what really happened?"

Evan nodded. "Four innocent Muslims, not terrorists, recruited because three of them were seen as friendly Muslims, often assisting the Police as mediators with other more politically motivated brethren. Three of them clean skins, manipulated and used by another Muslim agent."

"What are 'clean skins?" He asked.

"It means they had never come to the attention of the intelligence or the police authorities." He replied. "Neither did any of them fit the profile of a suicide bomber. Mohammed Siddique Khan worked with special needs children, as a teacher's assistant and also as youth worker, the Police trusting him as a mediator with more militant Muslims. His wife was expecting their second child at the time, all unusual factors."

John nodded. "I'm with you so far, but what about the fourth one?"

"They needed a radicalized fourth person with some connection to Al-Qaeda, so if it became necessary to justify their conclusions and get the media to incriminate at least one of them, there'd be evidence of militancy against that person."

"So explain how it happened?"

Evan took a deep breath. "They were asked to do a mock training exercise, which could help prevent a future terrorist attack, by allowing them to monitor and follow their progress, mimicking the carrying of mock explosives in backpacks. Although they would have been paid extremely well for their help, it was emphasized they had to keep this top-secret, even from their families, if the exercise was to work properly and efficiently, otherwise they would not be paid."

"But why would they do it?" John asked.

"They'd have been approached by someone with a becoming smile, a Muslim, or someone of their generation, probably the MI6 Agent Aswat, who would have told them this would help the authorities in preventing any potential terrorist attacks in the future and provide a service to their country." Evan took another large sip of his gin and tonic, allowing his head to fall back into the sofa again. "Remember, these were good people and certainly Khan was already providing intelligence information for the authorities, being on the periphery of an MI5 operation in 2004 called

Operation Crevice. This was simply another small step for him, even if it provided a good second income with his second child on the way."

"This is so difficult to believe." John said.

Evan nodded. "But that's exactly what you're up against." He said. "The ordinary person in the street wants to believe his government is protecting them."

"So Khan would have done this willingly?"

He nodded. "He probably took some self-esteem from the work."

"Wouldn't he have wanted his back protected?" John asked.

"He was an innocent, but I do know they cropped his photograph in their records, cutting it in half, for no other reason than to make it difficult for anyone to identify him from the only photograph in their records." He lifted his hands in the air. "It would end up nothing like the actual surveillance photograph and almost indecipherable, so subsequently discarded."

John shook his head. "Is this the way people in intelligence work?"

Evan nodded. "I also know they didn't show his photograph to an al-Qaeda super-grass in the United States, for obvious reasons, declining when questioned, to give complete and accurate information to the Intelligence and Security Committee of the House, as they needed to keep him sweet."

"Remind me about the man Aswat?" John asked. "I've heard his name before."

Evan smiled. "This is the man the US arrested and wanted to indict in 1999, but British Intelligence told their counterparts in the States he was a MI6 Agent, so they released him." He closed his eyes for a moment.

"Take your time." John said.

Evan opened his eyes. "The alleged leader Khan had helped the Police by acting as a go-between in gang problems in the Leeds area where he lived and worked. He was a man normally beyond suspicion who had been taken around the Houses of Parliament by his local Member of Parliament only a matter of weeks before the events of the 7th July."

John shook his head. "It's unbelievable."

"I've told you that's the problem for most people." Evan said. "Remember they'd have gone up to London to do the same thing once before, as they'd have wanted a dummy run to ensure he was reliable and would carry out the instructions precisely. They'd have had a considerable amount of money for their trouble."

"Wouldn't someone have asked questions?"

Evan shook his head. "They'd have been told they could have given their wives or girlfriends a real treat in London the next time with the promise of an even bigger pay-day."

"Is this how they work their contacts?"

"Of course." Evan replied. "They'd have needed three people, though I suspect a decision was made to take an extra patsy for the real event, just in case someone failed to turn up and they needed to be able to incriminate at least one of them if questions were asked."

John read another document, noticing it referred to two Israeli companies based near Luton Train Station, one in charge of the CCTV cameras on the London underground and at Luton Train Station. He held the document in the air. "Mossad?"

Evan nodded again. "The four men were told to meet at Luton Train Station, though three of them had travelled together, as two of them were friends of Khan in the Leeds area." He looked up. "The fourth had been recruited separately with a different agenda."

John read one particular document. "This is hardly believable."

"British Intelligence has done its cover-up more professionally than its American counterpart on this occasion. If something went wrong, they'll deny they recruited Khan, but will suggest he was consorting with terrorists, which he was bound to do if he was working undercover for them."

John shook his head. "But wouldn't they need to produce evidence to explain why they weren't following him, if they allege he was consorting with terrorists?"

"Not necessarily." He sounded evasive.

"This sounds outrageous."

"Because it is outrageous." Evan looked up, eyes widening. "They could simply say there were insufficient funds to invest in the surveillance and it didn't pass the threshold test."

"What's the threshold test?"

"If they've no direct evidence of any planning or commitment to a terrorist event, they'd argue there was no justification in spending the resources." His Welsh lilt creeping into his accent.

"So if they've got evidence of him consorting with terrorists, they'll interpret it as evidence of terrorist intentions?"

"They'd know he'd need to consort with potential terrorists, if he was going to do his job properly, as a friendly Muslim recruited to work undercover." Evan hesitated. "It's the beauty of our game."

John screwed his face up. "It's more than a game."

"But it's not as if they'll ever admit it or produce evidence of their complicity."

"So his name will be smeared wrongly with no hope of redemption for his reputation or for his family?"

"Of course." Evan said, a ragged edge to the tone. "But there are still inaccuracies and mistakes, if you examine the evidence carefully." He pointed to the folder. "There always is."

"But why would they want to kill and maim their own people in the first place?" John's face carried pain, eyes holding anger barely in check, as he recalled the lingering images of the injured and dying, crawling out of the tube stations, blackened and charred, images stained into his psyche.

"If you're asking these questions and doubting the evidence, imagine how difficult it's going to be for ordinary members of the public to accept it?" He rolled his eyes. "They'll be more sceptical, especially as they'll be frightened by the truth."

"You're right." A bleak expression crossed John's face.

"These were not men whose minds had been poisoned and warped by the deviant teachings of Jihadism or capable of committing multiple murder in the normal course of events, at least as far as three of them were concerned/" Evan said. "Yet their families' good names have been stained by the stigma of breeding terrorists."

John noticed another document referring to the cancellation of the 7.40 a.m. train to from Luton to Kings Cross and looked up. "What's the significance of this cancelled tube train?"

"If the alleged bombers were going to get to Kings Cross by 8.26 a.m. then ideally they needed to catch the 7.24 a.m. train from Luton because the 7.40 p.m. train was cancelled and the next one would have been 7.48 p.m., too late to get to Kings Cross on time."

"So did they catch the 7.24 a.m. train?" John asked.

Evan shook his head. "The Luton Station photograph is stamped at 7.21.54 and the 7.24 train departed one minute late at 7.25." He paused to ensure John was following his narrative. "They only had three minutes to climb the stairs, pay for three tickets, wait for the printing of three tickets and move to the platform."

"Are you saying it can't be done?" John asked.

"I've checked it all. It takes three and a half minutes to walk to the platform alone and that would have been without the alleged unstable TATP explosive on their backs, which is very volatile. You don't run with that on your back." He moved his hands in front of him. "They had to buy the tickets and wait for them to print and it takes thirty seconds to print each ticket, so from the evidence of the CCTV footage alone, it would have been impossible."

"But why haven't the Police re-enacted it and realised that themselves?"

Evan smiled, a weary smile, frustrated this man of intellect could not follow the argument. "Because they couldn't." He looked intensely at John. "They had their suspects and weren't looking for anyone else." He hesitated. "Why complicate the investigation?"

"So they didn't place the time and resources together to properly investigate the U.K.'s worst terrorist atrocity?" John mopped his forehead with a handkerchief.

"It's the way it works." Evan looked around, then back at John. "There's always some complicity with the intelligence services. It was the same with the IRA when some of the bomb supplies and arms dealing involved a level of knowledge and compliance with the intelligence services." He smiled. "It's never coincidence."

John's mouth dropped open, but he said nothing. Years of investigative journalism had given him a glimpse of the seedier side of life, but his instinct always sought to look for the good in people.

"They'd have known from examination of the CCTV footage on the underground system that they couldn't have been the bombers." Evan said. "Otherwise, they'd have been seen them on the CCTV at Kings Cross and they'd have produced the evidence for the media, so everyone could judge for themselves."

John nodded. "Of course, no-one has ever produced any CCTV footage of the alleged bombers in the underground and certainly not at Kings Cross."

"They couldn't produce it because no footage existed at the appropriate time." Evan sighed. "Don't you think it's puzzling, with London being the CCTV capital of the world, not one CCTV camera has been found with any footage of the bombers, other than the small footage at Luton?"

"It is strange." John said.

"They couldn't give the game away if they were to incriminate them, with imprints of times, which wouldn't have coincided with the schedules." Evan said.

"So their report and conclusions are based on speculation and probabilities?" John asked.

"Of course." He replied. "There has been no independent Inquiry, despite the event historically being the biggest ever terrorist event on the UK mainland. Even if one is convened later, the MI5 Chief of Staff will say they weren't responsible for the events."

"But he would say that wouldn't he?" Cynicism evident in the tone.

"Precisely."

"And the Police Report isn't even written by a named person as far as I can remember." John said.

Evan shrugged. "They'd have been ridiculed if a name had been placed on a vague report with conclusions based only on what may have happened."

"Would the alleged bombers have been told to catch any particular train?" Concentration lines etched deep into John's forehead.

"The cover could never have worked any other way." Evan replied. "They were supposed to be merely helping the security forces deal with the risks of a real terrorist atrocity." He looked across at John. "If that was the case, they'd have been given exact information, including the times of the train to catch and the precise route."

John shook his head, struggling to take in all of the information.

Evan moved his hands, palms upwards. "You'd have seen a video on television of them outside the train station, yet one of the photos is a fake. What the intelligence controllers hadn't bargained for had been the cancellation of the 7.40 a.m. train to Kings Cross, which would still have got them there in sufficient time. When they missed it, they couldn't have made Kings Cross in time on the 7.48 a.m. train. Each of the trains had been primed to explode independently, but simultaneously with each other." He paused for a moment, recalling the information from the documents. "Do you think the simultaneous explosions were the work of a genius?"

"I suppose not." John replied, though a puzzled expression remained.

"Then the conclusion is obvious."

John nodded.

"So you now have the evidence of the dirty hands of the intelligence services tainting the events." Evan said.

"They couldn't possibly have planned for the cancellation of the 7.40 a.m. train." John sighed. "Always, the hand of God interferes."

"Exactly." Evan said.

"So you're saying these four alleged terrorists were nothing whatsoever to do with the events of 7/7?" John struggled to understand the devious sophistication of it all.

"They always need the scapegoat and the false flag operation." Evan said.

"Who thinks up these plans?"

"It's what we do." Evan replied. "The Israelis benefit from anything which is anti-Islam."

John shook his head. "There has to be more to it."

"Of course, there are vested interests who since the time of the Permindex Corporation will assassinate anyone revealing a technology not dependant on oil." He shrugged. "If any foreign government threatens these people's overseas investments or become a threat to the petroleum interests of these elite, they'll be undermined."

"Even if it leads to deadly wars and the death of millions?" John asked.

"It makes no difference."

"So what about these four men alleged to be involved?" John asked.

"They were patsies and there has to be at least one, but they must die for the truth to be buried. They were being well paid and three of them thought they were being patriotic." Evan hesitated, shifting his position. "They only had dummy explosive packs on their backs and they would certainly not have run up the stairs, as is suggested by the CCTV cameras, as sensitive TATP explosives on their backs would have been very unstable." His eyes widened. "You'll also recall how the British Prime Minister was becoming very unpopular at the time for his pro-US stance and that he also took on a Jewish advisor at this time."

"I remember." John said. "But what's TATP?"

"It's an explosive."

"I understand, but what type of explosive?"

"First, it doesn't generate any heat or flame during the explosion, but it's most unstable. More often than not, it's used as a detonator for other more stable explosives, so it's different from conventional explosives." His eyebrows raised. "When it detonates its molecules simply fall apart and it doesn't use oxygen, so doesn't combust or burn like ordinary explosives."

"I'd heard terrorists use things like hydrogen peroxide and fertilizer?" John asked.

"Although TATP explosive is stated as being used in the original report, I suspect some other explosive was used."

"What makes you reach that conclusion?" John asked, beginning to wish he had made more notes.

"Well, first there's evidence of burns to survivors and witnesses refer to seeing a flash, but there'd be no burns or flashes with TATP. What they should have investigated was the use of a military-type explosive, as I'm convinced this is what was used." He hesitated again. "But they wouldn't want the signature of the military attached to this event, would they?"

"So what do you think was used?"

"Probably C4 military-type explosive, but if they had concluded in the Police Report that this was the type of explosive used, then it would have immediately linked the bombings with the military and the intelligence services." He held his palms out. "The cat would have been out of the bag."

John shook his head. "It's a deceitful web of intrigue."

Evan relaxed his head back into the sofa. "They'd gathered the information they needed by conjuring up documents to support the conclusions they needed and called it Operation Thesis."

"Do you know this for certain?" John shifted his position.

"I was part of Operation Thesis." He moved his hand across to the file, pointing to a document. "There's my signed witness statement confirming the events, in the event something happens to me."

John moved straight to the back of the file and read the witness statement.

Evan shrugged. "In any event, the upshot of all this is that the backpacks didn't contain bombs, as they could easily have gone off by accident, especially with the type of explosives alleged to be used, even if TATP was being used only as the detonator." He looked across at John. "As they ran up the stairs they'd only have carried mock explosives, so they didn't have to take any particular precautions to nurse their backpacks."

John shook his head, remembering another image from television. "But what about these excerpts of the suicide videos we've all seen on television?"

"But you'll remember no-one says anything at all about any target because they'd have thought it was part of the drill and would have been asked to make it like actors."

"What do you mean?" John asked, shaking his head.

Evan smiled sourly. "This is always the way it works."

"I don't understand?"

"Let me explain." Evan sounded exasperated, his face contorting. "Two of these young men would have been told to do these videos as part of the training exercise, at least the eldest would have been told to do it and one other as back-up, in case one of them didn't turn up on the day, as I explained. If you study them carefully, they're flippant, certainly not serious or sinister in the tone, only in the content. There's no hate or anger contained in the intonation of their voices. They'd have been told beforehand what to say and prepared by their handler, believing this was part of the mock training exercise."

"It's still hard to believe." John said.

"This is always the problem facing the public." Evan replied. "But what's really cute is that although their handler was a British citizen, he'd have gone to Pakistan for some weeks prior to the events so that telephone calls could be recorded from there." He raised his both hands in the air and smiled. "Khan would have been given two or more mobile telephones and told to answer any calls on them. He'd have been told not to ring him and the calls would have been made from public telephones in Pakistan, but as you must know, both the U.S. and Britain would have had significant operational intelligence outposts there with the full support of the Pakistan authorities."

"So their handler would be pulling the strings in Pakistan with the full backing of the intelligence services in this country." John said.

"You're getting the picture." Evan said. "He may even have been asked to start practising what he would say in the video on a home camcorder, without realizing the significance of what he was doing and the evidence it could provide for the intelligence services later when the Police would raid his home." He finished his gin and tonic in one swift movement. "You also must remember that these videos were not posted on a website, as you'd normally expect if the event was genuine."

John's shoulders hunched. "So these telephone calls coming from Pakistan are not what they appear to be?"

"Of course not." Evan replied. "They knew they'd be recorded, so the evidence would point to Pakistan." He smiled. "And one of the telephone calls from Pakistan would have been after the events, which would have been absurd if they'd been part of a suicide mission."

"So why was this man mixing with other potential terrorists?' John asked.

He looked at John quizzically. "I've told you he was acting as a go-between for the authorities in this country, as a friendly Muslim, but he could only do that by carrying out meetings with these people, so he could give the authorities intelligence."

"I understand."

"They're sophisticated and clever, but it was always part of their plans." Evan raised his eyebrows.

"Did any organization ever admit responsibility for these events?" John asked.

He shook his head. "Other than a 'fake' al-Qaeda website, which was traced to Texas, no-one claimed responsibility. There are other clues which give the game away and if it had been al-Qaeda they'd have been more than happy with the publicity and wouldn't have hesitated to claim responsibility."

John looked bemused. "What are these other clues?"

He pointed to another document. "You'll see they all bought return train tickets from Luton." He paused, as John looked at the document. "Why would suicide bombers do that if they were all going on one way suicide missions?" He pointed to another document. "You'll note they even paid for the car parking tickets at Luton Station and allegedly left home-made bombs in the boot of the car." He smiled again. "Now why would they need to do that if they were never intending to come back?"

John looked at the documents, then back to Evan. "So are there any witnesses who saw these Muslims carrying back-packs in the bombed trains?"

"No legitimate witnesses could have seen Muslims with back-packs on any of the trains, only on the bus."

John nodded. "So what did they see?"

"It's possible one of the alleged bombers reached his train, but most unlikely. The real evidence suggests no-one saw anyone carrying backpacks onto the bombed trains that morning at all." He stopped for a moment. "Neither is there any reliable evidence these four alleged bombers had been motivated by any political or religious beliefs to bomb. Even the Police acknowledge the evidence is incomplete and their report contains uncertainties and speculation."

John looked up from reading the documents in the file. "So those passengers on the train at Aldgate Tube Station who said the bomb exploded upwards from underneath the carriage were all absolutely right?"

Evan nodded. "It's easy to dismiss the odd evidence of witnesses who are still in shock, but the factual evidence is much more difficult to dismiss."

John took a deep breath, blowing his cheeks out as he exhaled. "But didn't they find a paper I.D. of Khan at one of the locations?"

"John, you should know better." Evan sounded exasperated. "A paper document surviving an explosion?" He hesitated. "It's like the paper passport of one of the alleged hijackers in New York, which they found near the Twin Towers, miraculously surviving the fireball, floating down to the ground. Scarcely believable, unless they've invented explosive-proof paper."

"So what really happened that morning?" John asked.

"This is where the other evidence comes in." Evan pointed to the folder again. "Read it and reach your own conclusions."

John read the remaining documents carefully.

Evan pointed to one document in particular. "You'll see from the reports that not one witness saw anyone carrying backpacks in the trains. Despite the Police pressing some of the witnesses, they refused. One witness even refers to a Police Officer pointing to the hole in the floor of one of the trains and telling a witness to be careful because that was where the bomb came up through the floor."

John shook his head, remaining silent as he read.

Evan pointed to another document. "That's the information about the involvement of Haroon Rachid Aswat, the alleged mastermind of the 7th July bombings, because they found a telephone number to the bombers from him, but as I've already told you, he had been an MI6 Asset, though there's some evidence he was turned and become dirty. I can't be sure." He tilted his head. "In any event, if he was working for the intelligence services and contacted the alleged bombers, what does that tell you about the alleged bombers?"

"They were set up." John replied.

"Right." Evan pulled out another one page document from the folder, pointing to a part of it. "This is what I referred to earlier, the evidence of the communication to the authorities in the United States asking them to release Aswat after his arrest there for organising terrorist training camps."

"So he was released after British Intelligence told them he was their asset?" John asked.

"It happens all the time." He handed his empty glass to John. "Even when he travels to Pakistan twenty four hours before the 7th July events and is subsequently arrested, he's again released on instructions from MI6. You'll see from the documents there that they told the Pakistani officials they were no longer interested in interrogating him."

"It's compelling evidence, even if it's only circumstantial." John said.

"At the very least, it's very strange behaviour. Don't you think?" Evan asked.

"Wasn't there something in the media in the US about this man to the effect he was a British Agent?" John asked.

"Fox News did a piece about it." Evan replied.

"Back to the events of the 7th July, what else can you tell me?"

"The bombs were definitely made from military-grade explosives." He turned to John. "Did you know that former Israeli Prime Minister Netanyahu was warned at 8.40 a.m. not to leave his London hotel that morning. This was later confirmed by an Israeli General. The Mossad Chief referred on the same day to the bombs being triggered simultaneously, but how could he have known that detail when the information wasn't even disclosed until the 9th July?"

"Doesn't that suggest it was a joint Mossad/British Intelligence operation?" John asked.

"You'd think so, but there are many other clues. Even the Prime Minister made reference in a press conference on the same day to knowing this was done in the name of Islam."

John nodded. "I remember it."

"But how would he know whether it was done in the name of Islam when no-one had claimed responsibility whatsoever and the Police hadn't even begun their investigations?"

John shook his head. "There's so much misinformation."

"That's why these people always win because no-one wants to believe it and the biggest put down is to be told you're a conspiracy theorist."

John nodded. "I can see that."

"You may even remember the then Metropolitan Police Commissioner, in a press conference on the same day made a similar mistake, making reference to surviving 'four miserable bombers'. He visibly flushed when he realised his mistake, correcting himself immediately when the significance of his mistake became apparent to him, changing the reference quickly to four bombs, obviously hoping no-one would realize his faux-pas."

"I remember." John said.

"But the expression he used makes it absolutely clear he knew exactly what he was saying the first time."

"I see your point." John said.

"He couldn't possibly have known there were four bombers at such an early stage of his investigation."

John nodded. "The human element again."

"In the same way as the cancellation of the train at Luton."

"So what would have happened to the bombers?" John eventually asked the obvious question.

"If they were not caught up in the explosions, and I don't believe they all were, then someone whose face was familiar to them, possibly even Aswat, would have picked them up as they made their way to Canary Wharf, perhaps to one of the tabloid newspaper offices."

"They'd have realised by this time they'd been set up." John said.

"Undoubtedly, but they could have been traced from their mobile phones, even when they were switched off, so it would have been easy to pick them up."

"And then?" John asked.

"A second person would have been in the vehicle, probably a blacked out and sound-proofed van. They'd have been told to get in the back where the second person would have been waiting for them."

"And what would have happened then?" John asked.

"They'd have been transported somewhere on a one-way ticket." Evan noticed John shaking his head. "I appreciate you find this information unpalatable, but they'd have been desperate and unable to think straight by this time, too frightened to do anything else and happy to see someone they trusted. He would have probably told them something had gone wrong."

John nodded, but said nothing.

"But they were doomed, one way or another, from the moment they turned up at Luton Station." Evan said.

"Ruthless." John said quietly. "But you seem to know exactly how these things happen?"

"I certainly know someone on a suicide mission wouldn't have paid for a car parking ticket when leaving their car or purchase return tickets. It doesn't happen that way."

"You're right. It doesn't make sense." John said.

"Neither does the recovery of a paper I.D. at the location of a bomb." Evan said.

John stared ahead blankly, his brain struggling with the acceptance of such a barbaric subterfuge.

"One other piece of information needs to be placed in the equation." Evan said, waiting to ensure John's attention. "If they were on a suicide mission why would they have left bombs in their parked car?" He hesitated again. "There'd be no reason for it."

"It makes you doubt the rule of law." John said ruefully.

"There are some people above the law."

"It's scarcely believable." John said.

"Well that's the way it works." Evan shrugged. "They convince everyone they're providing an invaluable service to their country."

John shook his head. "Receiving honours and promotions for their services too."

Evan nodded. "Always investigate who gets promoted after the event and you'll have your answers."

"What other discrepancies should I investigate for my piece?" John asked.

"Contrary to the indications given to the press and the media, the fourth recruit from Aylesbury didn't arrive at the same time as the other three, so you'll never see anything other than a still-framed photograph of the four together and that would have been created by computer software."

"But he still had time to catch the bus to the pre-arranged place?"

"He did." Evan said. "In fact, he took a long and indirect route just to get to the place where he was told to go, Tavistock Square. He caught a number 91 bus first, which would have taken him there, but for some reason took a number 30 bus going back on the same route. It was an illogical thing to do, unless he was obviously following a set script which had been given to him."

"It does seem strange." John stifled a yawn, but tried to maintain a level of concentration.

"He was even told exactly where to sit because a bomb had already been placed on the bus and all four CCTV cameras on it de-activated, despite the technician working on the cameras the previous weekend, working longer than was normal to maintain them or the fact he was not the normal technician who worked on the CCTV cameras."

"Wasn't there an advert on the bus saying 'outright terror—bold and brilliant'?" John asked.

"An advert for a play, but it's the sick way their minds work and may well have been done on purpose to affect the psyche of the people."

John offered him another gin and tonic, but he surprisingly refused.

"If you look at the videos or even the still photos of the bus after the demolition, there's a white van parked opposite the bus when it blew up. If you look at the company name on the van, this company just happens to be a demolition company, which has undertaken controlled demolition

contracts for the government and the intelligence community in the past."
He hesitated, noticing the puzzled expression on John's face.

"Are you saying they're responsible for the explosion?" John asked.

Evan shrugged. "All I can give you is facts, but you must reach your
conclusions." He smiled. "If you look at their vans, they advertise they
undertake robotic demolition work."

"There are so many coincidences." John said.

Evan nodded. "Even the fact that none of the four CCTV cameras
on the bus were working." He looked across at John. "Do you believe in
coincidence?"

"You know I don't."

"Well, there you have it."

John shook his head. "Isn't it strange how the public are persuaded
to pay for CCTV cameras to spy on themselves, yet at the first crisis they
never seem to work."

"The same thing happened at the Pont D'Alma Bridge in Paris when
Princess Diana died." Evan shrugged. "But the public are getting wiser to
the ways of spin and misinformation."

John picked up a document relating to De Menezes, recalling
the Brazilian electrician worked as a sub-contractor on the London
underground, later being assassinated. He read the document carefully, his
mouth dropping open.

CHAPTER TWELVE

There were a number of inconsistencies with the modus operandi of usual suicide attacks or the profiles of normal suicide bombers in respect of the 7th July 2005 bomb attacks in London. The alleged bombers purchased return tickets AND paid for their cars to be parked in Luton. They allegedly carried the supposed explosives in their bags, rather than strapping them to their bodies and wearing them, as would be normal for suicide bombers.

The alleged bombers included a university graduate, two were recent fathers and one had a wife pregnant with their second child. Another was a teacher of disabled children—none of which fitted the normal profile of a suicide bomber. Could there be a simple reason for it?

The time-scales did not allow sufficient time for them to arrive at the location for the Tube Station bombings and set off their alleged bombs.

The bus, which was bombed, did not follow the correct route and had its CCTV cameras switched off prior to the attack and the normal maintenance work on the cameras in the bus the previous weekend was undertaken by a "different" engineer who worked for far longer than was normal, yet still the CCTV cameras did not work.

A van, pictured alongside the bus when it exploded, is a company, which had been used before for contract demolition work by the government.

The alleged bombers all had personal items on them at the time, such as wallets, driving licences and bank cards, contrary to the normal actions of terrorists about to depart on a suicide mission.

FBI Agents based in the US Embassy in London had been told not to use the London underground, according to a posting on the Newsweek website.

Even Meir Dagan, then Head of Mossad, confirmed in an interview with the German magazine, Bild am Sonntag, on the 10th July 2005 that the Mossad office in London had been alerted to the impending attacks in London before the first bomb exploded.

John sat back, allowing his eyes to close, drifting into a place beyond himself for a moment, as he considered the documents he had read. A part of him wanted to deny it, but the evidence appeared irrefutable. He opened his eyes, leaning forward and turning to Evan. "So they used this power surge to detonate the bombs on the underground?" He asked, defying him to repeat it.

Evan nodded. "Hard to believe, isn't it?"

"No-one is going to believe it."

"It's intended to be difficult to believe." Evan said.

"I don't understand this power surge?"

"It's why the first reports of problems on the tubes that morning all related to a power surge affecting the trains with no initial report of a terrorist alert." He hesitated. "That came much later."

John re-examined the file again. "So what was De Menezes' involvement?"

"He was always dispensable." He replied. "He had no working visa, so it was easy to blackmail him."

"The reports said he was a sub-contracted electrician, but doing what precisely?" John asked.

"Doing what he was told." Evan replied coldly.

John turned his eyes away from the file. "Would he have known this power surge would have triggered explosive devices?"

"Almost certainly not."

"So he created the power surge on the underground without knowing its purpose?"

"Sure."

"But blackmailed?" John moved from the sofa to the window.

Evan's eyes followed him. "The likelihood is some authority figure approached him, saying he was likely to be prosecuted and deported." He waited until John turned back to him. "At this point, he would have been feeling at his most vulnerable and open to cooperation, especially if a working visa was promised."

"Would he have understood the implications?"

"Of course not." Evan shook his head. "He may have assumed some disruption on the underground, but certainly not the consequences of what he was doing."

"But he'd have asked questions?" John asked.

"But he'd have been given inaccurate answers." Evan replied. "Perhaps told it was a training exercise because it's an old chestnut they use from time to time."

"I suppose he'd have had no-one to turn to."

"Of course not." Evan replied. "These were the authorities."

"Even so, why would they kill him so brutally?"

Evan sneered. "John. John."

"Tell me?"

"He'd begun to talk." Evan replied. "They couldn't have a loose end, capable of letting the cat out of the bag."

"So the Police shot him, several times to the head and body in broad daylight in front of witnesses?"

Evan pointed to one of the documents. "There was a newly-formed organization called 'the Special Reconnaissance Regiment'. They were sure he was going to blow the whistle."

"So they shot him?" John asked again.

"They do what they always do, but too many Police Officers have run into problems with the Independent Police Complaints Commission and are reluctant to risk losing their pension, so it could have been someone on the outside."

"I'm losing you, Evan." He said. "Who did the killing then?"

"I can't be sure, but the way the man was shot repeatedly in the head, it had to be someone from this regiment, probably ex SAS."

"That's shocking."

"It's what happens, John, except the public usually never know."

"What about those who give the orders."

"They honestly believe they're doing it for the greater good of the country."

John sighed heavily. "I remember at the time thinking that this shooting, so soon after the bombings, was a strange coincidence."

"But you don't believe in coincidences."

John nodded.

"As always, check who gets rewarded afterwards, perhaps a promotion or an honour." He moved his hands outward. "I've told you it's the way the game works, John."

"You're talking about the commander of the operation, which led to the assassination of De Menezes?"

"Of course."

"I'm curious Evan." He felt weary. "Was it always intended that one of the alleged terrorists would get on that bus?"

"It was all strictly scripted and they followed the script." Evan replied. "At some stage, he was bound to realize he was being set up."

"But couldn't he have telephoned the Police?"

Evan laughed. "His mobile phone wouldn't have worked because of the events on the underground and how could he really turn to the Police?" He pointed to the file. "You've missed one document."

John began reading.

"You'll see the one alleged terrorist on the bus was killed in the explosion, as it had all been rigged beforehand." He pointed to one paragraph. "There's some evidence about how this was done."

John tapped the document with his index finger. "This suggests the usual contractor who maintained the CCTV cameras on that bus was replaced by someone else the weekend before."

Evan nodded. "And taking an inordinate amount of time for simple maintenance, yet none of the CCTV cameras operated on the day." He smiled. "Work it out."

"Has there been any official explanation for the cameras not working?" John asked.

"No" Evan replied. "As an intelligence officer with some knowledge of explosives, I can tell you the bomb on the bus didn't explode consistently with a peroxide-based explosive."

John stifled a yawn. "I'm not sure I understand."

"I suspect this was C4 military-based explosive, as on the underground."

John shook his head, but remained silent.

"Their mobile records will confirm they all tried to ring each other, but by that time they'd been closed down."

"Were they afraid they'd talk to the Press?" John asked.

"They'd never have been allowed to reach the offices of a national newspaper." He raised his eyebrows. "It would never have happened."

John nodded. "Didn't the Home Secretary announce in March 2004 that an attack was likely?"

"They had to prepare for the events."

"I recall seeing a BBC Panorama programme when they did a mock exercise based on three bombs exploding on the London underground and one on a London Transport bus."

Evan laughed. "Perhaps it was coincidence again, John."

"I don't believe it."

"I thought not." Evan replied. "Peter Power undertook the exercise in London based on almost identical events, with bombs going off at precisely the same time, even the same tube stations on the same day. It was done allegedly as a mock terrorist drill for a large company, but has remarkable similarities to the Operation Trojan and the FEMA exercise in New York at the time of the 9/11 events."

"Similar to what happened in the States?"

Evan nodded. "In the States, they'd set up Pier 92.for a proposed emergency centre in a planned trial bioterrorism exercise for FEMA, the Office of Emergency Management, as part of Operation Tripod, and all the staff were in place for it on the 11th September. It conveniently became the actual emergency centre, when the original command centre at World Trade Centre Building Seven was demolished."

John's eyes glazed. "It's frightening."

"It gets scarier." Evan replied. "The U.S. government used war games to create the confusion on the day of the 9/11 events and they combined it with a drill held by the National Reconnaissance Office and a Department of Defence Agency."

John looked back from the window. "So they used the same principle in the events in the U.K., even down to the mock exercise for the emergency services."

"But British Intelligence had perfected it, covering it up more subtly than the Americans."

John shook his head. "I may need more evidence of this if people are going to believe me."

"There are more coincidences?"

"What coincidences?" John asked.

"The evidence of massive short-selling of sterling in the ten days before the events of the 7th July 2005, similar to the unusually high stock bets on American Airlines and United Airlines immediately before the 11th September 2001 events."

John stared blankly ahead. "The problem is that it's only circumstantial evidence."

"You're right, of course." He buttoned up his coat, moving towards the door. "Their footprint is still obvious."

John moved to the door, opening it. "This is the advantage the Establishment has over the ordinary citizen who don't want to believe these things."

Evan walked through the door, but turned back. "Despite being pregnant, they kept Khan's widow in custody for six days until she condemns her husband to protect her young daughter." He shrugged. "If you have the widow of the bomber condemning him, it adds to the public mind-set."

"Why do they do these dreadful things?"

"They'll convince themselves it's for the public good."

John shook his head. "I couldn't live with it."

"But John, you're naive." He said. "At the time, the Prime Minister was being criticized for his stance on the war on terror and involvement in the Iraq war, especially as people had realized the intelligence report about Saddam's Weapons of Mass Destruction was mere propaganda and spin."

"Everyone now understands it was regime change, but they didn't have the courage to call it by its correct name."

"It's also been lucrative for some, John, but in due course they'll try to expand its powers to monitor email exchanges and website visits of every person in the country."

John nodded. "You mean mass surveillance with the network operator intercepting communications between say Google and a third party?"

"Eventually." Evan replied.

"As always, Evan, they use excuses to erode freedoms and increase the intelligence and military budgets."

"It always works, John."

"There's even been suspension of the Human Rights Act to allow alleged terrorists to be kept in custody for up to 42 days without going before a Court."

"And what about the Inquiries Act of 2005." Evan said. "It slipped through Parliament unnoticed, so all future public enquiries have to be supervised by the government minister, meaning any Inquiries are now neither public nor independent."

John nodded. "I'd forgotten about the Inquiries Act, but a High Court Judge went on record as saying that as a consequence a Minister could thwart an inquiry at every step."

"The legislation appears nondescript, as if it doesn't affect the ordinary person, but it prevents proper investigation into events which deserve a public inquiry." Evan pulled his coat collar up.

"But I suspect these things would never have got through Parliament without these events, Evan."

"As in the United States, the Patriot and Homeland Security Acts would never have been passed without the 9/11 events." Evan hesitated. "It's the way it works."

"What about the other document you promised?"

"You'll have it within a week." He handed him a business card. "Can you memorize the number?"

"I didn't think spies had business cards?"

"As you can see, it doesn't quite suggest I'm a spy, only that I work in the Foreign Office, with a telephone number, rather than an address." He replied. "I'm asking you to memorize it because I don't want to leave it with you."

John nodded. "Do you think I'll lose it?"

"No." He grunted. "But someone could take it from you and that would be embarrassing."

"Who could take it from me?"

"They'll be coming for you, John, and the card could incriminate me."

John felt a shiver run down his spine. "Really?"

"If it's a genuine emergency, John, text the word 'priest' and follow the message with a public place to meet. I'll do my best to meet you, but borrow someone else's mobile or buy a pay as you go because they'll monitor it."

John took another look at the card, using an old memory association trick he'd learnt at Cambridge, to memorize it, before handing the card back.

"Don't forget text the word 'priest' and I'll meet you."

"I'll remember."

"You'll need to be more savvy, John." He walked into the hall, looking back. "You're in a different ball game now and they don't play by your rules."

"But what's the foreign policy behind these events?"

Evan looked up and down the hall. "The U.S. policy strategy is based on what was suggested by Israeli official, Oded Yinon, back in the eighties, when he suggested turning the Middle East into small ethnic mini-states to make them easier to control."

John shook his head. "And so the U.K. supports it?"

Evan nodded. "Of course." He replied. "The war on terror is intended to de-stabilize the Middle East and compel them to eventually form these mini-states, controlled by western governments."

"And the link between Mossad and U.S. intelligence?"

Evan smiled. "When you've a physical Mossad presence at CIA Headquarters in Langley, what would you expect?" He replied. "But don't think the situation is too different in this country."

John's eyebrows raised. "You surprise me."

"In all intelligence operations, look for any connection with Israeli companies." Evan smiled. "They're often set up by the Israeli military intelligence, as fronts, so examine them closely. In the United States, they've a little-known aircraft leasing company connected to the Mossad-run airport security and passenger-screening company at the centre of their operations."

"You're taking grave risks by divulging these things, Evan, so be careful."

Evan nodded. "I don't pretend to be comfortable about these things, but I live by my conscience."

"I'll undertake research on this material, Evan."

"Look at a video released on the 1ˢᵗ September 2005 by Al Jazeera and you'll notice it's heavily edited, even the lip synchronicity is all out." Evan said. "It wouldn't hold up in a Court of Law because it's not authentic."

"So what do I look for?" John asked.

"The Israeli companies in this country operate in a similar way to the U.S." He whispered now. "If they're connected to the security industry or to screening at airports, be suspicious, as nothing is straightforward with intelligence. If you think you know the truth about something, take a second look. It'll never be obvious and when you think you know everything, you'll often be wrong."

"It's unsettling." John said, quietly. "Not my world at all."

"The more you know, the more paranoid you'll become." Evan said. "It's impossible to avoid cynicism."

"I did research some years ago for a piece about an operation called Operation Gladio, in mainland Europe." John said. "It made me very cynical about the intelligence services at that time."

Evan nodded. "It funded groups killing prominent politicians."

"As they were extremists, nothing fell back on the intelligence organisations, which funded them." John said.

"It's a simple way to sub-contract work too dirty for the intelligence community." Evan shrugged. "It happens all the time, as intelligence officers distance themselves from events."

"So my piece was right?"

"Sure."

"But wasn't there a downgrading of the terrorist risk in the UK in the weeks before the 7th July bombings in London?" John asked.

"You're right." Evan replied. "A reduction in the risk from severe general to substantial, even though a G8 meeting was due in the UK that month with all the leaders of the G8 nations in the country." He smiled. "Quite extraordinary, unless you see the pattern."

"But they did the same thing in the United States."

Evan nodded. "They changed the basis for intercepts of commercial aircraft shortly before the 9/11 events, despite sixty seven military intercepts having already taken place that year." He smiled again. "They took the decision-making away from the Commanders in the field, giving it instead to the Secretary of Defence, so on the day he took himself out of the loop, simply closing his door."

John sighed. "Very convenient, of course."

Evan looked furtively around. "It created the environment they required for the operation."

"On a separate issue, Evan, how far does surveillance on the public extend in the UK?"

"Further than the public imagines because no telephone call or e-mail is private anymore and every digital communication is recorded. They use this knowledge to suppress the truth and ultimately, they'll dispose of anyone who gets in their way."

"You mean kill them?" John's eyes bulged.

"For them it's lawful killing because they've got the power of the State behind them." He looked at John. "It works like this." He hesitated. "A burglary will go wrong or a mugging, like Lynne. For some, it'll be a suicide and they even have drugs mimicking all the symptoms of a heart attack."

"So I can't win?" John asked.

"It's possible, if there's no benefit in disposing of you because they don't just kill out of vindictiveness with all the risks attached to it."

"So what will they do with me?" John asked.

"I can't be sure, but improve your security."

"Is it that bad?"

"In a word." He smiled. "Yes."

"So what will they do?"

"They may break into your apartment again, administer a drug leaving no trace for an autopsy to find and induce a heart attack or get one of their agents to do their bidding, a drug addict perhaps, who'll do an anything for another fix."

CHAPTER THIRTEEN

"The dark repressions of consciousness create chaos . . . and the army of darkness will dwell in the world of man." (Revelations)

The damage to the planet will create its quarantine. The ritual killing is done in full knowledge, but only too late will they discover they have sacrificed their souls.

"They (referring to the middle achiever classes) are dangerous because there are so many of them. It is one thing to have a few nuts or dissidents. They can be dealt with, justly or otherwise, so that they do not pose a danger to the system. It is quite another situation when you have a true movement—millions of citizens believing something, particularly when the movement is made up of society's average successful citizens." (William Colby—former Director of the CIA) He also said: "The Central Intelligence Agency owns everyone of any significance in the major media."

Photographs of the wall of the Pentagon before it collapsed, (or was demolished), show a hole with a dimension of approximately sixteen feet, (the dimensions of a Global Hawk or what could be caused by a missile), but not a larger hole, which would reflect the impact of the forty feet plus dimensions of a Boeing. Furthermore, there are no large holes where two sixteen ton engines of a Boeing would have hit the structure on either side of the impact hole. Even after the wall collapses or is demolished there is a 65 feet width of damage whereas a Boeing is 124 feet 10 inches across. Close examination of the damaged area shows wooden filing cabinets undamaged by heat or smoke. A book rests open on a wooden table undamaged, totally different from the damage caused at the Twin Towers, yet as the Boeing was a trans-continental flight it would have still had 8,600 gallons of fuel at the time of the alleged collision. The foundations are undamaged and a column remains in place.

There is evidence of "thermite" residue in the dust found throughout the area of the demolished buildings in New York and in apartment blocks in the vicinity of the Twin Towers. It is an intense incendiary device used by the military, though significantly it does not have the high sound of some explosives. It has a unique chemical signature and reaches a temperature high enough to melt steel, which is why it is used to cut steel. Further, it burns under water so the Fire Fighters pumping water into the wreckage would not extinguish the fires, which also explains why some fires were still burning three weeks later. It is a mixture of iron oxide, aluminium, manganese and sulphur oxide, which increases its intensity. If it is part of a gel explosive it leaves a distinct fingerprint and a Professor of Physics has analysed four samples of dust around the vicinity of the WTC buildings and found active thermitic material in the dust in the form of micro spheres and particles of iron oxide manganese and aluminium and the red and grey chips found at the scene show clear evidence of thermite. Iron is a by-product of thermite, though it has not been used in the constructions of skyscrapers for more than a hundred years. The micro spheres all drew towards a magnet. Sulpher residue has also been found in the wreckage and on building structures and dust in the vicinity of the WTC buildings and it cannot be explained as a result of fire.

The front door smashed open with a noisy clatter, then the bedroom door banged open. John made out four large men, hooded in balaclavas, marching in, two of them pointing guns in his direction.

He was vaguely aware it was the middle of the night and dark outside, but hardly had time to rub his eyes, as a torchlight shone into his face. Another of the men grabbed him violently turning him face downwards on his bed, pulling his arms painfully behind his back and handcuffing him. It may have been a time for nightmares, but despite his disorientation this was painfully real.

"Show me your warrant and caution me if you're arresting me." John shouted, though the sheets and pillow muffled the strength of his voice, as he felt his face pushed down. Someone had a knee in the small of his back, making it difficult to breathe.

"Just shut the fuck up." The person holding him down on the bed shouted back, pushing his arms further up his back forcing John to cry out. He felt someone hit him across the back of the head with a hand. "We've got a warrant to take your laptop computer and any documents unlawfully in your possession." The same man said.

"Let me see your warrant?" John asked again.

"Are you stupid enough to think we need these things?" A second man said, placing his hooded head against John's face. The waft of a strong aftershave drifted into John's nostrils. He tried to identify it. Paco Rabanne he thought.

"Nadia." John cried out, before remembering she had taken a holiday with her brother and was safe.

"She's not here idiot." The second man said. "Now where's your briefcase?" He hesitated. "I want the laptop."

Before he could respond, the person holding him down on the bed joined in, pushing his arms forcefully behind his back again. "Tell the nice man where your laptop is please."

John remembered backing up all his material after the last burglary and leaving the memory stick and folder from Evan in a safe place, but didn't want to make it look too easy. He felt his arm being twisted again and grimaced. "Alright. It's hidden behind my clothes at the back of the wardrobe over there." He moved his head in the direction of the wardrobe. "But I want a receipt for it, if you are who I think you are."

The men laughed loudly and the one holding him down on the bed spoke. "And we thought you're supposed to be intelligent."

"Now tell us, who do you think we are?" The second man asked.

He heard rummaging about in the wardrobe and the sound of clothes being dumped on the floor. "You tell me." John trembled. "You're the one holding all the cards."

"Got it."

John felt himself being turned around face up on the bed and the man placed his hooded face closer and spat into his face as he spoke, through a slit around his mouth. "Now tell me, Mr Intelligent, do you have any backups for this material or do we have to rip the apartment to bits to find out."

"I haven't any back-up discs or memory sticks here." John said, factually correctly. "I promise you."

"Are you certain?"

"I used to be a priest you know. I don't tell lies." John breathed heavily, feeling weak.

Another of the men had opened the laptop and started it. "Password please?" He asked aggressively.

John hesitated and the man holding him hit him with what felt like the butt of a gun, much harder than before. He slipped back on to the bed groaning, blood trickled into his eyes and he struggled to speak. The same man who had hit him, placed his hands around his neck, squeezing and making it even more difficult to speak. "We've got authority to undertake lethal violence, if necessary." The second man said. "I warn you for the last time, give us the password now."

John groaned, but said nothing.

The person with the laptop came close to him. "Please understand we can get the contents of the laptop without it, but it'll take longer, so this is the last time you'll be asked politely."

The man holding him twisted his arm again.

"Alright, alright. It's priest1." He barely scratched out, still finding it difficult to breath.

"What did you say?"

The man holding him released his grip, turning him around and slapping him across the face. "Tell the man the password again."

"Priest1." He shouted, sitting up on the bed, breathing heavily. The accents of two of the men were unrefined, but definitely English, probably ex SAS, he thought. They were certainly not orthodox British Police Officers.

The accent of the third, giving the orders and taking control, could have been American. He approached John, speaking more quietly than the others. "You're lucky. It's not you we want this time, but if you continue to rock the boat with your investigation into matters of no concern to you, the next time it could be you. For now, we'll take your laptop and documents." His voice increased in intensity. "Do you understand?"

John sighed, a deep sigh, and took a deep breath, reassured there would be no lethal violence. Not that he was afraid to die. In fact, even though his body still trembled, at some mental level he had readied himself for death, almost accepting it, but the body still clung to life, reacting accordingly. Strangely, his body appeared to act separately from his mind and as with all the great spiritual truths it was a paradox. For a former priest, he found this experience of the mind and body working differently enlightening, even smiling at the thought.

The first man slapped him across the face again. "Do you find this funny?" He put his hands to John's throat. "He asked you if you understood."

"I understand." John spoke through gritted teeth.

"We've disconnected your telephone and taken your mobile phone, so there's no point in telephoning the Police because they'll not be able to do anything." He felt a key in the handcuffs and the release. Finally, he was pushed back forcefully onto the bed and within a few seconds they were out of the room and gone.

For a moment, he did nothing, relieved he had survived the ordeal, but instinctively reached for the telephone. The line was dead.

* * *

The following day, John borrowed a friend's mobile and text the word 'priest' to Evan, suggesting they meet at an Italian restaurant in a Soho back street for lunch. He arrived early, choosing a quiet bay for privacy, ordering a glass of the house red wine, whilst he waited, listening to the three tenors in the background.

Within ten minutes, Evan walked in. "What's the problem?" He sat down. "I didn't expect to hear from you so soon."

John looked around furtively. "I've had a visit from some thugs last night. They've taken my laptop, mobile telephone and some documents."

Evan groaned. "Was my private mobile number in it?"

"I can't remember."

"If it's the old number, it may be alright, but there's a good chance they'll trace it."

"What will you do?"

"I'll have to get out of the country, but not yet." Evan replied. "There are things I must do first."

"Is the mobile traceable?"

"It's not a contract mobile, only a pay-as-you-go sim card. If you're a priority target, they'll soon find out." He sighed. "They can trace mobiles easily enough."

"I'm sorry."

Evan nodded. "It's a complication, but it can be overcome."

"Can I e-mail you if I need to discuss anything with you?"

"No. It'll be intercepted." Evan took a deep breath. "The clever thing to do if you don't want the security or intelligence forces to intercept sensitive e-mails is to give someone a laptop with an encrypted password, then do an e-mail, but save it in draft rather than send it. The recipient can read the draft and no-one knows about the content of the e-mail."

"It sounds complicated." John said.

"Too complicated sometimes."

"What are you going to do now?"

Evan shook his head. "I'll have to be more pro-active, bringing forward my plans, but I'll remind them you were my contact."

"Do you want to confide in me?" John sensed something awry.

"Not really." He replied. "I've been asked to become First Secretary and Political Advisor at their Embassy in Sofia in Bulgaria."

"Is that a euphemism for spy?"

Evan smiled. "Some staff work on trade links and others are there to assist with British Nationals travelling or living in the country, but most are not. The secret intelligence agencies always place their agents on the staff of their embassies. It's merely a front to spy on foreign governments with the protection of diplomatic immunity."

"I suppose all countries do it?'

"Of course."

"It's a dirty job."

"You don't know the half of it." Evan grunted. "They even contract out sensitive work, using journalists and bankers." He hesitated, as menus arrived at the table. "They've an advantage of not being so conspicuous."

"Is there any significance to the placement in Sofia?"

"It would be easier to dispose of me there with the Russian Mafia presence in the country. Life is cheap and they'll do their dirty business if the price is right."

Concern etched on John's face. "Then you can't go."

"You're probably right, but it's not easy to avoid their clutches anywhere."

"Then you'll have to resign."

He laughed. "You're still naïve, John."

"It's difficult for a former priest to understand the machinations of the intelligence world."

"It's why you'll always be one step behind."

"So what will you do now?"

"I'll do what a former colleague did." He replied. "Shayler moved to Paris to avoid being prosecuted under the Official Secrets Act, courting as much publicity as possible. It made him a difficult target, too high-profile and too high-risk."

"I remember the publicity surrounding him. He made a number of DVD's and wrote articles on various intelligence matters, all with a level of apparent immunity."

"That's right."

"So you need to court publicity, Evan."

"I suspect he had other information ready for release if something happened to him." He shrugged. "It had to be a factor in protecting him."

"Can you do the same thing?"

"I've been preparing a detailed dossier since my colleague disappeared in the Balkans, so if something happened my Estate and lawyer wouldn't be bound by the Official Secrets Act." He said calmly. "I've encoded sensitive parts, a simple code, but it would give me time if it fell into the wrong hands."

"Then you must leave the country as soon as possible."

"I'd like to give you a copy of the dossier before I leave, if you can you meet me tonight?"

"Sure, but where?"

Evan searched his pocket for a receipt and gave it to him. "This is a receipt for a briefcase I've left at Waterloo Station. If, for any reason, I can't make the meeting, you'll find helpful documents in the briefcase."

"What documents?"

Evan smiled. "It explains how they compartmentalized the intelligence before the 9/11 events, with the Air Force Intelligence and the rogue unit within the State Department."

John hummed. "What will you do?"

"Perhaps I'll go through the Channel Tunnel, but first I'll pass on some additional information tonight." He replied. "I need to check something else."

"What?"

Evan tapped his index finger against his temple. "If I can't make the meeting, use the receipt."

John nodded. "I will."

*   *   *

A cold shiver, bringing fear in its embrace, grabbed John as he waited patiently for Evan to arrive. They had chosen to meet inside the Mysteries bookshop in the London West End, but patience was not one of his virtues and after an hour-long delay he wandered out into the drab autumn night. He felt cold, pacing the pavement in frustration.

Eventually, a familiar figure turned the corner, walking straight past him into the shop, with no acknowledgment. He carried a small briefcase, looking like a typical City worker calling into a bookshop on his way home from work. John followed him inside through the arched entrance into the quieter annex of the shop.

"You'd make a poor intelligence man." Evan turned to face him in one of the aisles of esoteric book titles packed into the quaint little shop.

"What do you mean?"

"You've no patience and are too visible."

"But I've been waiting for more than an hour and I thought something had happened to you."

"How long do you think we wait on observation duties or stake-outs?" He asked.

"Patience was never my best quality of character."

"I've noticed." Evan said. "Things have become difficult my end."

"I don't understand." John picked up a book and opened it. "What do you mean difficult?"

Evan opened the briefcase and handed a file of documents to him. "Everything about the activities of the colleague who disappeared in the Balkans is in the notarized documents within that file."

John placed the book back on the shelf and took the file and documents. "What difficulties?"

"I had problems getting into my flat and some colleagues were monitoring the place. I needed to retrieve some stuff, including a copy of a memorandum, which the Defence Secretary sent to the US President on the 30th September 2001." He picked up a book, avoiding all eye contact with John. "I felt it would help you."

"In what way?"

"It completes the circle of information you'll need and includes memoranda between the British Prime Minister and the US President, revealing they always intended to provoke Saddam into a war he couldn't possibly win."

John opened the file.

"Not here." Evan raised his voice. "It's not safe."

"Sorry."

Evan rolled his eyes. "And don't leave the shop with the file visible or it'll give the game away."

"I was curious."

"Read the documents when you're in a secure location"

"What's secure?"

"Your apartment is definitely not secure."

"I suppose not."

"In the meantime, stuff the file out of sight or under your coat please."

"O.K." John placed the file underneath his coat, wedging it under the waistband of his trousers, buttoning his coat afterwards. He smiled at what an assistant might think as he loosened his trousers.

Evan shook his head. "Sometimes I wonder how you've survived so long."

"God must be on my side."

"God can't stop a professional assassin."

"What do you mean by a professional assassin?"

"I mean a sub-contracted assassin."

"Don't frighten me." John said.

"Forewarned is forearmed."

"So what's in the Secretary of Defence's memorandum you mentioned?"

"It called for the administration to focus on supporting the Sheikh, not taking him down, as he was going to assist in their agenda."

John raised his eyebrows. "Now there's a surprise."

Evan picked up a book, browsing it, before looking around. "It called for the establishment of new regimes in a series of states by aiding local peoples to rid themselves of militants, freeing themselves of regimes supporting terrorism."

"What states?"

"Obviously, Afghanistan primarily, and you don't need to be a brain of Britain to work out the reason."

"Did he name other countries?" John picked up another book, as a shop assistant passed.

Evan turned his back, ignoring him until the assistant was out of earshot. "They wanted to take down Iraq, Iran, Syria, Libya, Sudan and Somalia." He replied. "They've been happy with Egypt, as their leader has been supportive of their agenda and they needed to stop the Muslim Brotherhood, but they fear he could be ousted at some point, so they've work to do there."

"There's no real surprise in any of those, except perhaps Syria?"

"Initially they placed a major goal of US policy as getting Syria out of Lebanon, but I think they want Assad out now."

John shrugged. "What do you mean by 'they'?"

"The Defence Secretary and our old friend 'Project for the New American Century' Paul Wolfowitz, who prepared the paper."

"Interesting."

Evan pretended to read a book. "Intelligence work is full of meticulous routine and corroboration of simple facts." He turned a page. "It's why they recruit people at University who have the potential to focus on the mundane, without losing their concentration."

"What else is in there?"

Evan spoke without a sideways glance. "There's a page in there, part of a Pentagon campaign plan, referring to both the Taliban and Saddam Hussein regimes being state regimes against which plans and operations might be mounted."

"I suppose this isn't unusual." John said. "They're bound to prepare plans, as part of their routine war games."

Evan waited for a customer to pass and remained browsing. "Do you realize how long it would take before these things could be released under the Freedom of Information Act?" He replaced the book on the shelf. "Even then they could deny access on the grounds of national security."

"I understand perfectly."

Evan pointed to the file under John's coat. "One particular paper in there was given to the US President after he'd already approved plans to invade Afghanistan. The paper called for postponing US air strikes indefinitely and using ground forces in support of the anti-Northern Alliance."

"They change sides so quickly."

Evan nodded. "It was their money, filtered through the ISI, which turned the Taliban from a bunch of religious students into a movement which took over Afghanistan in the first place."

John ground his teeth unconsciously. "Anything else I should know?"

"Whilst I remember." He turned to him. "One of the papers in the file refers to the strategic vision of the US government, endorsed by the then Director of the Joint Chiefs of Staff, after consultations with the outgoing Chairman of the Joint Chiefs of Staff and the incoming chairman."

"I don't understand?"

Evan smiled. "Just think about this for a moment because this policy was against the official White House line at the time."

John waited as another customer squeezed past them in the narrow aisles, moving through the archway towards the exit. "I recall the Director gained promotion to Chief of the United States Central Command, CENTCOM, after the invasion and occupation of Iraq in 2003."

"Correct." Evan nodded. "He took over military responsibility for the whole of the Middle East, but it's all in the documents."

John placed the book he had picked up back on the shelf without reading it. "I suppose I'll not see you for some time?"

Evan looked around furtively. "I think I'm being followed, so I must go. Everything else you need you can get from the documents, except one final thing."

"What's that?"

"There's some evidence al-Qaeda have hidden a nuclear device somewhere in Europe and they've threatened to detonate it if anything ever happens to the Sheikh or the Egyptian."

"Jesus Christ!" John said, quite out of character.

"I'm not sure he can help you." Evan said.

"Do they know where?"

"They may hold on any move against the Sheikh until they've better intelligence on the matter."

"Is there anything in the folder about it?"

"Too sensitive, John."

"I understand."

Evan nodded. "I'd like you to leave first." He said. "I'll wait a few minutes and buy one of the books before leaving, but be careful." He hesitated. "And don't look back please."

John shook his hand, leaving the shop without turning back. He quickly scanned the area outside for signs of surveillance, but saw nothing unusual with untrained eyes. After walking for about three hundred yards and down two different streets he became uneasy. Perhaps simple doubt, a nervousness or even intuition made him look over his shoulder, but he noticed nothing immediately. The feathery feeling in the area of his solar plexus was something he had learnt to trust more than logic and he became wary, so walked towards the next tube station, stepping into the shadows of the entrance. After moving towards the ticket machine, he fiddled with it, delaying inserting any coins, instead searching for money in his pockets, monitoring everyone in the vicinity for signs of anything unusual. Only one person, an immaculately dressed man with a bodybuilder's physique, could have been following him from the direction he had travelled, so watched as the man approached the entrance, talking to someone on his mobile phone. He could have been straight out of the male model catalogue with good looks to accompany the build. As he neared the entrance, the man beckoned to another person walking from the other direction. At that moment, he knew it was time for flight and took a ticket from the machine, moving quickly down the escalator. After the killing of De Menezes at Stockwell Underground Station in broad daylight, he knew that even the underground was not out of bounds for those with sinister motives and Establishment support.

CHAPTER FOURTEEN

The contributors to the 'Project for a New American Century', outlining the new strategy for American global dominance in the twenty-first century included Dick Cheney, the Vice-President, Donald Rumsfeld, Secretary of Defence, Paul Wolfowitz, (his deputy and its author), Jeb Bush, brother of George and Governor of Florida and Lewis Libby, the leader of Bush's 2000 election campaign team and later one of the White House team who was pardoned by George W. Bush, after being convicted of a criminal offence relating to the outing of a CIA Agent, Valerie Plame, for the actions of her diplomat husband in criticizing the invasion of Iraq.

Can it be mere coincidence those contributing to the report are also the ones responsible for failing to prevent the attack and for coordinating their desired global response? Is it also coincidence that both the CIA and New York City counter-terrorism offices, based in Building Seven of the World Trade Centre, were destroyed, along with any potentially incriminating evidence contained in their offices. Strangely, no aircraft collided with the building and no part of the Twin Towers collapsed onto it, yet it became only the third steel-framed building in history, after the Twin Towers, to collapse, allegedly due to fire, though obviously contrary to the laws of physics.

The strategy stated within the infamous think-tank policy document makes it clear there was "a need for an event, like a new Pearl Harbour", to gain public support for their Middle East strategy.

"Beware the (self-perpetuating) Terrorist Industrial Complex." Colin Powell—Secretary of State stated—when talking about the costs of Homeland Security etc.

John breathed heavily as he jumped on the underground train about to leave the station. His heart pumped hard, even his ears pained from the exertion. He smiled, recalling what a girlfriend had once said to him about his love of good food and wine being the old man's orgasm, but he sobered quickly as he noticed a man bounding down the stairs, just failing to get to the doors of the train before they closed. It was the same man who had been using the mobile outside the Station, the stylish suit, probably Saville Row he thought, and strained for a closer glimpse for future reference. Their eyes met and in that moment he knew their paths would cross again.

Until the documents in his possession could be copied and deposited safely he felt vulnerable. Alighting from the train at the next stop, he changed platforms and transferred to a different line, before the trail became obvious. Recalling Evan's comment about his naivety, he resisted the temptation to use the new pay-as-you-go mobile he had acquired, instead using a public telephone to his lawyer.

"Julian. I'm in trouble."

"What's new?"

"Someone is following me."

"Not again."

John smiled. "I need your help."

"Are you on a mobile?"

"I'm on a public telephone, but I do have a switched off mobile." He remembered only belatedly Evan's comment about being able to trace them even when they were switched off.

"Then dump it immediately or take out the battery." Julian said firmly.

"But it's a pay-as-you-go mobile and all my telephone contacts are in it."

"If matters are as bad as you think, you've no choice."

John nodded instinctively. "They're bad."

"I've experienced first-hand these situations after what happened in Paris the last time you asked for my help." Julian remembered vividly being kidnapped after John had tried to publish secret scrolls taken from the Vatican vaults. "When you asked me to set up the website, I hoped this time it was a mere precaution and I wouldn't hear any more from you."

"How can I forget Paris?"

"So it's a stark choice between your contacts or your life." Julian said.

"I see your point."

"Then break it up and dump it."

"I'll do it, but I need to leave some documents with you."

"Oh God."

John smiled. "Did you get the last lot from Nadia?"

"Sorry, I've not seen her." He replied, hesitating. "What documents do you mean?"

"Do you mean you've not seen Nadia at all and she hasn't telephoned you?" Tension strained in John's voice.

"Not at all and I've certainly not received any documents." Julian replied. "And my staff would have told me if they'd had anything from her."

"Shit." The words came out involuntarily.

"You'd better come to my home." Julian said. "I'll be waiting."

"I'll see you soon." John said.

"Would you rather I arrange for the Police to collect you?"

"I don't trust anyone at the moment, not even the Police. These people could have access to the Police computers logging the call." John hesitated. "I'll be alright."

"Good."

"I'll explain everything when I see you."

"When shall I expect you?"

"I can be there in about thirty minutes, but give me ten minutes leeway before calling the cavalry."

Julian grunted. "Will do."

John replaced the telephone and looked around, destroying his mobile and disposing of it in the nearest waste bin, before moving towards the platform. His mind spiralled, wondering why Nadia would retain the original documents. As he waited for the next tube, alert eyes panned the platform area. One person in particular looked suspicious, so when the train arrived, he positioned himself behind the inside door to the next carriage, so there was cover between him and this man at all times. He resolved to leave the train before the doors shut, if the man stepped onto the train, but he would remain on the train, if he stayed on the platform. In the event, the man ran alongside the carriage, peering inside as he passed. John timed his movement between the two carriages and the connecting door, so he would not be visible at any time, managing the operation and speeding back into the back carriage as the man ran to the second carriage. Soon afterwards the doors closed and he breathed more comfortably.

Another station arrived quickly. This time, no-one was visible on the platform, so he jumped off quickly, spurting up the escalator two steps at a time. He inhaled deeply, feeling the tension in his shoulders ease, telling himself to relax and repeating the word 'relax' helped. In his paranoid state of mind, he decided against taking the first taxi in the queue at the station, instead hailing one from the road outside. He shouted Hampstead, intending to give the full address when he neared his destination, after the driver had moved off.

At Julian's house, adjoining Hampstead Heath, he was ushered into the study. Shelves full of thick and imposing book titles overlooked the old mahogany desk like sentinels. Patio doors led to a landscaped garden, with the Heath stretching into the distance beyond the garden. Julian sat down nimbly on a leather swivel chair, neatly placed between the mahogany desk and a smaller computer desk behind him, so he had to turn around completely to use the computer. On the wall with no shelving, various framed photographs of dignitaries and high-profile clients lined the wall, all placed equidistant in two rows, parallel with each other. He studied them, recognizing some of the functions when he had been a top table guest. His desk remained remarkably clear, though one paper tray contained various letters and two files overlapped each other at the front.

"This is such an attractive place to live." John pointed to the garden and the Heath. "But would you patronize me and close the curtains?"

Julian duly obliged, returning to his desk, moving two files and pulling out a pad of paper from a drawer. "But it's hardly the place to walk the dog at night without attracting attention."

John felt more at ease, removing the file from underneath his coat and slid it across the desk. "You need to look at this because I'm in serious trouble again and this needs to go on the website in readiness."

Julian took a deep breath. "I realised you must have been in trouble again, but I'm puzzled about the documents Nadia is supposed to have handed me?"

John groaned. "I trusted her with some original documents I'd been given by the Chair of the Parliamentary Committee on Security and Intelligence and from an intelligence contact."

"So what's happened to them?"

"I don't know, but they were important documents I needed you to hold for me in the event of anything happening."

"Where is she now?" Julian asked.

"New York I think, from the note she left."

"Why don't you try to contact her?"

John sighed. "I'm not sure who to trust anymore."

"I'm pleased you trust me." Julian undid a top button from his shirt.

"She didn't know, but I've kept copies of most of the documents I gave her and retained some other original documents." He shook his head. "Are copies legally as credible as originals?"

"It's the difference between primary evidence and secondary evidence."

"In layman's terms please, Julian."

"It's not ideal, but it may do, though it's easier for copies to be discredited." He smiled. "Though you can put anything you want on the website initially because it's ready to go."

John pointed to the file. "Those documents must be kept safe, but can you copy them and give me a file with the copies tonight."

"Is this for the website?"

John nodded. "All of it can go on the website when it goes live, if it becomes necessary, but I need the copies for another reason."

Julian leaned back into the leather chair, browsing the documents, swivelling around in the process. He pointed towards his photocopier/printer. "It's not as fast as the one in my office, but it'll do the job."

"You're a life saver."

He smiled. "This isn't going to be another Paris, is it?"

"I hope not." John said, with little confidence. "But I need all of these documents to go on the website ready for release to the press immediately if anything suspicious happens to me."

"I understand."

"I'll prepare a Press Release referring people to the website and you've kept the contact details of my friends in the business, Julian.".

Julian listened, taking notes. "I've kept the contact details."

"Try and set up a deal as you've done before."

"No problem."

"Good."

"So what do you think has happened to the documents in Nadia's possession?"

"I assume she still has them." John replied.

"Did you notify the Police of the burglary and assault in your house?"

"Naturally." He replied. "I needed to protect my back and wanted a crime number for my insurers."

Julian took some stationary with his left hand from the shelf on the wall. "I suggest we fax a letter to the Foreign Office, with a copy of it going to the Home Office." He places some headed paper in his printer. "I'll put something together tonight."

"What are you going to say?" John asked.

"I'll confirm my instructions to act for you and list the recent events at your house, including the fact you'd been with Lynne immediately prior to her death. It should grab their attention."

"Is it relevant or wise?".

"It's too significant to be ignored, especially if they fear it may be published subsequently." He swivelled around and started typing something on his computer, then turned back around to face John. "I'll remind them if anything happens to you, they'll not be able to sweep events under the carpet."

"Will it protect me?" John asked nervously.

"It'll make them think twice."

"It's still a worry."

"If something happened to you in suspicious circumstances and this letter found its way into the public arena, there'd be an outcry?"

"I suppose so."

"Sometimes you forget, John, you're someone with a public reputation and it's a big asset."

John shrugged. "What about a press conference?"

"I can organize it."

"At short notice, so the authorities can't block it?"

Julian nodded. "If anything happens to you, I'll give a detailed press conference and release all the information in my possession, including the faxed letters to the Foreign and Home Offices."

"Good."

Julian thought for a moment. "Perhaps it would be a good idea to fax Scotland Yard, as well as the Ministries, if only to put the cat amongst the pigeons."

"What's the likely outcome?"

"I'll be asking for a reply by return to the faxed letter, if they want to prevent documents going into the public domain." He replied. "It's bound to trigger a response."

"I hope so."

"They can't ignore it."

John sank back into his chair feeling tired. "One final thing."

"What?"

"I don't feel safe in my apartment." He rubbed the back of his neck. "At least, not until these faxes have had their effect."

Julian nodded. "You can sleep in the spare bedroom."

"Can I have copies of the fax transmission sheets?" John asked. "It'll give me peace of mind."

Julian smiled. "I'll give you copies first thing in the morning."

"What time?"

"I'm in Court at ten in the morning, so it'll be about 8.30 at the latest, but the letters will be ready."

"I'm sorry for the trouble."

Julian shook his head. "This is the nature of my profession. I deal with problems people can't resolve themselves. It's what I do." He smiled again. "In fact, it adds a little colour to an otherwise drab job." He handed John a terms and conditions to sign to comply with the bureaucratic demands of his profession. "I'll need to copy your passport or driving licence and I'll need to copy a bank statement or utility bill for my file."

"Is this your charge-out rate?" John pointed to the terms and conditions.

"But I'm worth it." Julian smiled.

John signed the document, returning one copy. "I'll try not to get you into dangerous situations."

"That's a relief."

"If you get any calls asking you to meet me or any intelligence operative, be suspicious."

"If I ring you and it's genuine, I'll use the words 'lawyer' and 'priest' somewhere in the conversation."

"Fair enough."

"If I end up in a Police Station in this country, I'd rather not use one of these young solicitors on the duty solicitor panel rota."

"You probably could do with a stiff drink?" Julian gestured towards the lounge.

"Please."

"I have a question?" Julian moved from the study into the lounge.

"Only one?"

Julian smiled. "Over the last few days, I've come across a man on the Heath, too frequently for coincidence. He's tried to engage me in conversation and I've been suspicious."

"Describe him?"

"He was too well-dressed for the normal person I meet on the Heath and a body-builder's physique."

"Oh my God." John said. "It sounds like Saville Row man." He hesitated. "Is he dark with male model looks?"

"It sounds like him, John, but the only other thing I recall was a distinctive aftershave."

"Paco Rabanne."

"That's it."

John's mouth dropped open. "He's definitely one of the men who followed me into the tube station." He said. "I'm sure he was also one of the men who assaulted me in my flat, taking my laptop."

"Hmm." Julian thought for a moment. "Let's put this in the faxed letter in the morning and give a description of the man, even down to the aftershave."

"Will it help?"

"The more detail we provide, the more difficult for the authorities to ignore it."

"You give me confidence, Julian."

"It's my job." He moved towards the drinks cabinet. "Would you be prepared to give them what they want for a price?"

"What do you mean?"

"The intellectual property value of your material must be high."

"Too many people have sacrificed to betray them for greed."

Julian grunted. "It may get them off your back if they know you're not going to divulge or publish anything."

John shook his head.

"But you'd cease to be a threat, John."

"I understand, but it's not possible." John said firmly.

"If you change your mind, I'm a good negotiator."

"I'll not change my mind." He gave him a stern look. "But you can do something practical, Julian."

"What?"

"I'm not going back to the apartment whilst this goes on, so if I gave you a list of things I need and some clothes, could one of your staff collect them?"

Julian nodded.

"I'll give you the keys."

"One of my staff will do it." He hesitated.

"I've hidden the copy documents from Nadia in a folder in the attic, which isn't visible, even if you lift the hatch." John said. "Could someone collect those at the same time?"

"Not a problem." Julian replied. "My trainee will be happy to assist, but I'll tell him some background, so he can look out for trouble."

"Good."

"My staff are trained in confidentiality, so your secrets will be safe."

"I'll only be here for a couple of days." John sighed. "I hate to impose on our friendship."

"It's not a problem."

John nodded.

"Although I like your company, John, I could do with a simpler life." He passed over a gin and tonic.

"If Saville Row man is in the vicinity, then they're carrying out more detailed surveillance than I anticipated."

"Do you know who they are, John?"

"It must be connected to the intelligence services or else contracted by them."

Julian nodded. "I suggest you stay inside for a day or so and work behind closed curtains." He raised his glass. "The faxed letters will have an impact quickly." He took a sip. "At the least, it should hold off any premature action."

John raised his glass, looking around the lounge, noticing a large flat-screen television on the far wall and three leather chesterfields, all well-worn and inviting in his frame of mind. The matching cushions and curtains had the touch and look of an interior designer's work and he remembered Julian had recently endured a messy divorce. The walls had different colours, contrasting perfectly, and a beige ceiling, rather than white. Expensive light fittings were placed strategically for the best lighting and exclusive ornaments rested on the mantelpiece of the marble fire surround. "There's a legal issue concerning me, Julian." He relaxed into the soft chesterfield, taking a large sip of his gin and tonic.

"And what's that?" Julian settled into the chesterfield opposite.

"There've been articles about the abuse of the anti-terrorism legislation in this country and the implementation of draconian powers, far beyond the intention of Parliament." John adjusted himself. "Could they arrest me without charge and lock me away in Belmarsh or another of Her Majesty's institutions?"

"Hmm." Julian thought for a moment. "It's not easy to answer."

John smiled. "You remind me of the joke in your speeches about the man in the Royal Courts of Justice who insisted on having a one-armed barrister. Eventually, someone asked him why and he said he wanted a lawyer who wouldn't say on the one hand you have this, but on the other."

Julian laughed. "You must understand it's not that simple because although Parliament passes legislation, it's the Courts which have to interpret it and they often distinguish one case from another, if the facts are different."

"I'm not sure I understand."

"Well, the first rule of interpretation of statute is called the literal rule." Julian said. "This means that words in the legislation must be given their ordinary and everyday meaning, even if that meaning was not what Parliament intended when they passed the legislation."

"Sounds complicated?" John finished his gin and tonic in one large gulp.

"It gets worse." Julian replied. "There's a second rule of interpretation called the mischief rule. The problem is you can only move on to this second rule of interpretation if the first rule leads to an ambiguity." He hesitated, turning his hands up. "The mischief rule allows the Courts to look at the intention of Parliament when they passed the legislation, but only if there is an ambiguity in the literal rule."

John shook his head. "It's typical lawyer's gobbledegook." He placed his glass on the coffee table in front of him. "This is why you make so much money."

"I wish it was simpler."

"So what are the risks I could be arrested?"

"In my view, remote, but they wouldn't do it if they thought the newspaper industry would splash front page stories about the abuse of legislation." He stretched back into the sofa. "In any event, if they did arrest you the maximum period of detention would now only be 14 days, since the 28 day period of detention is being allowed to lapse."

"I hope the newspaper industry would support me."

"You're a journalist and they'd close ranks, especially if they thought it could be their turn next."

"I hope so."

"Establishment people like to hide in the shadows and would hate any publicity in newspapers." Julian smiled. "It would make them feel vulnerable."

John nodded. "And the government?"

"The Prime Minister could be asked questions in the House."

"Good."

"Precisely, but as a lawyer, I don't believe in worrying about obstacles before they appear."

"There's another point of view, of course."

"Enlighten me, John?"

"I'd be out of harm's way from government agencies and the publicity would give me more options when it comes to publication of the material."

"Now that's thinking like a lawyer." Julian offered him another drink, which he willingly accepted. "But would you be prepared to suffer incarceration for the sake of publicity?"

He thought for a moment. "I may not enjoy it, but it wouldn't frighten me if it was a means to an end."

*   *   *

Two days passed and John wondered if the faxed letters would trigger any response, but a telephone call from Julian's office late in the afternoon of the second day resolved his concern.

"I've had a telephone call from the Foreign Office." Julian said. "They want you to attend a meeting in Whitehall with an Under-Secretary tomorrow and someone from the Home Office will also be present."

"Will you be there?"

"It's up to you." Julian replied. "There's no question of police involvement or formal interviews, but if you'll feel more comfortable, I'll happily attend."

"I definitely want you there."

"No problem."

"What time do they want to see me?"

"Ten in the morning."

"I'd feel more relaxed if you're there."

"One of the Under-Secretaries responsible for intelligence matters will be present and another of similar rank from the Home Office."

"I was hoping someone from the government would be present."

Julian shook his head. "They can't be seen to be involved, but the Under-Secretaries will have authority to act and will have to liaise with someone in MI5." He brushed hair back from his forehead. "Ultimately, the Chair of the Intelligence and Security Committee in the House will have to be informed at some stage."

"Shame." John raised his voice.

"What do you mean?"

"That used to be Lynne, of course."

"We'll talk when I get home, but they've hinted there's money on the table if, to use their words, 'you're reasonable'."

John groaned. "If that's the purpose of the meeting, it's a waste of time."

"We'll talk about it when I get home."

"Alright." John replaced the receiver, pondering his dilemma, for his principles had already cost him his marriage and perhaps his life was now at stake. In his heart, he should not compromise and when there was conflict between his heart and head, the frenetic beating of a sensitive heart normally held sway.

CHAPTER FIFTEEN

An American lawyer and former Chief of Staff to a Republican Presidential Candidate told newsmen al-Qaeda was simply a CIA creation and that the 9/11 events were "a government ordered operation." He referred to documents in his possession when he said, "The President personally authorised the attacks. He is guilty of treason and mass murder." He claimed he had information from top military officers, FBI Agents and others confirming high-ranking government officials were complicit in the attacks of 9/11, which were carried out under the cover of a war games exercise code-named "Operation Tripod", under the command of the Vice President. The action, on behalf of 400 families of victims, charged that certain administration officials "all conspired with the government of Saudi Arabia prior to 9/11 knowingly to finance, encourage, recruit, permit, aid and abet certain individuals to carry out the attacks on the World Trade Centre and the Pentagon in order to orchestrate a contrived, stylized and artificial Second Pearl Harbour event for the purpose of galvanizing public support for their military adventures in the Middle East and in order to persuade Congress to enact their repressive Patriot Acts I and II for the purpose of suppressing political dissent inside the United States." Judges quoting obscure law, (similar to the Crown Proceedings Act 1947 in the UK, which gave the Crown immunity from prosecution for any actions during the Second World War), would not entertain the action or allow him to outline the evidence he had accumulated.

> **The Vice President at the time of the 9/11 events, when subsequently interviewed on television on the 8ᵗʰ December 2011, confirmed the rules of engagement with the President and stated that "after the three other planes had hit their intended targets" (i.e. before Flight 93 went down) he gave the Order to shoot down any hijacked plane which did not agree to divert" and that "frankly I did not hesitate."**

It had been a sleepless night and John's mind craved clarity. When he looked up at the brass plate outside the Whitehall offices marked 'Foreign and Commonwealth Office', uncertainty still plagued him like a soiled coat he had been compelled to wear. Security measures slowed his progress, with security machines and telephone calls necessary to verify their appointment. He walked with Julian through high-ceilinged corridors with ornate coving and cornices. The smell of a recent polish made him sneeze and the scurrying of the starched shirt brigade, hurrying from one room to another along lengthy corridors, reminded him of hamsters running around a circular ladder, getting nowhere. Eventually, they were ushered into a large room with two civil servants already seated. One sat directly behind a large teak desk with a leather inlay, old and marked, in its centre. Incongruously, only one set of documents had been placed on the desk. The second sat in an upright chair to the side of the desk. Sunlight shone brightly through the window behind the desk and John squinted in its reflection. He guessed from the greying hair and rutted furrows of the man behind the desk he would have been the elder, perhaps in his late fifties. Each wore a dark suit; the one behind the desk had a black pin-striped suit with a white collar on a blue shirt and a bright red silk tie. The man sitting to the side may have been late forties and wore a charcoal suit with an old-fashioned fob and chain linked to what appeared to be a pocket watch in his waistcoat. He wore a plain white shirt with a blue tie and his blond hair, thinning at the crown, had been brushed back. Tea and coffee facilities had been placed on a table to the side of the desk, together with a plate of custard creams.

The person sitting behind the desk gestured to them to sit on two upright chairs placed immediately in front of the desk, introducing himself as Anthony Buller-Smith. He pointed to his colleague, introducing him as

Gerard Quinlan. Buller-Smith waved his arm towards the tea and biscuits. "Can I interest you in some tea or coffee?"

John shook his head. "Not at the moment."

Buller-Smith looked directly at John, addressing him. "Mr O" Rourke, we're happy to give you the opportunity to discuss the matters contained in your lawyer's faxed letter."

He turned to Julian. "What do you want?"

Julian took a copy of the letter he had faxed from his briefcase and lifted it in the air. "The letter invites you to respond to me."

"But we've responded, which is why you're here." Buller-Smith said. "Our problem is we're unsure how far you want to go with this matter."

Julian shrugged. "First, I'd like some assurances as to my client's safety and well-being."

"In so far as it's in our power, I can give you that assurance, of course."

Julian nodded. "I suspect the contents of my client's laptop have been disclosed to you, so I anticipate you're aware of the material in my client's possession." He hesitated, but no response came. "Certain vested interests may regard my client as an embarrassment."

Buller-Smith grunted disdainfully. "I can't confirm these matters, nor can I formally acknowledge knowledge of material in your client's possession, but would be prepared to discuss things on a without prejudice and hypothetical basis."

"Fine." Julian nodded. "Let's discuss matters on that basis, if it helps." He placed his hand on John's arm. "Do I take it you wouldn't object if my client disclosed material in his possession?"

Buller-Smith shook his head. "Let's assume your client has possession of sensitive material." He said. "If he tries to disclose any such material he may well regret it."

"Is that a threat?" John asked sternly.

"Of course not." He looked towards his colleague, rolling his eyes and raising his eyebrows. "My colleague can be more specific, as it's his department, but I'm talking about applications to the Courts, which would be made in camera for national security reasons, as is allowed by recent legislation, so he'd have no publicity." He leaned back into his chair. "And perhaps more serious consequences would follow."

"What sort of applications and consequences do you mean?" John asked.

"Perhaps an Injunction may be necessary." He hesitated, adjusting his tie. "It would prevent you publishing any controversial material and defamation writs would be issued very quickly by specific individuals who wouldn't hesitate to protect their good names."

"I'd challenge any applications made in the Courts." Julian intervened. "And I've given him quite contrary advice and truth is a complete defence to defamation proceedings."

"Nevertheless, you'd have to take your chances in the Courts." Quinlan interrupted.

"Let's move past the preliminaries and get to the nitty-gritty." Julian said. "What are you proposing?"

"We're happy to place a proposal to your client, but it's important your client understands his precarious position." Buller-Smith replied, nodding towards Quinlan. "Legal advice has been taken on the potential breach of the Terrorism legislation and there are some within his department who would like to issue a warrant, which could result in your client's arrest and detention without charge initially."

"Nonsense." Julian said loudly. "The press would have a field day and they'd close ranks, as fellow journalists, if you tried to go down that road, so let's cut the bullshit."

"The government can't allow the press to dictate matters of law." Buller-Smith said.

Julian shook his head. "They'd be tainted by an abuse of the intention of Parliament when they passed this legislation and the press would ensure the country understood the government's machinations." He hesitated. "If you go down that route, you risk public opinion falling on the government like an avalanche."

John smiled. "In any event, you should know I'm not easily intimidated."

"Before this gets unpleasant, we've a proposal to make, which can resolve all matters to everyone's satisfaction." Buller-Smith picked up the documentation on the desk and walked across to the other side of the desk, handing it to John, before passing another copy to Julian.

John took a cursory glance at the document and its recitals in particular, recognizing it immediately, the confidentiality clause jumping out of the page at him. "I'll not take blood money." He said firmly.

Quinlan intervened for the first time. "This isn't blood money, but rather it's a reasonable commercial contract for the exchange of intellectual property rights and any copyright you may have in the material." He moved his hand to the side. "It's a very fair and reasonable business deal." He adjusted his waistcoat. "Especially when you consider you could never publish this stuff in the first place."

"Quite frankly." Buller-Smith interceded. "We thought any reasonable man would bite our hands off because it's a very attractive offer and deserves reasonable consideration." He looked directly at John. "Look at it this way." He looked away, then back to him. "If you published the material in your possession, particularly in the biased and slanted way you've structured it, there could be significant unrest in the Muslim community. If they believed your version of events, even if it wasn't true, they could react to the perceived injustice in a way which could have serious repercussions for the country and the government can't allow that to happen."

"What are you saying to me?" John asked.

"You're wrong in some of the assumptions and conclusions, but if the Muslim community believed you, then they could deviate from lawful behaviour." Buller-Smith said. "In that respect, you'd be doing your country a service by avoiding any risk of unrest and instability."

"Is that it?" John asked.

Buller-Smith frowned. "You'd be well paid for placing the interests of your country first and it's a fair recompense for your time and research."

"Most people who were offered a million pounds after tax wouldn't dispute it's a reasonable price for the material." Quinlan said. "Especially as much of it is already in the public arena."

Buller-Smith, playing the good cop routine, leaned forward, the palms of his hands resting on the desk. "All you have to do is agree not to disclose any of this material, directly or indirectly, verbally or in writing." He looked across at Julian. "It's straight forward."

John sneered. "If the material is in the public domain, why would you pay me a million pounds after tax for it?"

"It does suggest its content is true." Julian said.

"Making me this offer simply validates the truth of my claims." John added.

"No it doesn't." Buller-Smith blew his cheeks out. "There are certain matters, which are way off the mark and you couldn't possibly know the truth."

"We don't want to be drawn into an exercise in semantics." Quinlan said.

Julian turned to John. "I think we need to discuss it."

"There's no point." John replied quickly.

Quinlan intervened again. "You must realise there are freelance agents who could take matters into their hands."

"We'd have no control over them, even in this country." Buller-Smith said. "You must appreciate we can't control the U.S. government agencies, if you don't agree to this proposal."

"Don't threaten my client." Julian raised his voice.

Quinlan turned to him, then again to John. "Be reasonable." He pointed to the one document. "This is a better offer than you're ever going to get again and you've children to think about, so why don't you ensure you live long enough to watch them grow up?"

Julian interrupted noisily. "I've warned you not to threaten my client." He clenched his fist. "You're making a huge mistake if you continue to threaten my client and this meeting will end immediately."

"Calm down." Quinlan said, moving the palms of his hands down. "I'm dealing with facts."

"Let me remind you I've signed no confidentiality agreement and have specific instructions from my client if anything happens to him." Julian said. "And I'd make life as difficult as possible for you."

Quinlan shrugged, adjusting his waistcoat again, looking up at the ceiling, then back to Julian. "All I'm saying is there are some people in the arena over which we've no control."

"Let's calm things down." Buller-Smith raised his arms in the air. "We'd be as disappointed as you, if anything untoward happened, but it's a dangerous world out there." He sighed. "And it would be far more dangerous if it were not for the work of the unseen hands of our intelligence services."

"Just use common sense." Quinlan said, tension evident in his voice. "We'd make certain all our brother agencies would know you're bound by a confidentiality agreement not to disclose anything sensitive and it gives you complete protection and freedom."

Buller-Smith turned towards Julian. "Are you prepared to give him good advice?"

Julian shrugged. "I'd like the opportunity to give him advice, but he's very much his own man." He stretched out an arm to towards John, touching his shoulder, before looking back at Buller-Smith. "How long can you give us to consider the proposal?"

Buller-Smith looked at Quinlan and gestured for him to respond. "We'd like a decision within thirty minutes. It's not an offer that can remain open indefinitely and it'll have to be withdrawn immediately if your client is not going to accept it." Quinlan said. "And obviously we don't intend an unsigned agreement should leave the room because frankly we couldn't risk your client acting in bad faith and using it in anything he writes."

"Impossible." Julian spoke firmly. "I must give him advice and it's not unreasonable he should be given a decent amount of time to consider it."

Silence filled the room in a time-warped stand-off until Buller-Smith eventually spoke. "How much time do you want?"

"The end of the week?" Julian watched, as they looked at each other. "It may be in everyone's interests he should be given time to sleep on the proposal and reflect on its merits."

"We'd have to keep the documentation?" Buller-Smith said.

"You can keep it." Julian said. "I've read it and know now what's in it."

John turned towards him, raising his voice. "Julian."

Buller-Smith turned towards his colleague, then back to Julian. "We'll give you forty eight hours." He looked at Quinlan. "If he can't make his mind up in that time, he's never going to do it."

"We may need longer." Julian said.

Buller-Smith shook his head. "That's my final decision and it's a take it or leave it proposition." He said firmly. "I don't intend to negotiate on it."

"Who shall I contact?" Julian stood up, placing the agreement on the desk, gesturing to John to leave.

"Contact me." Buller-Smith replied immediately, taking a white business card with bold black print out of a drawer in his desk and handing it to Julian.

He read it aloud. 'Anthony Buller-Smith'. 'Under Secretary. Foreign and Commonwealth Office.' He noted an e-mail address and telephone number at the bottom of the card.

*   *   *

John returned to his apartment, preferring solitude and satisfied no danger existed for at least forty-eight hours. Too many thoughts filled his mind and the following night he chased intermittent nightmares with images of conflicting outcomes flitting in and out of his mind like butterflies in the summer sun. Outside the night was dark, with no moon, darker than he had ever known before and he moved to the window of his apartment, watching ghost-like figures in the shadowy streets below, wandering through the night like lost and kindred souls. He wondered how he had moved so far from the vocation he had intended for himself when he began his language and theology studies at Cambridge University all those years ago. The problem was one of principle, but principles had cost him so much and almost his life. He moved to his bureau, sitting on a hard chair with a small desk light creating eerie shadows across the room. The sensible thing to do was take the money and run, using it to support his family and projects of worth, but he struggled to crystallize his thoughts. He noticed an e-mail had arrived in his inbox from Nadia and he clicked on it, reading it to himself.

"There's a secret agenda relating to the New World Order and it's all calculated to events in the future when they fear the world will degenerate into chaos. Banking systems will collapse and conflicts will create fear in the population. Those in positions of power know fear feeds on fear, but there's an occult agenda behind the events too." He stopped reading for a moment, moving to the kitchen for some water, before returning to the bureau to finish reading the e-mail. "My brother tells me they've far greater power than even you imagined, so take a sensible approach because they'll not allow you to derail their plans centred around Jerusalem. I'm sorry John. I've done what I can to protect you from the intelligence services over here, but I needed the documents as leverage. My brother has connections and has helped, but I can't tell you whether the steps I've taken are enough. You mustn't trust George, as he's betrayed you, but I've taken care of him. I can't return to the U.K. yet, so whatever you want to do with the apartment is up to you, but I can't say more now. I've probably said too much already for my own good because I've no doubt every email is being intercepted. If only things could have been different. I hope in time you'll forgive me because I've always had your best interests in my heart. One day, I'd like to prove it to you."

John slumped back on the chair; his heart aching at what he saw as another betrayal. He noticed another paragraph down the page and scrolled down to a final paragraph. "I know about the offer you've received and I urge you to accept it. If you don't take the money, they'll sub-contract your assassination to a Swiss man with no direct connections with British intelligence. He's not failed yet and they use him because he can't be traced back to them. I suggest you pass a copy of this email to your Solicitor friend. It may help."

He shivered, but felt a need to print off the e-mail, as if he might forget it, taking the printed sheet and reading it again, but it still sounded like the same betrayal. His mind spiralled, as he wandered around the room, with sleep more elusive than ever, He eventually returned to his desk to respond to the e-mail, feeling better for the release of angry feelings in its transmission.

Two days passed quickly, too quickly, and strangled thoughts still scuttled around his brain. The pre-arranged meeting with Julian, late in the afternoon of the second day, gave him an opportunity to hand over the printed copy of the e-mail and the reply, which had arrived more than twenty four hours later. John arrived at his office in the centre of London early, entering the reception area, with its modern furniture and computer systems incongruously contrasting with the shelves of old books framing the room, encyclopaedias of Forms and Precedents on one side and old Halsbury's Statutes on the other, both out of date. After a few minutes, the receptionist ushered him into Julian's office, gesturing towards the chair opposite him. As usual, he had managed to keep most of his desk clear, except for two yellow files on it, one of which he opened, swivelling around on his leather chair, taking a sheet of paper from a shelf behind him and turning back he wrote the date at the top of the sheet.

Julian wore his traditional black pin stripe suit and white shirt, with a red silk tie and handkerchief to match in his top pocket. "What have you decided to do?" He asked, hesitating only to stop all telephone calls. "I've not troubled you, as I wanted you to think it through, without interference or pressure from me."

"I think you know the answer without asking." John handed over the printed copies of the two e-mails received from Nadia. "What do you make of these?"

He took the e-mails and read them, leaning back in his chair, before looking up. "I'll pass them to a senior Police Officer from Special Branch, to see if there's any way they can track down this Swiss guy or protect you."

"What about the documents she's taken?" John asked.

Julian placed his hands together, almost in prayer, moving forward in his chair. "You may have evidence in the form of admissions that she's taken documents from you, but I can't see them doing anything when they may be deemed only to have a notional value." He shrugged. "In any event, it's outside their jurisdiction if she's in the Big Apple."

"I suppose so." John said. "But can we retrieve the documents?"

Julian tilted his head to one side. "I don't think that's really your major concern is it?"

"Surely, they'll have to protect me?" John asked impatiently.

"John, you're right, but you're an idealist." He said. "They should do something to protect you, but let's be pragmatic."

John sighed. "So you don't think they'll do anything to help me?"

"I'll do my best to press the Police to do something, but I can give you no guarantees, as no crime has yet been committed."

John lifted his hands in the air. "So they'll have to murder me before they'll do anything?"

Julian shook his head. "Not exactly, but you must remember they work hand in hand with the intelligence services and the mandarins in the Foreign Office, so why would they do anything, which may cut their own throats."

"But they're supposed to protect the people."

"They've only limited resources and must justify their costs." He fiddled with his pen. "For that reason, they tend to be interested in offences already committed, rather than transfer resources into the threat of offences which may or may not be committed in the future."

John shook his head, but said nothing.

Julian shrugged. "I'm sympathetic about your documents, as you know, and the potential threat to your life is far more serious, but they may simply say there's insufficient evidence about the threat to your life to be able to justify doing anything."

"And the documents?"

"It's a civil matter and they've no jurisdiction on matters of intellectual property rights." Julian held out his hands, palms up. "They may even say you had no intellectual property rights over the documents in the first place and that it's out of their jurisdiction."

"I'm disappointed."

Julian nodded. "The warnings implied by Nadia can be easily dismissed as hysterical rants from someone in love with you or they may simply believe you're paranoid."

"But it'll be too late if something happens to me."

"Of course and we can place the threat in the public domain, so they can't be ignored easily and if the danger crystallizes, I'll ensure quick action."

"And if I'm dead?

"They'll apologise and I'll create a big stink."

"But nothing will change?"

"They'll admit mistakes, but it'll make no difference."

John dropped his head into his hands.

"I'll do what I can, of course."

John looked up again. "I'll speak to a good friend of mine, a Member of Parliament on the opposition benches, and see if he can place any pressure on the Police."

Julian grunted. "The more people who are aware of the threats, the more difficult it'll be for the intelligence services to undertake lethal action." He moved the paper on his desk and wrote some notes. "If you give me his name, I'll write to him too, so he'll have evidence of the deal offered to you."

John looked up, dropping his hands down. "My friends in the newspaper industry will help, so I'll call in some favours."

Julian nodded. "I assume from the e-mails you don't trust your Editor with any of this information?"

"Damn right."

"The problem is it's easy to become paranoid." Julian said. "You end up not knowing who to trust."

John shook his head. "When Nadia mentioned George, something instinctively told me she was right. Of course, when she told me in the second e-mail he had raped her, it's not something you'd make up, whatever else I think of her right now."

Julian sighed. "Perhaps you should reconsider the monetary offer?"

"It's not possible." He shook his head. "My instinct has always been to decline the money."

Julian's face twisted. "If you want my advice I'd urge you to take the money and get a life." He sighed. "It resolves all of your problems instantly."

John's eyes pleaded for understanding. "But I must live with myself and I can't build my life on someone else's shattered dreams."

"I can't pretend to understand, John."

"But there are grieving people around the world who need the truth."

"For my sake, give it a little more thought." Julian said.

John sighed. "I've given it thought every minute of the day and the answer comes out the same every time."

"It's your decision, of course."

"What about this Swiss man referred to in Nadia's email?" John asked.

"What about him?"

"Is there any way we can make some enquiries about him?"

Julian shook his head. "It's not as if there's a directory of assassins we can look up on the internet."

"Shall I ask Nadia if she can find his name?"

"Even if she knew it, would she give it to you?"

"It could have serious consequences for her, but something tells me she'd still give it to me."

"You still want to believe the best in people, John, and I guess you care about her."

"Of course."

"You're a good man, John."

He shook his head. "I've too many flaws in my character."

"Do you have Nadia's telephone number in New York?"

John nodded. "She put the number in my diary some time ago."

"So why don't you ring her from here?"

"I'm not sure I want to speak to her at present."

"It'll be morning there." He paused. "What have you got to lose?"

John thought for a moment, his eyes moving upwards for inspiration. "Can you record the conversation and place it on a conference facility?"

"Sure. If that's what you want."

"Within a minute, the telephone rang and eventually Nadia answered.

"Hi Nad." John spoke softly, still unsure what to say.

"Hi John." Her voice cracked. "I'm sorry about what's happened, it's not what I intended at all."

"I'm ringing from my lawyer's office because it's time to make a decision about the money I've been offered."

There was a moment's pause. "Would anything I say make a difference to what you're going to do?"

"It might."

"Then take the money." There was another pause. "The freedom it'll give you will allow you to do many of the things you've always craved to do and publishing this material won't make any difference."

"But" John said, without finishing the sentence.

"It's a simple decision isn't it?" She asked.

"The problem is I can't really trust you anymore, Nad, so how can I trust your judgment?"

"Then why did you ring me?" Her voice raised and agitated.

"Because I wondered if the feelings you said you had for me were ever real."

"For what it's worth, I've never really loved anyone as much as I loved you. That was the problem."

"How can that be a problem?" He asked, forgetting the purpose of the call.

"John, anyone who knows you will know precisely what I mean."

He hesitated and neither spoke for maybe half a minute. "Can you tell me anything else about this Swiss assassin?" He paused, before asking a second question. "Do you know his name?"

"John, that word you've used is one of a number of key words, which will be picked up by the echelon software on the computers at the listening stations in Menwith Hill, Yorkshire and at GCHQ, Cheltenham." She replied. "They'll play back this telephone conversation within a day or two or even sooner, if they've picked up the e-mail."

"So what?"

"But you're placing both of our lives in grave danger."

John sighed. The ill-feeling he had felt the previous night dissipated in the light of day. "I genuinely don't want you to be hurt, Nad, believe me."

She groaned. "I know, I know."

"What went wrong, Nad?" He asked, emotion staining his voice.

"You were always too honest and too principled John." She replied. "I was afraid to tell you the truth, as I knew it would be the end for us, so I clung on to the remnants of what was left."

"I'm sorry," He nodded unconsciously, understanding the problem too well.

"It's just you." She said.

"So can you help me now?"

"I can tell you very little about the Swiss sub-contractor and I don't know his name." There was a short pause. "By definition, he doesn't publicise himself, but he works out of Brussels, which should give you the clue as to his paymasters."

"That may help." John said.

"I've asked my brother and he tells me he's a tall thin man, gaunt in appearance and an expert in modern weapons technology and chemical agents, which can mimic heart attacks."

"Anything else?"

"He speaks English with no trace of an accent."

"Are they really going to do this Nad?"

She raised her voice, almost pleading. "For the sake of everyone who loves you and your children, take the money."

"I'd like to take the money."

"Then do it." She pleaded again. "Any reasonable man would take it."

"Perhaps I'm not a reasonable man, Nad."

*   *   *

Heavy rain clouds moved rapidly across the city sky, splattering John, his hair matting across his face and drips of water ran unpleasantly down the back of his neck. He entered the same office in Whitehall as before, with Julian at his side. It was the last throw of the dice and it had taken considerable pressure to get another meeting.

Julian kept a voice recorder hidden in his pocket. This time the meeting was with Buller-Smith, though an attractive secretary sat alongside him, a pen and notepad on her lap.

"You've asked for the meeting and against my better judgment, I've agreed to it, so the ball is in your court."

"I'm grateful to you for your forbearance." Julian said.

"Your client has had a generous offer and should make up his mind."

Julian fidgeted with his brief case, taking out a file, placing it on the brief case in front of him. "My client is still in two minds about the offer."

Buller-Smith turned towards the secretary. "For the record, there's been an offer to purchase intellectual property in certain written documents, which Mr O'Rourke has yet to publish." He grunted, as the secretary scribbled away on her notepad.

"What will happen to my client if he refuses to take up the offer?" Julian asked coldly, looking at some bullet points he had written.

Buller-Smith sat back in his chair. "Nothing to my knowledge and I don't know why you ask because it's simply a business decision for your client."

"Can you guarantee his safety, if he declines the offer?" Julian asked.

Buller-Smith's face contorted, furrows crossing his face. "I can guarantee this department will not do anything to harm your client."

"But on the last occasion, your colleague indicated you couldn't guarantee his safety or protect him." Julian waited for a reply, but none came. "You even went as far as suggesting there were freelance agents out there who may take matters into their own hands."

Buller-Smith cleared his throat. "If you're recording this conversation, you're doing it without my permission." He said. "You must be taking things out of context. I'm sure my colleague would merely have been advising that it's a dangerous world out there, but we've a duty to protect the public."

"My client is a member of the public, so how far does that duty go?" Julian asked. "Will you guarantee to protect him?"

"I'm not into rhetorical questions and it's impossible to give guarantees to anyone, as my responsibility is only for Foreign Office affairs." Buller-Smith replied starkly and vaguely. "Perhaps you've come to the wrong place."

"What does that mean?" Julian asked.

"Make of it as you will."

"Do you know a Swiss contractor who does work for the intelligence services on an out-sourcing basis?" Julian asked, raising his voice.

For the first time, Buller-Smith paled, eyes narrowing. There was silence, a long silence, before he finally responded. "I really don't know what you're talking about and if you've nothing further to add, I think you should consider this meeting at an end."

"What are you afraid of?" Julian refused to move from his chair

"Nothing."

"Then what's the problem?" Julian asked.

"I must assume, unless you tell me to the contrary, that the generous offer made for your client's work is rejected?"

"I'd like to have one final moment with my client, before I confirm my instructions."

"But the offer had a time-scale attached to it, so I'm bound to withdraw the offer formally today, if it's not accepted."

"I understand."

"We'll leave the room for a few minutes, but this can't go on any longer." Buller-Smith stood up, leaving the room, his secretary in tow.

Julian turned to John. "This is the best offer you're going to get and your last opportunity." He shook his head. "There's no turning back from this point, John." His eyes pleaded again. "Take the advice of a friend and accept the offer please."

John shook his head. "I can't."

Julian groaned. "But you reject my advice at your peril, John."

CHAPTER SIXTEEN

The Washington envoy to Canada stated that the President had ordered a shoot down of Flight 93 over Pennsylvania.

The Idaho Observer related that state police officials reported residents claiming a second plane was in the sky and of burning debris falling from the sky with debris found up to eight miles from the crash site and to one report of the plane falling apart on their homes.

There is also rare footage proving Flight 93 did not crash in a single piece, but came apart in mid-air, scattering over a wide area with human remains found miles from the crash site.

A Mayor stated "I know of two people, one served in Vietnam, who heard a missile." He added, "Military F-16 fighter jets were very, very close."

Another report talks of hearing some sort of explosion and seeing white smoke coming from the plane. This article rapidly disappeared from news websites when it did not fit the official story.

Reuters: The opening remarks at a Guantanamo trial by Naval Officer stated: "If they hadn't shot down the fourth plane, (Flight 93), it would have hit the dome."

Much of the technology developed in the United States can remain secret for years before it is divulged. The public know little about the extent of the use of the Global Hawks or the secret unmanned space plane, the X-37B, which can shoot down satellites and stay in space for at least six months or high energy lasers or microwave technology. Further, any Russian missiles confiscated at the time of the breakdown of the Soviet Republic would be regarded as top secret.

A United Airlines employee noted on 10th April 2003 that both Flight No: 93 (Tail No: N591UA) and Flight No: 175 (Tail No:N612UA) were still very much in use as he spotted them at O'Hare International Airport in Chicago and were marked as "Still Valid" in the manifests. Neither were scheduled to fly on the morning of 9/11 according to the manifests.

For several minutes, Julian stared blankly ahead in the back of the taxi, as it trundled slowly back through London's chaotic traffic, unchanged by the imposition of congestion charges for vehicles in the City centre. His face looked ashen and demeanour so different from his normal ebullient self. Rain pelted frenetically on the roof of the taxi, creating kaleidoscope patterns across the windows. He felt claustrophobic in the back seat and still puzzled at how John could turn down so generous an offer when his life was at stake. As much as he respected his values, he feared the worst for his good friend, even though he understood his distrust of the arbitrary use of executive powers of government. In his profession, he had acquired pragmatism by necessity after a career spent fighting the Establishment through the courts. He craved justice as much as the next man, but accepted the imperfect nature of the country's legal systems.

After several minutes of painful silence, he turned to John. "Let's put some precautions in place back at my office." He took a deep breath. "There are some things I can do."

"Whatever you think is best." John spoke without even looking at Julian, having withdrawn into that hidden part of himself where he could seek refuge.

"What made you reject the offer, John?"

"I had no choice."

"And the money?"

"What about the money?"

"Would it have changed your decision, if I could have negotiated more?"

"No, no. It's not the money." He turned to Julian "I've never been interested in money or things."

"You're right, of course." Julian said.

"I make my decisions according to what's right."

"I understand you've never done things for monetary reasons, but I'd like to understand your decision because I've got to live with it too."

John sighed, compassion in his eyes. "If I'm true to myself and to the principles in which I believe, then I had no choice."

"Patronize me, John, because I don't understand."

"Every thought which has ever been thought still exists." John said. "The energy behind my thoughts expands the more focus is placed on them and the longer I hold the thoughts." He ignored the puzzled expression on Julian's face. "They don't die if I die, but the world would deteriorate a little if I focused on different and less worthy thoughts, which would also have the effect of poisoning my soul." He smiled at Julian, suspecting he would never understand. "It's a price I can't pay."

"But John, you've so much to live for."

"So you think I'm a dead man walking already?" A twisted smile crossed his face.

"No, no." Julian replied, his face flushing. "But why take any chances?"

John spoke softly without looking at him. "Even physicists can establish that energy is indestructible, and thoughts are energy, so the energy I send out to the God within me is indestructible." He looked at Julian. "This is what I believe, so how can I act against those beliefs?"

"But John." Julian began a sentence he could not finish.

"There are no buts, Julian." He interrupted immediately. "I must be true to myself if balance is to be restored to humanity, as inevitably it must, whether I live or die." He caught Julian's eyes. "Don't you see?" He asked. "It's my contribution to the building of the Temple."

"This is all beyond my comprehension."

John smiled again, seemingly unaffected by the consequences of his decision. "You forget this is my territory, Julian. Not only was my uncle a Cardinal, but I was trained into the priesthood and practised as a priest for years, so what I believe in is what I am." He sighed. "And I've told you I must be true to myself."

"But what if you die?" Julian's voice arched.

"My training tells me this life is an illusion and the truer reality lies beyond death. It's death itself which is the great illusion and everything we do in this life prepares us for that transition." He spoke calmly. "It holds no fears for me."

"I don't see it."

"It doesn't matter, Julian, because the issue of dying had no part in my decision, other than the thought of its effect on my children."

"Then what about your children?"

"In its way, what I do is for my children because I'm creating a better world for them by following my truth."

"I still don't understand."

"Julian." He raised his voice, furrows emerging on his face. "Every thought matters if the world is to become a better world. If I denied the thoughts, I'd be staining my humanity."

Julian thought for a moment, but shook his head. "I can't pretend to understand, but I do know the world would be a worse place without you."

"The thought of not being there for my children grieves me, but I've already grieved for them when I had to leave them after the divorce. I don't blame anyone." He wiped rain water from the back of his neck. "They'll be materially and emotionally cared for in the event of my death."

"But you're such a good father."

"I'm not convinced I was cut out to be a father."

"That's nonsense." Julian said. "I've seen you with them."

"Perhaps we all have different destinies, but the thought of my death crystallizes what's important in my life."

"You're a brave man." Julian said. "And you've proved you're resilient, so let's be positive."

"I'm not any braver than the next man." John took a deep breath. 'But I don't fear death, it's the mind killer."

"What do you mean?"

"It attracts to it the thing you fear, so you can't live freely if you're afraid to die."

Julian shook his head.

John smiled. "In some ways, it would be a blessed relief, though to hasten it would be against everything I hold sacred."

Julian sighed. "I'll send letters to Special Branch and you must use your network of friends to get things published." He wrote notes in his pocket diary. "I'll get your website active and generate traffic to the site."

John felt strangely at peace. "Don't worry, Julian." He said. "I've a feeling everything will work out as it should be."

"Let's still make this difficult for them."

John nodded. "You've retained my Will and know what needs to be done in the event of my death?"

"Let's not look at this too bleakly." He replied. "I'll also fax and post letters to the Foreign Office referring to our meetings and my concerns about your safety." He replaced the diary back in his inside pocket. "They'll have to think carefully about the course they set."

"As you think fit, Julian." John sighed, the relief he felt palpable. He knew some of the great truths often came as paradoxes in the observations of them and the thought of facing death had strangely brought vitality into his life, which made him feel more alive than he could ever remember.

Julian turned to him. "I'd create such a stink if an assassination took place."

John smiled a peaceful smile. "I know, Julian. I know."

*   *   *

A week elapsed, a week of canvassing friends in the publishing world, of submitting information and various pieces of work to both the established and new order. He had written the profile for the website, a strange experience, placing his affairs in some sort of order, as if he was suffering from a terminal disease. He had managed to see his children, even if he had been reluctant to take them from their secure environment to avoid inadvertent targeting, but after the healing an urge to escape it all took over. Against Julian's advice, he had chosen mainland Europe and in particular Italy for his final destination, as he had promised himself he would return to Rome as a final pilgrimage and a reminder of the times spent there with his late uncle, but he attended Julian's office one last time.

"I'm leaving tomorrow, Julian." He said. "In an emergency, you know how to contact me."

"I still don't think it's wise, John." He paused. "Who'll protect you on the continent if there are difficulties?"

"I have faith."

"But you'll be on your own, with no witnesses to record events. If they've already engaged this Swiss man, you'll be on his territory on the Continent."

You're right, as always, but I'm not going to live my life like a prisoner in a cocoon." He said. "It wouldn't be living at all"

"But John, I'm concerned about your welfare."

John raised his hand. "Let them do their worst."

"I've always admired your courage, John."

"But I'm no different from anyone else."

Julian shook his head. "You've more courage than anyone else I know, John."

"My decision has set me free, Julian."

Julian nodded. "Will you be taking your mobile with you on your travels?"

"Why not?"

"Because you can be tracked from it, whether it's switched on or not."

"The intelligence man, Evan, told me the same thing, but I'm taking it."

"It's a matter for you, of course."

John smiled. "Evan has been very helpful and he may ring you, as he knows you're my solicitor and friend." He hesitated. "He's the source of some of the documents in your possession."

"John. I'm not sure you're wise to trust people in the intelligence community."

He nodded. "I understand completely, but you make a judgment and I'll not hide in the shadows."

"You're my most difficult client, John," His voice resonated with exasperation.

"Have you had replies to the faxed letters?" John asked.

"Only acknowledgments saying they're looking into the matter and a detailed reply will follow when investigations are complete." He shrugged. "A standard response."

"I didn't really expect anything else."

"What about your itinerary, John?"

"I'll leave it with you and approximate timescales."

"What about the names of hotels where you'll stay?"

"I'm sorry Julian, but I can't." He said firmly. "I'm going to drive through France and enjoy whatever time I have left and I'll stop when I feel like stopping."

"You're so stubborn." He shook his head. "It's not sensible."

"I know, Julian, but I'm not going to crawl into a bunker." He smiled. "I simply won't do it."

"There's a part of me, which admires you, John, but the lawyer in me thinks you're an idiot."

John laughed. "I'll ring you every second day with my location." He looked directly into his eyes. "If you've not heard from me after two days, you may have something to worry about."

"I suppose it's the best I'm going to get."

"It would be good to get to Rome, almost like going home."

Julian nodded. "A part of me admires you, even if you refuse to take best advice."

John stood up. "I'll go through the Channel Tunnel because I want to drive."

Julian shook his head, unable to reconcile his friend's choices. "Whatever you say, John."

"Do you need anything else?" John asked.

"Not really." Julian stood up, moving to the door of his office. "You're obviously going to ignore my concerns about your safety, particularly travelling in mainland Europe."

John smiled. "I know you think I'm mad, but don't worry about me."

"But I've no contacts on the continent to assist you in the event of any problems." His eyes showed concern. "It would be easy for a mugging to appear random."

"I've made up my mind, Julian." He offered his hand. "You've been a good friend, so there must be no guilt over decisions I freely make."

Julian shook his hand and walked with him to the outside office door. "Do take care of yourself, my friend."

John smiled confidently, turned, and left.

*   *   *

Paris had always been his intended first stop and he stayed at the Hotel Mercure, near the Eiffel Tower, where he always stayed when visiting the city. He should have stayed at a small guest house outside the City with no modern computer systems to pick up his passport on the grid, but he wanted to roam around familiar places on the Left Bank and to indulge himself at Le Grand Café, at Opera.

After two days in the City he continued his journey, surprised no confrontations had occurred. He wondered whether he had become paranoid, but sixty kilometres south of the City on the A6, La Route de la Sud, he noticed a Mercedes Coupe pull alongside him. The driver looked directly at him and when their eyes met, the man smiled. He must have been in his forties, bespectacled with a brown moustache, flecked with auburn and grey. To the whole world he represented an image of respectability, but when he pulled in front of him, staying forty metres ahead for more than ten minutes, he suspected the worst. As they approached the next service station, the driver lifted his arm out of the window, pointing to the sign and repeating the gesture with his hand, beckoning him to follow. His indicator flashed. John knew if he did not follow, it would acknowledge fear and he would learn nothing, but if he followed it would have its risks. Many thoughts spiralled into his mind and, instinctively, almost before he had decided what to do, he placed his indicator on and followed him. For safety reasons, he telephoned Julian on his mobile, outlining his predicament, asking him to remain on the line. He gave him the registration number of the Mercedes and placed the telephone in his shirt pocket, pulling his jacket over it, before driving alongside the Mercedes Coupe. A lean man fitting perfectly the description of the Swiss man alighted and he did likewise. The green countryside adjoining the car park sloped away to the south and many people milled around, voices mainly and unsurprisingly French. There was little time to observe anything else, only this innocuous-looking man dressed in an old fashioned trilby hat and a short brown coat. The man pointed to a wooden bench nearby with a picnic table alongside. John took a deep breath, the warm air invigorating his lungs and adrenaline rushed into his veins bringing a flood of energy.

"I've heard so much about you." The man turned to John, gesturing for him to sit first.

He obliged without hesitation. "I've heard a little about you too, though not your name."

He smiled and fenced with him. "Yes. What about names?"

"Do you want to give me yours?" John asked.

"They're just tags for those who want to be tagged." He replied. "They mean little in the scheme of things."

John searched the man's eyes for access to his soul, but the spectacles contained a tint and deflected his gaze. "You've nothing to fear from me, so why are you afraid to give me your name?"

The man looked around. "In different circumstances, I'd be happy to oblige you."

"It's going to make conversation difficult."

"If it helps, call me Eric?" He said, playfully. "It's as good a name as any."

"What do you want from me, Eric?"

"I don't want to play a game of cat and mouse with you because it shows no respect for a man of your substance." He smiled, charmingly. "You deserve better."

"I don't understand." John said.

"You wouldn't be alive now, if I didn't respect you."

"What do you mean?" John's eyes narrowed, frowning.

"I've had many opportunities to implement the conditions of my contract, but have purposely held back to observe you." He took off his spectacles and smiled. "This is most unusual for me."

John looked into his eyes, large pools of water, deep water, not the empty receptacles he anticipated. "You're a strange man with a strange occupation."

He smiled again. "By talking to you, I'm breaking all my rules."

"So why are you doing it?" John's face showed tension for the first time.

Eric looked away, but carried on talking. "Most men, knowing what you know, would run or hide." He replaced his spectacles and turned to him. "You've done quite the opposite and I'm curious about the reason."

"So you want me to satisfy your curiosity?"

"It's quite extraordinary and I needed to know the reason?"

"But why should I tell you anything?"

"That's true, of course." He looked at John, searching for an old memory. "I thought perhaps someone had hurt you so deeply in the past that you were already dead inside." He shrugged. "In those circumstances, there'd be no fear of death, but with you it appears something more profound."

John smiled. "Perhaps it's why you're not doing what you normally do, but I doubt whether someone in your position would understand."

"But my profession is much misunderstood."

"I doubt it."

"But it's my paymasters who make the decisions, not me." He said. "I'm just the mechanic, a meticulous one, but nevertheless a mere mechanic."

"You talk coldly about killing in a matter of fact way, as if it's normal." John said. "But what about the damage to your soul?"

Eric looked up and thought for a moment, before adjusting the buttons on his coat to open it, revealing a plain blue shirt underneath with top button open. "It happens like this." He placed his fingers against his lips and immediately took them away again, looking directly into John's eyes. "You become a soldier first with ambition to climb the ranks, so you obey orders and learn how to kill. It's patriotic and crowds come out to welcome you home when you return from a war zone in some obscure place. The place is of no consequence, but you feel good about yourself." He noticed a perplexed expression on John's face and smiled. "Honestly you do feel like a hero. Perhaps it's part of the indoctrination, but you learn many skills, all intended to help you kill, but you persuade yourself you're on the side of the good guys, doing this for your country."

John sighed, interrupting. "I can understand from a soldier's perspective, but now you take money to kill innocents, as a mercenary."

"It's no different." He said. "I just happened to be a good soldier and instead of killing for my country on orders from people I didn't respect, I freelance."

"In what country were you a soldier?" John asked, if only for Julian's benefit.

"Please." He replied. "I'd be disappointed if you treated me as a fool and whatever else you may think of me, I'm not a fool."

"Of course not, but you've already admitted you kill for money."

"Didn't you play with toy soldiers as a boy?" Eric asked.

"Of course I did, but that's different."

"How is it different?" He asked. "You learn about the great battles as part of your history lessons. In your case, Waterloo or Trafalgar and you learn that victory is glorious and you admire the great soldiers and their tactics." He moved his hands to the side. "It's the same when you freelance because there's a strange satisfaction in doing something meticulously and strategically well."

"It's an absurd analogy." John said.

"Perhaps you'll never understand it, but it's there. I assure you."

"So you don't think there's anything wrong in what you do?"

Eric pursed his lips. "The first contracts you take are often from the same line of command as those you take before you become a civilian, so you don't notice any difference." He inhaled a large breath. "Maybe you convince yourself this person is a bad guy and you're still soldiering, but after the first freelance contract, it's a routine you deal with in the same way a soldier does."

"But your soul; the damage you do to your soul?" John's voice arched.

"Of course, I'd forgotten." He replied. "You trained as a priest."

"However we're trained, whether it's priest or soldier, you're doing damage to yourself." He felt a need to redeem this man's soul.

"Not really."

"Don't you ask yourself if all of the people you murder are good or bad people?"

"It's not personal, it's just business." He replied. "And after watching so many people die, I'm convinced death is the end and there's nothing else."

"So, you don't believe in the survival of the spirit?" John asked.

He shook his head. "I've never seen anything to suggest there's anything beyond the physical body."

"Do you take every contract offered to you?"

He thought for a moment. "I've taken every contract offered to me." He shrugged. "It's the nature of my profession and difficult to refuse."

"You call it a profession?" He asked.

Eric looked sternly at John. "Of course." He replied. "There are skills involved and although anyone can learn to kill, the real skill is making it appear as a natural death."

John shook his head. "We're all projections of the group soul and one day you'll discover you damage your soul when you take someone's life."

"Life is flimsy and I've seen many people die, John." He placed his hands to the side. "When I see them take that last breath, there's nothing. If they're good or bad, it doesn't matter. For me, this idea of a soul is an illusion weak people create for themselves because they're afraid to die."

"So we're a freak accident of nature, a chemical reaction, leaving nothing behind us when we depart from this world, no inspiration, no joyous memories?"

"Correct."

"What about sacrifice, honour and heroism?" John asked. "As a soldier you must understand these qualities?"

Eric smiled again. "I've seen those qualities, but the heroes have left widows who survive with only medals and hardship to show for it. Even my mother suffered when my father died a soldier's death, with no money for food or for the education you now take for granted."

John nodded. "I begin to understand."

Behind the spectacles, Eric's eyes blazed. "Don't patronize me." He said, an edge in his voice. "I'm not looking for your understanding."

John raised both his hands and lowered them, surprised a man so cold and calculating could be so emotional. "I'm not patronizing you." He smiled. "You talked about being a soldier and I wouldn't have argued if what you did was in self-defence or in defence of your family or your country, if there was no other alternative, but what you do is because of your father's legacy."

"Please don't try to understand me."

John grunted. "As a former priest, I sense you're troubled and it's possible I can help you?"

Eric laughed loudly, a deep guffaw.

"What do you find so funny?" John asked.

He stopped laughing. "Forgive me. It's rude to laugh, but you misunderstand my motives in talking to you because I'm not looking for absolution or salvation."

"Why not?"

"I've made a pact with myself to provide security for my family, using skills my government developed." He replied. "I'll do whatever is necessary to make a better quality of life for myself and my family."

John shook his head. "It's a mistake."

He turned his head to the side. "The die is cast and I'll not change."

"But it's the pain you've suffered in childhood, which has triggered your lifestyle."

"I don't think so."

"Then the pact you've made is a pact with the Devil, for it'll damage your immortal soul."

Eric sighed. "Now you disappoint me, John, because I expected something more than platitudes."

"What happens now?" John asked.

"Aren't you the least bit afraid to die?"

"You were a soldier." John replied. "Were you afraid to die?"

"I suppose so." He replied. "But I was trained not to think, whereas you were trained to think." He looked at John. "Perhaps this is the difference between us."

"I've suffered pain too and at times death would have been a relief, but you go beyond the pain." John said. "The mystics call it the long night of the soul."

"Is that what takes away your fear of death?" Eric asked.

"I've studied the mystics in many cultures and religions, not merely as a scholar." John shifted uncomfortably on the hard bench seat. "Eventually, from studying those things and turning within, you gain an absolute conviction that there's a part of us which is indestructible and immortal."

Eric smirked. "I simply don't believe it."

"I know, but even modern quantum physics proves energy is indestructible." John observed him carefully. "You can call it spirit, energy or anything you wish because the label isn't important, but once you believe these things, you don't fear death afterwards."

Eric stared at him for perhaps half a minute, almost trance-like. "That's more what I expected from you."

A French family with four young children carrying picnic baskets and a rug noisily passed them, skipping playfully, innocently ignorant of the events in front of them. The conversation stopped as they exchanged a 'bon jour' with the parents, watching as the family moved to the table beyond them.

Eric spoke softly. "I understand you turned down a million pounds for your work on the complicity of the western governments in the terrorist events in New York and London." He turned to John again. "Why?"

"I'm not sure you'd understand."

"It'll make no difference in the scheme of things, but try me."

John took a deep breath, looking across at him. "We all have choices in life." He said. "It's called free will."

"Everyone wants to believe this illusion." Eric's eyes turned away.

"You sound as if you're afraid of the truth."

Eric smiled again. "So why did you turn down the money?"

"I couldn't sit back and allow the information to stagnate into malignancy. I believe justice will eventually be seen to be done." John's eyes questioned him. "So many innocent people have died and it's not right that the guilty should be immune from the consequences of their actions, so I couldn't be a part of a cover-up." He hesitated. "Anyway my death won't stop the truth emerging."

Eric nodded. "An idealist, as I suspected." He smiled. "I thought your justice is administered after death?"

John nodded. "You're right, of course."

"I like your ideals, John, but the real world is full of greedy, imperfect people"

"But what wonderful ideals, Eric?" He replied immediately, catching his eyes, hidden behind the spectacles, unflinching in the contact. "What if no-one had done anything about Hitler after his rise to power?"

"That's completely different."

"You're wrong, Eric." John said. "Eventually you'll end up with nightmares, unable to sleep at night."

He laughed. "Don't worry about me."

"But I do."

"I'll accept your answer, John, even if I don't understand your logic, but in the world in which I live, I see things from a different perspective."

John still felt a strange need to redeem this man. "It's true." He said. "Our worlds are separate and different because we've created them with our individual thoughts and imagination."

"I'm not sure I understand, John."

John smiled. "Be more careful with your thoughts because they have the power to create worlds."

He shook his head. "You're an exceptional man, John, and I wish the circumstances were different."

"They can be, if you wish."

"In my profession, it's not possible."

"Then change your profession."

"Once I've taken the contract, there's no turning back." Eric smiled. "The best I can offer is the opportunity to choose the time and place." He stood up. "Even the method, if you want?"

John wondered how this man could discuss these matters so coldly, but aware that Julian was listening, he played along. "How will it happen and where?"

"You choose if you wish." He replied. "It's the least I can do in the circumstances."

John shook his head. "I've not done this before, so what do you have in mind?"

"You could be walking down a dark street at night when some young thugs, high on crack cocaine or heroin, mug you, but it's no ordinary mugging." Eric spoke softly. "They've already been paid, normally enough for fixes for a month, and there's no risk of any evidence tracing back to me because I'd be far away." He hesitated for a moment. "Of course, I may have to stop the suffering of one of life's victims, a miserable man, probably with an overdose of heroin or cocaine or simply contaminated powder, but the trail would end in a brick wall."

"As simple as that?"

"It sounds simple, but it's not." He replied. "Nothing could be traced back to me and my principals would be happy." He turned to John. "This would lead to more lucrative contracts and so it goes on."

John stood up and they walked back to their cars together. "What about me?" John asked, struggling to engage in the surreal conversation.

"I'm told the preference is for your death to appear an accident or even natural causes, but it's the only restriction placed on me."

"Mugging sounds unpleasant." John said.

"There's always the chemical in your drink." He said. "The Micky Finn, as the Americans call it."

"Is it painful?" John prolonged the conversation for Julian's sake.

"Almost painless, perhaps twenty seconds of unpleasantness, but it may show the symptoms and appearance of a heart attack" He looked at John. "I can arrange it, if you wish."

"How would you do it?"

"A waiter in a bar or restaurant would normally do it for me, if I pay him enough." Eric spoke coldly, no emotion in the voice, as if discussing a scene in a soap opera. "If given the choice, it's what I'd do."

Some instinct of self-preservation still hovered within John's psyche and if he knew where it would happen, then he thought it would be easier to track him. "I'd like to see Rome one last time." Even if death held no fears, he had no intention of making it easy for this amoral man and Eric underestimated him if he thought so. "And I suppose the Micky Finn sounds the least painful alternative."

"I can always arrange for a gentle anaesthetic to be administered, allowing you to drift into a sleep state first, so that a lethal poison can be injected later, probably in the inner ear, so there'll be no marks on the body capable of being picked up in an autopsy." He spoke methodically, as if proud of his skills.

"The gentle way please." John said, as if observing events from a place outside of himself.

"Very well." Eric held out his hand incongruously, as if shaking hands on some business deal. "Shall we meet in Rome then?"

John nodded. "Rome."

"I should warn you if you fail to cooperate, I must reserve the right to keep all options open." Eric tilted his head. "I'm sure you understand the nature of my contract."

"Where shall we meet?" John strangely took his hand, almost subconsciously.

"Don't worry." He smiled his charming smile. "I'll find you if it's necessary because I've all sorts of surveillance devices, some you can't even imagine."

John returned to his car and watched as the Mercedes drove back onto the motorway. "Did you hear it all?" He asked.

"I heard it."

"Can you use any of the clues from the conversation to track him?" John asked

"I'll contact the Rome Polizia to warn them of a contract killer loose in their city, but there's no way the registration plate of the vehicle is lawful, so I doubt anything can be done before he gets to Rome, but I'll try."

Many jangled thoughts, all frenetically demanding attention, fought for supremacy and John wondered who he could trust. He purchased a mobile telephone from the Service Station to text Evan the message 'priest' and 'Rome—Spanish Steps. Saturday 1700 hours'. A long shot, he thought, but worth the try.

CHAPTER SEVENTEEN

"Islam can teach us today a way of understanding, which Christianity itself is poorer for having lost. At the heart of Islam is its preservation of an integral view of the Universe—as also with Buddhism and Hinduism (and with the Gnostic Christian gospels). It refuses to separate man and nature, religion and science, mind and matter and has preserved a metaphysical and unified view of ourselves and the world around us. But the West gradually lost this integrated vision of the world with Copernicus and Descartes and the coming of the scientific revolution. A comprehensive philosophy of nature is no longer part of our everyday beliefs . . . . There are things for us to learn in this system of belief which, I suggest, we ignore at our peril . . . . Young Britons need to be taught by Islamic teachers how to learn with their hearts, as well as their heads." (Prince Charles—in speeches from 1996).

Qur'an Chapter 2, Verse 62: "Verily, those who believe and those who are Jews and Christians . . . . whoever believes in God (Allah) and the Last Day and does righteous good deeds shall have their reward with their Lord, on them shall be no fear, nor shall they grieve."

Qur'an Chapter 57, Verse 27: " . . . . We sent after them our Messengers and we sent Jesus, son of Maryam (Mary), and gave him the Gospel and we ordained in the hearts of those who followed him, compassion and mercy . . . ."

"A great liar is also a great magician." Hitler.

John reached Rome early on the Saturday, booking a hotel room not far from its centre. The Eternal City in the beautiful month of May was everything he remembered, with so many people milling around, enjoying its unique atmosphere and culture. It was the perfect month for shirt-sleeve walking and al-fresco dining in the beautiful restaurants scattered around the piazzas and its medieval cobbled backstreets. The smells of freshly-baked pizzas and the buskers, the street vendors, even the fortune-tellers, all invoked old memories and lifted his spirit. He had reported to Julian, as promised, using a public telephone he thought would be difficult to trace. The sound of the exquisite language, with its rifts of staccato highs and lows, so romantic and vibrant, invigorated him. Arriving early at the Piazza di Spagna, at the foot of the Spanish Steps, he noticed no-one familiar. As usual, the area was full of the young of Rome, la Bella di Roma, sitting on the steps, watching life pass, naively unaware of its mortal dangers. He stopped momentarily to study Bernini's famous Barcaccia fountain. A little child with groping hands, obviously of Eastern European extraction, tugged at his shirt. These beggar children spilled around the tourist spots, their mothers hovering in the background, gesticulating wildly if they refused to pursue their victims relentlessly. Dismissing the child with a wave of his hand, he subconsciously felt for his wallet.

He walked to the top of the Spanish Steps, dodging the children and the courting couples sprawled across almost its entire length, navigating the climb to the top carefully. At the top, he looked towards the dome of St Peter's Basilica in the distance, bringing back memories of his uncle, who had been more like a father to him. A jolt of apprehension, like a sinking feeling somewhere deep in his stomach, reminded him of a darker destiny and he scoured the area looking for Eric, his intuition sensing his presence nearby. He felt like a condemned man, counting down the hours to his death, clamouring for more time, but knowing it was inevitable. It wasn't fear in the traditional sense, but rather a body demanding the right to live its allotted span and resisting the spirit's impulse to return home.

Patience was a virtue that John had never mastered and after waiting for more than an hour with no sign of Evan, he took one final glance around and left. It may have been a long shot and his last trump card, but it was time to accept whatever fate offered. He wandered around aimlessly for perhaps an hour or two, refusing to look over his shoulder, as he walked past the expensive designer shops in Rome, eventually reaching the popular Piazza Novona. A series of fountains drew the tourists, particularly the

Fontana Dei Quattro Fiumi at its centre. It was too expensive to eat there, he thought, but smiled to himself, as if the cost of the restaurants was important in his precarious predicament. Nevertheless, he moved away from the artists and the caricaturists and crossed one of the river bridges, ambling slowly along the narrow streets towards Trastevere. He loved walking along the sun-dappled cobbled streets, with their strange intertwining properties, draped with ivy and wisteria-covered balconies. The haphazard restaurants always attracted him, all punctuated with the multi-coloured flowers and window boxes and all likely to fail the fire regulations and modern health and safety obligations. The smells, the architecture, all mingled in the melting pot of cultures which inhabited the area, but he determined to enjoy every minute granted to him, even purposely ignoring the sounds of heavy footsteps echoing around and behind him in some of the quieter and more secluded alleys and streets. The journey to Trastevere was as enjoyable as the destination, as he passed a restaurant with Dean Martin's 'That's Amore' seeping out. He walked on towards the next piazza, smiling to himself at the unashamed commercialism of the place, even within the shadow and earshot of the Vatican. Finally, he entered a familiar small restaurant and sat down in a quiet corner, sighing as he sank deeply into the comfort of a cushioned chair in a corner of the restaurant away from any window and shielded from prying eyes.

He remained in a world of his own, grounding himself only for a few minutes to enjoy the menu and anticipate its culinary delights until the noise of the chair opposite being moved drew his eyes upwards. At first, he didn't recognize the figure hovering above him, with the full beard and tinted spectacles. His attire seeming more akin to the artists at the Piazzo Novona, with light blue ragged linen trousers and a shirt opened at the top with a strange cravat of sorts tucked around his neck.

"I'm sorry I couldn't make it to the Spanish Steps, John, but you were being watched."

John squinted. "It's you, Evan." He said. "I didn't recognize you."

"Do you mind if I join you?" He asked.

"Of course not." John replied instantly, gesturing to the chair with his hand.

Evan grunted as he sat down, removing tinted spectacles and sitting across the table from John.

"Evan. I'm sure your eyes were blue the last time we met."

"They're contact lenses."

John nodded, offering his menu. "Are you joining me for the food?"

"Why not?"

John related the events of his journey and, in particular, the meeting with Eric at the service station south of Paris.

"Bizarre." Evan said.

"It was surreal."

"That's not normal, of course, and I can't explain it." Evan examined the menu.

"Is this the sort of life you live, mixing with these type of people?"

Evan shook his head. "Definitely not." He replied firmly. "Most of our work is routine and boring, but it sounds as if your conversation could uncover clues about the man's identity."

"My lawyer friend is working on it."

"When is the hit likely to happen?" John asked.

"It's difficult to say because so far he's broken all the rules."

"What do you mean?"

"He's been so unprofessional." He replied. "But you've been naïve too, John." He placed the menu back on the table. "You know I've worked for the Foreign Office and for all you know I could be an assassin too." He raised his eyebrows and smiled.

"I suppose so."

"Yet you're happy to talk to me." He said, looking over his shoulder for a waiter. "Many assassins are quite personable and it's often the reason they're successful."

"I'm not going to worry about it, Evan."

"But how do you know I don't have a contract to assassinate you?"

John sat back. "Life is full of risks."

A waiter arrived, taking their order and mundane conversation followed, as they ate their food and shared some house wine.

"It's a dirty job you do, Evan." John wiped his mouth with a serviette.

Evan shook his head. "There's a strange sense of satisfaction when you've followed a plan meticulously."

John felt uneasy, remembering a similar expression used by Eric. He looked at him differently in the moment, trying to search for the man behind the mask, as he would have done as a priest years ago. "Does that mean you've been responsible for killing people, Evan?"

"Not directly." He replied vaguely.

"I thought field officers' license to kill was a fiction and you sub-contracted out that sort of work."

"I had a colleague who was killed in the Balkans and I know someone in the community did it"

"What's happened to that man?" John asked.

"Nothing."

"But surely there's no satisfaction in killing someone?"

Evan took a last sip of wine from his glass. "I'm no expert in these matters." He lied. "But this is what colleagues tell me and I simply meant that I could see the satisfaction in doing something well."

"So you've not killed anyone?"

Evan's face flushed. "As you must know, no-one within the intelligence services will ever admit to killing anyone." He replied vaguely again.

John finished his glass of wine quietly, recalling both Lynne and Evan had mentioned his friend who had disappeared in the Balkans, but nothing had previously been mentioned about him actually killed. It made him strangely suspicious and he stood up. "It's time for me to go."

"I'll wait here and leave separately." Evan said.

He turned to Evan. "When will I see you next?"

"I'll be looking out for you and when it's safe I'll find you.'"

"Then I'll go now." John started to move away from the table.

Evan caught his arm as he passed. "I'll wait a respectable time and leave, but tell me the route you're taking back to your hotel, so I can remain a reasonable distance behind you."

"I haven't even thought about it."

"Are you walking back to your hotel?" Evan asked, before ordering a limoncello from the waiter as he passed.

John shrugged. "I love walking around Rome, especially at night, so I guess I'll walk."

"Fair enough." Evan said.

John walked away feeling uncomfortable with unanswered questions flitting in and out of his head. It wasn't the awareness of the risks he faced, but something else. Too many discrepancies had arisen in the conversation and he recalled Evan's failure to protect Lynne, despite his friendship with her. He had no conviction he could be protected either and he walked slowly back from Trastevere in a different mood, listening for every sound and sight, attaching himself briefly to a young courting couple until he crossed the bridge. For an unfathomable reason, he decided to take a taxi from there. The idea of changing hotels occurred to him, but instead he asked the receptionist at his hotel to change rooms, insisting the receptionist ensure secrecy, sleeping only in fits for most of the night. In the morning, he telephoned Julian, needing detached advice to take stock of his position and recognizing for the first time that more than anything else he had a strong desire to live.

"You must return home now." Julian said firmly. "It's not right you take these risks."

"Perhaps you're right." John said.

"If you leave Rome, don't take your car because it'll have a tracking device attached to it by now."

"But I feel more in control when I drive my car"

Julian laughed. "In control?"

"I've realized something, Julian."

"What's that?"

"I want to live."

"You're normal, after all." Julian said. "I'll send my trainee down to collect your car and drive it back."

"I don't want any harm to come to him."

"They'll not be interested in him, so bring the keys back with you."

"So you want me to fly back?"

"It's the best and quickest way to get back."

"I'm not sure." John said.

"I need to discuss some developments on your articles."

"What developments?" John asked.

"One of the Sunday newspapers want to publish your material and serialize it, but they want to do a profile first. I've told them about the deal offered to you by the government and it's whetted their appetite." He hesitated. "But they need you back here quickly."

"That makes my decision easier." John said.

"Don't use your laptop to book the ticket, but use the hotel facilities and either fly schedule back into London from the Leonardo da Vinci Fiumicino Airport or get a regional charter flight and fly into Stansted or Bristol from Ciampino." It sounded as if he was turning over pages. "It's the airport used by both Ryanair and Easyjet."

"But something might happen today." John said.

"Then get on a flight back to the U.K. without delay." Julian said. "I'm sure it can be arranged, but don't waste time."

John thought for a moment. "I think you're right." He said. "I couldn't sleep last night and I've some doubts about this man Evan."

"What did he say?"

"Only little things, but I think after drinking he mentioned something about a friend in the Balkans being killed." John replied. "In any event, I've become wary of the man."

"I'll make some enquiries by the time you get back." Julian said. "In the meantime, I want you to telephone the Guardia di Finanza and ask for an officer called Luigi Bellastroni. Apparently, he deals with terrorist incidents and intelligence matters and acts as a liaison officer with the Carabinieri. He'll be expecting your call and wants your itinerary. He was most concerned at the thought of a contract killer in his City."

"I'll contact him after I've booked a flight." John said. "But what shall I do if Evan turns up at my Hotel?"

"Why don't you ask him to speak to me?" Julian said. "If he refuses, then it'll place you on enquiry."

John smiled. "Inventive."

"He'll know I've placed him in the City at the same time as you." Julian said.

"I hope I'll see you soon, Julian."

"By the way." Julian said, shuffling some papers. "Your friend Nadia telephoned me and said she was back in London and needed to contact you."

"Nadia."

"Yes and she's left her new number and asked if I'd pass it to you."

"Very strange" John said.

"I didn't tell her anything or even how to contact you, as I wanted to speak to you first." Julian said. "I'll not give her your new number unless you instruct me."

"Thanks Julian."

In reception, John booked a flight with remarkable ease, the Hotel printing off the ticket, before speaking to the Police, informing them of the time of his flight out of Fiumicino and his itinerary. He felt comfortable with his decisions and took a deep breath as he walked out into the Roman sunshine, groaning as he noticed Evan almost immediately, realizing it was too late to avoid him.

"What are your plans today?" Evan asked, as he reached him.

John felt renewed energy and in daylight felt more positive. "If it were not for the dangers, I'd go to the Cistine Chapel." He lied.

Evan nodded. "Then why don't you go?"

"What about you?"

Evan smiled. "I'll do what I said I'd do last night and stay a respectable distance from you, but you took a taxi last night?"

"I was tired." John lied again. "Was it a problem for you?"

Evan shook his head. "Not really, but it's your life."

"So if I'm approached by Eric, what should I do?"

"Nothing." He replied. "I'll deal with it, just trust me."

"One minute." He raised his left hand, using his right to use his mobile, contacting Julian quickly.

"Who are you telephoning?" An uneasy expression crossed Evan's face with furrows on his forehead.

"Hi Julian." John said. "As you know, I'm in Rome, but I want you to have a word with Evan." He hesitated. "I've mentioned him to you before and I thought that if there's anything you need to know to pursue your investigation, you can ask him now?" He offered the mobile to Evan, but he declined it.

Evan shook his head, waving his right index finger back and for, holding his left hand up, palm facing John, his mouth dropping open. "I can't speak to your lawyer." He said. "Don't be absurd."

"Evan, please talk to my lawyer?" He pressed him. "He'll retain confidentiality and won't repeat anything you say."

"No way." He said firmly, waving his hands so they crossed in front of him.

"Why not?"

Evan shook his head and walked ahead.

Out of earshot, John spoke to Julian: "I can't get him to talk to you, but he knew you were my lawyer, even before I mentioned it."

"It tends to corroborate your suspicions, John, so you'll have to be very careful."

"I agree." John said. "I don't know if he's freelancing or whether he's acting on instructions from his superiors."

"There are grave risks, John."

"I know."

"Have you spoken to Bellastroni?" Julian asked. "I've been assured he'll protect you."

"I've spoken to him and explained my itinerary, including my flight time out of Fiumicino and into London."

"Be careful John because I'm not sure what else I can do from here, but I'll meet you at the airport, if you give me your flight number and time of arrival."

"I'll ring you when I'm through immigration control." John said, giving him the details he needed and ending the call, before running after Evan and gaining his attention.

"Why wouldn't you talk to him?" John asked, breathing hard.

"Don't be ridiculous." He replied. "I'm not even supposed to be in Rome."

"But he's my lawyer and he's trained in confidentiality."

Evan shook his head again. "You and I are going to have a serious falling out, if you're not careful." An ugly expression distorted his face into a caricature. "I've told you I'm trying to escape the clutches of the intelligence services and I've left the country without informing them, so there's no way can I incriminate myself."

It sounded plausible, though John remained unconvinced. "I don't like your attitude, Evan, if you're supposed to be helping me, so I'll return to the hotel." He turned back in the direction of the hotel.

"You're not safe there." Evan shouted, but John ignored him, walking quickly.

A loud noise, like a gunshot, rang out, echoing across the city and John jumped out of his skin, his heart pumping with adrenaline. He looked back over his shoulder only to see Evan lying in the street, blood seeping from a wound in his chest and a handgun alongside him on the floor. He hesitated, wondering if he should run back to the hotel or duck behind a stationary car nearby. These were natural instincts, but he ended up doing neither, literally frozen to the spot for what must have been a minute. Enough time for a sniper to have shot him too, but getting his body and mind to work in unison proved impossible. Eventually, he ducked down behind the stationary car and searched the area, but noticed nothing suspicious. Police officers, guns drawn, arrived at the scene quickly with crowds morbidly gathering. He backed away towards the reception area of the hotel, where staff had come out onto the street to satisfy their curiosity and inspect the scene. Within about five minutes, the telephone in reception rang and one of the staff returned to answer it, calling to him and holding out the receiver. He took a deep breath, composing himself and taking the telephone.

"It's Bellastroni here, Mr O'Rourke. I'm afraid the shooting outside was nothing to do with my men and although it appears the victim was armed, his gun had not been fired." He hesitated. "It may have been drawn, that's all."

"Very strange." John replied

"I assume this was one of the men planning to kill you, but I need someone to identify him." He paused on the line again. "Can you do it?"

"Of course I'll do it." He replied. "His name was Evan."

"What about this man Eric, your lawyer mentioned to me?" He asked. "Can you give us a description of him?"

"Of course."

"I'm assuming that this incident can't be coincidence."

"I'm sure you're right." John said. "I've a good idea he is responsible."

"I had a man near the hotel, keeping an eye on things." Bellastroni said. John grunted. "What did he see?"

"He heard the gunshot, but saw absolutely nothing." He paused. "It had all the hallmarks of a professional hit."

"That's worrying." John's voice cracked. "There's only one man who could have been responsible for a professional hit."

"I'll need a witness statement from you before you leave, Mr O'Rourke." Bellastroni said. "I need to see you immediately?"

"I'm relieved you're taking over personally, but I hope it doesn't cause you any embarrassment because the man killed may have been an operative working for British Intelligence."

"I'll discuss it with you when I arrive in about five minutes, Mr O'Rourke." He said. "But I've received some further information I need to discuss."

"Will this prevent me leaving Rome today?" John asked.

"It shouldn't do, provided you give me the signed witness statement and agree to return for any hearing."

"Not a problem."

John replaced the telephone, but almost immediately it rang again and she held the telephone up in the air again, beckoning him forward. He picked it up, expecting Bellastroni, but instead heard Eric's distinctive voice.

"I've been watching the events outside your hotel." He said, quietly.

"Was that you who shot Evan?" John asked.

"Perhaps."

"What do you know about him?" John asked.

"His former paymasters weren't happy." He said. "He'd been freelancing and they don't like loose cannons."

"So he wasn't acting on instructions from British Intelligence?"

"I don't believe so, but I think his drinking had become a problem." There was a pause on the line. "They allowed me a free hand if he encroached on my territory and the time had come to take up the option on my contract."

John grunted. "I'm not sure I understand?"

"It's simple."

"Did Evan wanted to kill me or do you mean he'd turned against his paymasters?"

"You know he had a gun and was pointing it at you."

"So you killed him?"

"The man was a professional, but I'd been given the sole contract."

"I guess I'm not very popular at the moment." John said.

"Are the authorities controlling the events?" Eric asked.

"You probably know more than I do."

"Are you prepared to meet me today or have things changed?" Eric asked.

"I can't meet you today." John stalled for time. "It's simply not possible."

"Mm," Eric hesitated. "I'm afraid this changes things from my point of view, but at least I've warned you, John."

"Really?"

"Really." Eric replied.

"What exactly do you mean?" John asked.

"Take care." Eric said coldly, before hanging up.

John replaced the telephone again, leaning against the reception desk and took a deep breath. His life mattered to him now and to avoid a victim's bondage he determined to trust the Italian Police authorities to protect him. In less than five minutes he met Bellastroni, a tall good-looking man who spoke impeccable English. They borrowed the Manager's office and Bellastroni sat down at the desk, taking off his hat and inviting John to sit opposite him.

"First, I must tell you within seconds of your telephone call, I received a rather sinister call from the man Eric. He more or less admitted responsibility for the killing and hinted he would carry out his contract on me."

Bellastroni opened his briefcase, taking out a pad of documents. "It doesn't normally happen this way." He said, a puzzled expression crossing his face.

John nodded. "He said something about an option in his contract on the man shot in the street."

"Is that right?"

"Can you trace the call?" John asked.

"Perhaps."

"If you could get a transcript, you may find it useful as evidence." John shifted in the chair uncomfortably.

Bellastroni sighed. "Unfortunately I can't get a transcript quickly enough to benefit us this morning, but it'll be done."

"What's your advice?" John asked.

Bellastroni looked up from his paperwork and thought for a moment. "Don't leave the hotel." He scratched his head. "I'll place one of my best men here and personally drive you to Fiumicino Airport, a journey of about 26 kilometres."

"Thank you."

"But it's down to the British Police to protect you in London.

John sighed. "My lawyer is sorting that out for me."

"What do you know about the man who has been shot?" Bellastroni asked.

"As I've told you, I believe he'd been working for British Intelligence, but the telephone call I had from Eric inferred he was a rogue agent of some sort and an embarrassment to them."

"Even more interesting." He took down some notes. "I'll have to pursue enquiries with London."

"Of course."

He completed the witness statement, the whole process taking perhaps an hour to finalise by the time he outlined the historical matters. When John left the Hotel he ducked under a large white sheet, on Bellastroni's advice, as he walked from the rear of the Hotel into the back seat of his personal unmarked car.

"Is this absolutely necessary?" John asked, uncomfortable with the fuss.

"Trust me." He replied, pushing John's head downwards into the car. "It works against any sniper danger, as they'd be unable to either identify the target or hit with any precision. It may not stop him trying, but it's the best protection I can offer you over a short distance."

"Very well."

"I need you to lie down in the back of the car please, Mr O'Rourke."

In no time, the vehicle was speeding towards the airport with Bellastroni at the wheel, a marked Carabinieri vehicle in close proximity behind. For the first part of the journey, everything appeared uneventful until a dual carriageway was reached at at about half distance when John heard a loud expletive. He lifted himself up in the seat sufficiently to be able to glance through the back window and noticed a large white Toyota running to the side of the marked Carabinieri vehicle and positioning itself between that car in the outside lane of the carriageway and the wall separating the two carriageways. Bellastroni was on his radio in seconds.

"Tell me the registration number and make of the vehicle, Mr O'Rourke, please?"

John strained his eyes, reciting the Toyota make and the registration number, which was relayed to his control centre. He heard the screeching of brakes and the sound of crashing metal signifying a collision behind. Looking back he noticed the Carabinieri vehicle had been pushed into another vehicle to its side and turned around so it faced the other way. "Did you see that in your mirror?"

"I did." Bellastroni pushed his foot on the accelerator, beeping his horn continuously and weaving between slower traffic. He drove the car only as Italians do with their love of motorsport, always imagining they are driving Ferraris on a racetrack, rather than Fiats on congested roads. "Just five miles to go." He said, dropping down a gear for increased acceleration, as he weaved past another slower vehicle, this time on the inside instead of the outside.

"Can I do anything?" John felt useless in the back of the vehicle.

Bellastroni handed him the radio with one hand. "Speak to the operator in the control centre and relay any information they give you. I need to concentrate on the driving."

He willingly took it, introducing himself to the operator in his fluent Italian, his Cambridge education and linguistic skills proving useful. "They're finding the time of the next intercept." There was a pause. "There are cars driving towards you, so within minutes they believe they can protect your rear."

Before Bellastroni could respond, he felt a bump, as the white Toyota ran into the back of them. John strained again in his attempts to look inside the driver's compartment, but the windscreen had tinted glass and it proved impossible. "The windscreen has tinted glass, but it can only be Eric."

"Hold on tight to something." Bellastroni said. "I'm going to try and slow him down."

John just about had time to hang onto the back of the seat in front when the car braked hard. His face forcibly pressed forward into the back of the seat in front, then a huge bump from behind as the Toyota hit the car hard. This time, he was thrown back hard into the rear seat, dropping the radio on the floor on impact, immediately picking it up again. He felt the car accelerate again and noticed the white Toyota had fallen some way behind. A signpost for the next exit appeared and the radio operator chimed in. "One of our vehicles will be joining you at the next entrance." He relayed the message.

"About time," Bellastroni shouted as he manoeuvred around slower traffic again.

John heard the sound of a police siren as they passed the exit. He could see a traffic police car move onto the carriageway and signal for Bellastroni to go ahead. The officer in the passenger seat of the vehicle drew a gun and aimed at the tyres of the white Toyota, as it moved alongside. A screech of brakes followed and he saw smoke coming from the wheels of the Toyota and the sound of metal crashing. The next moment, he saw it veer to the side and across the hard shoulder and into a field alongside the road, before turning over on to its roof and noisily coming to a complete stop with a thud against a tree. He saw the driver struggle to get out and reach for something which looked like a handgun. From a distance, it looked as if he was taken down. As they pulled away, all he could pick out was a man on the ground and two uniformed officers standing over him. He was too far ahead now to positively identify him.

John breathed a huge sigh of relief. "I think he's down."

"Good." Bellastroni visibly relaxed into the back of the driver's seat, slowing down to a more manageable speed. "Without wishing to be rude, Mr O'Rourke, don't be in a hurry to return to Rome."

John smiled, a lop-sided smile, borne of relief.

*   *   *

Back home, he related events to Julian, receiving assurances a Police Officer would be assigned to watch his apartment, so he felt reasonably secure. In the moment, he had forgotten Nadia was back in the country and retired to bed early before she had returned to the apartment. He needed some sleep and recuperation and was in no mood for confrontational conversation.

It must have been about three in the morning when he awoke out of a deep sleep by the sound of the bolt opening on the front door. Assuming Nadia was returning, he listened for other familiar sounds, as she always took a bottle of water from the refrigerator in the kitchen before going to bed, but he heard nothing. He jumped out of bed, feeling anxious, but before he could open the bedroom door, it pushed open from the other side, hitting him in the head. Reeling back, it took him a few seconds to come to his senses, by which time he could see the unmistakeable figure of Eric standing over him with a gun in his hand.

"I thought you'd be lying at the roadside in Rome." John said, fear gripping him and his voice fading away.

Eric smiled. "Sorry to disappoint you."

"So who was in the white Toyota in Rome?" John groaned, sitting down on the edge of the bed, trying to kick-start his brain.

Eric moved the gun from one gloved hand to the other, closing the door with the free hand. Once the task had been completed, he held the gun with two hands. "I told you I use sub-contractors, rather than place myself in danger or at a crime scene. The man in the car was an associate, but they'll not connect him with me because the gun I'd given him isn't traceable." He smiled. "A little subterfuge and guile is necessary occasionally."

"The driving did appear desperate and not your style at all." John touched his head, but felt no blood.

Eric nodded. "A car chase with the Police isn't professional or advisable, but there's always someone who needs the money and will take the risks. Give them a gun and they think they're Al Capone."

John pointed to the gun. "But you can't use that gun because your instructions are to make my death look like an accident."

"It's true." He pointed to a glass of water on the bedside table, taking a vial from his pocket. "But I've told you about the Micky Finn and I can use the water over there."

"Do you really think I'm going to make it easy for you?"

"If necessary, I can still use the gun and make it look like a bungled burglary."

"But the Police would investigate it."

"They'll accept it because the alternative is a trail leading back to them." He hesitated. "But I agree that's messy."

"I don't think it'll be that simple." John said.

"It'll happen something like this." Eric said. "The Senior Police Officer in the case will get a telephone call from someone high ranking in your intelligence service and they'll be told it'll cause embarrassment if there's a finding of anything other than a bungled burglary." He placed his index finger to his lips. "The message will filter down the ranks and the investigation will be completed quickly with no arguments or dispute and they'll be grateful for the saving on paperwork."

"You seem to have it all planned." John said. "But there's always human error." He lifted his head up, his senses almost back to normal. "What if you leave DNA behind?"

"You're clutching at straws, John, and I'm disappointed."

"I can live with it." He replied.

"More to the point, can you die with it?" Eric moved to the bedside table, keeping his eyes on John at all times, placing the vial on the table.

John didn't know whether Nadia had returned to the apartment and wondered if Eric had already killed her. He dismissed the thought, as he would have heard some commotion and he had the impression Eric did not kill unless there was a contract for it. "Can I go into the kitchen?" He asked, hoping to alert her.

"Why would you want to go into the kitchen?" Eric's eyes never left him.

"I want to show you something."

"What?"

"I've a large bag of money and some documents your paymasters may be interested in acquiring." He hesitated, getting up from the edge of the bed. "I'm sure this will be in your interest."

Eric moved back towards the door and thought for a moment. "I suppose it can do no harm, but no tricks please because it would be foolish." He opened the door slowly, without looking, beckoning John through it and ahead him, the gun pointed at him at all times. "Do you know your problem, John?"

"What's that?"

"You're too rigid and never protect your back."

He thought about rushing him, but was always more than an arm's length away and decided it would only be a last act of desperation, otherwise it would be futile. Walking slowly ahead, he noticed Nadia's bedroom door open, but decided not to give his hand away. "What do you mean?" John asked loudly

"As an example, a hacker would only hack into a sensitive intelligence computer system if he knew he had a back-up, which would make it counter-productive for the intelligence people to kill him?"

"I'm not sure I understand?" John raised his voice again.

"He'd plant a virus so that the system would crash if he did not go in the back door from time to time and confirm he was still alive." Eric replied. "That way, they could never kill him because it would cost them too much and they'd lose too much sensitive information." He hesitated. "You see, John, you've no back up."

"Is that what you think?" John hardly blinked.

"What about these papers and the money?" Eric asked.

John moved to his briefcase on the floor and opened it, taking out a large file and a bundle of documents, moving out to the bureau and placing them down, pointing to them. "These are the documents, which caused all the problems." He hoped Eric would turn around or try to pick them up and give him a moment of distraction and one last opportunity. "Although I've only a few hundred pounds in the briefcase, I could get you considerably more by morning if you'd walk away from this contract and leave me alone."

Eric smiled and walked towards the bureau. "You don't understand my profession." He said. "A contract is a contract and if I walked away, I could never do business again." He moved his eyes to the briefcase. "Sorry, John."

"All the papers they want are there."

Eric turned slightly towards the bureau, moving forward, but hesitated. "Don't even think about it." He returned his attention, targeting the gun directly at John's head.

Eric picked up the file with one hand, his eyes slightly deviated, which was the signal for one desperate lunge, but Eric turned expertly away and John fell to the side of him, the butt of the gun catching him to the side of the head, as he fell. He felt blood trickle down the side of his face, but strangely no pain. When he tried to get up, he fell down again, looking up at Eric one last time.

"You give me no choice." Eric said, pointing the gun directly at him and preparing to shoot.

Nadia, hiding behind her bedroom door, listened to the conversation and waited for the right opportunity. She took her gun and moved silently towards the lounge, pointing the gun at Eric's chest, thinking it was a larger target than his head.

"There's always a choice." She said, firing the gun as she spoke. Eric just about had the time to turn, but nothing else. A startled look reflected in his eyes, the look of a rabbit trapped in a car's headlights. His spectacles fell to the ground first and he followed them, landing heavily with a thud, blood seeping from a hole in his chest all over the carpet, pooling underneath his body. She noticed his eyes remained eerily open and would swear she saw a glimpse of his final moments in the pupils.

CHAPTER EIGHTEEN

"If any one slew a person . . . . it would be as if he slew the whole mankind and if any one saved a life, it would be as if he saved the life of the whole mankind . . ." Qu'ran 5:32.

Order out of Chaos—they (governments) create the problem, then they offer the solution—just as Goering had said all governments do at the Nuremburg Trials. Even Nazi propaganda referred to "Neuordnung" or New Order, intending to create a dictatorial regime throughout Europe and in this respect German National Socialism was very much a precursor of the New World Order.

Secret evidence, closed trials, false imprisonment, warrant-less searches, involuntary drugging, the seizing of private property all seem like something out of the Nazi era, but fear has resulted in many Americans pushed into passively accepting it.

Referring to Section 213 of the Patriot Act, a Congressman said: "The worst part of this so-called anti-terrorism bill is the increased ability of the federal government to commit surveillance on all of us without proper search warrants . . . . anyone who thinks of this as anti-terrorism needs to consider its application to every American citizen."

6th to 10th September 2001:

Unusually large options (bets that stock prices will fall) are placed on American Airlines and United Airlines stock at the New York Stock Exchange.

1963—J. William Fullbright, Chairman of the Senate Foreign Relations Committee spoke at a symposium and stated " . . . . The case for government by elites is irrefutable. Government by the people is possible, but highly improbable."

George Bush Senior addresses the United Nations and talks of an historic movement towards a New World Order. On September 11th 1990 he addresses Congress and states—" . . . a New World Order can emerge in which the Nations of the World can emerge . . . . today the New World is struggling to be born."

Endorsed on the dollar bill—"Novus Ordo Seclorum"—New World Order.

The Director of the CIA twisted in the chair in his office, looking first at the Secretary of State, across the desk from him, then at the General commanding the Afghan operation on his right with the Admiral from the Joint Chiefs of Staff on his left. He recorded the meeting, as usual, but trusted each of them, purposely restricting the meeting to the four of them.

"You know we've had intel on the whereabouts of the Sheikh's safe house and located his compound in Abbottabad in Pakistan since August 2010." He addressed the Secretary of State, hoping she could exercise some leverage on the President.

She nodded. "I've been at some of the ghost meetings."

"But he still refuses to sanction an operation."

"So what's the problem?" She asked, puzzled.

"Time is passing." He hesitated. "The President has been procrastinating now for six months and refuses to take a position."

"But why?" She asked.

"The negative influence of his Chicago aide."

"In what way?" She asked.

The General intervened. "She's told him if he's seen undertaking another act of aggression against Muslims or if things went wrong it would destabilize the Middle East and adversely affect his chances of re-election."

The Admiral passed a file to her. "This is the red team exercise and the independent report showing their analysis suggesting only a forty to sixty per cent chance of success, but as the commander of the Joint Special Forces I'm convinced the odds are considerably higher." He gave her a few moments to consider it. "Seal Team Six have already been training in a special compound in Nevada."

She looked at the Director. "The intelligence services have had great damage done to their credibility by the Iraq WMD black farce. We knew Saddam had weapons of mass destruction because we supplied them and still had the receipts." She placed her hands together. "I need to know the source of your information?"

"The Pakistani intelligence officer who passed the information has been offered a new identity and passport, so we could cause severe problems for him if the intelligence was wrong." The Director looked at the General, then at the Admiral. "We've also had a covert in a safe house on the high ground since last September and he's confirmed the intelligence."

The Secretary of State leaned back in her chair. "We must take him out."

The General nodded. "We all agree." He looked at each of his colleagues. "The problem is how do we do this, still protecting our backs and bypassing the President?"

The Director turned to the Secretary of State and shrugged. "That's why we need your help to resolve this problem."

She raised her eyebrows. "He's unlikely to get a second term on current ratings, so what has he got to lose?"

"We must act quickly or the secret will eke out and the ISI will warn him off." The Director said. "We know an Islamic state, friendly to Pakistan, is passing money to Pakistani intelligence to keep the Sheikh out of sight."

"We can't delay any longer." The General said.

"And you've told the President?" She asked.

"Of course." The Director replied.

"I'll have words with him tomorrow." She said.

"It may not be enough." The Director said. "We've had repeated resistance from his aide and all we get from the President is that he'll think about it, but after he discusses it with his aide, he never comes back." He shrugged. "We can't go on like this without losing our man."

"So what do you want me to do?" She asked.

"I've thought of using my general operational control in the Afghanistan arena to bomb the compound." The General took off his spectacles.

"Have you suggested it to the President?" She asked.

"I've suggested it." The General replaced the spectacles, sitting up straight-backed.

"And what did he say?"

"He's had three options put to him." The Admiral interceded. "A bombing raid using B2 stealth aircraft with cruise missiles, but the risks are that there will be collateral damage with private citizens killed and no clarity on the identification of our target."

"And the other options?" She asked.

"The second option was to work with the Pakistani ISI to develop a joint ground action, but that has been dismissed on the basis that knowledge of the operation will leak out and our man will disappear." The Admiral spoke calmly.

"And presumably that only leaves the third option, Admiral." She said. "Use your special forces and implement a stealth hawk helicopter raid into Pakistan."

The Admiral nodded.

"But the President is still afraid it'll result in innocent Pakistani casualties." The General said. "I've tried to reassure him it would result in a successful operation and the Sheikh's death."

"But he still doesn't trust your judgment." She said.

"Obviously not." The General said.

"The President said his preference would be for a ground operation, so I've made plans for it." The Admiral said. "It's called Operation Neptune's Spear and will involve two stealth black hawks, codenamed Razor 1 and 2, with 23 Seals leading the initial attack group, even a sniffer dog called Cairo. There'll be two Chinooks, codenamed command bird and gun platform, with 56 men following up five minutes behind as back up."

"And he still won't act on your ground operation?" She asked.

"No." The Director replied. "I've threatened to resign, but it makes no difference."

"So what do you want me to do?" She asked.

"I want to work around the President's persistent hesitation, but I need your help."

"How do you propose to do it?"

"The operation will report to me and it's ready to go." The Director grimaced. "But I want to ensure there's no comeback."

"I'll support you, if it's necessary." She began coughing and placed a hand to her mouth.

The Director nodded. "We'd be prepared to leak the extent of his procrastination if he tries to create problems for us afterwards."

"We refer to the Sheikh as Geronimo, so the President will know it as Operation Geronimo." The General said. "We'll go ahead with it under the auspices of my operational control in Afghanistan if it becomes absolutely necessary, but we can't wait any longer if we're to take the Sheikh out."

She sighed. "I'll have a word with the Vice President. I'm sure we can get him onside."

"We've got to take him out." The Director looked at the General. "There can't be any question of capture. He knows too much and his old links with the Agency must remain secret." He hesitated. "In any event, we don't want detainees."

"We're currently coordinating the operation between us and excluding the President." The General said.

"I've got a direct reporting chain from our Pakistan Station, bypassing normal channels." The Director said. "Once we begin the operation, the Admiral will be at our base in Jalalabad, relaying events to us from there."

She took a deep breath. "Don't tell me anymore for the time being, perhaps it's better I don't know, but I'd like to bring the President on board, even if it's kicking and screaming."

The Director looked directly at the Secretary of State. "What do you suggest?"

She leaned back and thought for a moment. "There's a way of manipulating events."

"How?" The Director asked.

The Secretary of State pushed hair back from her forehead. "We must point out to his aide that there'd be a huge public backlash if he did nothing and the Sheikh got away."

"But we've already explained this to the President." The Director said.

She smiled. "I'll tell his aide if the Sheikh evades capture due to his procrastination, then it'll be impossible to keep it out of the press."

"She's a hard nut and won't be bullied." The General replied.

She shrugged. "I'll also suggest there's a way of implementing the operation without any risk of comeback on the President."

"In what way?" The Director asked.

"By suggesting she advises the President to pass operational control to you."

"Will that be enough?" The General asked.

"With a little subtlety." She smiled. "I'll suggest the effect of passing operational control to you would guarantee a delay in the operation, as you'd probably be reluctant to act quickly without the President's express consent."

"It could work." The General nodded towards the Director. "His aide may think you'll hesitate once operational control is passed to you and it deflects responsibility if things go wrong."

"I'll still need everyone's agreement to support me, if we go ahead on this basis." The Director said.

"You've got it." The Secretary of State said. "I'll defend you if it becomes necessary."

"Of course." The General said, before turning to the Secretary of State. "Are you certain you can manipulate events for operational control to pass to the Director?"

"Let's try it." She nodded. "We can inform the President last minute."

"I'll pick a day when he's playing golf and we can drag him off the golf course." The Director said.

*   *   *

The President, still in his polo shirt and golf jacket after a morning game of golf, sat amidst thirteen of his closest advisors within his administration, his eyes fixed to the screen, with its video link and audio feed piped from Langley to the high-tech Situation Room on the ground floor of the White House's West Wing. Admiral McRaven relayed information from Jalalabad. "I hope they're right about it being our man." A concerned look etched into the President's face, knowing any chance of a second term would be gone if this messed up. "What's the codename?" He asked, looking towards his National Security Advisor.

"Geronimo, Mr President." He replied.

"How has this happened so quickly?" The President asked.

"The time is right." The Director replied.

His Vice President sat quietly alongside him in open collar and shirt sleeves, feeding rosary beads between his hands. Behind him stood the Chairman of the Joint Chiefs of Staff and alongside him on the other side in full uniform sat the General, his hands hovering over the laptop in front of him. Opposite sat the Secretary of State, wearing a tweed jacket with piped collar and buttons, a diary, pen and notebook resting on her lap. The White House Chief of Staff stood next to the National Security Advisor.

"Perhaps I should have been more involved." The President said.

"Don't worry, Mr President, they're certain he's our man." The Director spoke from the audio feed in his Langley basement. There was a short pause on the line. "Our operatives in Abbottabad have confirmed it and the sophisticated eavesdropping equipment and infrared imaging has all been analysed." The Director waited, but the President remained silent. "Even the microphone smuggled into the compound has recorded his voice and they've even measured the shadow of our man in the compound." The Director's voice had an urgent edge. "They're sure it's him."

"His photograph has been examined by technicians many times." The Secretary of State interceded. "All the satellite and spy-plane images have been poured over dozens of times. We've used drones and intercepted mobile phones, even using radar from the satellites to search for possible escape tunnels and to establish how many people are in each room. It has to be him, Mr President."

"We've followed the two brothers, the couriers, to the compound and they're in there now." The Director said from Langley. "There can be little doubt."

"Is there likely to be loss of life?" The President asked generally, without looking at anyone in particular. He had deliberated for months over the decision to proceed with the deadly game, reluctant to send in an assassination squad with no process of law, whether international law or otherwise. His man would be executed, plain and simple, as part of a kill operation and his mind remained in turmoil.

"This was your preferred choice if you recall, Mr President." The Director said. "They've left Jalalabad airbase, crossing the border at 22.50 hours local time, finding gaps in the Pakistani's radar systems by contouring the curve of the Earth at about 100 feet high and travelling between 110 and 130 miles per hour."

"I suppose it's necessary." The President recalled the basis of the stealth ground operation to be used and knew the stealth helicopters had additional sound insulation to prevent noise alerting anyone in the compound. He knew the Sheikh could never be allowed to stand trial with the knowledge he possessed. On the other hand, a bomb would have killed too many women and children, perhaps even innocent neighbours.

"Trust your commanders, Mr President." The Director hesitated. "We're following the more favoured of your three options, a raid by Special Forces."

"As a lawyer, this is anathema to me." The President shook his head. "All my life I've espoused the principles of democracy and the rule of law, even for those people my country deems terrorists."

"Mr President." The Secretary of State interrupted firmly, eyes turned towards her. "The stakes are high and there are times principles have to be abandoned for pragmatism."

"But an act of vengeance makes me look a hypocrite."

"Loss of life is always a possibility, Mr President, but we need you to support the kinetic actions your commanders have implemented in good faith." She replied.

"We can't wait any longer." The Director's voice echoed on the audio feed from Langley. "They're in Pakistani air space and I must give the O.K., Mr President."

The President shook his head, taking a bottle of mineral water in front of him and taking a sip. "What do you mean by kinetic?"

"It's the Pentagon's language for lethal, Mr President." The Director said.

The President nodded. "They tell me this compound is only a few hundred metres from the Kakul Military Academy where three army regiments are based?" He looked at the Secretary of State, his jaw clenching. "How could he be living in a Pakistani garrison town close to this Academy?"

"Mr President, you know my belief that Pakistan has played a double game on terrorism for years and the money they've had from us in Aid has been channelled to government and military personnel." The Secretary of State set steely eyes on him. "I suggested last May they were harbouring him, but they poured scorn on my comments."

The President sat back in his chair. "I suppose there could be significant consequences for a Muslim country involved in the capture or killing of the leader of al-Qaeda."

She nodded. "You're right, Mr President."

"But I expected better intelligence from them, so we could do the job." The President said.

"Of course, Mr President, but these are matters for analysis later." The Director of the CIA said.

"What about the violation of Pakistan's sovereignty?" The President asked.

The Secretary of State shook her head. "What can you do, Mr President? If you give them the information and allow them to do it, they could tip him off and we'd have to start all over again. What would the American people say about your decision?" She hesitated. "In any event, you'd be giving the Pakistanis a poisoned chalice."

The President nodded. "I suppose they'll make a fuss for a few days, but then they'll be glad someone else did the dirty work."

"Sure." She fixed eyes on him.

"How many helicopters did you say are going in?" The President asked generally.

"Initially twenty three members of Seal Team Six will go in two of our night stalker MH-60 stealth black hawks, Mr President." She hesitated. "They've been extensively modified and adapted secretly with stealth equipment and for reduction of rotor noise, so they shouldn't be detected until it's too late." The Admiral spoke from his link in Jalalabad. "Two Chinooks with 56 men will be in reserve to go in immediately afterwards."

"And your men, Admiral?"

"They're highly-trained commandos from our Naval Special Warfare Development Group, Mr President, Navy Seal Team Six, the elite of the elite, together with a translator versed in Urdu and Pashto." The Admiral said, awaiting the final confirmation. "They've completed their training at Bagram and at the Tarbela Ghazi Airbase, Sir, and they've had two dummy runs." He hesitated, but the President said nothing. "There's no moon and the weather is cloudy, so the helicopters can travel at low level, skimming over the houses with their lights off and there's no way will they be seen until it's too late. By the time, they hear or see anything, they'll be over the compound. The plan is for Seal Team Six to be dropped onto the roof from the two helicopters and within thirty minutes on the ground it'll all be over." He waited impatiently.

The President sighed. "We can't afford to have a public trial of this man."

"Of course not." The Director said. "He knows too much."

"And they understand the lethal instructions?" The President asked.

"They understand, Sir." The Director said. "But the Press will be informed Seal Team Six were instructed to capture only if the Sheikh conspicuously surrendered."

"Good." He paused. "And they'll take the body away afterwards?" He fidgeted in his chair.

"Of course." The Director said. "They'll be taken back to the USS Carl Vinson in the North Arabian Sea, via Bagram."

The President looked at his watch. "Then it's go, Mr Director."

They listened as the Director of the CIA radioed affirmative to Admiral McRaven in Jalalabad. "You'll see everything from the Stealth Drone flying at 4,600 feet and the head cameras on the Navy Seals, Mr President. It's a live feed and you'll hear everything from their microphones." After a short silence the Director spoke again. "The pictures may change to a drone flying at 20,000 feet, but I'll try to give a commentary on events as they happen, but there's radio silence at present with secure texts only."

Soon the helicopter hovered close to the compound and the codename 'Palm Beach' echoed. At one stage, a whining noise signalled a Black Hawk crash-landing in the compound.

"Christ. What's happening? Was it hit?" The President shook his head, remembering the loss of life of eighteen US servicemen when a Black Hawk was brought down in Somalia and seeing his second term vanishing before his eyes.

The Secretary of State clasped her hand over her mouth, recalling the same event.

"It may just have caught the wall of the compound with the rear rotor-blade or it could just have been mechanical, Mr President. Perhaps it's the Green Unit." The Admiral said from Afghanistan. "We've prepared for this contingency, Sir, and my men will deal with it."

"Trust them to do their job, Mr President, there'll be a Plan B." The General moved forward, placing his hand on the President's shoulder. "We must let them do their job."

Time seemed to stand still, but soon the President heard the sound of gunfire, small arms fire, seeing the flashes of stun grenades from a small building within the compound, then the return fire from Seal Team Six. He sat impassively, as this return gunfire silenced the defenders within the compound, two falling dead. More elite troops slid down ropes dangling from the remaining helicopter onto the roof.

"One of those shot was the courier, Mr President." The Director said on his link. "They'll drop into the room on the third floor and others will work their way up to the third floor from the bottom as part of Plan B."

The President heard someone shout for the breach man. His eyes fixed to the screen, observing the same scene as Seal Team Six, watching as they approached and entered the main building, a third man, a much younger man, appeared on the staircase. He moved for something, but before he could move much further, a shot fired and a bullet hit him in the chest and he fell backwards.

"I think that's the Sheikh's son Khalid." The Director said.

The cameras picked up a room full of children, but the Team moved up the stairs. Another man feverishly pointed to a bedroom when questioned at gunpoint as to the whereabouts of their prey, then darkness for a moment.

What's happening?" The President asked.

"As well as night armour, they've got night-vision goggles and are equipped with laser targets, Mr President." The Director said. "They're on the landing outside the bedroom."

The President heard the sound of a woman wailing tearfully.

"We've a visual on Geronimo." The Team Leader said from the landing outside one of the bedrooms on the third floor, his voice clear and firm. A shot fired at him and missed. The Sheikh ducked quickly back into the bedroom, but Seal Team Six followed.

The President watched as his man stood defiantly in pyjamas in front of the Seal Team Leader, making a move for his fabled AK47. He wore a prayer cap on his head. Two women, his wives, stood in front of him in the bedroom, the younger one, Amal, screamed something and shouted her husband's name, moving towards the Team Leader and in front of the Sheikh.

Another member of Seal Team Six lowered his sights and after the sound of a shot firing, the woman fell to the floor, screaming hysterically and clutching a wound to her leg. Another Seal member took the other wife, Khaira, blinded by a white strobe light, out of the line of fire, holding her before tying her wrists, so he could protect his colleagues from the action of any suicide vests. Their target, though unarmed, had to be silenced. The infrared laser of a sawn-off M4 gun showed on the target's chest. There was the sound of two further shots and two flashes of gunfire, the first round hitting its target in the chest with a high-calibre 5.56 mm bullet, the target falling backwards onto the bed, then hitting the floor. The same member of Seal Team Six stood over the limp body, administering a double tap, this time the target was hit with a bullet in the head, in the region of the left eye, blood and brains spattering gorily everywhere in the process. "Geronimo EKIA. For God and Country Geronimo, Geronimo, Geronimo."

The sound of the woman groaning and weeping hysterically came across vividly in the Situation Room in Washington.

"What's EKIA?" The President asked.

"Enemy Killed in Action, Mr President." The Director said.

"We got him." The President released a huge sigh.

"Is this your husband?" The Seal Team leader asked the injured woman still groaning and weeping on the floor.

She nodded. "Yes." Her reply tearful, voice cracking.

It was all the leader of Seal Team Six needed, but he shouted for a tape measure, before realizing they didn't have one. "We need someone six feet four to lie next to the body to ensure we've the right man and we need DNA."

"I don't believe it." The President said, listening to the audio feed. "We've donated a sixty million dollar helicopter to this operation and we can't afford a damn tape measure."

A member of the Seal Team Six lay next to the body and confirmed the height. He wrapped the Sheikh in a white sheet and organized the removal of the body into one of the waiting helicopters, one of the Chinooks had arrived to take away the men from the downed Black Hawk.

The remaining members of the Navy Seal team searched the house. In another room, the cameras showed another woman in the far side of the bedroom cowed in the corner, crying, a small boy huddled underneath her body. All non-combatants were quickly bound with plastic ties.

"Get all the hard drives in any computer in the building, any mobile phones, any memory sticks or DVD's and any diaries or paperwork you find, handwritten or otherwise." The Team Leader shouted. "We'll never get a better chance for intel."

"There are about five computers in the kitchen and some mobile telephones and thumb drives." Someone else shouted.

"Then bag them all." The sound of computers being smashed came across to those gathered in the White House.

"I've found about a hundred memory sticks and flash drives and dozens of DVD's." Another voice said. "And there are about eleven hard drives."

"We need them all." The Team Leader shouted, pointing to an AK47 and a small Makarov hand-weapon. "Take that AK47 over there and the hand-gun."

"Are there any casualties?" The President asked, his question relayed by the Director.

"None." He heard the Team Leader relay the answer back to operation control.

"Can they all get away in the remaining helicopters?" He asked the Director.

"No problem, Mr President." The Director replied. "But there's no room for the wounded wife or any of the other dead."

"What about the downed Black Hawk?" The Team Leader asked.

"It must be destroyed to protect our technology from being discovered." The Director said, hesitating. "Use the explosives."

A member of Seal Team Six set charges and fired up detonators. Minutes after the explosion, the remaining helicopters were airborne. The Admiral's voice rose sharply. "We've been forty minutes and the Pakistani's have scrambled their F16 jets."

"Jesus Christ." The President said. "Get me someone over there quickly."

"It'll not be necessary, Mr President." The Admiral interrupted. "I've calculated that we'll be out of Pakistani airspace and back in Afghanistan before the jets can get near to us to do any damage."

The President sat back in his chair, relaxing for the first time. "Well done everybody." He sighed. "Do you think we should spread the word about the Egyptian's involvement in betraying and locating the Sheikh's hiding place?"

"We've connections in the Saudi Press and could leak the information to them, perhaps running a piece in the Saudi newspaper, Al-Watan?" The Director paused on the audio feed, adding almost as an afterthought. "But he's such a divisive influence within the Jihadist movement, it's not necessarily a good idea."

"We should use the information and intelligence we've collected to follow the money trail, closing down the Islamic Charities, which act as fund collectors for these terrorists." The Director said from Langley. "We can also destroy al-Qaeda's command structure."

"I agree Leon." The President looked around. "Well done everyone and thank you. Remember this is only the first chapter in a very long book and it isn't over."

The Secretary of State edged up to the National Security Advisor. "Do they all know the extent of the part played by Sheikh's fourth wife, Khairiah Saber, and by Al-Qaeda in locating the Sheikh?" She whispered. "She was jealous of the Sheikh's sixth wife, young Amal."

"I don't believe so." He replied quietly.

"What about the reward?" She asked.

"We wouldn't want to pay it if it goes to anyone connected to Al-Qaeda."

She nodded. "It'd be supremely ironic at a time when Al-Qaeda was broke and the Sheikh had become delusional and an irrelevance, if the

$25 million reward went to one of their operatives to get them back in the game?"

"We both know this operation was a political event, but we can't give money to these people to resurrect their operations." He took her arm. "You must make sure the Director doesn't hand over the reward money to them."

She nodded.

EPILOGUE

"A time comes when silence is betrayal"—Martin Luther King.

"Say. We believe in Allah (God) and that which was revealed to us and that which was revealed to Abraham and Ishmael and Isaac and Jacob and the tribes and that which was given to Moses and Jesus and to the Prophets from their Lord; we make no distinction between any of them, and to him we submit." Qu'ran 3:83.

"The children of Israel must remember the favour bestowed upon them by God and fulfil his covenant. Then God will be true to them." Qu'ran 2:40. (The term 'Israel' standing for all people in search of God within themselves, being the name that God gave to all people in the world.)

Dust samples have the clear evidence and signature of thermite, a military explosive incendiary device, often used as part of a gel explosive. Iron oxide and sulphur oxide residues are also found at the scene of WTC, again proof of thermite. Thermite reaches temperatures of 4,500 degrees, hot enough to melt steel and burns, even under water, explaining why molten steel is still red hot twenty one days later.

"We are on the verge of a global transformation. All we need is the right major crisis."—Bilderberger and Club of Rome executive member.

"In searching for a new enemy to unite us, we come up with the idea that pollution, the threat of global warming, water shortages, famine and the like would fit the bill . . . . all these dangers are caused by human intervention . . . the real common enemy of humanity, then becomes man himself"—The First Global Revolution (1991)—published by the Club of Rome (a globalist think-tank).

Insight Magazine: "With one vote by Congress and the sweep of the President's pen, say critics, the right of every American fully to be protected under the Fourth Amendment against unreasonable searches and seizures was abrogated."

"What we do in life . . . . ripples through Eternity"—Marcus Aurelius.

As Libya's now deceased Gaddhafi once said, there is no need for guns or terrorism as there are 52 million Muslims currently living in Europe and with the birth rate for non-Muslims far below what is needed to sustain each country's culture, Muslims do not need to use violence for its Islamic ideology to eventually infiltrate every European country.

The doctrine of the Hegelian dialectic—being the study of opposing forces maintains that thesis encountering anti-thesis results in synthesis. Simply offer a draconian solution to a problem you have engineered . . . . and it advances the secret agenda of those who created the problem in the first place.

The evidence compiled by the Architects and Engineers for 9/11 Truth demonstrate beyond a reasonable doubt that "the official NIST explanation for the destruction of World Trade Centre Towers 1,2 and 7 is simply not true. The evidence shows they were destroyed by explosive controlled demolition."

Letters of Rabbani: Allah (God) . . . the substance of these beings which he created is but nothingness . . . He created ALL in the sphere of senses and illusions . . . The existence of the Universe is in the sphere of senses and illusions and is not material . . . In reality, there is nothing in the outside except the Glorious Being: Who is Allah (God).

Qu'ran: "We created man and we are nearer to him than his jugular vein."

Al-Qaeda is from the Arabic root 'qaf-ayn-dal', which can mean the base or foundation and it can mean the principle or the model or the rule. It has been interpreted in many ways. A training manual discovered and marked al-Qaeda may well refer to the basic rules. It may also refer to the foundation of the expected society to come.

In this book, it has given the interpretation and description used by former UK Foreign Secretary, the late Robin Cook, four weeks before he died, when he referred to it in a newspaper article as the base, particularly the computer database of CIA mercenary recruits fighting with the Mujahadeen against the Russians in Afghanistan—al-Qaeda—and paid for and created by US taxpayers to wage jihad against the Russians.

In this context, Militant Islam has been created by the West. It may not be a sinister impulse in itself, but rather in its human deviation, more often rooted in the social inequality and the desolation of extreme poverty. From this spiritual and material desert, they see a glimpse of light and the possibility of healing the divisions within the Muslim world and, in its turn, all of humanity. They clamour for the joy it brings, sacrificing anything and everything for the hope of an escape from their hitherto meaningless existence. The ecstasy and meaning within that mere glimpse, in a world otherwise bereft of meaning, is the impulse which is resonating across the Muslim world, with its concentration on the lesser Jihad, rather than the more important greater Jihad, being the internal struggle to improve one's soul. It is this social inequality which is the breeding ground for all revolutions, but it must be countered by an intellectual argument and an emphasis on the greater Jihad, even if it means having the courage to face the truth no matter how painful and unpalatable it may be. Truth has a similar resonance, as it stems from the same spiritual source. The theological principle of oneness or unity is within all religions and in the Qur'an is called Tauhid. It is the fundamental basis behind all true spirituality. No-one can doubt the purity of the revelations of Mohammed, (unlike the teachings of the New Testament), nor in its pure form should Christians be frightened of its teachings. Christian teachings have been formulated some 325 years after Christ, when Emperor Constantine negotiated with the Vatican as to what would or would not be included in the gospels at the Council of Nicea, so it is not for us to question the purity of Islam, only in its deviation from the revelations.

The Tauhid in its accurate interpretation can only relate to the unity of ALL men (not merely the Ummah or Muslim community) and if this word is understood and explained by the spiritual teachers in its true meaning, then maybe one day all of us (Muslim and non Muslim) will be called 'brother'. Until that time, it is critical the West understands and accepts the life of an Afghan or an Iraqi or a Muslim is no less valuable than the life of an American. Fear or anger is not the answer, nor is the demonization of a figure or group, as you may discover the financial backers, and sometimes even the perpetrators of terrorist activities, are neither obvious nor apparent. Spirituality and Love are the only remedies. They are the key, as they transcend all religions, which so often are the great divider of peoples.

The Twin Towers could not have been a haphazard or random target. It has too much archetypal significance and those with knowledge of its symbolism knew fear would result. Fear is a way of controlling the population and creating the secret agenda. The events of 9/11 were intended to strike at the hearts and minds of everyone and at what Jung referred to as the collective unconscious, from which all archetypes of myth emanate. It was intended to be an attack upon our imagination, as the physical world is but an extension of the imagination thrust outwards, something which would sear a lasting memory into the world's consciousness. Those with knowledge of this symbolism planned the event, for they also understand the power of fear, self-perpetuating and corrosive, undermining the secure mind-set and subsequently used to control the population. The horror and trauma of the televised 9/11 events created 'denial' as a psychological defence to the insecurity it created. This, in turn, prevents us from looking at the empirical evidence. The emotion of fear and vulnerability can turn to anger and the desire to ridicule the messenger.

The archetypal image of The Tower, as expressed in the Tarot card of the same name, (and in the Tower of Babel in Christian scriptures), is an image of sudden violence and destruction. The whole structure of life is collapsing, never to be the same again and people are falling to their deaths from The Tower. The interpretation of the Tarot card relates to the collapse of the structures, which hold the Querent's life together. It is the one card, which makes people recoil in fear at its appearance in a reading. The explosion of the lightning bolt, as revealed in the card, can amongst other things reveal in its meaning a physical external natural disaster. The drops of fire falling on each side of the card of The Tower in the Rider-Waite Tarot cards are shaped like the Hebrew letter Yod, the first letter of God's name in Hebrew. They symbolize the fact the Universe and the human mind cannot stay imprisoned within our tower of illusion and repression. The Universe will free us, if necessary with violence, if we cannot rise out of our dark repressions, which imprison us, of our own free will.

Carl Jung once described consciousness as like a dam blocking the free flow of the river of the unconscious and The Tower blows away the dam completely. The fact that the events of 9/11 were situated in the heart of one of the most important financial centres in the world are not insignificant and is a clue to the events, which will strike at and erode the fundamental security structures upon which we have become to rely. The erosion of the financial structures were bound to follow. The combination of these various events may take more than a generation to unravel. Fear not only gives those in power control over the population, but if manipulated and unchecked can be an excuse for almost any action they care to contemplate.

Perhaps the Death card of the Tarot has a similar effect as The Tower in that the Querent recoils at its sight, though the esoteric and divinatory meaning of the Death card involves a far gentler end to one phase of life and the beginning of another. It is a re-birth and a slow transition, so its archetypal image is less frightening at a deeper level. The essence of what we are is indestructible and immortal and must never be feared, for fear is the mind killer.

However, there is a positive aspect to the card of The Tower. Its structure has been destroyed because it has not been erected on stable foundations. In its destruction, there is an opportunity to re-build from firmer foundations, which can lead to freedom and new beginnings. If the collective unconscious can focus on different values and its reconstruction, then the world can still be healed and trust can replace mistrust, but only love can overwhelm the divisions of hatred and fear, whether caused by religion, race or greed. We must all make a contribution to the building of the Temple or the imperfection of our work will destroy us and the first step is the restoration of individual values based on the heart. It is not insignificant the true teachings of Islam are also based on the heart and not the head or intellect, as Mohammed was an illiterate man who merely channelled divine revelation without the limitation of language to restrict consciousness. Is it surprising mystics tell us that revelation comes as a lightning bolt, destroying the illusions of the material world in one blinding flash.

Any corruption of Islam, and there is much corruption, is the work of those who resist that which is good. It is merely the flaws intrinsic in the inherent nature of the human interpretation of what is a divine revelation. It is not to be feared and can be overcome by compassion and understanding.

If we tune into intuition (the heart) rather than the mind (the head), then instinctive feelings emerge. We need the input of our positive intuition as well as thoughts into the collective unconscious, even if we may not see individually the consequences of our contribution and our thoughts. The energy and thoughts we introduce now are the foundation of the world in which our children and grandchildren will live. The physical universe is expanding, so our personal universe must also expand too. This eternally expanding universe must be allowed to flow, not resisted. Evil is but a resistance to that which is good. Any resistance can only be temporary in the spiritual scheme of things and every dark era has eventually emerged into a new dawn of inspiration.

The true meaning and use of the Tarot, as a psychological tool in the transformation of the mind, using archetypes, is a path of liberation. It brings out the divine spark in all of us, uniting it with our conscious selves and eventually ends the duality of God and human. However, it is necessary to take the first steps down into the darkness of the self to discover the trapdoor of joyous light. It is such joyous light that we are almost blinded by the lightning bolt when confronted by the only true reality, which is the indestructible and immortal spirit.

The Tarot card of The Tower is card number 16 in the Major Arcana or Trump cards of the Tarot and it is followed by number 17, The Star, which is symbolic of Hope, for after the storm there is peace. It is the card representing healing. The Star Maiden pours down wisdom freely from a chalice, which can never be emptied. Dew was regarded as the sweat of the stars and as a consequence was used for healing. The Star also represents wholeness and freedom and is the light beyond the trapdoor. It is a transformation of the darkness of the unconscious changed into the glorious light and awareness of the super-consciousness. In the Tarot card, the stream of water flowing back into the pool is a representation signifying that all archetypes must blend back into the one formless truth, for the archetype has done its purpose and re-connected us to the source. Love sees itself only by the grace of hatred and in the existence of its opposite in this Universe of duality. There is an opportunity for people to awaken from their hypnotic dreams and exercise their free will and for the first time become consciously aware of the unity of all things. The time is almost upon us when spirituality will meet religion and stare it in the face. As a consequence, the duality, which is man, will return to the unity of the One and the broken personality will be salvaged and finally heal. It is the time for truth, honour and a new beginning based on these ideals, for freedom and inspiration begins with all of us.

Lightning Source UK Ltd.
Milton Keynes UK
UKOW051812040712

195483UK00001B/146/P